CRIMES OF ARROGANCE

MITCH ENGEL

Outskirts Press, Inc.
http://www.outskirtspress.com

Paperback ISBN: 978-1-4787-9069-3
Hardback ISBN: 978-1-4787-9091-4

Library of Congress Control Number: 2017909175

Cover Photo © 2017 thinkstockphotos.com. All rights reserved - used with permission.

Outskirts Press and the "OP" logo are trademarks belonging to Outskirts Press, Inc.

PRINTED IN THE UNITED STATES OF AMERICA

To Lauren, Brent, and Matt

For finding the joy in being yourselves

Prologue

THURSDAY, JANUARY 9, 2014

Somehow the arrangements didn't feel right to Chen. Neither he nor his partners were required to sign a single document at the closing. In fact, none of them even bothered to show up. Yet each of the six had walked away with forty-seven million dollars.

For months, a battalion of ever-so-willing bankers and lawyers had produced endless paperwork. The sizable cuts they received off the top would more than compensate them for whatever family dinners or Saturday tee times they missed to get the deal done.

It would be hard to argue that four hundred and ninety-seven million was anything short of astounding for less than two years' work. Still, at the last minute, Michael Chen had tried to convince his partners to hold out for another four million, solely because he thought it might sound cooler if the final sale price topped half a billion. Then, as usual, Laffy spoke up like he was the last remaining adult on the planet. Anthony Lafferty had been pulling the same tired act since the very beginning, though this time his high-handedness at least had served a purpose. Reopening the negotiations would have been pure lunacy. Even Chen recognized that fact, but veering off-course was how he kept things interesting.

Despite being the youngest of the group, at twenty-seven, Michael Chen shouldered a feeling of parental responsibility for the group. The whole enterprise stemmed from his work at MIT. But he also knew that if it hadn't been for Conks, he would have shared his proprietary algorithms with the rest of the tech universe

1

in some academic journal for no money at all. He'd never been wired for commerce, or plenty of other facets to everyday life. Thank goodness she interceded. In one way or another, Teresa Conkle had been looking out for him since his freshman year at Caltech.

For almost two years, the six partners had worked together practically round the clock. Common purpose had bonded them in ways he never could have anticipated. But he also recognized a significant portion of this closeness was born out of their common backgrounds. Each of them was a bona fide genius. Academic prowess had set them apart since childhood. He knew first-hand how advanced intellect made one different from other kids on the playground. Different from classmates, and even from siblings.

Eventually a kid grows accustomed to the feelings of isolation. Watching one's peers from the outside, an adolescent will find greater and greater comfort from science projects and mathematical equations. As years pass, human-to-human contact becomes more and more peripheral—at least until entrepreneurial chance brings six kindred souls together. After the formation of the partnership, Michael and the others, in their own peculiar fashion, had melded into a close-knit family—cerebral dysfunctions and all.

Moving forward, each now would have the means to chart his or her own course. Odds were good they individually would go on to reap millions or billions more through subsequent new ventures. Maybe some of them would be lucky enough to hook up with another like-minded group—not that any of the six ever could admit to deriving emotional fulfillment from social interaction. Regardless, Michael anticipated a void in his life, and he presumed the others did as well. A return to intellectual isolationism. Sure, the partners had vowed to stay in touch. Conks was likely to organize an occasional lunch or dinner. But things would never be the same. That common purpose, that unifying element would be missing.

———◇———

Anthony Lafferty was counting on his five associates experiencing an emotional vacuum over the months ahead. Two years earlier, when he'd been introduced to the others, he immediately recognized the roles they might play in plans he'd been formulating for as long as he could remember. Now, with the company sold, the financial means were in place. When the time was right, he would strengthen the bond of these newly minted millionaires in ways they couldn't possibly imagine.

TUESDAY, OCTOBER 14, 2014

The conversation was getting pretty hard to stomach. Or more precisely, the guy doing most of the talking was. Webb Tremont allowed his eyes to wander, surveying the room's large open space. After almost eight years, he still was amazed by the attention to detail. The long wooden bar with a half-dozen beer taps standing in ready formation. The vintage pinball machines. The work-out equipment in the corner. She had created a masculine utopia. The ground level of his private domain contained everything an adult male could want—or at least a forty-one-year-old version who refused to grow up.

The upstairs living quarters were a far cry from Webb's original decorating, which had consisted of a second-hand sofa, a battered table he used as a desk, and shelves fashioned out of barn wood and cinderblocks. Hiring Corrie to redo the coach house turned out to be the best decision he'd ever made. Sure, she was every bit the talented interior decorator her credentials suggested. But he also had fallen head-over-heels for her from the moment he poked his head into her place of business.

Corrina DiMarco was the first and only woman with whom Webb Tremont willingly had practiced the unnatural act of monogamy, though that subject barely was discussed. They simply had become committed to one another from the onset. How or why she still tolerated him after all this time remained a mystery to him— one he decided was best left unsolved.

Webb forced himself to refocus his attention on the matter at hand. Sitting directly across from him was a living, breathing caricature—the president of CBS Programming and his full battery of sycophants dressed in tailored suits. Heads bobbed up and down in unison as each sacred work rolled off the man's celestial tongue. The underlings sat to either side of their small-framed, curly-haired messiah—his teeth glimmering from expensive veneers, his fingernails from the polish of a morning manicure. Elmore Brogan. Even his name had the air of someone who took himself far too seriously. Webb wondered how the parents of a newborn possibly could have known.

He wasn't sure what was supposed to impress him most. The six-million-dollar guarantee lying before him in writing, or the fact that Brogan had taken time away from his busy schedule to travel to Lake Forest and present it to him in person. After all, the nearest place to land the network's corporate jet was more than half an hour away. No small inconvenience for a man of such epic self-importance.

Brogan had spoken slowly, pausing between sentences to drink in the salaried adoration from his flanks. Webb would receive the full six million for his creative contributions on the front end. This amount would double to twelve once the expected audience ratings were achieved, and more than triple after reruns of the show went into syndication.

Webb wasn't taken in by any of it. He recognized that the only things Brogan and CBS really wanted were his name and the rights to his books. The other promises were nothing but gratuitous decoration. No matter. Webb didn't really care that he would be listed atop the writing credits. The real scriptwriters could pull whatever material they wanted from his eleven books. He knew that any legitimate creative input on how content was to be presented would be nonexistent, which also was of no consequence to him. Webb had entered the negotiations under no false pretenses. For him, the deal was about one thing and one thing only. The money.

FRIDAY, OCTOBER 17, 2014

The final paperwork was completed late in the day on Thursday. Elmore Brogan was eager to unveil his latest brainchild, so a press release went out early the next morning. In the fall of 2015, CBS would launch *Serve & Protect*, a weekly crime drama based on the popular book series of the same name. What's more, the author, Webb Tremont, had signed on as a senior writer.

The thirty-eight-year-old Brogan was the network's acclaimed "boy wonder," but Webb figured the source of most of that acclamation was the man himself. Before accepting his senior position with CBS, Brogan already had banked tens of millions as an independent producer. Each year he continued to collect outrageous sums from the syndication rights to such timeless classics as *Mayhem at Midnight*, *Fog Harbor*, *The Mercenaries*, and *Untold Marital Secrets,* to name but a few.

Elmore Brogan claimed to have harbored a weakness for crime stories since before he entered the business. Apparently, this proclivity was genetic. His grandfather had been a scriptwriter on the original *Dragnet*, back in the Fifties. Then his uncle worked with Steven Bochco as one of the producers on *Hill Street Blues* during the Eighties. For years, young Elmore had been looking for his own opportunity to extend the family's legacy of bringing police work into America's living rooms.

He was yearning to do a cop show like the ones from the old days. Those iconic programs that offered viewers gritty, unvarnished police stories on a weekly basis. No concocted special units. No futuristic crime labs or choreographed martial arts. Just real, everyday crimes solved by real, everyday officers of the law. For close to fifteen years Brogan's creative instincts had proven infallible and he was convinced that a substantial, demographically attractive audience would join him on his nostalgic journey.

Tired of waiting for some zealous program developer to bring him the right concept, he decided to take matters into his own hands. He closely followed the "Best Seller" lists. Time and again over the past decade, books published under the banner of "Serve & Protect" had climbed toward the top. They were anthologies of genuine police stories, collections of real criminal cases. The author had an uncanny knack for researching and writing about intriguing crime cases and the police work required to solve them; plus he stuck close to the actual facts.

The network's pockets were deep. For the right amount, Elmore Brogan had been certain he could convince this Webb Tremont character to become part of his landmark project. Promoting the show as "Webb Tremont's *Serve & Protect*" would carry tremendous marquee value.

———◇———

With the announcement made, Webb anticipated that book critics and others in the writing community would accuse him of selling out. No matter, the last laugh was his. He'd never envisioned himself as a serious writer in the first place, and after eleven successful books he still didn't. Writing hardly had been his first occupational pursuit.

His books already had raked in millions. By all rights, the staggering amount now added by CBS should be enough to impress his father, since money was the only language he spoke. But Webb knew otherwise. The dollars he earned were tainted because the eldest son of the vaunted Brandon Tremont had chosen to write about something as untoward as crimes. Despite the success and acclaim that had come Webb's way, his father's attitude was, at best, indifferent. Such subject matter was not in keeping with the family's standing.

Still, Webb assumed his father and the rest of the Tremont clan were a helluva lot happier than they were over his original choice of careers. Bounding out of college, Webb Tremont had become a cop. If things had turned out differently, he still would have been carrying a badge.

SATURDAY, OCTOBER 18, 2014

Anthony Lafferty had disappeared to the Cape for a few days. Returning home to Boston, he was scrolling through the news on his laptop when s small headline leapt off the screen. "CBS Inks Webb Tremont for New Crime Show in Fall." Reading through the details, his mind started processing the possibilities.

The timing, the situation couldn't be more perfect. By the time autumn rolled around, his five puffed-up geniuses would be ripe for the picking. Anthony Lafferty prided himself as an analytical being, as a person who approached all matters rationally. Fate or karma didn't exist in such a world. Nonetheless, he now found himself wondering.

Chapter One

A YEAR LATER, NOVEMBER 7, 2015 ... THE FIRST OF MANY WEEKENDS

Spencer and Julie Anne McFadden were regulars at Armando's, or at least they had been prior to the second round of corporate downsizing at DrillMax. Now Spencer hadn't collected a paycheck in over a year. But the first Saturday of November was their seventeenth wedding anniversary and such an occasion warranted a table cloth, wine list, and menu that wasn't laminated—especially since Julie Anne's parents were watching the boys for the night.

A bottle of Chianti Classico and two glasses of limoncello later, the couple arrived home at close to midnight, anticipating a nightcap in the hot tub they'd installed when times were healthier for petroleum engineers. Music was blaring through the wide-open front door of their twice-mortgaged Colonial and any thoughts of late-night romance quickly were dashed. At ten, Danny was their oldest. Even if he'd snuck away from his grandparents' house a few blocks away, he wasn't likely to be throwing a party. Someone else was inside, or at least had been. The McFaddens wisely elected to stay in their car as Julie hit 9-1-1 on her cellphone. Within minutes they were joined by the Bellaire Police.

Inside, the signs were obvious. Intruders had paid them a visit. Skillful ones at that. Every drawer, closet, and secret nook where valuables were kept had been discovered and laid bare. Oddly, the couple's most valuable possessions were neatly arrayed across the dining room table. An antique watch. A jade bracelet. Gold and silver necklaces. Diamond earrings. Two wooden boxes filled with silver coins. A cut-glass nativity set inherited from a favorite aunt.

The large flat-screen over the fireplace and four other TV's throughout the house were turned on—as was the expensive sound system pumping out the Dirty South hip-hop that had been heard from the street. Attached to an oil painting on the living room wall was a Post-It Note that read, "Thomas Redding, 1947—current value, $1,785.00." Three more pictures were similarly tagged with appraisals.

Only items of significant worth seemed to have been touched. Otherwise, the house was exactly as the couple had left it. Except for an envelope taped to a mirror in the front entryway. Printed on the outside was a note, "To help tide you over during difficult times." The envelope contained ten one-hundred-dollar bills.

That same Saturday night, Bellaire police officers were called to two other addresses where break-ins had occurred. In each instance valuables were neatly displayed, nothing was stolen, and envelopes containing the same note and cash amount were left by intruders.

In total, nine couples or families around the Houston suburbs arrived home to identical circumstances.

THE SECOND WEEKEND

As the highest-performing sales rep at Beesinger Steel Cabinets, Sherry Hargrove had been on the road for three straight weeks. Short on cash, Sherry decided to pop into her Mt. Lebanon office and fill out expense reports, so that she could submit them for reimbursement first thing Monday morning. Otherwise, it would have been another day before anyone realized the security system inside corporate headquarters had been breached.

Surprisingly, no one at the four other area businesses went into work on Sunday, November 15. Perhaps it was because the Steelers were playing the Cleveland Browns and the entire city tended to block out the rest of the world on game days.

By 9 a.m. on Monday, nearly two thousand employees around Pittsburgh logged on to their desktop computers and were treated to the same information that had awaited Sherry Hargrove the prior afternoon.

On the screens of every employee at five different office complexes were the serial numbers, balances, and access codes to the asset accounts of each respective company. If an employee chose to scroll past this first page of highly confidential content, they found tables listing the salaries, ages, and computer passwords for every one of their co-workers.

Whoever penetrated the computer security systems of these sizable companies had gained access to their most classified information. The person or persons responsible thereby possessed codes and passwords that would have allowed them to effect transfers of tens of millions of dollars. Yet not a single dime had been diverted.

A separate message was locked onto the computer screens of the top executives at each of the five organizations, "When controlling overhead costs, cybersecurity is a foolish place to underinvest."

THE THIRD WEEKEND

The first car to be noticed was a Porsche Panamera, parked in the spot reserved for the precinct captain. So, of course, it drew attention. By midday on Sunday, November 22, sixteen other luxury automobiles were found in police station parking lots across Greater Portland.

Each of the cars' owners reported they'd last driven their vehicle to a private club or high-end restaurant on Friday or Saturday evening—and most had handed their keys to a parking valet. When they'd been ready to depart the respective establishments scattered around the metropolitan area, their automobiles were nowhere to be found.

Before being relocated to the police stations, these seventeen stolen cars had been washed and filled with gas. In a few instances, worn wiper blades and burnt-out light bulbs were replaced. With one Mercedes coupe, a dent had been pounded out of a rear side panel. Taped to each dashboard was an envelope containing cards with the same simple message: "Please drive safely."

Chapter Two

"**G**ood evening, I'm Lester Holt, and topping the headlines for Monday, November 23, 2015, is a FBI press release which probably has police officials around the country scratching their heads ... and likely will have millions of citizens perched in front of their TV sets later this week to watch a new police drama on another network. For more details on this story, we go to Washington DC where Jed...."

The three of them were playing cards with the TV on in the background when the reference to *Serve & Protect* caught Webb Tremont's attention. As soon as the news telecast segued to details about a hurricane gathering along the eastern seaboard, Webb hit the off button. He hesitated a moment, trying to gather a semblance of composure, but finally flung the remote control into the cushioned leather chair he had vacated when the Washington correspondent started relaying the absurdities of the lead story. If Corrie and Sprig hadn't paid him a late-afternoon visit, he would have hurled his makeshift missile at some harder surface and the room would have been raining black plastic and triple-A batteries.

"This can't be happening. Another week or two and that godforsaken TV show would have been cancelled, buried, and soon forgotten. But now, because some anonymous group of degenerates wants to spice up their weekends, the ratings for the coming week are gonna skyrocket ... and my name still will be plastered all over the dreadful garbage."

———❦———

Nearly eight hundred miles away, on the top floor of a Boston high-rise, shot glasses were raised. This time they drank tequila—AsomBroso Gran Reserva, in fact. At eleven hundred dollars a bottle, it was a shade pricey even for the six young millionaires. But tonight was special. Anthony Lafferty, the eldest of the one-time business partners, eyed the others one by one, encouraged more than ever by the triumphant expressions on their faces. Finally he spoke, "It took 'em long enough, but now the real fun begins."

Chapter Three

He wasn't surprised that the public outcries ramped up as soon as the connection was made to the TV show. The clamor wasn't massive by any stretch, at least not yet—but it was enough to irritate anyone in a position of authority. The media's predictable cast of pundits were showing no hesitation in their assertions. Such an obvious pattern should have been noticed sooner. How could it have taken three weeks for the FBI to recognize what some unknown group was up to? But second-guessing was nothing new for law enforcement. Webb Tremont had seen the same routine countless times in the crime cases he chose to write about. Even on the best of days there were plenty of detractors eager to take shots at anyone with a badge.

In this case, not a soul had been hurt, not an iota of damage had been done. For the most part, the country's reaction was one of amusement, if not outright joy. The disparate criminal acts from the three preceding weekends were being lauded by many for their ingenuity. In a matter of hours, some group of nameless perpetrators had become social media superheroes.

The FBI hardly could be criticized for failing to identify the parallels to a television drama after the first two weeks. The population of the Houston area was approaching six million. Another three million lived in or around Pittsburgh. Yet despite extensive local media coverage of the prank crimes in those two cities, not a single resident had made the association with the prior week's episode of *Serve & Protect*. Or if they had, they'd kept that possibility to themselves.

But Portland was different. As the weekend car thefts were reported, local citizens who had watched the most recent Wednesday night episode quickly picked up on the correlation. Calls poured into the authorities as well as the media. At that point, linking the events in Portland with what had occurred in the other two cities was relatively simple police work.

Serve & Protect had premiered in early October, as the anchor to the CBS Wednesday night line-up. Elmore Brogan's reputation was on the line, so it was the most heavily promoted TV show on the fall schedule—arguably one of the most overly hyped programs in television history. The ratings on that first Wednesday night had been colossal, at least for the first half-hour. But apparently, America didn't share Elmore Brogan's passion for old-fashioned crime and Webb Tremont understood why. The content was tedious.

Viewership plummeted throughout the final thirty minutes of the premiere episode. The audience numbers for weeks two and three were even more anemic. The show was an unmitigated disaster. Cancellation should have been immediate, which would have ended Webb's misery in being associated with such vapid productions. But politics prevailed inside "Black Rock," the network's headquarters on West 52nd Street. He was informed that *Serve & Protect* would be allowed to linger until late November, then quietly disappear amidst a flurry of holiday specials.

The inaugural episode had centered on a prostitution sting in Atlanta that made national headlines in 2011, when six suburban housewives were arrested coming out of a Pilates class. The second telecast featured Martin Short as a stubborn small-town sheriff who solved what was thought to be a murder-suicide in North Dakota, but turned out to be a murder-murder after the sheriff's eight-year investigation led him back to a son who'd killed his wealthy parents. The third episode dealt with an alleged date-rape between two high-profile college athletes who'd been keeping their bisexuality a secret until charges were filed.

Each of the show's elaborate productions was based on an actual crime case from one of Webb's books, but few folks seemed to care. The number of people watching *Serve & Protect* bottomed out in week three and remained abysmal during weeks four, five, and six. Television critics were ruthless, and deservedly so.

The script for week four was based upon a raft of home burglaries from 2008, on the outskirts of Cleveland. Week five was about a series of cybercrimes from 2004, when more than ninety million dollars were absconded from a handful of corporations and transferred to secret offshore accounts. Week six featured a sophisticated ring of car thieves who stole hundreds of luxury automobiles across seventeen cities during the late 1990s.

Then the FBI made its announcement that an anonymous group was committing its own, more light-hearted versions of the crimes featured in the three most recent episodes. Cable news networks. Talk radio. Facebook. Overnight blogs. The country's airwaves and every dark hole of cyberspace instantly lit up. Tens of millions of Americans were accessing whatever source they could to catch up on back episodes of *Serve & Protect*. What had been an unmitigated train wreck was now television's hottest property. Webb's anticipated nightmare was just beginning.

Chapter Four

Fifty-five days short of the start-up's second anniversary, the highest bid had been submitted by a Minnesota conglomerate that licensed specialized products and services to financial institutions. Four-hundred and ninety-seven million dollars, no strings attached. Once the deal closed, Michael Chen wasn't required to stay another moment. He and his partners cleared out their work areas and walked away. The value to the new parent company was in the algorithms, the encryption solutions already patented and tested. The handful of banks that participated in the software's trial phase had signed long-term contracts without hesitation. The protections afforded their internal operating systems were superior to anything else on the market. Every major bank and brokerage house was sure to follow.

The principal partners of S.A.F.E., which stood for Secure Applications for Financial Encryption, separated to pursue individual opportunities. Once the investment bankers, the attorneys, Uncle Sam, and the balance of S.A.F.E.'s employees received their shares, each partner cleared forty-seven million. So the urgency wasn't what it might have been for a group of young professionals to land their next jobs. At the time, Chen was twenty-seven and all but one of the others had yet to turn thirty-one.

During the months following the January sale, two or three of the former partners would get together for an occasional lunch, or maybe hit a few of Boston's nightspots. Eleven months later, no one had seen fit to reunite the entire group. The chemistry was unusually good while they were working together, but personal relationships never had been a priority for any of them, so none of the group seemed interested in organizing an all-inclusive activity—that is, until the holidays approached and Chen received an email from Lafferty suggesting they meet for dinner at a new ethnic restaurant in the South End.

That evening's conversation and late-night drinking reminded them of how good it felt to be part of a cohesive group. Each had experienced so few in the past. The six agreed to gather again the following week at an obscure little brasserie in another part of town. After that, Michael was hooking up with the other three males and two females on an almost nightly basis. The subject never was discussed, but he knew they all had missed each other's companionship. Their success together had forged something special between them. And the fact that none of them fit neatly into other groups caused the six of them to fit especially well together.

They cared little about mainstream pursuits or mainstream relationships. Michael recognized that their rambling discussions in the past had exhibited varying degrees of pretension and intellectual elitism. Now, without business goals to unify the former partners, these affectations were becoming a more pronounced glue between them. But so what?

Soon the six were attending concerts, nightclubs and movies, or even basketball and hockey games … whatever events might attract a big crowd. Money certainly wasn't an issue. Except in one sense. The group enjoyed observing first-hand how average folks wasted theirs. How the general population occupied itself. After their outings, the six usually would assemble at a coffee shop or wine bar, or back at one of their apartments or condos. There, for hours, they could debate how mentally bankrupt the vast majority was—pondering how low the lowest common denominator actually might be.

By the time the marketing assault behind *Serve & Protect* was thrust upon the American public during the late summer of 2015, the six of them were practically inseparable. Professionally, Beaumont and Conks were applying their talents to full-time positions inside firms which had lured them with huge salaries to develop new product concepts. Michael and T-Man were developing concepts on their own that they planned to launch independently. Blake was freelancing as a high-tech trouble-shooter, while Laffy, the oldest, continued to keep his options open. But regardless of what occupied their daytime hours, the six increasingly looked forward to their evenings together.

When October rolled around, someone in the group had suggested they order Thai food and watch the first episode of the new cop show that was being promoted non-stop. Concurrence was immediate. None of them could remember a television network promoting one of its properties so aggressively. They were curious to see what type of program would persuade TV executives to engage in so much blatant pandering.

Ten minutes into *Serve & Protect*, the group's expectations had been met. The instincts of network decision-makers were as banal and insipid as ever. The first episode was even lamer than the mind-numbing books the show was based upon. And that hadn't seemed possible.

As the premiere episode drew to a close, a suggestion was tossed out almost flippantly. The ensuing discussion ran well into Thursday morning.

Chapter Five

Over the six weeks that followed the premiere telecast, Webb Tremont had laid low to avoid the slings and arrows. He'd been awaiting the onslaught since July, when he prescreened the initial episodes of *Serve & Protect*—recognizing immediately that the general public was going to reject such unmitigated garbage. His expectations had been met. The media critics unloaded. *Webb Tremont has bastardized his artistic soul. Blah, blah, blah.* What hurt were the knocks from his fans, his loyal readers. He hated to disappoint the folks who liked his books. He didn't disagree with them; he just hated to disappoint them.

Webb still found it amazing that he'd actually sold books in the first place. Millions of them, in fact. Until he started writing about crimes, his most notable literary accomplishment had been the B+ he earned for a fifth-grade essay about tree snails. Thirty years later, it wasn't unusual to see his published work occupy a full row on airport or drug store bookracks—his name emblazoned in bold red letters. He presumed that finding the hallowed family moniker attached to something as crass as crime story paperbacks was completely odious to his fellow Tremonts.

After all, Webb was one of "THOSE" Tremonts. The very same Tremonts who appeared annually on the *Forbes* list. The billionaire Tremonts. Webb's father was Brandon Tremont, the foremost contemporary Tremont in a line of wealthy Tremonts that dated back six or seven generations. Maybe eight, because it was difficult for Webb to distinguish where one generation ended and another began inside a family whose prosperity and influence had taken root in the first decade of the 19th century.

There may have been other Tremont authors during the family's prolonged history. He had no idea. But Webb was certain that no other Tremont, past or present, would have written about crime, let alone become obsessed with the subject.

Police work was Webb's inner passion. For as long as he could remember, he'd been fascinated by the law and the people who enforced it—like thousands of other young kids, he imagined. But as Webb transitioned into adulthood, those feelings held. Even intensified. In rare moments of reflection he was inclined to attribute his preoccupation to a need for a higher standard, some grander purpose. So much in his privileged life seemed shallow and superficial. From birth, he'd been guaranteed access to virtually any experience or possession by having the Tremont name and checkbook at his disposal. Respect, admiration, popularity; those also came conveniently to a Tremont. At least on the surface. In the land of the well-heeled, limits and boundaries didn't exist. There was no black or white. Only green.

For Webb, the unfettered dichotomy of the law appealed to him. It made sense. Right and wrong. Good guys and bad guys. Guilty or not guilty. The law provided a simple, natural order for how the world should operate.

He had paid his dues by working the late-night dispatch desk until his twenty-fifth birthday, when he finally was eligible for the police academy. Granted, as a suburban cop, his five years of patrolling tony north shore neighborhoods didn't afford Webb an opportunity to fight crime in the streets the way he had envisioned as a kid. But he did feel good about himself for shouldering whatever responsibility he could in upholding the balance of common decency.

After a series of events eliminated his opportunity to serve in blue, he lost this sense of inner purpose until he happened into an opportunity to write about crimes and police work. It wasn't the same as carrying a badge, but it was the closest thing available. He decided to give writing a shot. Webb Tremont didn't really fancy himself a literary person, but stories about the sacrifices and achievements of everyday cops deserved to be told. A cop of any kind, from small-town sheriff or village constable, to big-city beat cops and detectives; they all should be heralded. So, he applied himself and somehow struck a chord with a sizable reader base that seemed to share his desire to hold officers of the law in higher esteem, as pop culture and special interest groups worked overtime to tear down authority figures.

Then his worst fear from that first meeting with Elmore Brogan had been realized. Webb was hoping that Brogan's pet project might capture the human side of cops in more realistic proportion—without all the stereotypes and overly contrived melodrama about persons who enforce the laws. And without glorifying the actions of those who elected to break them. But Hollywood's stilted view of the world again had prevailed. Thankfully the public saw through the cardboard cartoons and decided not to watch the weekly drivel. Until that infernal announcement from the FBI.

Now anyone with a pulse would be tuning in for the next ghastly installment of *Serve & Protect*, waiting to see what inspiration might be drawn by some unknown collection of clowns who wanted to play loose with the law.

Chapter Six

B y the time Wednesday evening, November 25, and the seventh episode of
Serve & Protect rolled around, folks across the country had spent forty-eight
hours rollicking over every salacious detail from the first three faux crimes. Michael
Chen and his fellow collaborators secretly basked in their acclaim. The cable news
networks had latched onto the public's infatuation and essentially placed other national events on hold. Panel after panel of talking heads worked overtime dissecting
and belaboring the peculiarities of what had occurred in Houston, Pittsburgh, and
Portland. The theories as to who the perpetrators were and what they might be up
to ran a wide gamut—from absurd to more absurd.

They'd instantly become America's sweethearts. Bold. Masterful. Ingenious.
Maybe what they were doing wasn't as important as penicillin or manned space
flight, but it was a lot more entertaining.

Even the president got into the act during his regular Tuesday-morning press
briefing when he made a light-hearted remark about the antics of "some cop show
copycats." Within hours the label became permanently affixed. In subsequent media coverage, the unknown group was uniformly referred to as the "Cop Show
Copycats," courtesy of an inadvertent decree from the White House.

During the final hour of television prime time on the night before Thanksgiving,
over 34 million households, almost 71 million people, were tuned to CBS. It was easily the most-watched TV event since the prior winter's Super Bowl. The eager audience was treated to a re-enactment of an especially disturbing crime case from 2001.

Two Arkansas anarchists had been tracked down and arrested for injecting hallucinogenic drugs into unsold packages of a popular over-the-counter pain medication. After ingesting one of the capsules, a mother of three drove off a freeway ramp, killing herself and two of her children.

The morning after the show aired, much of the national euphoria had toned down. Commentators were more subdued. Water cooler conversations around the country turned somber as viewers came to grips with the fact that *Serve & Protect* was based on real crimes that produced real victims.

The six bright minds who'd gathered to watch in Boston were unfazed by the challenge before them, confident in their ability to gain additional public favor against whatever backdrop a lame TV show might present them.

Chapter Seven

When the ensuing weekend came to a close, the newly named Cop Show Copycats had obliterated whatever hangover remained from Wednesday night's broadcast. Social media again was buzzing with triumphant reactions. News reporters were tripping all over themselves with praise for what had taken place in California.

On the Friday after Thanksgiving the six Bostonians traveled to California and invaded the shelves of supermarkets and mass merchants around Sacramento. By Sunday morning customers from seven local retailers had found a sweet surprise inside their just-purchased packages of Sinu-Care. The copycats replaced capsules of the sinus relief medicine with multi-colored M&M's. On an even sweeter note, each of the seven lucky customers also discovered a one-hundred-dollar bill folded neatly among the candies.

For the first time, Michael Chen and his cohorts could follow the immediate aftermath of their weekend antics because of the wall-to-wall media coverage. Authorities promptly pulled Sinu-Care from every store within a radius of seventy-five miles—a decision that proved unpopular when it was reported that thirteen additional unsold packages of candy and currency were discovered. Thousands of Californians had been denied their chance at one of the treasured bottles. The pharmaceutical giant that marketed the product sent in a flock of representatives who soon were mystified because the factory seals on the affected bottles appeared to be untouched.

The media reveled in every sensationalized aspect. A few voices tried to raise concerns, but they were drowned out by legions of others who waxed on and on about the brilliance of the copycats. Sure, tampering with over-the-counter medications was a federal offense, but officials needed to lighten up. No one had been hurt—in fact, just the opposite. Those lucky enough to purchase them were rewarded. If anything, the audacious acts of the copycats had served the public interest by demonstrating how much the existing protocols for distributing and selling such products needed to be tightened. The public reaction was everything the six of them hoped it would be.

But there was one outcome they hadn't anticipated, at least this soon. Sacramento was the second city where this group of pranksters had spread one-hundred-dollar bills like confetti, so a few commentators already were likening the Cop Show Copycats to modern-day Robin Hoods.

On Monday evening the former business partners reconvened as they always did, for a detailed assessment of the prior weekend. Though the logistics of getting to and from Sacramento had proven more difficult than the first three weekends, everyone agreed that in total their latest lampoon had been relatively simple to execute. In fact, they'd been able to enjoy an added benefit. They each completed their assigned tasks on Friday night, leaving them all day Saturday to tool around Central California before heading back to Boston on Sunday. Unfortunately, they were obliged to do that separately, so as not to draw unwanted attention to a group of unfamiliar faces.

In traveling to Sacramento, five of the six had flown out of Logan on Thursday afternoon. Of those five, only T-Man was allowed to book a direct flight—because he drew San Francisco when they'd pulled their cities from a hat. The others needed to make connecting flights in order to reach their destinations of Reno, San Jose, and Modesto. With few major airports within reasonable driving distance of Sacramento, they agreed to make an exception to one of their standard protocols. Blake O'Meara and Michael Chen were allowed to fly on the same plane to San Jose.

Cars were rented and all but Gregory Beaumont converged in Sacramento on

Friday morning. During their respective drives from their assigned arrival cities, each made stops at local convenience stores or Mom & Pop groceries along the way to purchase packages of Sinu-Care. They had identified establishments in advance that weren't sophisticated enough to employ security cameras. It often required much extra planning, but avoiding visual trails of any kinds was another of their mandatory protocols. The product needed to be procured locally so that authorities couldn't use lot numbers to trace an advance purchase to the Boston area.

Beaumont's work schedule for the week included a Friday-morning staff meeting that he couldn't miss without raising questions, so he flew to San Francisco later that day and caught up with the others in time to help Blake access the computer systems inside the predetermined mass merchants where the tampered packages were to be placed. The pair worked from a room inside a rundown motel the group had selected as "central command" for this particular weekend's activities. According to their ground rules, the seedier the accommodations the better. Lower-end, less-reputable establishments were likely to have fewer, if any, security systems to avoid or immobilize. Also, most cheap motels required guests to pay in advance, preferably with cash. No credit cards meant no paper trails. Once the appropriate amount of cash was sitting visibly on a registration counter, the owners or employees working the front desk weren't inclined to spend much time checking a potential guest's ID. Not that this issue posed a major concern, since each of the six carried an ample supply of counterfeit driver's licenses.

While Gregory Beaumont and Blake O'Meara worked their computers from the motel, the other four hit the highways and byways of Sacramento in teams of two. Each twosome visited five stores. One team member watched for an appropriate moment, then signaled the other to insert two new packages of Sinu-Care among those already on the shelves. Twenty in total. Reverse shoplifting.

Upon arriving at the parking lot of a specified store, the assigned team would phone O'Meara and Beaumont back at central command. Any store employee who happened to be paying attention to that store's computerized video surveillance would notice the security system inexplicably had gone down. But within minutes the system again would be up and running normally—once O'Meara and Beaumont had received an "all clear" call from the designated team, indicating that they'd completed their task and exited the store.

Earlier in the day Teresa Conkle had handled the unsealing and resealing of twenty Sinu-Care packages, as well as the substitution of candy and cash. Earlier in the week she'd studied the exterior cartons and plastic bottles used by the manufacturer. She brought along a small steaming device for opening the packages, as well as the exact glue formulation for resealing them.

The events during this fourth weekend went as perfectly as the three before. With proper preparation, the six former business partners were convinced they could amuse themselves indefinitely. Public response to their latest adventure was no surprise. The public was accustomed to the mundane, to warmed milk for the masses. So, of course, people were going to be amazed when finally confronted with legitimate inspiration.

However, the group did experience one disappointment during their first week of national attention. That ridiculous name—Cop Show Copycats. Granted, it had been coined by no less than the President of the United States. But still, they deserved better.

Chapter Eight

With an entire nation rejoicing the exploits of the Cop Show Copycats and eagerly anticipating their next installment, Webb Tremont was amazed how the newspaper and broadcast coverage chose to ignore a rather obvious truth. These unknown parties were breaking the law at every turn. They were criminals.

Surely the top brass at the FBI had to be aware of this fact and were placing a high priority on identifying the culprits. They needed to put a halt to these antics as quickly as possible, before someone got hurt—which invariably happened when folks toyed frivolously with the law—and also before these troublemakers managed to embarrass every arm of law enforcement.

***

The intensity of the effort was being downplayed. Why turn the public against the Bureau for throwing a wet blanket onto all the fun being generated by an unknown group of sophisticated pranksters? Enough people already viewed the FBI as a bunch of heavies.

The manpower assigned to fieldwork on the growing case file was substantial, with more to be made available as soon as leads started developing. Heading up the investigation was C.J. Matthews—a plum assignment for a special agent with only eleven years on the job. The special agent had produced stellar results and earned repeated distinctions during that tenure.

But after the first week, results from the investigation were far from stellar. In fact, there were no meaningful results at all. Matthews and the field teams working the case quickly recognized that some number of renegade souls who'd captured the country's imagination were damned good at being criminals. Worse than good. Thus far, they'd been perfect. A deplorable word when attached to crimes and criminals.

In Houston, the copycats had entered nine private residences and pulled valuables out of countless hiding places. In Pittsburgh, they'd penetrated computer systems inside five respected corporations. Then in Portland, they'd removed vehicles from the parking lots of seventeen exclusive establishments and thumbed their noses at authorities by relocating them to the police stations of every local precinct. That same weekend in Portland, a mysterious epidemic of technical problems had plagued the surveillance systems monitoring the parking lots from which the vehicles were stolen, as well as the police facilities where they later were found. Most recently, the unknown group inserted modified packages of a controlled medical product onto the shelves of ten mass merchants during regular business hours on the busiest shopping weekend of the year.

As assigned federal agents in four geographic areas descended upon this unprecedented trove of crime scenes, expectations had been high. There surely would be eye witnesses. Security videos. Fingerprints. Fiber samples. Computer trails. It would be a matter of days, if not hours, before these practical jokers were identified and rounded up.

But a week later. Nothing. C.J. Matthews was strapping in for a long ride.

———◦———

Most people might experience a ripple of anxiety if an administrative assistant from the FBI were to call to request an appointment as part of an official investigation. Webb Tremont had the opposite reaction. Relief. He'd begun to worry that the nation's ridiculous love affair with the Cop Show Copycats extended to federal authorities. He might be forced to live with the *Serve & Protect* atrocity every Wednesday night into perpetuity. So, he was comforted by the prospect of meeting with some special agent named C.J. Matthews and helping this G-man in whatever way he could.

For the first day of December, Tuesday afternoon was unseasonably warm along the north shore of Chicago. Webb decided to shoot a few hoops on the driveway until the special agent arrived. The moment the nondescript gray sedan pulled up to the coach house and he saw the agent's face, Webb Tremont knew he was in trouble. Not with the law. No, his problem would be stringing coherent thoughts together.

First of all, this G-man was a G-woman. Secondly, FBI agents weren't supposed to look like cover girls. His immediate impression was that C.J. Matthews should be waltzing down red carpets instead of chasing down wanted criminals. Then it hit him that this gorgeous creature was trained to kill if circumstances required. With his penchant for police work, such a blend of beauty and vocation was a lot to absorb. He refused to allow his mind to wander any further. Tremont was a confirmed monogamist. Not necessarily the marrying type, but a monogamist nonetheless, and he knew how fortunate he was to have a girlfriend like Corrie who was willing to put up with his complicated ways.

Like a moth drawn to a flood light, Webb made a path to the driver's side of the car. As he politely opened her car door, the agent still was gathering a few papers. She glanced up from the seat. "A gentleman … why, thank you."

Webb responded with a simple nod. He needed a little more time to muster actual words. Up close she looked even more spectacular. Blonde with green eyes. Even while seated, she appeared fit. As soon as she rose and stepped away from the car, he knew he'd been too quick to judge. Fit was one thing. This woman was a physical specimen. Even dressed in a business-like suit it was obvious her body was firm and shapely in all the appropriate places. And tall. To make matters worse, she was sporting the hint of a tan. He refused to contemplate the possible location of tan lines. Webb Tremont was defenseless. If C.J. Matthews had decided to accuse him of a felony right there on the spot, he would have confessed merely for the opportunity of having her place him in handcuffs. To say nothing of her searching him for a weapon.

The agent extended her hand and smiled. "Pleased to meet you, Mr. Tremont."

The smile only made things worse. Bright, perfect teeth. Magnificent full lips.

29

Dimples on both sides of her smooth, bronze cheeks. She oozed outdoorsiness and athleticism. "Malibu Perfect" typically held little attraction for Webb, but C.J. Matthews also carried a badge and a gun. Any past rating scale was immaterial. He once again gave a slight nod, but this time also managed to expel a few syllables as he clasped her hand. "Miss Matthews." That was enough. He couldn't risk whatever else might tumble out of his mouth.

She didn't allow the silence to grow awkward. "An unexpected choice of residences," she observed. "Considering your success as a writer, when I pulled up to the front gate I assumed your house was the sizable one in the distance, through the trees. But the mysterious voice on the intercom directed me back here."

"That was Nessie. She started working for my parents before I was born. She's the one who really runs this place … at least since my mom died."

The agent tried to conceal her puzzlement, before finally surrendering. "Let me get this straight, Mr. Tremont. You're forty-one years old, you've made millions from writing books, and you probably have hundreds of millions more in family money, yet you're living here in your parents' coach house?"

Webb shrugged his shoulders. "It's a long story, so let me simply clarify two important points. First, I've never touched a dime of family money. And second, this is my coach house. I bought it from my father back when I was a cop. Wasn't easy making the payments, but I even paid more than it was worth so he'd never be able to claim I took advantage of him."

Now she was more perplexed than before. "Sounds like an interesting family."

"You have no idea, Miss Matthews. You have no idea."

Webb didn't think it appropriate to invite a federal agent upstairs to his living quarters. Especially one who'd just stepped off the pages of a swimsuit calendar. So he escorted her into the first floor of the coach house. Except for the assortment of weights and work-out machines in one corner, the large open space resembled a Wisconsin roadhouse. Hardwood floor and knotty pine walls. The middle of the room contained a slate pool table. An authentic Irish dart board hung on the adjacent wall. To the side was a seating area with oversized dark leather furniture.

He grabbed two bottles of water from the vintage fridge behind the bar. "Would you like a glass?"

She shook her head. "No thanks. Somehow drinking from a bottle, even a plastic one, seems more appropriate in here."

"I guess I should apologize for the décor. It's …."

She cut him off. "No apologies necessary. This room is incredible … I just wasn't expecting something so rustic, considering the stateliness of the overall grounds."

Webb couldn't let that go. "Stateliness. Nice try … my father would like that. How about pretentiousness … or ostentatiousness?"

C.J. Matthews allowed his questions to become rhetorical ones, so he continued, "My girlfriend designed this room … the upstairs, too. A buddy from the police force recommended her for the job, and that's how we met."

"Mr. Tremont, I'd have to say you scored a double victory." The special agent let loose with another one of her smiles.

"Miss Matthews, perhaps we could dispense with the formalities. Please call me Webb."

"Considering your background, I'll assume you're familiar with the rules, Mr. Tremont."

It had been worth a try. Over the next two hours, Webb surprised himself by fashioning mostly complete sentences, but there still were multiple occasions when his mouth went a little dry.

The primary purpose of the special agent's visit was to probe Tremont about people from his present or past who might want to harass or embarrass him. Could he think of enemies he'd made, or individuals who disliked him enough to plan and implement a series of weekend crimes that parodied his TV show?

Webb was quick to distance himself. "Please make no mistake, that program is anything but mine. I may have sold my name and the crime cases from my books, but I've had nothing to do with the final scripts or actual productions."

"I'm sorry, Mr. Tremont; I understand the distinction. But regardless, your name is closely associated with the show. If someone was looking to make a statement either to you or about you, *Serve & Protect* provides them a highly visible forum."

In response he quipped, "Based on the audience numbers prior to the most recent episode, 'highly visible forum' would have been a gargantuan overstatement. Have you met Elmore Brogan? I wouldn't put it past him to have concocted this whole copycat thing to bolster ratings and salvage his reputation."

"Not the first time that possibility has been suggested, I assure you. We have agents in New York interviewing Brogan and other executives at CBS, just to be sure ... as well as investigating whether he or others at the network might be intended targets for the copycats."

Webb responded, "I imagine that well-paid gang in New York isn't short on enemies. It's quite a group to whom I've prostituted myself."

"We can drop the self-flagellation, Mr. Tremont. We're fully aware of where your money from the TV show is going."

As a crime writer and former police officer, he should have known the FBI would have dug into his personal dealings. His arrangement with CBS was going to generate somewhere between six and twenty million dollars. After the contract was signed, his attorneys completed another flurry of paperwork to establish Legacy Blue, a foundation that assisted the children of fallen police officers. This second arrangement was never publicly announced. Every cent Webb Tremont earned from the TV show went directly into the foundation—as would a quarter of his book royalties going forward.

He preferred not to talk about the foundation and changed the subject. "Let's get back to your original question, Miss Matthews. As you might have guessed, I've already been pondering the possibility that the copycats could be targeting me for some unknown reason. I won't deny there are plenty of folks who have reasons to dislike me ... considering my family, my upbringing, my years as a cop, and then my second career as a writer. And, let's face it, my personality can be something less than endearing from time to time. But I can't come up with anyone who might hate or resent me to this degree, let alone have the smarts and resources to pull off what these copycats are doing."

She asked him to keep pressing his memory over the days ahead and pass along any names that popped into his head, no matter how tenuous the likelihood might seem. She assured him the FBI would be discreet in its follow-up of individuals, and also forewarned him that she'd be calling him periodically to make sure he stayed on task.

Regular phone calls with a divine spirit from law enforcement. At last Webb Tremont had unearthed a benefit to the whole copycat debacle.

Chapter Nine

As another Wednesday approached, anticipation built over the type of crime that would be featured on the next episode of *Serve & Protect*. What would the Cop Show Copycats be given to work with for their fifth weekend? CBS dispensed with releasing advanced descriptions of the coming week's broadcast. The network execs figured viewer interest would be piqued to even higher levels if people were left in suspense about the subject matter.

Interest also climbed in Washington DC. With the attention being drawn by the Cop Show Copycats, the powers at FBI headquarters quietly upgraded the investigation to its highest domestic crime category. Though media and special-interest groups weren't applying pressure on the federal authorities because of the perceived harmlessness of the parody acts, it was only a matter of time before such a leap would be made. Questions inevitably would get raised. After all, the copycats weren't simply mocking a prime-time TV show, they were mocking the competency of law enforcement. And due to a spate of fatal shootings by overzealous police officers in recent years, law enforcement was under enough attack already.

Much of the pressure fell on Special Agent C.J. Matthews. Though she'd yet to submit a request, more field teams were assigned to her as the sophistication of the unknown perpetrators became increasingly evident. Nothing of consequence had been revealed through comprehensive reviews of airline records for the flights into and out of the four cities where mock crimes had occurred. The search was expanded to include airports in cities within reasonable driving distances. Still nothing. There was no recurrence of groups of any size booking flights to a common destination. If the copycats were flying commercially, each in the group was likely booking his or her own flights separately and possibly using multiple identities with corresponding documentation. Air travel under an alias was difficult with the security procedures in effect since the rise of terrorism, but not out of the question for individuals having appropriate technical skills and resources. The FBI expanded its scope to include private airports and charter services, plus train and bus routes.

———◇———

Webb Tremont was having frequent thoughts about C.J. Matthews, and not simply because of the lasting physical impression she'd made. He recognized the challenge handed to the special agent was a daunting one. Intelligence. Technical ability. Creativity. Mobility. Access to financial resources. Patience and preparedness. The Cop Show Copycats seemed to possess a formidable set of skills. But each weekend they also revealed a characteristic that authorities had been counting on since police forces first were formed. A trait which inexorably caused criminals to slip and fail. Arrogance.

The group's decision to emulate cases from a weekly television program was in itself an act of unbridled arrogance. This arrogance was amplified through the manner in which each parody crime was executed. The subtle twists on the actual crimes. The messages and cash left behind in envelopes.

The pretentiousness of these copycats was accentuated by how the media exhausted every nuance with its coverage. As talking heads glorified the wondrous intricacies of each weekend frolic, Webb looked forward to this same fervor proving to be the group's undoing. Their activities to date made one thing abundantly clear. The Cop Show Copycats were grandstanders of the highest order.

The copycats' first foray had been spawned by the fourth episode of *Serve &* *Protect*, which centered on Ohio burglaries committed over a four-month period during 2008. Due to the economic difficulties of that particular year, the owners of nine homes in and around the Cleveland area had found it necessary to tighten their household budgets. Each cancelled their service contract with a local home security company. As it turned out, that firm employed a hard-working young woman with an entrepreneurial itch. For every customer residence, the security company maintained active files which contained floor plans and an inventory of artwork, jewelry, and other valued items covered by added insurance riders. This female supervisor launched a side business by recruiting two convicted thieves and supplying them with the copies of files for expensive homes where security service had been suspended.

With detailed floor plans in hand and their alarm systems deactivated, breaking into these homes and robbing them of valuable possessions was a walk in the park. Until several months later, when a police investigator noticed something in the background of the photos taken at the various crime scenes. On the windows of several of the homes were decals indicating the residences had been protected by the same security company. A little digging revealed all nine homeowners had suspended service contracts with HomeGuard Security, and from there it was a matter of days before the trail led back to the entrepreneurial supervisor.

On November 4, 2015, the fourth episode of *Serve & Protect* stuck close to the facts from this 2008 case, which Webb had researched for his eighth book. Over the ensuing weekend, nine similar break-ins were perpetrated by the Cop Show Copycats outside of Houston. Since then, Webb and the rest of America had learned a great deal more about their approach.

The prank burglaries took place in a handful of communities, meaning no single police department investigated all nine incidents. And with nothing missing from any of the homes, none of the local investigations were given an especially high priority. So, the cancellation of the nine security contracts had been missed. But two weeks later, after the FBI made the connection to the TV show, federal investigators noticed that just as in Cleveland, all nine homeowners had run into financial problems. Security service to each of the homes had been suspended during the previous year, and those contracts happened to be with one particular provider that served the upper end of the Houston market.

Because the service contracts were suspended instead of cancelled, the floor plans and information about the contents of these residences were retained in the company's computer system. By hacking into that computer system, the copycats were able to determine which homes no longer were protected by active alarm systems, and what valuable items could be found inside. Exact pieces of art were itemized in the files, which meant the copycats could enter each residence with their own updated appraisals typed on Post-It notes. With the nine homeowners strapped for funds, the envelopes containing a thousand dollars in cash were well-received. "To help tide you over during difficult times."

But the Cop Show Copycats really weren't out to help anyone. They were showing off. Nothing more. That had been Webb Tremont's opinion from the moment the FBI issued its first press release and those sentiments grew stronger by the day. Webb was taking the whole insane situation personally. Not because the copycats were making a mockery of the TV show that had his name plastered all over it. The show already had been a mockery without their help. And not because he worried the copycats were targeting him with their actions, since he had no tangible reason to jump to that conclusion. No, the part he took personally was the burlesque they were making of the law.

Webb may not have looked or acted like a straight arrow, but when it came to the law, he was a card-carrying puritan—especially as the behavior of police officers was being called into question at every turn amidst the national discourse. Sure, he knew there were a few bad cops in most any city, but he also knew they were the exception. Good cops were getting raked over the coals by mere association, and now a bunch of dandies was trying to make fools of the whole profession.

Webb Tremont had gone to college on a wrestling scholarship and still looked like he could manage a decent take-down or reversal. He was on the tall side, at six-two. He rejected any type of fitness regimen, but instead ran or worked out whenever the mood struck. Occasionally he showed signs of the limp that served as a memento from his final case as a cop, but overall Webb felt like he was in reasonably decent shape. His hair was more than dark. It was ebony, like his mother's, but in recent months he'd noticed random specks of salt amidst the pepper. He usually needed a haircut, as well as a comb—a style Corrie had taken to describing as "floppy." His father was less tactful when he addressed his son, or anyone else for that matter. "Webster, just because you purport to be an author, you shouldn't feel obligated to go out in public looking like a rag doll. My heavens, you're forty-one years old."

His nose and chin were angular. Emphatic. His eyes were dark brown, almost black against the backdrop of hair and eyebrows. His skin tone likewise was dark. His beard was heavy, and Webb was borderline obsessive about being clean-shaven—a trait he attributed to wrestling coaches from his past who had insisted he shave all applicable body parts in the never-ending quest to make a lower weight class.

Webb hadn't worn a suit or tie since his mother's funeral, eight years earlier. He occasionally would throw on a sport coat, but never of the tweed or corduroy variety. Those were the uniforms of the literary profession. Even after eleven books, mostly best-sellers, he refused to be categorized as a writer. On most days, he randomly pulled clothes from the back of his closet—though front or back wouldn't have much mattered.

In terms of personal comportment, Webb Tremont took pride in at least being consistent. He tried to remain carefree, but he often pushed this envelope to the point of irreverence—especially when Brandon Tremont was anywhere near. The lone exception were his years with the Lake Forest Police Department. On-duty, his behavior had been straight arrow to the core.

———◆———

The eighth telecast of *Serve & Protect*, on December 2, featured a case from Webb's very first book, published in late 2006. It dealt with a string of kidnappings committed along the Carolina Coast during the summer of 1997. Over the course of ten days that July, a deranged vagrant climbed through windows into four children's bedrooms, abducted three girls and a boy, and tried to convince these preschoolers he was their rightful birth father and that they'd been stolen from him as infants. Fortunately, the kidnapped youngsters were found two weeks later, sleeping inside an old Volkswagen van that looked suspicious to a deputy sheriff in Warsaw, Indiana.

On Sunday, December 6, four days after the original crimes had been reenacted during prime time, the Arizona State Police called a televised press conference. Webb watched from Lake Forest as each disgusting detail was revealed. The Cop Show Copycats had spent their weekend in the Tucson area, where four couples notified local authorities that their homes were broken into. At each residence, unknown parties had entered a child's bedroom during the late hours between Saturday evening and Sunday morning. Oversized envelopes were left beneath the pillows of four sleeping children, whose genders and ages happened to precisely match the four kids abducted in the original Carolina case.

The four thick packets were addressed to the children by name, with a card inside containing a message for his or her parents: "We apologize for violating your privacy, but we hope our actions will encourage you to better secure your home. Please accept the enclosed as a token of our heartfelt concern." Accompanying each note was a stack of fifty hundred-dollar bills, or $5,000.

The media ate it up. The Cop Show Copycats were passing out C-notes like Halloween candy. They no longer were being referred to merely as playful pranksters. Now they were anonymous benefactors who cared about kids. Webb cringed with every new superlative. This anonymous group knew exactly how to play to the public. These characters had defied the sanctity of a child's bedroom not once, but four times, yet they weren't being criticized, or even questioned. Instead, thanks to four parcels of cash and a few well-chosen words, they were progressing toward sainthood.

Adding to the insanity, by midday on Monday the four sets of parents were making the rounds on the news networks, enjoying newfound celebrity and their windfalls of cash. With each successive interview, they heaped higher praise on the unknown individuals who had slipped into their homes while they and their children were sound asleep. The Cop Show Copycats weren't simply mocking the law; now their efforts were undercutting parenthood and human decency.

Chapter Ten

By late Sunday night Michael Chen had made his way back to Boston from Arizona. When he and the other five assembled for their regular Monday evening meeting, Michael suggested they select more accessible cities for the next few weekends. Thankfully everyone concurred, even Lafferty for once. Remaining fresh and clear-headed was vital to their continued success. Schedule-wise, traveling to Tucson on the heels of a weekend in Sacramento had been more grueling than anticipated.

Michael had drawn San Diego. The drive to Tucson was six hours each way, given his strict adherence to the speed limit—which was another of the group's specified ground rules. The last thing they needed were documented face-to-face encounters with law enforcement over something as avoidable as traffic violations.

The easiest drive had been T-Man's, from Phoenix. Less than two hours. But poor Conks, she was stuck with a nine-hour slog from Orange County.

Like everything else, the inconveniences of travel had been anticipated when the six did their original planning. Hardships would be required to fit each epic adventure into a discrete weekend, but they had felt the sense of accomplishment would more than compensate. Thus far this assumption had proven true, but there was no need to make themselves martyrs. Especially since no one outside the group was ever to understand the extent of their sacrifices.

They agreed that every objective again had been met over the previous weekend. With the mock kidnappings in Arizona, the six bright minds had recognized they might lose favor with the public by sneaking into children's bedrooms, but the significant bump in cash had done the trick. Just as predicted. Beaumont quipped, "If we'd have thrown in another five grand, I think some of those parents would have been okay if their kids had gone missing for a day or two."

With the postmortem out of the way, plans for the coming weekend could begin. Blake O'Meara handed out folders and Chen began leafing through the inserted pages. Once the group had committed to implementing the mock crimes back in October, Blake navigated her way into the computer files of a CBS programming executive, which provided the group a copy of the final script to every mind-numbing episode of *Serve & Protect* for the entirety of the broadcast year.

The room went relatively quiet for the next half-hour as each of the six absorbed the details of the coming Wednesday night broadcast. Then one by one they powered up their laptops to research the original crime that was the basis of the next episode. By midnight the group had compared observations, shared their ideas, and committed to a preliminary course of action that would be finalized when they gathered around a TV two nights later.

The featured crime case for the second Wednesday of December was gorier and more cold-hearted then any episode to date. The stark realities would require careful steering. After thorough discussion, the group decided to shake things up. The months ahead would be a lot more fun if they kept the public guessing.

With a full season of program content in hand, the group could have chosen to plot their elaborate weekend schemes well in advance. But they'd agreed at the onset that allowing excessive time for preparation was akin to cheating. Michael still was amazed at how quickly the group had coalesced on so many fundamentals. In the commission of perfect crimes, there could be no shortcuts. Legendary performance required rigorous standards. Tackling the featured cases on a week-by-week basis was in keeping with that spirit. They had debated about waiting for Wednesday night and learning about each new crime with the rest of the country. But they'd recognized such tight turnaround times would be too taxing, even for them, since five of the group were gainfully employed during the intervening daytime hours.

Their accomplishments indeed would be legendary. Of this they'd been certain from the beginning. True geniuses should be capable of perfect crimes. Leopold and Loeb had made huge headlines in 1924 because they were drawn to the same alluring challenge. But the six partners dismissed that pair's attempt as feeble. If those two allegedly brilliant students from University of Chicago had been legitimate geniuses, they wouldn't have murdered an innocent fourteen-year-old. How fulfilling could that have been? Not to mention the fact they were caught and sentenced to life in prison. They were so careless with their attempt that even Clarence Darrow couldn't dissuade a jury of their guilt. Leopold and Loeb had been just two more pitiful fools with wasted intellect.

No, the grandest achievement would come from executing a perfect crime and gaining the public's favor. Not just once, but again and again. Maybe dozens of times. For as long as the weekly exercises continued to stimulate them. Once their creative endeavors turned into drudgery, the group pledged to call it quits and move on to new challenges in their lives. The public would be left guessing. Marveling. Erudite minds could dissect their criminal artistry for centuries, pondering who might have been the responsible parties and what had become of them.

Michael and the others had joined forces as novices to the world of commerce in early 2012. It was commendable that two years later their start-up had been sold for a staggering amount in record time. But lots of techies were sporting similar notches on their belts. There even was a growing number of new wave entrepreneurs who'd launched and sold multiple successful concepts before the age of forty. Michael was confident he and Conks, and probably Beaumont and T-Man, were destined to do likewise.

But no one in the world of technology, or any other world, had accomplished anything remotely close to what they now were pulling off on a weekly basis. Perfect crimes with the whole world watching. Few in history would have dared to consider such an outrageous undertaking. And therein lay the motivation. The psychic reward. The measuring stick. They privately would know how they stacked up with the greatest minds of all time.

They waited for the fourth episode of *Serve & Protect* to unveil their first parody crime. Credit for that foresight went to Conks. They all had figured the lame TV show was going to bomb, but Teresa Conkle was the one who suggested this likelihood could be used to their advantage. As things turned out, the ratings disaster was on the verge of outright cancellation before they introduced their weekend mastery. The resulting upswing in audience levels only served to accentuate the colossal disparity between the ordinary and the extraordinary.

⊶⊷

Webb Tremont worried about the dangerous tightropes the Cop Show Copycats might be walking over the weekend ahead. The original murders had taken place in April of 2000, and he was only too familiar with the triple homicide being portrayed on Wednesday night's episode. Months earlier, Brogan's team of script writers had asked Webb to forward his research files from the case he had profiled in his third book. His signed contract with the network gave him no choice but to comply and then watch as Hollywood bastardized the actual facts.

He felt a deep connection to every case from his books. He had researched hundreds of criminal investigations for each volume, before choosing the twenty or so that struck a deserving chord for law enforcement. During his first few years as an author, Webb was cranking out a new volume of *Serve & Protect* every six months before he discovered the value of pacing. He finally accepted that no matter how hard he worked, he couldn't possibly tell all the stories worthy of being told. It was impossible to resurrect more than a small portion of the incredible police work that went virtually unnoticed.

Despite the soaring popularity of his books, their success never fully registered with Webb, because he knew his writing career had started as an act of desperation. He had resigned from the Lake Forest Police Department near the end of 2004, once police work no longer was viable. After five months away from the force, he'd yet to uncover a single new marketable skill—let alone a career direction that could hold his interest. Worse, his savings were nearly depleted and he sure as hell wasn't going to touch any of the trust funds that had his name attached to them. If his sister and brother wanted to live off family money, he wasn't one to question how they led their lives. But he'd rather stand in a soup line than reach into the Tremont treasure chest—or the money generated by the Emerson Publishing dynasty on his mother's side of the family. With this same stubbornness, he had declined medical disability payments from the police department.

Aimlessly unemployed, he faced the prospect of informing his father that his payments for the coach house were going to be late for a few months. He had known that Brandon Tremont would have relished such a moment. *No problem, Webster … you know I wanted to give you that wretched building in the first place, but your mother acquiesced to the irritating purchase agreement you sent me. Perhaps it's time we find you a suitable position in one of our family holdings.* For Webb, there definitely were fates far worse than death.

Timing was everything. When the associate editor from *Atlantic Monthly* called, how could he possibly have turned down her offer? She was willing to pay him $10,000 to do nothing more than jot down his personal accounts of two crimes that had made national headlines—two incidents in sleepy Lake Forest that generated so much notoriety for Webb Tremont that he no longer could go about normal duties as a police officer in Lake Forest or anywhere else. He wouldn't even have to fret over how the article might read, because she would have some paid staffer at the magazine rewrite whatever Webb submitted, to assure that he came across as literate.

His pride kicked in. Webb took the writing assignment seriously, working round the clock to be certain the smallest details were conveyed exactly the way he wanted them. Not a single dangling participle or improper syntax.

The finished piece was nothing like the associate editor had expected. Or wanted. She'd been hoping for graphic descriptions of how Tremont startled and shot a raging lunatic on the verge of murdering four innocent victims inside a stately Lake Forest mansion. Or the frightening details of how his routine rounds at a local public school had brought him face-to-face with a whacked-out gunman looking to make a name for himself a few years after Columbine. Or the bullet that tore apart his hip and sealed his decision about giving up police work.

Instead, Webb wrote a more generalized article about suburban cops, the special training they received and rarely were called upon to deploy; the daily constraint and humility they exhibited among the dismissive constituencies they were charged to protect; and ultimately their readiness to put their lives on the line on behalf of those very same constituents. To the degree references were made to the two highly publicized crimes that had brought him notoriety, the mentions were incidental. And "far too self-deprecating" for the young associate editor's taste. Nonetheless, her bosses loved what Tremont submitted and he refused to change a word, so that was how the piece ran during the summer of 2005.

As stacks of mail were received by the magazine, he was encouraged to learn that a lot of readers agreed with his approach. Some of the most heartfelt letters streamed in from small-town police chiefs, rural county sheriffs, and hundreds of suburban police officers around the country. Webb Tremont had tapped an emotional mother lode for police officers everywhere.

A month later Webb was given carte blanche to submit another article. He could write about whatever crimes he wanted, and this time they were going to pay him fifteen grand. Webb was convinced the magazine was running recklessly out of control, but figured he might as well grab the money before some adult in a corner office woke up and recognized what was going on.

For days, he buried himself in Chicago's central library, thumbing through old newspapers and wire stories. Finally, he retreated to his coach house where words miraculously started flowing from his fingertips onto a keyboard. He wrote about three separate crimes: a brutal beating, a sexual assault, and an armed robbery. They'd been committed in three separate cities—Des Moines, Savannah, and Salt Lake City. The three felonies had nothing to do with one another, except for the fact they'd been stopped in progress by three separate police officers from three different police departments on the very same night, within a single hour of one another. And that was the point.

At any given hour, on any given day, there were countless criminal acts being contemplated and committed. Likewise, there were thousands upon thousands of law enforcement professionals who couldn't possibly put a stop to all of them, but nonetheless were committed to make whatever difference they could. Webb Tremont wanted readers to imagine how different any night in any city might be without that kind of selfless commitment. Once again, he struck a powerful chord.

The magazine put him on retainer and ran whatever he sent them over the months that followed. Content-wise, Webb didn't stray much from what quickly became a comfort zone. He stuck to real crimes, the real police men and women who solved them, and the real lives and families behind those officers and the risks for which they'd signed on. His passion for what he was writing grew, and surprisingly, so did his reader base. In addition to old newspapers and libraries, Webb gained ready access to police officials, and in many instances their files and computer systems. Apparently, he was perceived as an advocate, a voice for law enforcement. He could pick up the phone and doors would magically open.

Most importantly, he'd unearthed a profession that allowed him to work outside the mainstream. No staff meetings. No public places. No public at all. Just him and his trusty keyboard in the privacy of a coach house.

In early 2006, an insufferable character from Simon and Schuster started phoning him. The publisher's rep had been "ravenously following" Webb's magazine work, and felt his pieces were "unflinchingly organic." The relentless pitchman was "irrefutably convinced" that Webb's *Atlantic Monthly* articles provided an ideal launch pad for a successful book or two. The guy had a way with words, but Webb decided to give him a try just the same. Seven months later, *Serve & Protect* was published. Within three weeks, the book had climbed to fifth on the New York Times list. Over the next nine years Webb researched and wrote ten more editions in what became the *Serve & Protect* series.

Now, a decade later, Webb's happenstance journey as a crime writer had spawned a god-awful TV show and a band of lunatics who were thumbing their noses at the law and every man or woman committed to enforce it. He gladly would toss aside his keyboard and never construct another sentence of prose if the whole farce would just come to an end.

Chapter Eleven

The audience ratings blew through every record for a Wednesday night. Nearly 80 million viewers. Webb figured the suits at CBS must have been erecting private shrines to the Cop Show Copycats. But he recognized that anyone watching the December 9 episode would have found the experience a great deal less joyful.

The case from 2000 involved three homeless African-American women in Baltimore. During the late-night hours they were lured to Federal Hill Park, where all three were bound, tortured, and eventually burned while still barely alive by a group of inebriated Neo-Nazis. In the end, five males in their thirties and forties were arrested and prosecuted for cruel, senseless acts committed during the fourth month of a new millennium.

While researching the case more than seven years after the fact, Webb flew to Baltimore to interview investigating officers and other parties familiar with the events. The responsible individuals had been members of the Aryan Disciples, a not-so-secret secret organization of white males, ranging in age from twenty-one to upwards of eighty. Legal drinking age seemed to be the most stringent qualification for membership. After all, no group of hate-mongering bigots would want to promote the consumption of alcohol by minors. Monthly meetings were held in the basements or private party rooms of local Baltimore bars. "Meetings" was a loose term for rancorous drunk-fests.

Following official adjournment of the April gathering, five of the Disciples decided to carry their spewing and drinking to a second nearby establishment. And then a third and a fourth. By one in the morning, they'd convinced themselves that the vitriol of that night's occasion needed to be commemorated in some appropriate fashion. They headed for The Block, a section on East Baltimore Street where late-night companionship could be readily secured. There they persuaded three seasoned ladies of the evening to join them for an intimate outdoor party in a remote corner of Federal Hill Park—to celebrate the advent of spring. The women couldn't possibly have anticipated the type of intimacy these cretins had in store for them.

Their lifeless forms were still smoldering when a pair of pre-dawn joggers happened upon the gruesome aftermath. Several days were needed to identify the victims. No permanent addresses could be found for any of the three. But each turned out to have children—eight in total. Now all motherless.

Paternity could be established for only three of the eight kids, and none of those biological fathers were deemed suitable for guardianship. Social services eventually placed all eight with other family members or into foster care.

In their drunkenness, the five Disciples had been careless and the ensuing trial was a slam dunk for the prosecution. The crime scene was teeming with forensic evidence, so only a handful of the available witnesses were needed to testify to the abhorrent behavior displayed by the group in various bars during the hours leading up to the murders. Each convicted killer was given a life sentence, and none of their attorneys saw fit to appeal.

Almost sixteen years later, Webb now joined millions of others as they waited and wondered about the weekend ahead. How could the vaunted Cop Show Copycats possibly parody such horrific crimes? And if they did, which of the thirty thousand big or small municipalities across the nation might they select for staging their insufferable re-enactment?

The answers arrived during the early-morning hours on the second Sunday of December. Police and fire department teams were once again called to Baltimore's Federal Hill Park. If nothing else, the copycats were unpredictable. They had returned to the scene of the original crimes. But not to recreate some clever trivialization of the senseless murders. Just the opposite. The copycats instead paid overdue homage to the three victims and their orphaned children. Webb had read the newspaper stories and screened the file footage of news broadcasts that reported on the original crimes. The media coverage from 2000 had focused on the brutality of the crime, along with the killers, while minimizing the human loss because the three females happened to be prostitutes. Webb was forced to admit, if only to himself, that the copycats demonstrated a great deal more compassion and respect than had been expressed a decade and a half earlier.

Shortly after 2 a.m., authorities received a call from an unidentified female voice. She reported a small blaze in the park—in the same isolated section where the three original murders had occurred. Once the flames were extinguished, a fireproof metal box was found among the ashes. Inside were seven envelopes, each labeled with the name and address for the three surviving daughters and four surviving sons of the three slain mothers. An eighth child, a son, had died from a drug overdose in 2009. Contained in each envelope was $2,500 in one-hundred-dollar bills, and a note that read, "As small token for the exploitation of your family's tragedy."

Webb was no math wizard, but including these latest envelopes the copycats now had handed out close to $50,000—hardly chump change for a string of weekend larks. Add to that the weekly cost of traveling to different cities, which now numbered six. The anonymous creeps seemed to have access to plenty of financial resources, so maybe the Cop Show Copycats robbed banks on the side.

———

Special Agent Matthews arrived in Baltimore on Sunday afternoon. After spending a few days at the four faux kidnapping crime scenes in Tucson, she'd flown up to Portland and completed her circuit of cities thus far visited by the copycats. Things in Federal Hill Park were proceeding as expected. Forensics was practically dissecting the whole corner section of the park, while field teams were hitting the streets looking for persons who might have witnessed relevant activity over the prior twenty-four hours.

Meanwhile, a series of unexpected surprises was occurring forty miles to the southwest, at FBI headquarters. Later that evening, C.J. Matthews was bombarded by phone calls from members of the Records & Information unit. These normally unflappable research professionals were practically frantic because of the names and addresses on the envelopes left for the daughters and sons of the original victims.

Back in November, as soon as the connection was made between the first three mock crimes and the *Serve & Protect* television show, FBI teams began delving into every crime case that was to be featured over the remainder of the broadcast season, compiling intensive dossiers on each. For the Baltimore murders, that dossier included updates on every person with meaningful ties to the case—the victims, the convicted killers, police and fire investigators, attorneys and trial witnesses, plus each of the seven surviving children who now were adults. But after three weeks, when the Baltimore murders episode aired, federal authorities had been able to confirm the current whereabouts of only five of the seven children.

Over the decade and a half since their mothers' deaths, the surviving kids had traveled divergent paths to adulthood. Only one of the seven still went by the surname on his birth certificate. Two had bounced through various foster homes. Three had spent their teens with relatives, while two others had taken to the streets at an early age to fend for themselves. But somehow the copycats managed to track down an exact location for each of them. One girl was married, living in Lafayette, Louisiana with a husband and four children, while another had married and divorced twice by the time she'd reached the age of twenty-two. One son was serving a sentence in a New Mexico state penitentiary. Another was living among the homeless in New York City, so for him the copycats simply addressed an envelope to the shelter where he most often slept when the weather turned cold.

A request was promptly issued to the relevant local authorities, asking them to locate the seven individuals based on the addresses printed on the envelopes filled with cash. Each address was confirmed as accurate. The Cop Show Copycats had outperformed the Federal Bureau of Investigations, which claimed to oversee the most elaborate missing persons system in the world. C.J. Matthews strapped in for a long ride.

Chapter Twelve

F our stars. Two thumbs up. A grand slam. On any scale, by any magnitude, the performance in Baltimore had earned the Cop Show Copycats top ratings from the public. For Webb Tremont, watching the non-stop media tributes became a gut-wrenching experience. The previous Wednesday's murder case on *Serve & Protect* had presented a delicate challenge, but America's newest superstars proved up to the task. The reverence shown the three original victims and the generosity directed to the seven surviving children was a combination that hit all the right buttons.

Webb was relieved that another weekend had passed without the copycats inflicting harm on anyone, and he assumed the sons and daughters could use the cash, but the public's love affair with a group of renegade misfits was dispiriting. Their popularity was soaring to celestial heights. Shirley Temple. Elvis. The Beatles. They were entering a stratosphere with very thin air. The Cop Show Copycats were now cyber-champions of the highest order according to the boundless blogs, twitters, tweets and social media postings. People of all ages were obsessing over their ingenuity, scrutinizing the intricate configurations of each successive masterpiece, the nuances to every action, and the carefully crafted words in the messages left behind.

According to FBI press briefings, the execution of this latest pseudo-crime again appeared to have been flawless. No fingerprints. Not a trace of DNA. The group's signature envelopes and notecards could have been purchased anywhere. Same with the fireproof metal box. The only possible items that might prove traceable were the hundred-dollar bills, but the currency the copycats left behind was always well-circulated with no sequence or pattern to the serial numbers. These newest packets could be added to a growing stack of bills that FBI specialists were trying to source.

As a result of the murders in 2000, the section of Federal Hill Park where the copycats struck was under constant video surveillance. As with previous crimes, the group temporarily had disabled the monitoring cameras without triggering an out-of-service signal inside the central system. Likewise, none of the dozens of cameras which canvassed adjacent streets had picked up activity that might be attributable to the copycats. Authorities were given no choice but to acknowledge the continued dearth of leads.

The media unleashed hordes of psychological profilers to paint hypothetical pictures of this collection of nameless individuals. Opinions on the group's dynamics, composition, and size seemed to shift by the hour. The only consistent characteristic offered up was that the Cop Show Copycats were smart. From the standpoint of law enforcement, frighteningly smart.

Somewhere walking the streets was a unified group of gifted minds who were taking it upon themselves to intrigue and entertain the public at large. As average folks went about their day-to-day lives, millions now were on the lookout. Could the copycats be those eight people huddled around the back table of the neighborhood coffee shop? Or maybe the bunch that assembled every afternoon at the bar on the corner? The oddballs who did tai chi on the rooftop at dawn? Or the group of eccentric characters playing chess and reciting poetry in the park?

Webb felt helpless as he watched the circus ramp up. Somewhere these Cop Show Copycats must be gathering to put the finishing touches on another virtuoso performance for their adoring public.

"Credit goes to you, T-Man. Using the original crime scene caught the bovine masses by surprise and, more importantly, we underscored the manner in which the Baltimore media trivialized the lives of three murdered prostitutes. Maljanne!"

Glasses were raised, then tentatively sipped. Michael Chen could tell the others were a little uncertain, wondering how iced tea made from Tieguanyin leaves was going to taste, or whether he might be playing a trick on them.

Conks had been teasing when she threw out the idea during their return drive from Baltimore. But he called her bluff by agreeing to give it a try, though he found the idea of serving such a delicate brew in this form completely repugnant. Tieguanyin tea was produced in the Fujian province of China and was considered the rarest, most refined blend of oolong tea. Michael appreciated the difference these exquisite leaves made because he'd grown up drinking tea with every meal. Now he had a standing order with a local importer for a pound to be delivered every two months, at the contracted price of $1300 per pound.

It had been Chen's turn to host their next Monday-evening brainstorming session. That afternoon he brewed enough leaves to fill two pitchers and then allowed the tea to cool to room temperature. He tried not to cringe as he poured the abomination over six glasses of ice. Harder still was actually putting one of those glasses to his mouth. Surprisingly, the flavor was almost pleasant.

Michael would do most anything for Teresa Conkle—which now included the metamorphosis of sacred tea leaves into a common, everyday soft drink. Conks always had detested hot tea or hot anything. Her parents owned a horse farm outside of Lexington, so she was partial to sweet tea and Kentucky bourbon. On the nights she hosted the others, she invariably kicked things off with a round of mint juleps.

He and Teresa went way back, to their college days at Caltech when they'd become study partners. She was a sophomore and he was a seventeen-year-old freshman. In her own way, she'd been looking out for him ever since, and Michael would be the first to admit he usually needed shepherding. There was so much about everyday life that he found tediously unimportant.

After Caltech, he had accepted his first graduate fellowship at Stanford while she opted for Carnegie Mellon, but they stayed in regular touch until they both wound up in Boston—Michael working on his doctorate at MIT, Teresa working for a prestigious management consulting firm. At MIT, his focus was encryption development, and that's where he conceived a series of algorithms for advancing the security protocols inside the operating systems of financial institutions. He was preparing an article for an academic journal that would detail how an embedded one-way trigger could completely transform the dynamics of secondary and tertiary passcodes. That's when Conks flipped out. She was convinced his innovation would save big banks billions of dollars over time, so why shouldn't he be meaningfully compensated before they benefitted? She persuaded him to forgo scholarly acclaim and form a private company instead. His only condition for agreeing was that she quit her job and team up with him.

Early on they'd seen the need to bring in partners. Maybe six had been over-kill, but Michael felt a larger group would make this first journey into commerce more interesting, more fun. And he'd been right. In truth, he and Teresa Conkle had planned on five equal partners, but once the others were on board, the group still lacked needed depth in certain areas—primarily the boring stuff that no one wanted to touch. Pricing models, structuring contracts, and lots of legal garbage. Setting up meetings with banks and brokerage houses. That's when Conks suggested Anthony Lafferty. He was a few years older than the rest of them, but he'd taught classes at Carnegie Mellon on the business applications of emerging technologies. Upon meeting Lafferty, Chen recognized the guy wouldn't add much to his fun quotient, but he figured a little adult supervision couldn't hurt.

Gregory Beaumont had been a 28-year-old doctoral student at MIT with Chen, and the two had gotten along rather well. That was a rarity for two overdeveloped minds, so Michael reached out to his light-skinned African-American friend. Beaumont seemed to have had a tough childhood in the Oakland area and was thrilled to be given a chance at a financial jackpot.

Conks had met T-Man during one of her consulting assignments and thought his mind was pretty bent—in a good way. His demeanor could be a bit distant, but he always was thinking outside the grid, so T-Man had blended well with the others from day one.

She also suggested Blake O'Meara. The two had grown close during her final year of grad school at Carnegie Mellon. Blake had gone on to work for some IT knucklehead in New York City, so convincing her to move to Boston and take a flyer on a new partnership was as simple as a phone call.

Michael had wanted to call the company G.R.E.E.D.——Get Rich Easy through Encryption Development. The others would have gone along if it hadn't been for Lafferty. He warned the group that a name like that wouldn't sit too well with the investment community. So, they'd settled on S.A.F.E.——Secure Applications for Financial Encryption. It wasn't the last time the professorial stiff would step in and attempt to steer the group back between the guardrails. They recognized that Laffy was bright in his own way, but he unquestionably was cut from a different, less vibrant cloth than the rest of them.

In hindsight, the results were indisputable. Just twenty-three months later, they had walked away with forty-seven million apiece. Now, with two more years behind them, Michael still hadn't reached thirty, while Anthony Lafferty was a few months into his forties. The others fell somewhere between, but much closer to the younger end of the spectrum. Career-wise, he and Conks were in the latter stages of developing separate software concepts that likely would make each of them another bundle. T-Man was somewhat secretive about his pursuits, but he'd let it slip that he was developing a concept for children's television——sort of a *Sesame Street* for the tech generation. Meanwhile, Greg Beaumont and Blake O'Meara were pulling down large sums working for others.

When Michael reflected on the group he'd assembled, he recognized how all six resumes were loaded with graduate degrees, post-graduate degrees, prestigious scholarships or fellowship grants, and academic awards. Their combined list of alma maters was beyond elite. Yet whatever sense of achievement the six might have derived from academia, professional pursuits, or the resulting financial rewards, it wasn't enough to quench their intellectual appetites once they'd allowed their active minds to cross into uncharted territories. He always had advocated pushing out boundaries in the pursuit of fun. But now he wondered if they'd pushed too far.

Chapter Thirteen

The vibrating sensations against his inner thigh were unexpected but not unpleasant. Once Webb pulled the cellphone from the front pocket of his khakis and glanced at the name on the screen, he felt a sudden twinge of guilt. Certain male impulses were beyond his control when C.J. Matthews called. Without any provocation, his imagination could start sprinting down trails he knew were off-limits. As Corrie eyed him from across the table, he figured there was at least one adjustment he could make. Until the copycats were captured he would carry his phone in another pocket—someplace less erogenous.

Webb excused himself to an adjoining room. The special agent was phoning from Baltimore to see if he had come up with names of possible enemies the FBI should be exploring. The Cop Show Copycats were treating her to a whirlwind tour of America. The previous week she'd called him from Tucson, when he was forced to sheepishly confess that he had come up empty. Tonight was more of the same. He still had no one.

Following the brief conversation, he returned to his assigned chair in the dining room of the main palace, which was how Webb had referred to his father's house since his earliest teen years. It was the residence where he and his two siblings had been raised. Even as a kid, he'd felt no emotional attachment to the place. Three stories, twenty-eight rooms, and eleven bathrooms just didn't feel like a home. Especially since the enormous stone structure rested on ten acres of manicured grounds, secluded by hundreds of towering oaks and buffered from the outside world by an eight-foot ivied stone wall that snaked around the entire expanse. No swing sets or sandboxes. Not even a badminton net. Just a full-time maintenance crew. It was a monument to pure capitalism that dated back to 1918 and the noted architect, Howard Van Doren Shaw. Brandon Tremont had purchased the property in 1966, which signified to Webb that his father was horribly dull before he'd reached the age of thirty.

His father had moved to Chicago as an up-and-coming aristocrat right out of business school. His relocation was at the behest of his father, Webb's grandfather, who had wanted someone under his tutelage to oversee the growing number of Tremont holdings west of the Alleghenies. At first, young Brandon had opted for a city apartment along Lake Michigan, on Chicago's Gold Coast, where he lived until he met and married Webb's mother. The Lake Forest Estate was a surprise wedding present to his new bride upon their return from a two-month honeymoon in the Mediterranean. After two months alone with his father, Webb was amazed the former Janice Emerson still was interested in living anywhere with the man. His mother had been attractive, intelligent, and wealthy in her own right, so Webb was convinced that love indeed must be blind.

Webb blamed Sprig for the fact that he was suffering through a second such dinner in the span of forty-eight hours … first his regular Sunday penance and now again on Tuesday. But at least tonight's menu showed promise. Sprig had selected meatloaf and mashed potatoes for her birthday meal—a combination that hadn't been served on Tremont Estate since Webb was a kid.

On Sunday evenings all decisions on the main course, as well as the accoutrements, were made by Nessie. She was allowed to choose from an extensive list of Brandon Tremont's favorites—which meant prime rib or rack of lamb. Period. Accompanied by roasted potatoes, and a side dish of broccoli or creamed spinach. A mixed green salad to kick things off and sherbet for dessert, except during the two months each year when fresh strawberries were in season. The precision drills began promptly at 7 p.m.

Until Corrie met his father, Webb had managed to limit his Sunday-night dinners over at the main palace to no more than once a month. But his girlfriend struck it off with Brandon Tremont from the moment he introduced them, and soon the pair had formed an unholy alliance. Their cozy friendship had led to one nightmare after another for him—like the now standing invitation for Sunday-night dinners. Brandon Tremont insisted. A command performance. As a result, Webb had been enduring eight years of lamb or beef on a weekly basis. It wasn't bad enough that his girlfriend had become a turncoat, but her daughter was following suit. Webb had offered to take Sprig and a group of her friends to the restaurant of their choosing to celebrate her fifteenth birthday. She instead accepted the invitation from his father. Webb was surrounded by ingrates.

Sprig's real name was Melissa, but the only person who still called the spirited teenager by her given name was Brandon Tremont. Even her own mother had thrown in the towel and converted to Sprig after a few months. Webb had dubbed her with the nickname as soon as he laid eyes upon her, which was only a week into his relationship with Corrie DiMarco. The girl had been seven at the time, but he could see this precocious daughter was going to grow up to look just like her mother … a sprig off the same tree. He pitied the young men in her future, the hearts she was destined to break.

Webb knew his father didn't necessarily hate children—since after all, he had conceded to sire three of his own. He'd simply assumed the stoic Brandon Tremont was indifferent toward them, as he was toward so much around him. But his father had taken an instant liking to Sprig when they met, after she looked him square in the eye and started throwing out questions that most adults wouldn't dare pose to a powerful billionaire. Ever since, Brandon Tremont had been lighting up whenever she was around. Corrie and Sprig were the only two aspects of Webb's life of which he could be certain his father approved. Such high regard was particularly unusual, because Corrie never had married. A child out of wedlock was the pinnacle of unseemliness to this man who epitomized propriety. Perhaps other hidden sides to Brandon Tremont's personality were still to be revealed. But Webb surmised it more likely that the earth was slipping out of orbit as the end of civilization neared.

The intimate birthday gathering on a Tuesday night at least provided a welcome diversion for Webb's attention. The next evening would bring the ninth episode of *Serve & Protect*, and he was well aware of the unsavory crimes at the center of it. He'd written about them in his tenth book.

———◇———

After thirty-three years, Jerry Hollander figured Trina Steggman would be his last partner. He'd taken this latest newbie under his wing nineteen months earlier, after Leanne Stoltz busted her spine learning to snowboard. Hollander made no secret of his penchant for pairing up with young, unattached females. Maybe his choices reflected a touch of Southern chivalry, but mostly he enjoyed the long hours spent alone with them. Working the streets of Memphis in an unmarked car provided plenty of those.

Seniority carried its privileges. Trina Steggman was the sixth consecutive police department debutante that Hollander had snagged from the new detective pool, and he hoped to avoid a seventh. At almost sixty, he was inching closer and closer to mandatory retirement.

Prurient pursuits were the furthest thing from Jerry Hollander's mind when he shared the front seat with women half his age. The heart inside his burly chest forever belonged to his soulmate and high school sweetheart, plus the three daughters they'd raised together. These daughters were the reason Hollander preferred being paired with young females during work hours. He gained incalculable insights from the wandering dialogues of nine-hour shifts. The perspectives from his partners helped him understand the ever-changing complexities confronted by younger members of the opposite gender, which better equipped him for his conversations on the home front.

The character and compassion of Detective Jerry Hollander were but two of the traits that caused Webb to make him the focal point of the twelfth chapter of a book he completed in late 2013. The veteran detective played a pivotal role in solving an illogical sexual assault case which had occurred six years earlier.

Over a four-day period during May of 2007, the unclothed bodies of four females in their late teens and early twenties were discovered in obscure locations around the metropolitan area of Memphis. The first was found in an alleyway, the second in a deserted parking lot, and the third on the front steps to a foreclosed building. The last female, and the oldest at age twenty-three, was found in a greenside bunker on the seventh hole of Colonial Country Club in the suburb of Cordova. Thankfully, all four were alive and relatively unharmed, at least from a physical standpoint. None of the young women had been beaten or raped, but after having their clothes forcibly removed, each had been taunted and groped with their private areas repeatedly probed. The emotional harm likely would remain with them for years to come.

Each victim was abducted while walking alone after dark in secluded outdoor areas near their respective schools or places of employment. Each was found hours later by a different person. Each of the four citizens stumbled upon a blanketed form, only to uncover a naked and tightly bound young woman beneath. Because the locations were isolated, the victims had endured lengthy waits before being discovered. The golf course victim had spent an entire night in the sand bunker until a grounds crew worker arrived the next morning to mow the adjacent green.

The four young females provided nearly identical descriptions of their horrific ordeals. Each had been accosted by a group, thought to number five or six, maybe more. All male. All laughing and reeking of alcohol. The girls had been blindfolded and bound from behind so they were unable to catch a glimpse of their abductors. They were transported inside a van or enclosed truck of some type, during which time their clothes had been pulled off or hurriedly cut from their bodies. For a sustained period, maybe thirty minutes or more, they were poked and fondled amidst laughter, male-to-male banter, and what was believed to be the sounds of cameras clicking. The vehicles kept moving throughout the nightmarish experiences and when they finally came to a stop the women were carried out and left beneath the blankets. Two of the victims received meager apologies from some of their captors. The other two only heard laughter as the van or truck drove off and left them crying in the dark.

The accounts given by the four victims diverged on one important detail. The sounds of the voices. Some of the abductors were thought to be Caucasian, others

Black. Some Southern, others from parts elsewhere. Opinions varied as to how educated the perpetrators might have been, or how old. The young women seemed to be describing different groups of males who had behaved identically.

After four nights, the abductions ceased. On the day that followed each successive incident, the Memphis media covered the story in greater and greater detail, so many in the community theorized the abductors were scared to a halt as the city of Memphis moved into fuller and fuller alert. Detectives Hollander and Steggman came up with a different theory which they sold up the line and were granted permission to investigate.

Hollander had chased down plenty of crimes within the gang elements around Memphis. The abductions of these females carried earmarks of gang initiations, but the end results lacked the cold-blooded edge. Still, initiation rituals of some sort might explain why different combinations of males might adhere to the same prescribed methods, and also why four repeated acts took place over a concentrated period.

Hollander and his wife hadn't attended college, but their three attractive daughters did. Over the years, an assortment of frat boys had hovered around the Hollander household. Plus, Detective Trina Steggman had dated a few college guys in her day. The hazing of fraternity pledges might have been on the wane across the country, but it wasn't dead yet. Hollander and Steggman didn't want to believe a group of male college students would willingly push silly traditions over the line into acts of felony, but to them it was the most logical explanation for the crimes at hand.

The Memphis area was home to more than two dozen institutions awarding college credits. Less than half offered residential campus life, and a number of those were small schools with strong religious fabrics and no social fraternities. So, Hollander and Steggman focused their energies on a handful of schools and soon determined that only one local college had fraternities with pledge initiations during the May week in question.

Due to the relentlessness of these two detectives, thirteen freshmen and two sophomores were arrested and convicted as adults. With any luck, they hoped most of these young men might still accumulate the necessary credit hours for a college degree. For sure, their prison sentences would afford ample time for correspondence classes.

When all the ugly dust had settled, an unexpected twist emerged. The fraternity's upperclassmen hadn't instructed the eager neophytes to carry out the abductions and sexual assaults. No, this harebrained idea had been dreamed up by the fifteen new initiates on their own.

As a reflection of the changing times, the popular fraternity had dispensed with old-fashioned hazing and shifted its emphasis toward teambuilding. During the week leading up to spring initiation, more recent pledge classes had been instructed to plan and implement an "epic event" of their own making. They were to devise some unspecified scheme that would establish "a legacy of mythical proportions" for future pledge classes to follow. The output from this simple directive had proven to be entertaining in recent years—and not just for the fraternity, but for the campus as a whole. But this time around, a few demented minds along with gallons of alcohol had blurred the common sense and decency of fifteen young men who had wanted to make certain the pledge class of 2007 would leave a lasting impression. Sadly, on that particular dimension their efforts could be categorized as successful.

With the number of titillating details contained in the Memphis case, Webb wasn't surprised that Elmore Brogan had selected the fraternity abductions for prime time. The Hollywood crew would have an opportunity to push new boundaries with the network censors for the most explicit scenes. Webb had learned that one of Brogan's cardinal principles for programming was to push such boundaries whenever an opportunity presented itself.

Chapter Fourteen

The sixteenth of December was another red-letter night for Elmore Brogan and his cronies at CBS. Every Thursday morning, Webb received an email from the network that reported the overnight ratings. He shook his head at the latest one. More than forty million homes and eighty-three million people had tuned in for Wednesday's broadcast—and there was a special footnote. *Serve & Protect* was the first regular prime-time show to reach those levels since the last episode of *Seinfeld* in 1998. But according to Nielsen, the percentage of kids in the audience dropped precipitously after the first fifteen minutes, which Webb attributed to the vigilance of parents. With the number of graphic scenes jammed into an hour, he wasn't surprised to read that the ratings for adult males held strong all the way through the final credits.

At this point, viewership and production values had become almost immaterial to the journalists and babbling heads. Each of Brogan's cherished episodes was nothing more than a carrier—a dry piece of toast to a BLT. The only thing anyone really cared about was the weekend version still to come a few days later, when the Cop Show Copycats would satisfy the national hunger.

The location the copycats chose for their next re-enactment held little significance for most folks. Highwood was a municipality with a population of 5,400 and a colorful but mostly forgotten history. Even current citizens were unlikely to appreciate the town's melting-pot roots. Today's residents were more familiar with a contemporary claim to fame. On a per capita basis, Highwood, Illinois was home to more eating and drinking establishments than any city, town, borough, or hamlet across the fifty states.

The 445 acres of Highwood were sandwiched between two of Chicago's most upscale northern suburbs, and the town stood in stark contrast to its surrounding wealth. Highwood had been predominantly populated by working-class families since the town's inception during the late 19th century. The original settlement formed outside the gates of Fort Sheridan, a US Army base that was built on the bluffs overlooking Lake Michigan in 1887, to provide protection for the Midwest's most up-and-coming metropolis. Previously, the nearest soldiers to Chicago had been stationed two states away at Ft. Leavenworth, Kansas.

Over the next century, Fort Sheridan became one of the army's most vital officer training centers, and as was the case with many military installations, an adjacent community took shape. Highwood was where soldiers spent off-duty hours and where military family members could afford to reside. This affordability soon made Highwood an attractive place for immigrants to settle—the brothers, sisters, and cousins of live-in domestics who maintained the mansions dotting the shoreline of Lake Michigan.

The town grew symbiotically with its adjacent communities. Highwood offered a community where recent arrivals could sink their roots in close proximity to the relatives who had preceded them to a land they now would call home. This influx brought ethnic skills in cooking and crafts that spawned new businesses to better serve Chicago's expanding north shore. Generations of Italians, Greeks, and Eastern Europeans turned Highwood into a classic American story. More recently, Latino families had become an integral part of Highwood's cohesive fabric. The town's two main streets had long been lined with restaurants and bars, while the adjoining streets and alleyways had housed dozens of small family businesses.

Webb recognized the irresistible canvas that Highwood must have represented to the copycats as they sought to emulate the crude abduction of four Memphis females in more suitable fashion.

Shortly before midnight on Friday evening, the seventeen-year-old daughter of Highwood's mayor said goodbye to a group of high school friends who had gathered for pizza and a movie at one of their homes. Unlocking her car, she found a blanket draped over the driver's seat. Underneath was an envelope.

On Saturday morning, the forty-two-year-old wife of the commanding officer of the Ft. Sheridan Reserve Center finished her weekly spin class at a Highwood fitness center. After entering the combination and opening her locker, she found a similar blanket and envelope inside.

Later that afternoon, the Highwood Police Chief's fourteen-year-old daughter was babysitting several blocks from home. At slightly past 3 p.m., the doorbell rang. When she answered, no one was in sight. A blanket and envelope were waiting on the front stoop.

Finally, at one in the morning on Sunday, a thirty-three-year-old divorced wife, who now was the sole proprietor of one of Highwood's most popular restaurants, climbed the steps to her apartment above. Waiting on the floor of her bedroom was a blanket with an envelope beneath.

Inside each of the four envelopes was a single hundred-dollar bill. Plus a note that read, "Any girl from Highwood needs to be careful."

The cash amount was trivial compared to the munificence of previous weekends, but this monetary reduction was addressed on Sunday afternoon. As hordes of media types assembled in downtown Highwood to report the latest actions from the Cop Show Copycats, a fifth envelope was discovered on the windshield of a van belonging to a local TV station—and this last envelope might better be described as a packet. Printed on the outside was the name of a volunteer agency, "Lake County Woman's Abuse & Rape Services." Enclosed were 200 one-hundred-dollar bills. Twenty thousand dollars, but no note. Apparently, the copycats felt they'd conveyed enough messages for one weekend.

By selecting the daughters of the mayor and the police chief, the wife of a commanding officer, and the owner of a successful restaurant in a town renowned for eating establishments, the copycats were demonstrating how easy it was to target whomever they wanted with their mock crimes, and that secured locks of any kind were useless against them.

In leaving envelopes addressed to women under the four blankets, they delighted an adoring fan base with their clever touchstone to the crass manner in which four naked assault victims were left in Memphis. And with twenty grand earmarked for women's causes in the surrounding county, they again displayed a generosity steeped in social awareness.

As details of the weekend's events were released to the public, millions again were applauding the overarching message delivered by the copycats. Webb had to admit that the peacocks knew how to play to the masses with their insufferable grandstanding. For weeks, he'd been worried about taking the whole situation too personally. After all, his only connection to the copycats was a TV show they'd selected as some sort of platform for their lunacy. So what if his name happened to be attached? Webb was determined not to allow himself to become paranoid over a bunch of moralizing jokesters.

But Highwood changed his thinking.

Webb was notified by a first call around midday on Saturday—from one of the FBI field agents who reported to C.J. Matthews. She immediately wanted him to know about the first two envelopes discovered in Highwood. The news struck close to home with Webb. Literally. Highwood adjoined Lake Forest directly to the south. The center of Highwood was, at most, a six-minute drive from Tremont Estate and his coach house. More concerning were the messages the copycats left inside—"Any girl from Highwood needs to be careful."

This little missive contained a not-so-subtle insinuation for Webb and the most important person in his life. Those bastards didn't really mean "any" girl; they were alluding to one specific girl from Highwood. Corrie. Corrie DiMarco had grown up in Highwood. Her dad, as well as her aunts, uncles, and cousins still lived there.

Perhaps the copycats were cautioning Corrie to reconsider her romantic involvement with the current man in her life. This explanation normally would have seemed plausible to Webb. Plenty of his buddies had been offering similar counsel to Corrie for years. *How could someone as interesting and attractive as you be hooked up with a misfit like Webb Tremont?*

But these clowns weren't being cute. The terse notes scattered around Highwood were meant as a warning. "Any girl from Highwood needs to be careful." The copycats had issued a direct threat to his girlfriend.

Special Agent Matthews jumped on a plane and made her way to Highwood. Being in close proximity to Lake Forest, she called Webb Tremont to set up their second face-to-face meeting. She asked him to bring Corrie along because the FBI shared his concerns over the copycats' pointed threat. So at least he wasn't being overly paranoid, which was reassuring in an odd sort of way. But now Webb faced another menacing concern.

Corrie had yet to lay eyes upon C.J. Matthews. For some inexplicable reason he now regretted, Webb had seen no reason to elaborate on the personal qualities of an FBI special agent with whom he happened to speak at all hours of the day or night. Her physical attributes would become apparent quickly enough and leave Corrie wondering why the subject had never come up. He kept reminding himself nothing inappropriate had occurred—other than random thoughts beyond his control. Webb anticipated a degree of discomfort when the three of them met, his girlfriend watching his every move, waiting to see where his eyes might wander, looking for that first hint of drool to escape a corner of his mouth.

Perhaps the anxiety was misplaced. It had been a month since his initial impression of Miss Matthews on the driveway outside the coach house. Time could play tricks with one's memory—especially with males whose libidos hadn't advanced much beyond tenth grade. Maybe she wasn't as incredible as he remembered.

They agreed to an early breakfast on Monday, at a diner in Highwood. Webb and Corrie arrived first and were seated in a back booth when C.J. Matthews appeared through the front door. No luck. The woman was every bit the vision of flawlessness that Tremont had been toting around inside his skull. Accompanying her was a fellow agent, but his presence only made things worse. Her partner was standard-issue dull—the way agents were supposed to look. The contrast was stark. As the pair navigated a path toward the rear of the room, male patrons throughout the restaurant were craning their necks from every angle. Even female customers were following her movement. Corrie gave Webb one of those coded glances that indicated future discussion would be required.

Because of the dossiers the FBI had compiled on everyone close to Webb Tremont, agents working the case understood the implication of the copycats' message about Highwood girls. Of greater significance, these Highwood notes were the first clear indication the copycats were motivated by something other than public acclaim. They apparently harbored animosity of some sort toward Tremont, the woman in his life, or both. So now the FBI would be encouraging Corrie to dig through possible names from her past to see what leads might develop.

"Miss DiMarco, please excuse us for intruding on your private life, and if you would prefer not to talk about any matters in the presence of Mr. Tremont, we can do this at a different time. But we need to understand the circumstances surrounding the pregnancy with your daughter … and more specifically, who the father was and the nature of that relationship. Is it possible this individual resents your involvement with Mr. Tremont?"

Corrie was unfazed by the special agent's directness. She also didn't seem bothered by C.J. Matthews' physical appearance. On attractiveness Corrie could hold her own, especially with Webb. Her looks appealed to men on a different scale. Though she wasn't especially curvy or photo perfect, the naturalness of her facial features and the confidence with which she carried herself caused plenty of heads to turn. Webb had been smitten from the moment he laid eyes upon her in 2007.

She had been highly recommended to him, so he dropped by her office unannounced when he was looking for a suitable designer to renovate the coach house. Corrie was kneeling next to a file cabinet when she heard the door open. As soon as she stood, Webb forgot the purpose of his visit.

Corrina DiMarco was practically a full-blooded Italian, but her features weren't especially Mediterranean. Her hair was dark red and appeared to be long. While working she wore it in a ponytail pinned loosely to the top of her head. Fortuitous for Webb, as this left the view of her long graceful neckline unobscured. He could have feasted for hours on that vision alone. He recognized that most males tended to fixate on more populist parts of the female anatomy, but Webb was one of a small, discriminating faction of neck men.

He was surprised by her relative youth, considering the glowing professional endorsement she'd received from one of his hard-to-please cop pals. Her skin was smooth and light, punctuated with barely discernible smatterings of freckles. Dark-blue eyes. On the tall side, at what he guessed to be five-eight or five-nine. Her frame was narrow and almost petite. She looked fit. Her running shoes had logged serious miles. She was wearing a men's blue oxford cloth dress shirt with the sleeves rolled above the elbows of her well-toned arms, and the swell beneath suggested her breasts were small, firm, and braless. Her cream-colored Levi's accentuated legs and a backside that were likely to attract plenty of attention, if not outright ogling. But what sealed the deal for Webb was her sense of presence. Her first smile some-how revealed a penchant for mischief and adventure. The posture, the turns of her head, the gestures of her hands, everything in her being suggested Corrie DiMarco was completely comfortable in her own skin.

She possessed an inner toughness, a resolve that Webb admired more and more as their relationship developed. At fourteen she had lost her mother and younger sister in an automobile accident when a drunk driver veered over a median strip. Corrie was in the back seat and survived. In that instant, the balance of her teenage years were stolen from her as she became the primary caregiver for a terminally ill grandmother who lived in the family's small frame house. She also became an anchor in the life of her father, Salvatore, who owned a small masonry tile business. Eight years later, Webb continued to marvel at the manner in which she dealt with every adversity, large or small.

Now he was sitting in a coffee shop where any male in the place would have traded seats with him. If just one of those men had offered, Webb might have jumped at the opportunity in order to avoid the pending conversation. He knew how much Corrie detested dredging through the details of her ill-fated summer romance. She could deal with the fact that the guy turned out to be a cowardly pig, but she never would get over the embarrassment of her own naïveté.

At twenty-one, Corrie had been working part-time and going to design school when she met the man who would become Sprig's biological donor. He was attending grad school out East but had returned home for the summer because of some coveted corporate internship in downtown Chicago. He came from old money and she'd made the mistake of believing the louse was raised a North Shore gentleman. A few months later, she learned he had been interested only in a summer fling. When she told him she was pregnant, his parents offered to pick up the costs of an abortion at a discreet, upscale clinic. When Corrie refused, their family attorney presented her with an offer of sixty grand, a buy-out, if she simply went away and never contacted them in the future. Hush money. They gave her a week to think about it. She never bothered to respond, choosing instead to chart her own course and make the best of single parenthood.

"Agent Matthews, the man with whom I became pregnant was so self-absorbed that I can't imagine he has given me another thought ... that is, once he and his parents finally were convinced I wasn't going to re-enter their lives and demand money. His name was Philip Templeton and he wanted just one thing from me, and I too easily obliged. In return, fortunately, I ended up with the single best thing that ever happened to me ... Melissa, my daughter. So, I have no regrets, and Lord knows he didn't."

Webb watched the accompanying male agent take notes as Corrie responded to a series of follow-up questions from C.J. Matthews. When Corrie described Templeton as "some sort of gear-headed tech genius who was studying computer technology," eyebrows were raised around the table. Webb never had heard those details. High-level smarts and access to serious family money. Regardless of Corrie's nonchalance, this Philip Templeton character had the makings of a viable suspect.

As the conversation wound down and no other relevant names surfaced from Corrie's past, C.J. Matthews brought the meeting to a close, "Miss DiMarco, I'm glad you're at peace with the way your relationship ended with Mr. Templeton ... but I hope you understand that we'll need to check into him just the same."

The foursome slid out of the booth to shake hands and exchange goodbyes.

Webb grabbed his jacket from a hook on the nearby wall, hoping he and Corrie might simply follow the two agents out to the parking lot. Instead, he felt a tug on his sleeve.

"Not so fast, cowboy. Let's have another cup of coffee … I thought you might want to hear my impressions of the special agent."

Yup, he reflected, Corrie DiMarco definitely had a penchant for mischief and adventure.

More than a few newscasters referenced the fact that Highwood, Illinois neighbored Lake Forest, the high-priced community where Webb Tremont resided and wrote the books which served as the inspiration for the *Serve & Protect* TV show. The proximity simply was viewed as another amusing choice made by the Cop Show Copycats.

The FBI was starved for leads, and the talking heads continued to have a field day with how flummoxed the deified copycats were keeping the authorities. Regardless of whatever temptation there might have been to throw the media a bone, C.J. Matthews and her bosses chose not to go public about the Highwood connection with Webb Tremont's girlfriend. Why give the anonymous group of renegades any indication of what the investigation had or hadn't uncovered? Let them wallow in their unbridled stardom. Eventually carelessness would kick in.

The Highwood locations where the envelopes had been found by four female residents were in normally active areas of town. Federal agents and local police had hoped at least one local citizen would have seen someone or something suspicious. But again, nothing. The same with surveillance cameras. Nothing. Just as on previous weekends in previous cities, Highwood experienced a rash of temporary system malfunctions.

One or more of the copycats even had ventured into an area teeming with police officers and media people in order to place a fifth envelope on the windshield of a TV station van. Again nothing. The group was taking greater and greater liberties, yet still performing impeccably. They'd broken into a car, a gym locker, and an upstairs apartment. In broad daylight, they'd stepped onto the front porch of a house in a densely populated neighborhood. Yet not a trace of evidence was uncovered by Matthews and her field teams.

In total, the copycats now had given away $70,000 in one-hundred-dollar bills. A special section of agents in Washington DC who specialized in tracing currency confirmed that several of the bills from prior weekends had circulated through Las Vegas in October, around the time *Serve & Protect* first went on the air. With the amount of cash flowing through casinos, Las Vegas was arguably the most efficient place in the world for persons to collect a sizable quantity of a large US denomination without raising attention or leaving an incriminating trail. The Cop Show Copycats had contemplated every detail.

Most of the copycats had departed the Chicago area late Saturday night so that they could catch early Sunday flights to Boston from Milwaukee, Indianapolis, St. Louis, and Des Moines. Because Anthony Lafferty had no Monday-morning job obligations complicating his schedule, he volunteered to hang around the extra day and leave the fifth and final envelope at an appropriate location. Blake O'Meara had decided to stay and keep him company, which hardly surprised Michael Chen. She never missed an opportunity to be alone with her former professor.

But neither Michael, nor any of the others, had anticipated Laffy's being foolish enough to place the large envelope filled with cash on the windshield of a TV news truck parked in front of town hall. This kind of needless risk could undo everything they'd accomplished, and worse yet, create serious legal consequences for each of them if they were to be caught.

The tension in Gregory Beaumont's apartment grew palpable as soon as the six former partners assembled on Monday evening. Michael had grown accustomed to periodic disharmonies created by Lafferty during their two years of business partnership. He'd figured Lafferty's random bursts of condescension were some form of compensation mechanism. But in recent months, Anthony Lafferty had proven to be a model of collaboration and accord.

Teresa Conkle was the first to speak up. "Listen, Anthony, when you offered to stick around Highwood and handle the last envelope, we—"

Laffy cut her off. "I know what you're going to say." He paused and none of the others were sure what to expect because of Anthony Lafferty's mercurial temper. Michael braced for an outburst.

Instead, Laffy continued speaking in a soft, calm voice. "I owe you all an apology ... and that includes Blake, because she had nothing to do with a decision that was mine alone. When I left her at the motel on Sunday morning, I had no idea I was going to take that kind of chance with the fifth envelope. I'm sorry, but as soon as I saw all those media folks gathering in the center of downtown Highwood, I couldn't resist ... I knew the public would eat it up. You have my word ... never again."

Remorse was the last emotion any of them had anticipated. Anthony Lafferty never had said he was sorry about anything. Michael was at a loss for words.

After a few moments of awkward silence, T-Man finally spoke up. "We appreciate your sensitivity to our concerns, Laffy ... and we accept your apology. And, by the way, your instincts were spot-on ... the yapping dogs on television can't stop talking about where that money was left."

Grateful for how Lafferty had gone out of his way to absolve her of blame, Blake O'Meara decided to shower additional praise his way. "We shouldn't forget that it was Anthony who suggested Highwood in the first place. The news reports are highlighting the proximity to Webb Tremont. That sperm-lucky dullard has to be totally pissed that we would dare encroach upon his rarefied turf."

Michael watched Lafferty's response. Laffy said nothing, instead giving a simple nod to confirm his gratitude for the group's forgiveness. When he made eye contact with Blake O'Meara, Anthony Lafferty gave her a wink that suggested he appreciated her additional comments. But something in his expression seemed disingenuous.

———⚬———

Privately Anthony Lafferty was seething, wondering why the needy bitch couldn't keep her pitiful mouth shut for once. Why must she constantly go out of her way to please him?

The mutual disgust for Webb Tremont was intensifying nicely within the group, just as he'd hoped. Sowing the subtle seeds had required patience. The last thing Lafferty needed was Blake reminding everyone that Highwood was his idea. At least the press hadn't picked up on the more underlying relevance of Highwood. That would come out soon enough, he was sure. For now, at least, it was better that his associates not understand how the messages inside those envelopes were targeted threats directed at Webb Tremont's girlfriend.

Chapter Fifteen

The days immediately following the copycats' visit to Highwood weren't especially good ones for Webb Tremont. The awkward Monday-morning breakfast with C.J. Matthews and her fellow agent had kicked off the week. After the two federal agents exited the diner, Corrie kept her comments brief—but nonetheless effective.

"Webb, in all your various mentions of C.J. Matthews over recent weeks, I don't recall you saying a word about the woman's physical appearance. I guess I should be genuinely flattered that you don't even notice when another woman happens to be stunningly beautiful. For the life of me, I can't think of any other reasons why you might have chosen to keep that fact to yourself."

Webb had expected a second shoe to drop in rapid succession, but not another word was said about the matter. Instead, Corrie calmly suggested they leave the coffee shop and get on with their days. Outside, they separated to their respective cars and he drove off feeling utterly sheepish. As usual, her approach had been perfect.

Over the balance of Monday, it gnawed on him more and more that the meeting with the FBI had been required in the first place. "Any girl from Highwood needs to be careful." He was fuming that the anonymous morons had pulled his girlfriend into their nauseating games. For the time being, his top priority would be tending to Corrie so that she didn't start freaking out over the copycats' veiled threats. He was agonizing enough for the two of them.

On Tuesday morning, Webb threw on sweatpants and a parka for a brisk

December jog into downtown Lake Forest, though the four square blocks of low-rise commercial space barely qualified as a downtown. Corrie's design business was housed on the second level of a three-story building. She also rented the top-floor apartment for her and Sprig. This living arrangement allowed Corrie to balance an odd-hour career with being a single mom.

Before heading upstairs to Corrie's residence, he stopped at a nearby storefront for two mega-cups of high-octane coffee. Like him, Corrie didn't care much for the silly concoctions posted on the menu board. They both preferred strong regular coffee with a small splash of milk. Sprig was another story. Her preference was salted caramel mocha Frappuccinos, heavy on the whipped cream. Whenever he placed an order for her, the people behind the counter seemed to snicker at him. He was sure of it.

Worse yet, he was convinced the perky young baristas took extra time making the damned things just so they could watch him squirm a little longer. On this particular Tuesday morning, the wait was more excruciating than usual because everyone standing in line, everyone cloistered around the altar of sweeteners and whiteners, everyone who'd staked out their precious soft chairs by the gas fireplace, as well as everyone on the whole stinking planet, seemed to be talking about the pain-in-the-ass Cop Show Copycats. *How awesome it was that their latest conquest had been pulled off a few minutes to the south. How clever they'd been with their four choices of women to receive notes and money. How incredibly generous they'd been with that fifth envelope containing $20,000, and how smart to direct attention to the plight of thousands of abused and assaulted women.* Listening to the collective nonsense, one had to believe these imbeciles were saving the world all by themselves. As Webb endured the endless adulations spilling from the mouths of a man and wife standing next to him, he couldn't help but contemplate how the pair might look with a hazelnut macchiato or cinnamon dolce smoothie poured over their heads.

When he finally made his way up to Corrie's apartment, the morning didn't get any easier. Despite her mother being the possible target of a copycat threat, Sprig had her computer open on the kitchen table and was busily lapping up the most recent rave reviews from social media. When Webb was around, Sprig tried to disguise her enthusiasm for the beloved Cop Show Copycats as much as possible, but he should have known better than to swing by before she'd left for school. Sprig's first class on Tuesdays was Current Affairs and the teacher was now reserving the first ten minutes for the kids to discuss the copycats' latest round of weekend miracles.

After Sprig headed downstairs for school, Frappuccino in tow, Webb turned to Corrie. "I'm concerned about your state of mind after the weekend events."

She smiled. "And who said chivalry was dead? You Tremont men are quite the gentlemen."

The confusion on Webb's face caught her by surprise. "I'm sorry, Webb, I assumed your father would have told you. He called last night and invited Sprig and me to move in with him until the copycats are captured. Because of the notes they left in Highwood, he's beefing up security around Tremont Estate and thinks we would be safer there."

"Is Sprig okay with the idea?" he asked.

"I wouldn't know … I didn't bother mentioning it to her."

He wasn't sure he understood. "Are you kidding … you mean you're not accepting my dad's offer?"

"Of course not," she responded. "The copycats haven't harmed a soul, and I hardly can believe they have it out for me."

He chuckled. "I really wasn't thinking about the copycats. No one has ever dared to turn down an invitation from Brandon Tremont."

Webb wanted to strangle his father. The audacity of the man to call his girlfriend and invite her and her daughter to move into his sacred mansion, yet not have the common courtesy to inform his own son in advance. Or even after the fact. Let alone ask Webb if the arrangement would be acceptable to him.

But at the same time, he wanted to hug his dad for the first time in too many years to count. The offer to Corrie reflected uncharacteristic concern and compassion from his stoic father—not to mention the fact that Brandon Tremont actually made the call himself instead of instructing some paid underling to do it for him.

The more Webb considered the suggested arrangement, the more he approved of his father making the invitation. But he also recognized a losing battle when he saw one; Corrie's mind was made up. She and Sprig were staying put.

After leaving her apartment, the week's frustrations continued to mount. Webb barely had just entered his coach house, when the phone rang.

"Hey, Tremont, Fritz Westerfield here."

Webb glanced toward the nearest window and began calculating the probabilities. Ultimately, he decided the odds weren't favorable. A body hitting pavement from the second floor would likely suffer a few broken bones—at most, a severe concussion—while he was hoping to end his earthly miseries entirely. He was left no choice but to acknowledge the voice on the other end of the line.

"Hello, Fritz. To what do I owe the honor?"

He really didn't care, but he was obliged to say something. Fritz Westerfield was one of Elmore Brogan's rabid minions. The young man might have been a decent enough chap in an earlier life form, but Webb would never know. Members of Brogan's inner circle were required to forfeit their true personalities out of servitude to Saint Elmore.

"I think you'll be pleased, Webb. Elmore has arranged for you to be interviewed tonight during the *CBS Evening News*. He feels the timing couldn't be more ideal for you to comment on the popularity of *Serve & Protect*."

Pleased? Webb would have preferred bamboo shoots under his eyelids. During the month since the copycat story broke, Webb had been besieged by hundreds of requests from reporters looking for comments. But he successfully had avoided contributing a single sound bite to the media's three-ring circus. In responding to Westerfield, Webb mustered a litany of reasons to avoid this latest incursion. To no avail.

First off, Webb knew the guy with whom he was conversing had no say whatsoever on the matter. Zero. Elmore Brogan had issued a royal edict, and Fritz Westerfield was nothing but a highly paid messenger.

Second, Webb Tremont was contractually bound. Strings were attached to the selling of one's soul. A stipulation in his written agreement with the network required Webb to make as many as six personal appearances each year to promote the ghastly program. Thus far, he'd endured only three—book signings in New York, Chicago, and L.A. back in April, when the network previewed its fall line-up with major advertisers around the country.

Following the viewer reaction to the premier telecast of *Serve & Protect*, Webb had anticipated the series would be cancelled and he would escape further public humiliation. Once the copycats turned the show into a ratings beast, he had assumed the network no longer would waste time or resources to generate additional publicity. But it seemed Brogan wasn't going to be satisfied until every television in America was tuned in to his pet project.

He knew this type of media appearance was a classic ploy used by the networks—devising a trumped-up news segment to hype one of its own programs. In this case, a gratuitous live interview was to be conducted with the author of the books upon which the network's hottest show was based, and the whole thing conveniently would take place on the evening before the next episode. The terms of Webb's contract were explicit. Webb Tremont was forbidden from making negative comments about the show's scripts, the quality of the final productions, the network's executives, or the network in general. As far as Webb was concerned, that didn't leave much for him to talk about.

Webb had done plenty of media interviews over the years while promoting his books around the country. As a result, he wasn't subjected to the tortuous practice drills normally imposed by the network's publicity gestapo. After all, how much trouble could a guy get into by answering a few simple questions that were teed up in advance to make him and the program look good? On Tuesday, December 22, at precisely 6:19 p.m., New York time, viewers found out.

Webb was seated inside a studio at the CBS affiliate in downtown Chicago. He tried to appear congenial with his outward demeanor. Inwardly, Tremont was fuming. Brogan and his network henchmen were forcing him to publicly opine on circumstances he found repugnant. As soon as the "On Air" sign lit up, the network's anchorman started lobbing softballs from his studio desk in New York.

"Good evening, Mr. Tremont. Thank you for taking time out of your busy schedule to be with us."

Webb flashed his best TV smile. "Thank you, Collin. I have no comment."

Webb looked at the folks behind the glass in the production booth and smiled. They were starting to fidget. Surely Tremont had misunderstood what had been said. No question had been asked that even required a comment.

On a monitor, Webb could see the anchor in New York doing his newscaster thing of straightening a stack of papers in front of him. He started again, "Webb Tremont, since the *Serve & Protect* television series is based on your best-selling book series, you must be thrilled that the program has become such an enormous hit."

This time around Webb tried for a more understated smile, "Thank you, Collin. I have no comment."

"Okay, Mr. Tremont, let's move on to the Cop Show Copycats … what do you think of the attention they continue to garner through their imaginative weekend activities?"

"Thank you, Collin. I have no comment."

The network honchos might have a legal right to stick him in front of a camera, but they couldn't force Webb Tremont to contribute to the nonsense. The anchorman's frustration became evident as he worked through two more exchanges that wound up in exactly the same place.

Finally, he allowed his total exasperation to show. "Mr. Tremont, I have no idea what game you might be playing this evening, but we'll try one last question. How about the copycats themselves … do you think the sophisticated schemes they've been pulling off are an intellectual exercise of some sort, or do you think they are hoping to make a moral statement of some sort?"

It was only Tuesday evening, but it already had been a long, tough week for Webb. His nerves were raw. Emotions took over. This last softball demanded a homerun swing. He stared directly into the camera, and this time no smile was necessary. "I think they're nothing more than arrogant punks."

By the time the broadcast ran two hours later on the West Coast feed, the editors had deleted the entire segment. But viewers in the other forty-three states hadn't been so fortunate. At least Webb wouldn't have to worry about CBS execs holding him to any contractual commitments in the future. Regrettably, the indignation of his final answer did provide the rest of the networks a delectable sound bite. His lingering close-up filled the airwaves over the next twenty-four hours. "I think they're nothing more than arrogant punks."

On Wednesday, in the middle of the afternoon, Webb received a call from Nessie. "Your father was hoping you might join him for an end-of-day refreshment." At this point, his week couldn't get much worse, so he accepted the invitation.

"Very good then, Mr. Tremont will expect you promptly at five o'clock."

When he slogged over to the main palace around five-thirty, Brandon Tremont was waiting patiently for him on the lower level—in the tasting room outside his prized wine cellar. Maybe Webb had miscalculated and things could get worse. The wine cellar had been the scene of many a fatherly lecture.

Like always, Brandon Tremont sat in his favorite leather Chesterfield. Webb turned one of the Chippendales sideways and straddled it. The elder Tremont poured himself a nice crusted port, while Webb popped open an Old Style pulled from the side pocket of his jacket. In this timeless setting, watching his father slowly sip from antique crystal that had been passed through the family for over a century, Webb marveled over how little the man seemed to change. Thin face; narrow frame. Never an ounce of fat. His father was within a few years of eighty, but still disciplined himself to thirty minutes every morning on a rowing machine, along with squash four times a week. His fingers were long, nails perfectly manicured. His skin well-scrubbed, unblemished, and slightly pallid. Hair, neatly cropped; the silvery gray turning white in places. Eyeglasses worn only while reading.

Webb recognized that Brandon Tremont might be described as handsome, but he'd never heard a soul other than his mother dare utter such a comment. It was hard to think of someone who never smiled as visually appealing. Not that his father walked around with a frown on his face. He simply went through life with few outer emotions. His dad was a highbrow automaton who possessed all the creature comforts and none of the creature passions.

Webb sat patiently, nursing his can of beer and awaiting this particular late-afternoon dissertation. He knew the drill. Brandon Tremont would leisurely savor a few sips of vintage nectar before engaging in conversation. Webb was fairly certain of the subject matter, so he saw no need to hurry his father along. Even if Brandon Tremont hadn't seen the television interview, by now one of his lackeys would have briefed him on what took place.

At last he spoke. "I would hazard a guess that the people at CBS are regretting their decision to put you on live television, Webster."

"Oh, you saw that?"

"Not at its appointed time, but I've seen several replays since. You might have alerted me you were going to appear." His tone was neutral, non-judgmental.

"I didn't care to have anyone watching … in fact, I didn't care to be there myself."

Brandon Tremont's lips made a perceptible upward movement that almost resembled a smile. "I think you made that abundantly clear. I'm left to presume the appearance had something to do with the contract you signed with that hideous television program of yours."

Webb nodded.

His father took another sip of port before continuing, "I recognize your distaste for the moral delinquents that your creative venture has spawned, and I applaud you for not further dignifying their outrageous behavior while still managing to fulfill your legal obligations. That was very well done, Webster."

Webb was at a loss for words. His father was shrewd about business dealings, so he wasn't surprised that Brandon Tremont had understood the legal land mines he'd brushed up against by doing the interview. But the even-keeled Brandon Tremont actually was praising him. With most of the country now labeling Webb Tremont a killjoy for not embracing the Cop Show Copycats, his father picked this as an opportune moment to start handing out accolades.

Brandon Tremont slowly finished his port while Webb drained his Old Style, plus a second one extracted from the opposite pocket. His father's purpose had been served, so no additional words were necessary. But as the two stood to leave, Brandon shared a final observation. "For someone who makes his living with words, I would have thought you might have chosen more eloquent language. Nonetheless, I believe your point was made."

Webb looked at him quizzically, at which point Brandon Tremont spoke in a voice that attempted to mimic his son's. "Nothing more than arrogant punks." He reached over and patted Webb on the back. "Far from poetic, yet very well said, Son ... very well said."

Chapter Sixteen

The eleventh episode of *Serve & Protect* aired on December 23. An annual holiday special featuring the biggest stars of country music originally was scheduled for the Wednesday-night time slot, but there was no way Elmore Brogan and his cronies were going to let even a week of their ratings bonanza slip away. As Christmas approached, Webb was being widely portrayed as a Grinch for trying to steal the luster from the Cop Show Copycats.

Many broadcast-industry insiders still were speculating that the copycats were an elaborate PR hoax cooked up by Brogan. To allay the accusations being bandied about, the chairman of CBS Broadcasting did a sixty-second intro to the telecast, disavowing any network involvement with the copycats and remembering to wish the viewing audience "the happiest of holiday seasons."

Webb wanted to puke. For good measure, this duplicitous fat cat had wanted the public to know that the CBS family was cooperating with authorities in every way possible to help put a stop to the lawless pranks. His end-of-the-year bonus probably would double because of the copycats. Not a handful of people with a detectable pulse could possibly believe the network wanted its gravy train to get derailed.

On the strength of Wednesday nights, CBS had dominated the ratings race for four consecutive weeks. Advertisers were paying outrageous premiums to get their commercials into *Serve & Protect*. Manufacturers were working round-the-clock to crank out a wide assortment of *Serve & Protect* merchandise now available on the CBS website—just in time for the holiday shopping season. And courtesy of the attorney who'd hammered out his contract, Webb was receiving a small percentage on every item sold. So at least the "arrogant punks" were ringing the cash register for his Legacy Blue foundation.

After so many bad experiences, Webb had figured his disgust for Elmore Brogan couldn't sink any lower. He was wrong. For the previously unscheduled broadcast of December 23, Brogan reached ahead into February and pulled forward an episode that centered on churches—a seemingly perfect fit for Christmas week, except that the featured case dealt with molestation and desecration in the nation's heartland.

These libidinous aspects weren't the reason Webb had included the bizarre string of crimes in one of his earliest books. If anything, he shied away from sex crimes because he didn't want to sensationalize them. There were enough sickos already roaming the streets. But he'd felt this case merited special attention because of the combined efforts put forth by police departments across the state of Michigan.

Apparently, Brogan and his scriptwriters were concerned the viewers might not be satisfied with mere molestation and desecration, so they added another time-tested Hollywood element. Fabrication.

Thirteen Catholic churches had been robbed and vandalized over a 22-month period before authorities in Lansing were able to arrest their first suspect in 1998. By the end of that day, four others were taken into custody in four separate Michigan jurisdictions. In all, detectives from nine municipalities collaborated with Michigan State Police to piece together a trail that led them to five previous victims of sex abuse who were responsible for the unusual crimes.

The three males and two females ranged in age from twenty-two to twenty-seven. Each had been molested in their youth by Catholic priests or nuns and had struggled to overcome the emotional scars from their past. They'd connected to one another through an online "survivor network." As it turned out, all five were seeking something more cathartic than chat rooms and a website filled with pithy quotes. Sensing a mutual unleashed anger, the five agreed to meet in person. One victim's pent-up hostility led to another's, and before long they were a cohesive group plotting for payback.

They crafted a plan and methodically executed the complicated pieces to that plan for nearly two years. Every few weeks, one of the females would enter a Catholic church during the daytime, light a candle, and patiently sit inside the chapel in feigned meditation. All the while, she would be waiting for an opportune moment when no one was paying attention—at which point she'd slip into another area of the building. She would secure a hiding place in some empty office, classroom, or storage closet and wait until the premises were vacated for the evening. From inside the building, she then would unlock a back or side entrance for the others to join her. Having eight hundred Michigan parishes from which to choose, the group was able to scout out low-budget churches with primitive, if any, security systems.

Once they were inside the sanctuary of a church, the five went to work. The former abuse victims spray-painted epithets on walls, doors, and artwork—a litany of fluorescent commentaries on pedophilia, blasphemy, and hypocrisy. Confessionals were nailed shut. With red paint, they hand-lettered the names of area priests and nuns who had been convicted of past indiscretions onto the front pews of the central naves, as though permanently reserving seats for these guilty parties among the repentant. Lastly, they removed whatever cross was most visible within each church's principal worship area. In a few instances, this effort required dismantling heavy structures that were attached to walls or ceilings. Days after each break-in, that cross would be discarded in an alleyway behind a porn shop, massage parlor, or suspected brothel.

The required police work was tedious. No single department could have solved the crimes. Yet together they did. At the eventual trial the three young men and two young women received significant prison sentences, but much of that time was suspended upon appeal. A number of advocacy groups raised funds for their defense and also reimbursed the thirteen churches that incurred damages. It wasn't a happy story with a tidy, happy ending. But considering the unseemly issues at the core of the case, the end result was as good as could have been hoped.

The television version didn't really deal with those core issues or end results. It also paid little attention to the skillful police work required to solve the case. The

Serve & Protect episode instead devoted disproportionate time to the depiction of symbolic acts that never really occurred.

The final production included a flurry of flashbacks as supposed re-enactments of the sexual molestations the five principal characters had endured as teens or children. These haunting memories were interwoven with present-day scenes of the group meeting in person for the first time and conceiving a plan to assuage the pain they collectively carried. The episode showed the young women entering individual churches, secluding themselves, and finally reemerging during the afterhours to open doors for their accomplices to join them inside—which was pretty much how the real break-ins had happened.

But once the television intruders assembled inside each church, true facts essentially were ignored. The prime-time culprits quickly removed their street clothes and donned vestment robes, wearing nothing underneath. After committing assorted acts of vandalism to the sanctuaries, the emotionally charged group of five converged at the main altars and performed overt sexual rituals they'd contrived in advance. The final act of desecration was replacing the central cross at the front of each sanctuary with a gigantic wooden phallus. The filmed sequences were highly graphic and required careful editing just to make it on the air. The story's pivotal characters were portrayed as both victims and criminals, and it was no coincidence that the five actors and actresses looked like the cast from *Baywatch*.

Six fertile minds gathered and watched *Serve & Protect* in Boston with particular interest, adding nuances to the preliminary plan that took shape just two nights earlier. During the intervening forty-eight hours, their emotions had heightened due to an unexpected new element. "Nothing more than arrogant punks." Anthony Lafferty watched with amusement as the group's anger mounted over Webb Tremont's pig-headed statement. He couldn't have scripted the clueless bastard more perfectly.

C.J. Matthews was grateful Christmas Day went uninterrupted. She at least was able to enjoy the holiday with her mother and siblings in Bangor, where she'd grown up. On Saturday, she was back at work, busily working her phone and computer from the upstairs bedroom she'd shared with a sister as a kid. She was certain Sunday would find her on a plane to some new city, but she'd stopped trying to predict where the copycats might strike next.

Sunday morning she received a call. The answer was Central Ohio. America's anonymous heroes had left their mark at five churches within a sixty-mile radius of Columbus—the number of churches presumably chosen to parallel the original five vandals in Michigan.

The sanctuaries of these churches had been filled to capacity on Thursday evening, Christmas Eve. But conveniently enough for the copycats, those buildings would have been practically empty over the two days that followed, as clergy and staff spent time with their own families after a taxing month of holiday events.

On Sunday morning, December 27, when the Ohio congregations returned to their churches in Chillicothe, Springfield, Marion, Zanesville, and Dublin, a surprise awaited them. Strewn across the altar table at the front of each sanctuary was an old-fashioned Catholic cassock, or monk's robe. Spread atop each cassock were hundred dollar bills totaling $2,000, along with a typed note. "For children victimized by sexual abuse. We encourage churches around the country to address this travesty."

In those same sanctuaries, hundreds of cards were taped onto the seatbacks of pews. On each card, typed in red letters, was the name and hometown of an individual who had been convicted of sexual assault, rape, or molestation somewhere in the state of Ohio. Beneath each name, in smaller black letters, were the identities of their victim or victims. Also indicated were the ages of those persons at the time of their specific abuse. All had been minors.

These cards created an immediate problem for state and local officials—for two reasons. First was the legal requirement that the names of abuse victims remain undisclosed. Second, the pertinent lists of abuse victims were among the most protected data files maintained by Ohio's legal authorities. In fact, the names taped onto the pews at these five different churches didn't appear in a single central file anywhere in the state. No less than three secured databases had been penetrated without anyone's knowledge. In total, the names of more than sixteen hundred victims were displayed across the five churches as the copycats once again flaunted their ability to access the most classified information on whatever subject they desired. When Special Agent Matthews arrived later in the day, senior staffers from the state attorney general's office were still muttering among themselves as she made the rounds to each of the faux crime scenes. "Welcome to our world," she whispered to the field agent accompanying her.

Sundays were becoming an unwelcome routine for Webb, as he closely followed the media coverage. Interviews with people on the street revealed how much the public continued to feast on every tasty morsel. There weren't enough superlatives to describe the group's technical skills or the boundless generosity and compassion they were directing toward important causes.

During their Sunday morning worship services, each of the five Ohio congregations collected more than triple the dollar amounts left by the copycats atop the cassocks, donating those funds to organizations that supported abuse victims. Calls were going out to churches around the country to raise money for similar causes. Advocacy groups for the sexually abused were practically racing one another to issue statements of praise for the Cop Show Copycats.

Though the five churches were entered illegally during the night, no physical damage had occurred. No names were painted on pews, the copycats instead using tape to post the names on cards. No walls were spray-painted, no crosses stolen. No confessionals were nailed shut. In gaining entry, not a single door or window had been pried or scratched.

The selection of churches was markedly different than the original Michigan break-ins. Rather than smaller working class congregations, the copycats chose larger facilities with significant operating budgets. Each church was equipped with sophisticated security systems, yet all five of those systems had been compromised. The insufferable peacocks never missed an opportunity to posture. More irritating to Webb was a subtle personal message seemingly meant for him.

In a departure from the original Michigan case, the churches visited over the weekend weren't Catholic. For years, the Catholic Church had monopolized public attention on a variety of reprehensible issues surrounding sexual abuse of minors. The copycats instead targeted a denomination rarely associated with such cases. One could argue that the copycats were attempting to make a broader statement, that abuse problems were bigger than any single religion ... that people of all persuasions too eagerly pointed fingers as they swept their own issues under a carpet.

Webb was trying hard not to become irrational about this band of troublemakers, but the previous weekend they had left veiled threats for his girlfriend. And now came the churches in Ohio. If the copycats had wanted to make a statement that applied more broadly than the Catholic Church, why wouldn't they have left their precious messages and money at churches across a variety of denominations? Yet all five were Presbyterian. Webb and his family had been active members of a large Presbyterian church in Lake Forest since before he could walk.

Chapter Seventeen

"**Y**ou're sure no one noticed the two of you? A car with its hood up in an empty church parking lot might have been hard to miss." They were piling on again. Now even Beaumont sounded agitated.

Anthony Lafferty kept his calm, "I'm positive. Like I already told you, we were parked behind a row of dumpsters at the rear of the building."

Lafferty thought the group's questions had been answered sufficiently on Saturday night, in Ohio, when they'd met in Chen's motel room after everyone returned from their assignments. But back in Boston on Sunday evening, his five little lambs still needed reassurance and had called for a special meeting. If they were this flustered now, they were going to be basket cases a few weeks down the road.

Teresa Conkle did her best to bring the issue to a close, "I guess we should congratulate ourselves on the contents of our emergency kits since Blake was able to jerry-rig a fan belt."

But Chen, the little termite, wasn't ready to let go, "The fact that a lousy strand of nylon rope held out long enough for Blake and Laffy to limp into a gas station hardly merits celebration." He looked directly at Lafferty, "The two of you took unnecessary risks ... and after the crap you pulled in Highwood, you promised to stick to the rules. If that rope had snapped on a busy street, you would have drawn all kinds of unwanted attention. What you did was irresponsible. The whole reason for having a person assigned to central command was for occasions exactly like this.

If you simply had called, I would have purchased a new fan belt and brought it out to you guys in Dublin."

Lafferty didn't say a word in response, working hard to contain his anger. He didn't like his judgment being questioned, especially in front of the others. And more especially by a smug little wimp who rarely had the balls to make decisions for himself. On anything. He and Chen locked eyes in a protracted stare down.

Finally Michael Chen looked away and shrugged, "Let's move on to something else."

The group was unaccustomed to confrontations. In fact, everyone but Lafferty went out of their way to avoid them, which gave him a decided advantage when these types of situations arose.

The plan for the weekend in Ohio had been more logistically challenging than their prior efforts. As usual, they'd flown in separately on Friday—this time to Indianapolis, Cincinnati, Toledo, Dayton, and Lexington. T-Man got the worst of it, drawing Louisville and enduring a two hundred mile drive to the town of Westerville, just north of Columbus. The six converged at the predetermined Red Roof Inn. Anthony Lafferty and Blake O'Meara used a set of fake ID's and checked in as a couple, as did Teresa Conkle and Beaumont. T-Man and Michael Chen requested singles. They didn't have reservations but Conks had called in advance to make sure rooms were available. On Christmas weekend the place was practically empty.

Friday evening's Christmas dinner consisted of carry-out pizzas in Chen's room, the designated "command central" for the coming weekend. Michael stayed there, equipped with multiple laptops and cellphones, as the others called in with status reports at designated stages of the operation. The person manning command central maintained a timely accounting of the group's overall progress and communicated to the others as necessary, but also was available to help with anything unexpected that might occur—which was why Chen had felt the need to throw his little hissy fit. "Typical," thought Lafferty. "Oh, how they love their procedures."

Another of the group's established protocols was carrying an "emergency kit" in every vehicle used during the execution of a mock crime. Inside the duffel bags were assorted tools, rags and cleansers, glues, adhesive tapes, fasteners, a sewing kit, first aid supplies, a magnifying glass, latex gloves, disposable shoe covers, rain parkas, and much more. With two PhD's and nine masters degrees between them, the copycats hadn't left much to chance. In total, there were eighty-seven items the group had determined to be most useful if unforeseen situations were to arise—including a nylon rope that could be fashioned into a makeshift fan belt. So as far as Lafferty was concerned, Chen should stop his senseless whining.

First thing on Saturday morning, they'd gone to their assigned churches. Five churches, five individuals. One per person. But without consulting the rest of the group, Anthony Lafferty and Blake O'Meara had elected to team up and handle their two assignments in tandem. The others didn't like deviations from the collective plans made earlier in the week, but Lafferty knew they wouldn't raise an objection. By now they were accustomed to the complications that his personal involvement with Blake sometimes created.

After Blake had signed up for one of his classes at Carnegie Mellon, the two became romantically involved—unbeknownst to the young professor's wife and two children. Fortunately, that marriage had ended in divorce prior to his relocation to Boston, so he didn't have to split the millions he'd earned over the years since with his ex-wife.

When Anthony Lafferty joined the partnership, he had seen no reason to tell the others about his past intimacies with Blake and was glad to learn she'd also kept that aspect of their relationship to herself. But several months later, those details came to light after Blake stormed out of a conference room sobbing about some trivial comment he'd made. The woman was incapable of carrying on a genuine adult relationship. That reality, however, was what made her receptive to his advances in the first place. It also would serve him especially well in the future, which is why Lafferty had rekindled their romantic entanglement soon after S.A.F.E. was formed. In the meantime, she willingly fulfilled whatever needs he might have for female companionship. And more recently, her easy compliance had allowed him to explore an expanded range of latent urges. He figured he might as well take advantage of the availability while he had it.

Lafferty didn't do much to hide the one-way nature of his arrangement with Blake. The others clearly recognized the imbalance but continued to hold their tongues. Their collective resignation was on full display whenever he snapped at Blake because of her unrelenting neediness. The woman had a superior mind, but if her self-image was that abysmally low, none of them was inclined to intercede on her behalf.

The two of them had taken the churches in Springfield and Dublin. Beaumont went to Zanesville, T-Man headed to Chillicothe, and Teresa was assigned the church in Marion. By mid-afternoon on Saturday, they'd all returned to the Red Roof in Westerville, having scouted their assignments and made preparations to re-enter those same churches later in the evening, once the buildings were locked and theoretically secured for the night. Following another round of carry-out food early Saturday evening, they once again headed out to tend to their respective duties.

At 9:30, Lafferty assumed Beaumont, T-Man, and Conkle had returned to the motel according to schedule. The group would be congregated in Michael Chen's room, waiting for Blake and him so they could debrief and enjoy their customary round of celebratory beverages. This weekend was Beaumont's treat, and he'd purchased an interesting assortment of local craft beers. By ten o'clock, the four of them would be growing nervous. At eleven, with still no word, the group would be downright apoplectic. Blowing a timeline was unprecedented. For seven consecutive weekends, there hadn't been a single hitch—so perhaps it was time they be dealt a dose of reality.

The four young millionaires could wait in the crummy motel room as each agonizing minute crawled by. If something had gone wrong, they each faced a lengthy list of charges. The federal authorities would want their scalps as compensation for two months of torment. Plus, the media onslaught would eliminate any possibility of resuming a normal life. Most importantly, the group would have failed to pull off their beloved perfect crimes. Whatever they had accomplished over the weekends thus far would be meaningless. The acclaim, the ingenuity, the intricacy of their plans would have gone for naught. The end result would be no different than if they'd been common criminals. The four of them surely must have been wetting their pants.

When Anthony Lafferty and Blake O'Meara finally had joined the others at 11:40, the tension was palpable. Lafferty nonchalantly fielded the group's questions. "Why are you making such a big deal out of this? We had a broken fan belt ... that's all. It really was no problem. Blake was able to fashion a temporary solution with the nylon rope. Then we were stuck at a gas station for an hour or two until the mechanic could get there from home and install a new one. We had things under control the whole time."

Beaumont asked the next logical question, wondering why they hadn't bothered to call. Lafferty was ready for him. "To be honest, it never crossed our minds. We took a walk while the guy was working on the car and found a nearby park with a nice empty pavilion that seemed pretty isolated. I guess we became preoccupied in what we could discreetly classify as conversation. After all, it is the Christmas season."

There was nothing subtle about the innuendo, and he knew this particular subject matter would shut them up. It always did. He wasn't sure any of the four even possessed a libido, so he liked taunting them with his sexual references from time to time. There was great sport in watching them grow uncomfortable, and this time he also was making a statement about his calm under fire. They would be left wondering how he possibly could think about romance in the midst of committing criminal acts that were certain to make the next day's national headlines.

Blake kept silent for once, but her discomfort was obvious. Based on her demeanor, the others might have doubted whether he was telling them the truth. But they were more prone to be embarrassed for her, amazed that she would continue to allow him to manipulate her as his personal plaything. Blake's doleful predictability had provided more than adequate cover. The others would never know what really had delayed the two of them.

Chapter Eighteen

Webb recognized that Monday duties in Ohio would be more harried than usual for C.J. Matthews as she bounced between five churches and the field teams assigned to each. Still, she found time to phone him late in the day. His paranoia was allayed because the FBI shared his opinion that he again was being singled out by the copycats' choice of Presbyterian churches. The Bureau had no intention of publicly revealing this latest link to him, but eventually some hardworking reporter would start making the connections. Unfortunately, Webb still couldn't offer up a single person who might have it out for him.

Special Agent Matthews had continued her grassroots tour of America by arriving in Columbus on Sunday afternoon. Regardless of where that beautiful face and form might slide between the sheets on Saturday night, she would be heading to another new city the next morning. Such a lifestyle hardly was conducive to meaningful personal relationships, and somehow Webb Tremont took comfort in that fact. Until the copycats were identified and arrested, he wanted to believe this fantasy woman somehow was committed to him alone—or at least to the criminal case that was driving him crazy.

Webb hit C.J. Matthews with his usual barrage of questions. Mostly he wondered how the church break-ins were accomplished. In the middle of one explanation, she stopped. "It might be easier if you went to your computer, Mr. Tremont ... I've just emailed you a photo."

He downloaded the picture and stared at it for several moments before reacting. "It looks like a Christmas ornament ... the kind a kid might make in art class."

"Or maybe as a Sunday school project," she added. "So, seeing ornaments like this hanging in a church wouldn't feel out of place ... would they?"

The answer was obvious, but Webb obliged. "No, I wouldn't think so." He was intrigued, having no idea where the conversation was leading.

"It seems this time the copycats didn't bother showing off their technical skills by neutralizing the security systems inside the churches. Based on their efforts to date, the five installed systems would have been relatively routine for them to infiltrate and override. But apparently they're purists ... they opted to more closely align their method with the original break-ins in Michigan."

Webb still was clueless. "You'd make an excellent crime writer, Miss Matthews. I can hardly wait to hear the exciting conclusion to 'Mystery of the Fourth-Grade Christmas Ornaments.'

She chuckled, "I'm sorry, I don't mean to be cryptic ... it's just that our forensics folks were baffled all day yesterday and most of today until one of our agents went back to the Zanesville church and noticed a cluster of these ornaments hanging in one of the hallways. He had just visited the church in Chillicothe, where he remembered seeing a similar grouping. After a few phone calls, we established that ornaments like the one on your computer screen were hanging from a hallway ceiling inside all five churches. And not just any hallway. In every case, the hallway leads to an exterior door where security keypads are mounted on the adjacent interior wall ... and each of those keypads happens to be the one where the last exiting staff member punches in the security code at the end of a day before locking the door."

He stopped her. "Let me guess ... hidden cameras?"

"Very good, Mr. Tremont ... that's the conclusion Forensics also reached. On the inner surfaces of one ornament in each of the five clusters they found residue from adhesive tape. We believe those particular ornaments concealed micro-cameras pointed at the keypads. So, someone sitting at a remote monitor could watch the specific security codes being entered by the person who locked up each church. Then a few hours later, the copycats could enter that same church and disarm the security system by simply keying in the appropriate code."

"So, you believe the copycats visited the churches in advance and hung those ornaments?"

She answered, "Yes we do ... just like the original Michigan group, where one of their members went into each church in advance." Then she added, "As of right now, we have no better explanation as to how or why those ornaments ended up in the hallways of all five churches. Our agents have confirmed none of the ornaments were made by a Sunday school class ... and they weren't hung by anyone associated with the churches. Each building was locked on Christmas Day, which was Friday, so our working theory is that one or more of the copycats entered the churches during the daytime on Saturday, when the doors were open again. They waited for the right moment when no one was paying attention, grabbed a chair or something to stand on, and hung the ornaments with push pins into the ceiling tiles. We tried it. Even allowing a few extra moments to aim the camera inside the designated ornament, hanging the ornaments easily could've been accomplished in twenty seconds or less."

Webb probed further, "Those churches had to be pretty empty the day after Christmas ... so you're saying no one noticed any unfamiliar faces roaming the halls?"

"Yes and no," said the special agent. "In three of the churches, the few people onsite were preoccupied with specific tasks and don't recall seeing anyone else while they were there. But in two of the churches, we interviewed individuals who noticed some sort of utility serviceperson inside the facilities. Nothing seemed unusual about their presence, and neither individual bothered to check what the serviceperson was doing or got close enough to provide a meaningful description. We've contacted all the possible service providers to those two churches, and none of them made service calls on Saturday. So, we're assuming one or more of the copycats were disguised as uniformed technicians to avoid looking out of place."

Webb moved on to a rather obvious question. "Okay, that might explain how the copycats disarmed the security systems once they were inside the buildings later that night … but the doors still would have been locked by then. How did they get inside the churches to punch in the codes?"

Her response was surprisingly candid. "We're not sure. But if we had to guess, they used a simple time-tested method. In one of the churches, an associate pastor noticed a few items of furniture slightly out of place next to a window in a classroom near the entrance where the security system keypad is located. While the copycats were inside the churches earlier in the day, they very well could have unlocked windows inside nearby rooms on the ground floor … figuring staff members were unlikely to go around and check window latches before leaving on a Saturday evening after the building had been virtually empty all day. One of the copycats simply had to open that same window later in the evening, climb through, and get to the keypad in time to enter the code before a warning signal was transmitted. The installed systems allow anyone entering those churches a half-minute or more for disarming the alarm."

She paused before throwing in a postscript. "But to be honest, Mr. Tremont, we can't be positive. Perhaps the copycats somehow obtained duplicate keys … or maybe they also happen to be skilled locksmiths. Keeping up with these jokers is no simple exercise."

Each week, the copycats seemed to be expanding their set of criminal skills. Webb's mind was spinning with more questions. "So if your theories are correct, the copycats took the time to remove the cameras from one of the ornaments at each church before exiting on Saturday night. So why not take down the ornaments altogether … why leave items that have the potential of producing forensic evidence?"

He knew the answer, but he wanted to hear her say it aloud and she didn't let him down, "They obviously were confident the ornaments were clean … that they wouldn't provide any meaningful leads. So once again, Mr. Tremont, we have to presume the copycats merely wanted us to see how clever they were. They have a very distinct pattern of showing off."

Bingo, she'd said it. How comforting to have the Federal Bureau of Investigations recognize what he'd instinctively known from the very beginning.

Other details had emerged from the investigations in Ohio. The security systems of four of the five churches had been deactivated around 8 p.m., within twenty minutes of one another. Due to the driving distances between those churches, it could reasonably be concluded that at least four different copycats were involved in the break-ins. Based on the sophistication of the pranks to date, the FBI had concluded the number of copycats was likely between seven and ten, but the simultaneous events of Saturday night were the first hard evidence of what a minimum number might be.

Taping cards to the pews, along with laying out the cassock, cash, and envelopes in each sanctuary, could have been handled by single or multiple persons, depending on how much time the copycats were willing to spend inside a location. Since none of the security systems had been reactivated upon their exits, it was impossible to determine how long the intruders remained at each church.

The most ominous fact was released to the public a few hours after Webb's phone conversation with C.J. Matthews. A janitor who worked at the church in Dublin had not shown up for work on either Sunday or Monday. His name was Jorge Cabral and he hailed from the Dominican Republic. He'd been hired seven years earlier to assist the church's long-standing maintenance person, Bartek Kalinska, who was getting along in years.

Mr. Cabral was thirty-one and lived with three other Dominicans on one side of a rundown duplex. His roommates indicated he hadn't been to the house since Saturday afternoon, which they claimed was not unusual for Jorge.

During his interview with federal agents, Mr. Kalinska provided additional perspectives, which could be interpreted a number of ways. The elder janitor explained that one of Cabral's responsibilities was handling final clean-up on Saturdays, in preparation for Sunday morning services. It wasn't uncommon for his young assistant to go out on Saturday night and return to the church late in the evening to finish his duties. When he did this, Cabral often would sleep on a cot in the basement, so he could be there to open the church early on Sunday morning for the arriving pastors and congregation. "I always can trust my Jorge to get his work done no matter what … I not worry about what time of day he do his job. Jorge a good boy, a good worker. He always come through for me."

The Polish janitor had taken the Dominican assistant under his wing. When asked if Cabral had failed to show up for work in the past, Kalinska disclosed, "A few years ago, Jorge disappear for month almost. I afraid he go back to his country. But turned out he just worried about some man from immigration who asking questions around church."

Mr. Kalinska couldn't be sure if Jorge Cabral was in the country legally or not—which was a question the church's administrative head also seemed uncomfortable addressing. Agents made a few calls and determined the assistant janitor lacked proper documentation and was subject to deportation.

On Tuesday, Jorge Cabral again failed to appear, so more and more media hounds started sniffing around. Local police were obliged to offer theories about his absence. Sure, Mr. Cabral could have walked in unexpectedly on the copycats while they were inside the Dublin church. They may have enticed him to flee the area, or possibly done him harm because of the danger he represented as a witness. But the copycats had shown no propensity for violence, and there was a more plausible explanation.

Whether Jorge Cabral encountered the intruders or not, he would have recognized that the Cop Show Copycats had visited the church as soon as he walked into the sanctuary and saw what they left behind. He therefore could anticipate that the church soon would be inundated with authorities and news reporters. As an illegal immigrant, he wouldn't want to risk being near that type of attention.

The media uncovered Cabral's previous disappearance tied to his fears about immigration status, and the public quickly latched onto this explanation for the janitor's absence as though it were a proven fact. Alternative scenarios made no sense to a loyal fan base. The copycats wouldn't harm someone—especially inside a church on Christmas weekend. Besides, the authorities hadn't uncovered a shred of physical evidence that suggested an interaction with the copycats.

To Webb, the world was going mad. News stories were treating Jorge Cabral's disappearance as a minor footnote. No one dared to rain on the copycat parade by discussing the obvious possibility. An innocent man could be in peril, or even dead. Webb had dreaded such a moment. When a bunch of wise-asses decided they were above the law, mistakes were bound to be made. Someone eventually would get hurt. Maybe Jorge Cabral had surprised the self-righteous bastards while they were perpetrating more of their insanity in Dublin. The group or one of its members might have overreacted.

Their outrageous pranks had been going along swimmingly. Too swimmingly. Perhaps the copycats had nothing to do with the disappearance of Jorge Cabral. But it still was only a matter of time. Tremont had researched thousands of crimes. No amount of talent, intellect, or preparation could anticipate every unforeseen circumstance. And any group of people who believed they were impervious to mistakes were destined to become victims of their own arrogance.

Webb Tremont's familiarity with the topic of arrogance extended well beyond criminology. Since birth, he'd watched entitlement and condescension as modeled behaviors across his sizable family. The Tremonts were so steeped in stately prominence that a few years earlier, hordes of them had gathered privately to celebrate their very own bicentennial in New York City. Not so private, however, that the press was excluded. *People Magazine* ran a photo spread on the festivities.

The celebration marked two hundred years since Nathaniel Tremont had launched his trading company in coastal Maine. The family's revered patriarch had had an inkling that folks on distant continents would take a liking to New England maple syrup. With his own young nation now having a few decades of independence under its belt, he also figured there was a segment of hard-working former colonists who were ready to shell out some discretionary dollars—and that was his real brainchild. By swapping out barrels of syrup around the globe, he was able to enable his fellow countrymen to more easily take possession of alpaca topcoats, ivory chess sets, silk smoking jackets, and other basic necessities of life. As far as many of Webb's relatives were concerned, Nathaniel Wilfred Tremont stood as one of the unsung trailblazers to the American Way.

Over the two ensuing centuries, Tremonts had branched into logging, banking, real estate, oil refineries, and various other wealth-producing annuities. Not to mention riverboat casinos, franchised spray tans, and other assorted ventures that most self-respecting Tremonts avoided mentioning when family paths happened to cross in Newport, Jackson Hole, or St. Barts.

As best Webb could discern, few of his living relatives knew much about the generations of Tremonts that predated their most-beloved forefather, Nathaniel. For all Webb knew, the family's North American ancestry might trace back to the *Mayflower*. There may have been stowaway Tremonts on the *Niña*, *Pinta*, or *Santa Maria*. But none of that heritage much mattered. As far as contemporary Tremonts were concerned, the official family tree took root as soon as Nathaniel started socking away inheritances for his offspring and their legions of descendant lucky seeds.

Early in their relationship, Webb had made the mistake of revealing his full name to Corrie. Webster Alcott Sheridan Tremont. She responded in typical fashion, "You mean that in addition to every imaginable comfort money could buy, your parents also gave you two middle names."

From his perspective, he'd been saddled with those names and the silliness that went with them. She never would understand. Not many could, or would want to. His name was nothing more than a label of bloodlines. He'd learned firsthand that the broad assumptions made by most people were generally true. Money does attract money. Ever since Great-granddaddy Nathaniel moved his wife and kids into their first starter mansion in Portsmouth, Tremonts had been rubbing elbows with many of the country's most prodigious trust funds. The resulting marriages had produced a number of legendary asset mergers.

When babies were delivered into the Tremont fold, the proud parents didn't dare consider a normal name like Johnny or Katie or Sally. In fact, few were given first names at all. Inscribed on their birth certificates were collections of last names to commemorate the various bank books that fate had brought together for the purpose of procreation. In Webb's case, his name signified that somewhere along the line a descendant Webster, a descendant Alcott, and a descendant Sheridan each had managed to hook up with a descendant Tremont. Lord knows how many attorneys it had taken to keep all the inheritances straight.

His older sister, Emerson Westbrook Tremont, was another living, breathing testament to pooled fortunes. Webb's parents weren't big on nicknames, so from birth they expected everyone to call her Emerson. But by the time he'd reached his teens, Webb had convinced most of her friends to call her Brooke. When his father was around, he lengthened it to Brooklyn for the sheer irritation value.

The third and youngest sibling in Webb's immediate family really got hung out to dry. Sheffield Armstrong Worthington Tremont. Not even his prep school classmates were able to spin a decent nickname out of any part of it. Now in his mid-thirties, the poor guy still answered to "Sheffield." Webb had been calling him Spud since the time his brother could eat solid foods.

It was like that across the board. Generation after generation, Tremont parents had been unwilling to consider a normal name over fears they might offend those special deities who looked out for the privileged class. One distant cousin, Trey, was legally named Tremont Wilson Alden Tremont. Dropping the two middles, his name was Tremont Tremont. Webb long had suspected there could be something a little incestuous on that limb of the family tree.

Being a middle child, Webb had taken it upon himself to drive Brandon Tremont crazy. He once confided to Corrie, "For as long as I can remember, I've resisted every decision my father insisted upon making for me."

Like a good little first-born, sister Emerson had scampered off to Massachusetts and Dana Hall for prep school—which was two years before Webb reached high school age. The bar had been set. But Webb liked throwing outside curve balls when his dad was calling for a fast ball up the middle.

Brandon Tremont had been dispatched to Chicago as a young man by his father, and dutifully stood guard over the western frontier of the family empire. Webb wasn't able to come up with a single decent reason for leaving the sovereign state of Illinois to attend one of the Eastern academies that had the Tremont name engraved on the front of some science building or dining hall.

First, he pestered a concession out of his mother—which was his prescribed pattern for getting his way. She, in turn, convinced his father to surrender in what became a titanic clash for the ages—The Battle of Exeter. "For God's sake, boy, what are you thinking?" Phillips Exeter was where blazer-clad Tremont men had been boarding and prepping since the presidency of Rutherford B. Hayes.

Not only did Webb remain planted in the Land of Lincoln, but he also managed to convince his folks to allow him to attend the local public high school instead of some venerable Midwestern private academy. In fairness though, Webb had to admit that the high school in Lake Forest was not your typical public school. Lake Forest was a rather tony suburb on the shoreline of Lake Michigan, about thirty miles north of downtown Chicago. He'd seen first-hand that the eleven hundred kids who comprised the student body of Lake Forest High School possessed more than their rightful share of sports cars and affectations.

Next up was his decision on higher education. Webb's performance in high-school classrooms had been strong. He easily could have been accepted into a number of hallowed Eastern institutions without any help. But Brandon Tremont and his legendary checkbook had been priming the pump at a couple of the most exclusive ones. His father may have caved during the preliminary rounds, but this was college. The main event. The stuff by which careers and family pedigrees were made. Brandon Tremont had very definite plans for his eldest son and this time he wasn't about to succumb to adolescent stubbornness.

So, Webb outmaneuvered him.

Without his father's knowledge, Webb accepted a wrestling scholarship to Eastern Illinois University, in the downstate town of Charleston. If Brandon Tremont had found the time to attend one or two of Webb's wrestling meets, he might have recognized that his son was being recruited by a wide assortment of schools. His father went apoplectic, but Webb knew he had him boxed in a corner. A Tremont man always stood by his word, and Webb had given his firm commitment to both the wrestling coach and admissions director at Eastern. To Webb's knowledge, he was the only Tremont ever to attend a public institution of higher learning.

By the time Webb Tremont earned his college degree, he figured his father would have thrown in the towel. Nothing Webb could do from that point forward was likely to surprise or disappoint his father more than the choices he'd already made thus far in life. Unless, of course, it was his decision to become a cop.

Chapter Nineteen

The tension in Boston was escalating. By Monday evening, when the six gathered to initiate plans for the coming week, the normal spirit of accomplishment had been missing. The growing animosity between Michael Chen and Anthony Lafferty made the others uncomfortable. Michael wasn't going to let go.

"First there was your reckless grandstanding with that last envelope in Highwood, and now the blatant disregard for our ground rules with your car problems on Saturday night. Don't you think you owe the rest of us more respect than that, Anthony?"

Lafferty had watched Gregory Beaumont and Teresa Conkle bobbing their heads in support of Chen. Even these simple motions were amazing to him, because he hadn't thought they possessed the courage to challenge anybody on anything. T-Man, of course, remained indifferent. He always did. Then there was sorrowful Blake, who seemed to disappear into the woodwork.

In responding, Lafferty kept his tone calm, not allowing body language to reveal the agitation he was feeling for having to answer for his actions. "Michael, just lighten up. I've got as much riding on what we're doing as the rest of you … I'm not going to screw things up."

Now it was Wednesday, an evening typically filled with eagerness as the group reconvened to watch the network's pedestrian rendition of the real crime they would artfully memorialize a few days later. But a new fact had emerged since Monday to further complicate Anthony Lafferty's standing with the others. A missing janitor.

This time, he made no attempt to remain calm. "I don't know what else I can tell you, Chen. Blake and I didn't run into anyone at either church. If you don't want to believe what they're saying about this Cabral character hiding from immigration officers, that's your problem. You can take a flying leap as far as I'm concerned."

With another confrontation behind them, the subject turned to the coming weekend. Over the next few hours, Chen contributed little to the discussion. Lafferty figured the temperamental weed was either embarrassed from backing down so quickly, or hurt because none of the others had jumped in to support him.

Lafferty always could count on forceful conviction to prevail, and for once Blake had listened to the instructions he'd given her in advance about keeping her mouth shut. Group dynamics were progressing exactly as anticipated.

<hr />

Thursday would bring New Year's Eve, but people around Webb weren't feeling very celebratory. The dark cloud of the Cop Show Copycats had doused everyone's spirits. Except Sprig, who seemed to be enjoying the grandest adventure of her young life. The latest wrinkle was a rotation of dark-suited men and women who now were ever-present during her daily activities, courtesy of Brandon Tremont. The private security details that followed Sprig made her an instant celebrity with her peers wherever she ventured. Corrie wasn't too pleased to have armed professionals stationed outside her apartment and office, or trailing behind her on the simplest of errands, but she was willing to accept the bad with the good in the interest of her daughter's safety. Plus, she was touched by the extent to which Webb's father worried about the two of them. On a daily basis, Brandon Tremont continued to insist that the two of them move in with him until the copycat threat was eliminated. And on a daily basis, Corrie declined politely. Such repeated denials were totally unprecedented for the powerful billionaire.

Under normal circumstances, the security around Tremont Estate consisted of a closed gate that opened only when someone inside the main house pushed a button to allow entrance, plus private security personnel who drove through the grounds every few hours. But Brandon Tremont now had contracted for a pair of guards to be posted at the front gate at all times, along with a third guard near the main house and a fourth outside the coach house—despite Webb's protestations. Just to be safe, his father also arranged for a special security detail at the home of his sister and her family in Philadelphia. Webb's younger brother, Sheffield, was sent off to Paris on family business until further notice—which surely must have been a welcome assignment to Spud, who in his mid-thirties remained a familiar face at popular nightspots across most of the European continent.

Webb stayed in touch with members of the growing FBI team assigned to C.J. Matthews, closely following the investigation in Central Ohio and elsewhere. The results were to be expected. Countless blind alleys and very few leads. Agents in New York and Connecticut completed their discreet probes into Phillip Templeton, the man with whom Corrie DiMarco had become pregnant. He no longer was a suspect. His financial records and schedule for the past eight weekends confirmed what Corrie knew all along. This ghost from her past couldn't possibly be one of the Cop Show Copycats.

His name was added to the dismally short list of individuals who'd even been worthy of investigating in the first place. To date, Webb Tremont had supplied the FBI only two names. The FBI had no choice but to dig into them, though Webb knew it would be a waste of government resources. At first blush, Lyle and Ricky Mason may have seemed like obvious suspects. They were the older brothers of Ronny Mason, a crazed gunman who was shot multiple times when Webb made national headlines for the first time. But Webb couldn't imagine anyone in the entire Mason family having the brainpower to even spell copycat. Nonetheless, these Neanderthals needed to be ruled out. Which they were.

———◆———

Webb had graduated from the police academy three years earlier. Until an overcast evening in February of 2002, he'd never drawn his weapon for anything other than target practice. The life of a suburban cop was mostly routine and the sleepy tranquility of Lake Forest was especially pronounced during the winter months, when the town's snowbirds fled to their tropical getaways. Webb was bundled up and making his rounds on a remote lane lined with old mansions. "Rounds" in this instance meant pulling into the darkened driveways of seasonally vacated estates and parking his patrol car. He then would hoof it around each oversized dark house on their multi-acre dark properties to confirm that nothing looked out of place. He was fulfilling an important, time-honored duty of the LFPD. These nightly rituals allowed bronze-skinned Lake Forest taxpayers to rest more comfortably as they knocked back vodka martinis after another grueling round of golf or an afternoon of chasing marlins at some favorite winter retreat.

On this night, as Webb worked his way down his assigned addresses, he noticed a nondescript sedan driving up and down the dead-end street. The silhouette inside suggested a male driver and no passengers. The car would head one way, pull into a driveway, back out, and drive the opposite direction for a few blocks, then pull into another driveway and head back again. After eight or nine trips, the car failed to re-emerge at Webb's end of the street. Since there were no outlets in the direction the driver last headed, Webb presumed the man had arrived at an address he must have been struggling to locate. His hosts probably were waiting for him. But in protecting the upper end of the economic curve, a green suburban cop leaned toward caution. Best to be sure, so Webb jumped into his patrol car and drove slowly in the direction the man last traveled.

Several properties later, he recognized the sedan. The car was parked behind a tall hedge of arborvitae, partway up a long driveway, but far from the sprawling home to which it led. He left his patrol car at the curb and proceeded on foot. Approaching the empty vehicle with his flashlight, he spotted an open box of shotgun shells and a partial bottle of Bacardi on the front seat. He immediately radioed for backup officers, knowing their arrival would take several minutes. In the meantime, he thought it wise to walk the mansion's perimeter—to gather his bearings for whatever situation they might encounter.

Making his way into the backyard, the rear of the home was mostly glass, so he gained a full view of what was taking place inside. At this point, Webb only could hope his fellow officers got there in time to make a difference, because the situation wasn't going to wait. He quickly rushed toward the house.

He watched as an enraged man pointed a shotgun at two adult couples who appeared to be pleading with him. Looking around for something to throw, Webb grabbed two logs from a tall stack of firewood at the side of the veranda and hurled the first through a large leaded-glass window adjacent to a set of French doors. He waited a moment before throwing the second log through a separate window.

The armed intruder automatically turned and fired his shotgun at the first crashing sound, and then the next. By the time he'd discharged his second round, Webb had pulled his Glock semi-automatic from its holster and gone for a kill shot. In fact, several of them. His aim was effective, if not perfect. He missed the target's heart but managed to inflict serious damage to a number of other vital organs.

By the time backup arrived with flashing lights and sirens, Webb was busy hand-cuffing a totally incapacitated human form. He couldn't tell if the wounded man was breathing and didn't much care. Webb had seen enough movies with indestructible bad guys and was taking no chances. Ronny Mason eventually recuperated, stood trial, and received a lengthy prison sentence for his efforts.

As to the four individuals whose lives Webb was credited with saving, the women were sobbing uncontrollably and the men were practically comatose from shock. Webb couldn't offer much comfort, as he was pretty shaken himself. He'd never shot a man, let alone risked his life on a moment's impulse. Pure animal instinct. If he had bothered to think about what he was doing, he was sure he couldn't have done it.

The owners of this particular mansion were a married couple in their mid-fifties. The husband had made millions from flipping commercial real estate. Before the intruder barged in and ordered everyone into the family room, the couple had been watching a movie in their big-screen theater room with their adult daughter and the latest man in her life.

The lunatic with the shotgun had been the daughter's husband for a brief period. According to the parents, their youngest daughter had gone through her proverbial phase of dating "bad boys" and wound up married to young Ronny Mason—who hailed from a family of known troublemakers from Kenosha, Wisconsin. From the onset of matrimony, the daughter's attempts to tame her misfit had been futile. Ronny never adjusted to his wife's upbringing or the upscale lifestyle to which she was accustomed. Considering his attempts at murder, he didn't want anyone else adjusting, either.

The daughter was gorgeous. The parents were loaded. The crazed ex-husband had married way over his head. It was the kind of story the media gobbled up. In 2002, the cable news networks weren't as voracious as they later became, but they still milked every drop out of the story for several days. Unfortunately for Webb, his name and face were an integral part of the coverage, and he was ordered by his superiors to endure one endless interview after another, not to mention dozens of public appearances around the Midwest. Finally, after a month or two, he convinced the police chief to dial things down—reminding him that Lake Forest was a town of few words. Tax-paying, vote-casting citizens didn't want their patrician refuge associated with violent crimes or a gun-toting lowlife who had slipped into its esteemed upper crust.

Ronny Mason was incarcerated and would remain there for at least another ten years. Lyle and Ricky Mason also had seen the inside of a few jail cells but, to date, both had avoided serious prison time. At their brother's trial, when Webb's testimony and cross-exam stretched to over an hour, it became rather obvious to everyone in the courtroom that this young suburban cop had made himself a pair of enemies. He ignored the scowls and related attempts at intimidation from the Mason brothers, and instead smiled in their direction whenever an opportunity arose.

The bizarre incident thrust Webb into the spotlight for what he hoped would be his proverbial fifteen minutes. Ideally less. But what were the chances of lightning striking twice? Later that summer, fate once again would come calling and push him back to center stage. The population of serene Lake Forest was a mere twenty thousand people, yet Webb Tremont's number came up twice in six months.

The December 30 telecast of *Serve & Protect* featured a case from Webb's first book. Every chapter in that volume remained special to him. With the totality of modern criminal history available to write about, he had selected nineteen cases for his inaugural book effort. Telling people he chose each crime with loving care sounded a bit strange, so he kept that part to himself.

During the research phase, he became enchanted with a series of domestic robberies committed in Nashville—not the robberies per se, but the trio who committed them. This time out, he was pleased the Hollywood gang had recognized the inherent intrigue of the original case and elected to play it straight with the real facts.

A pair of prominent ex-jocks from the University of Tennessee showed up at a Nashville police station late one afternoon in the spring of 2003 to jointly file a burglary report. For years, the two close friends and neighbors had been locked in a genial competition of collecting autographed sports memorabilia that happened to be outrageously overpriced. As the expensive rivalry escalated, the pair grew careless about gloating over their recent purchases. Thefts were inevitable.

As they eventually learned, the most valuable items in their collections had been walking out the front doors of their homes for well over a year. One of the two finally noticed a framed basketball jersey hanging in his den. He remembered it being more faded from the sunlight that seeped through the plantation shutters. On closer inspection, he discovered irregularities with a number of other items displayed around the house and invited his neighbor to render a second opinion. Within hours they'd concluded that both of their collections had been seriously downgraded. A vast array of jerseys, hats, balls, bats, pucks, sticks, clubs, helmets, and gloves had been taken from frames or acrylic display cases and replaced with counterfeits.

What couldn't have been anticipated by the detective team who interviewed the hapless duo was the ingenuity of three high school girls. Each worked as a babysitter on the side, and by collaborating on their schedules, they made sure that the three of them secured all babysitting duties in the two upscale households. Both couples paid well, and the girls' original intent merely had been to keep other teenaged babysitters from getting their foot in the door.

But after months of working their healthy arrangement, the enterprising trio recognized a second, more lucrative opportunity. Soon they were taking turns in removing valuable sports memorabilia and replacing them with credible substitutes. They replicated original autographed items by buying identical but unsigned versions on eBay or elsewhere. One by one, they slipped them inside the two homes and meticulously copied the autographed signatures. By phoning around, they located a shady dealer from Atlanta who made quarterly trips to Nashville and purchased whatever lifted merchandise they had to sell.

To Webb, the fifteen dollars an hour for babysitting constituted robbery enough. But over the course of nineteen months, the teenaged triad appropriated a hundred and seventeen items. The three also happened to be honor students, which was no surprise considering the sophistication of their operation. The entrepreneurial girls would invest as much as six or seven hundred dollars for an unsigned item, confident the authentic signed one they stole would return thousands. They carefully monitored market pricing on every piece of memorabilia they moved.

Their Atlanta fence was the only reason the threesome got caught. High-end sports collectors comprised a relatively limited market. Detectives working the case discovered that an unusual number of recently sold items at one South Beach specialty store matched the list of pilfered merchandise from Nashville. In exchange for a lighter sentence, the middleman from Atlanta quickly caved on his trove of illegal sources throughout the South.

Preparations for New Year's didn't stand in the way of America's newest pastime. The twelfth TV episode of *Serve & Protect* attracted a huge audience and unleashed another wave of eager anticipation. The show was filled with plotting babysitters, grandstanding ex-jocks, high-school honor rolls, and outrageously priced sporting equipment. As New Year's Eve and New Year's Day came and went, the public waited for an entertaining interpretation from the Cop Show Copycats. Webb was much less than enthusiastic. But even he didn't anticipate the unexpected turn of events on the coming weekend.

Chapter Twenty

"Good morning, today is Sunday, January 3, and I'm Cecilia Vega in New York. Topping the national news is a story from New Hampshire that likely will cause people to question whether they want the Cop Show Copycats visiting their local communities … and, quite frankly, will dampen the public's enthusiasm for the Cop Show Copycats in total."

Webb Tremont had been awakened in the middle of the night by a phone call that provided him the details, but he still was glued to the television at 7 a.m., wanting to hear the national reports with his own two ears. The tables finally had turned on America's media darlings. Surely the copycats would carry a smaller fan base into 2016. Or ideally none at all. Out with the old and in with the new.

Webb should have reacted more negatively to the vandalism that had occurred out East on Saturday evening. The damage likely would run into the millions, if a value could be placed on the destroyed items at all. But to Webb, the financial loss was a minor sidebar to the fact that a bunch of heedless lunatics now would be revealed for what they truly were. Criminals.

Hanover was a town of 11,000 people just inside the western border of New Hampshire. The surrounding community featured a number of sizable properties, and one of those happened to have been owned by the same family since 1843. Forty-two acres, replete with an eight-bedroom manor house, riding stables, shooting range, two tennis courts, and an array of outbuildings. The current occupants of this historic country estate were George and Morgan Patterson, Webb's aunt and uncle.

As much as his father's programmed indifference may have confounded Webb over the years, he found this quiet propriety far more bearable than the personalities of Brandon Tremont's siblings. Topping the charts on unpleasantness was his father's youngest sister, Morgan Selby Tremont Patterson. The only positive observation he'd ever been able to make about dear Aunt Morgan was that she'd somehow unearthed a perfect soul mate. Together, she and George Patterson were as mortifying as any two people could hope to become—which he presumed was their intention all along. If they'd achieved this lofty status without really trying, he seriously had miscalculated the human potential.

Aunt Morgan possessed an ability to evoke feelings of unworthiness from anyone in her presence. "Webster, might you be so kind as to pass the cranberries?" The simplest of requests could sound like eternal condemnation as each word squeezed through her thin, pursed lips. Uncle George was worse, because the man never stopped talking. There didn't seem to be an important person east of Pennsylvania with whom he wasn't "intimately close" or hadn't recently "chatted up at the club." Of course, "the club" might allude to any one of the dozens to which he belonged. To Webb's knowledge, George Patterson never had worked a day in his life; he'd made a full-time profession out of being wealthy.

By taking residence at Tremont Farms, Aunt Morgan and Uncle George became the anointed custodians to many of the Tremont most coveted heirlooms—a collection of imported luxury items that dated back to the 1820s, soon after the family's grand patriarch, Nathaniel, had started his original trading company. One of Grandpa Nate's sentimental offspring must have thought it appropriate to set aside samples of all the early imports—most of which were geared toward leisurely pursuits. Dueling pistols plated in gold and silver. Chess sets carved from ivory, jade, or exotic woods. English riding saddles and a vast array of equipment once used for polo, cricket, and fencing. Subsequent Tremonts kept adding to the accumulation, and by the middle of the 20th century, this far-flung assortment was considered one of the foremost collections of antique sporting and gaming equipment in the Western hemisphere. On occasion the priceless collection was loaned out to museums, but its permanent home was the farm in Hanover, protected by the most sophisticated security systems on the market.

The country estate was an even larger family heirloom. "The Farm" had remained in the family since the land first was purchased by one of Nathaniel's sons. Over the ensuing years, there'd been little rhyme or reason as to which family members wound up as its principal occupants. When Webb was a teenager, his father once remarked, "For over a hundred and fifty years, Tremonts have needed only to look as far as New Hampshire to determine who among any given generation was most proficient at the art of manipulation." Morgan Selby Tremont Patterson and husband George had been the reigning champs for close to forty-five years— since wrangling their way onto the property as newlyweds.

As this was January, Webb assumed his aunt and uncle must have been wintering at their Santa Barbara home when the authorities contacted them about the break-in. Had it been one of the warmer months, they just as easily could have been passing time at their apartment in Manhattan. Either way, he was certain the pair would have been "distressed to no end" that such misfortune had befallen them. So few misfortunes had befallen them over the years.

Webb also figured they'd be clueless about the Cop Show Copycats and how vandalism in Hanover connected to a TV program from earlier in the week. Current events, pop culture, or the outside world in general held little interest to the Pattersons. But through his extended family, the copycats once again had managed to create a link between Webb and their latest weekend escapade.

At 10:39 on Saturday night, the Hanover police were beckoned to Tremont Farms by the property's automatic alarm system. Data stored in the property's various alarm systems ultimately revealed all security mechanisms had been deactivated for several hours from late in the afternoon until they were reactivated at 7:22 p.m. Three hours later, one of the alarms was triggered by some form of remote signal and local police were called into action. Once they were safely away from their latest crime scene, the copycats apparently had wanted their handiwork discovered in time to make the Sunday morning news cycle. What awaited the authorities, and soon thereafter a horde of reporters, was a scene filled with mixed messages border-ing on lunacy. While growing up, Webb had been forced to visit Hanover on several occasions, so for him drawing a mental picture was easy.

Off the front entry hall of the main residence was an enormous parlor that originally was designed as a grand ballroom. There the copycats had gathered every artifact from the family's extensive collection of sporting and gaming equipment. More than sixteen hundred items were pulled from display cases, storage closets, and vaults throughout the main house or adjacent buildings constructed for the sole purpose of preserving the valuable collection. The locks to these various outbuild-ings had not been damaged. But not so for the contents once contained inside.

The assembled items were arrayed across the floor of the parlor, where it ap-peared as though the copycats proceeded to mutilate the collection with heavy objects. More than half the pieces were shattered, misshapen, or severely dented—while others around the furthermost perimeter of the room were left unharmed. A portion of the damaged relics could be repaired and restored, but most had been completely destroyed. The loss would run into eight figures.

Two sealed envelopes had been placed amidst the rubble. The first contained a straightforward message: "To the privileged, the rest of us are nothing more than playthings." The animosity reflected in this statement seemed consistent with the damage rendered by the copycats.

But in this context, the second, bulkier envelope made no sense at all. It was ad-dressed to "The Boys & Girls Clubs of New Hampshire." Inside were one-hundred-dollar bills totaling $20,000, plus a note that read: "To be used for needed sporting equipment that can serve a legitimate purpose."

On Sunday morning in Boston, Michael Chen once again allowed his emotions to get the better of him. For the second time in fourteen hours, he was embroiled in a full-scale shouting match with Anthony Lafferty. The first had erupted inside the main house on Tremont Farms, but that confrontation was only a few minutes old when T-Man suggested the fireworks be postponed to a later time rather than stand in the middle of a crime scene screaming at one another. Michael had agreed, because at that point words couldn't change a thing. The damage was done.

The six partners had decided to stay closer to home for a few weekends because of the lingering tensions stemming from the car troubles in Ohio and the continued reports of a missing janitor. They would pull off their upcoming crimes within a reasonable driving distance of Boston and minimize the logistical complications until the group's chemistry could be restored. So, the suggestion of Tremont Manor in New Hampshire quickly had been embraced, but now it felt like that elusive chemistry was lost forever.

Both rental cars had been silent on the three-hour return drive to Boston on Saturday night. Further discussion of what had occurred in Hanover was put on hold as agreement was reached that all six should be together before they again jumped into the heated subject. Chen fumed in the back seat during the entire ride. Fortunately, the others had made sure he and Lafferty were in separate cars. Hoping a few hours of sleep might calm the situation, they elected to reconvene for an early breakfast on Sunday at Teresa Conkle's condominium.

The hours apart only piqued Chen's anger, and the others' too, as they individually absorbed what Lafferty had done ... the irreversible boundary that now had been crossed. Their efforts over the prior two months might have been criminal, but no one had been harmed. In fact, the public's general good had been served by their series of parody crimes. But yesterday's destruction of property was a prosecutable felony by anyone's definition. The situation in which they found themselves was insane; the consequences of Lafferty's wanton behavior were unimaginable.

From the very beginning there had been no room for even the slightest misinterpretation of the commitments they'd made to one another. Their so-called crimes were to leave no victims and produce no damage. Period. They wouldn't be actual crimes at all. How else would Chen have agreed to take such outlandish risks? Why would he or any of them have participated so willingly? Now the notion of perfect crimes in the purest sense had been shattered by a self-centered prick who had rushed into the room wielding a sledgehammer. In a matter of seconds, the lives of six successful geniuses had been turned upside down. The situation was irreparable. Regardless of whatever sized checks he and his associates could write, the destroyed items never could be replaced. Concealing the group's identities originally was deemed a pivotal part of the lasting lore they'd sought to create through their weekend activities. Moving forward, protecting this anonymity was essential if they hoped to avoid prison and total ruin.

Everything had been going according to plan with their latest escapade. They had obtained a list of the antiques preserved at the farm by penetrating the computer files inside the insurance company that provided coverage. The assorted items were located exactly as indicated by the inventory log. The first two hours actually were fun as the six of them worked their assigned rooms and buildings, retrieving hundreds of the ridiculous relics and bringing them to the parlor in the main house. Once the parlor was full, they let the remaining items spill into the foyer.

The full assembly of allegedly valuable heirlooms was laughable. It was a perfect counterpoint to the needs of inner-city kids. Blake pulled the envelope with the twenty grand from her pocket. The overall impression they would be leaving was exactly what they'd intended. How could they not have noticed that Lafferty had slipped away?

From out of nowhere, he came hurrying into the room with that sledgehammer over his shoulder and a look of pure rage on his face. How were they to know what he had in mind? Suddenly he was swinging at everything in his path. They had no choice but to back away out of a need for self-preservation. He was flailing away like a madman, words spewing out of his mouth as he smashed one item after another. "Meaningless rubbish, it's all such meaningless rubbish." He had repeated those words over and over.

As the reality of the situation registered, Chen finally started screaming, pleading with Lafferty to stop. Beaumont joined in, and soon they all were screaming at him. But Lafferty was oblivious. He moved further into the room, battering more antiques until their shouts eventually registered and he gazed their way. Suddenly,

Laffy loosened his grip and the heavy hammer fell to the floor, and he started yelling back toward the five of them, "You don't understand. You'll never understand."

After a few moments, Chen stepped toward Lafferty, raising his voice as he approached. In response, Lafferty started spewing more anger. The words were growing louder and louder before T-Man convinced them to postpone their screaming match—reminding them genuine crimes had been committed and that the property was periodically patrolled by local police cars.

To make matters worse, the wall-to-wall media coverage had started before dawn on Sunday morning, and that's when five of them learned about a second envelope. Apparently, Anthony Lafferty had left a message of his own: "To the privileged, the rest of us are nothing more than playthings."

Oddly, when Lafferty showed up at Theresa's condo, he said very little as he joined the group. In a gesture totally out of character, he brought croissants and pain au chocolat from a nearby French pastry shop they liked to frequent. In the four years Chen had known Anthony Lafferty, he couldn't remember the asshole doing anything kind for anybody. It was evident that Lafferty had no intention of kicking off the conversation, which was fine with Chen.

The runway was clear and Chen started by revisiting the mess-ups in Ohio. Conks soon pivoted into the lack of respect Lafferty had demonstrated toward the other partners since the earliest months of the software company. As they finally worked the conversation to what had transpired the previous evening in New Hampshire, Beaumont and T-Man launched into the oldest partner. Soon even Blake was castigating her sometimes lover for what he'd done.

As words continued to fly, Lafferty listened calmly, his composure remaining intact. He offered no rebuttal, showing no outward signs of anger or refutation.

This day of reckoning lasted less than half an hour, during which time the group's rage escalated, peaked, and eventually waned into awkward silence. Their backlog of pent-up complaints had been aired. As the stillness hung, Chen and the others braced for the explosion that was sure to follow.

When Lafferty finally spoke his voice was gentle, his tone contrite, even remorseful. "I agree with everything you've said this morning, and with what was said last night. I was completely in the wrong and am deeply sorry. I allowed my emotions to get the better of me."

He paused, allowing the words to sink in. No one knew what to say. The last thing Chen had anticipated was an admission of guilt—mostly because Anthony Lafferty never thought he did anything wrong.

He continued softly, "You know how much I abhor families like the Tremonts … how offensive I find everything they represent." He hesitated long enough to make eye contact one by one with each of them. "And I think all of you share these feelings to some extent."

As could be expected, Blake slowly nodded in agreement, but T-Man also tipped his forehead in concurrence. Now there was a nervous tremor to Lafferty's voice. "Yesterday, as we pulled all those ridiculous antiques into that ostentatious old ballroom, I was struck by how that collection symbolized one family's unde-served birthright … the endless generations of self-entitlement and the opulence in which they've languished. And there we were, standing on property that has served the Tremonts' protected interests for close to two hundred years … and how over those generations, they've contributed virtually nothing to society. So, by the time we'd completed our assigned tasks, I was seething. Suddenly my mind flashed to the sledgehammer I'd seen leaning against the garden shed behind the house and something snapped inside my head … it was like I no longer had control over my ac-tions." He looked directly at Chen. "What I did was reprehensible. I have tarnished everything we've accomplished to date, and only wish I could somehow make it up to each of you."

The group was speechless. After a few moments, Gregory Beaumont asked, "Laffy, we hear you, but if you acted out of emotional impulse, how do you explain the second typed note you left behind?"

Lafferty remained contrite. "Fair question, Greg. I prepared that note on Friday because of my personal disdain for what the Tremonts and families like them repre-sent. I intended to show it to the rest of you once we'd assembled all the antiques, and see if you would agree to leaving it behind with the other envelope. I guess I came into the weekend with my emotions already worked up. Once I flipped out, I certainly didn't think a second message could screw things up any more than I already had … so I quietly slipped it out of my pocket as we were hurrying out. For this, I also apologize."

In a matter of minutes, the volatile situation had been neutralized. Chen still wanted to strangle Lafferty for what he'd done, but strangely the connectedness among the group felt stronger and more genuine than ever.

Lafferty watched as the group came around. Angers and animosities were shelved. Disaster number one had been averted and turned to his advantage. Timing now was crucial. He allowed a few moments to lapse before addressing the elephant in the room. "I know you must be thinking we need to call the whole thing off … suspend our weekend activities, go our separate ways, and maintain a vow of silence about what we've done together over these past few months."

Another well-timed pause followed, as he watched his five naïve associates tentatively eyeing one another—each wondering if someone else was going to advocate for the group's disbanding. Clearly it would be the most prudent decision. But he knew he had them. Lafferty waited long enough for everyone to recognize their hearts weren't into splitting up.

He continued, "Trust me, if you all agree that it's best to call it quits, I will yield to the group's wishes with my heartfelt apologies. But personally, I think we'd be compounding my mistake by leaving the public with Hanover as the lasting memory. In the week ahead, we no doubt are going to take a beating in the media. Everything we've accomplished will have gone for naught and we'll be written off as a bunch of unstable sociopaths if we allow that to become the final punctuation. Granted, we never can fully erase the blemish of Saturday night, but I'm confident we're resourceful enough to resurrect our good standing with the public."

The others were being drawn into the possibility, and Lafferty could feel it. "I propose we give this coming weekend a try. Let's see if we can't conceive of a way to deliver a message within the context of this week's crime case that will reestablish us as the 'good guys.' Okay, maybe not with law enforcement, but with the general public … the millions and millions who still can appreciate what we've been delivering on their behalf. I think we should admit to the public that an unfortunate mistake was made in Hanover and proceed to win back much of their favor. It can't hurt. If the results are promising, we think about expanding on that momentum into the next weekend, and perhaps the ones after that. If they're not, we fold our tents and we're no worse off than we are this morning."

Lafferty had been prepared to offer other humble perspectives, but a key part of winning was recognizing when victory had been achieved. He sat back and let the others ruminate for another hour. Rationally they were going through the motions of weighing all the pros and cons, but the energy in the room was undeniable. No one was ready to call it quits.

In hindsight, planting the seeds and nurturing them had been surprisingly simple. After two years of working days and nights in close quarters, followed by their clandestine mock crime journey of recent months, the other five now shared Anthony Lafferty's antipathy toward Webb Tremont and the silver-spoon set. For different reasons, of course. Plus, the feeble clown, Tremont, had contributed mightily to the cause with his "arrogant punks" remark on national television. Tremont's crime books were nothing more than secondhand trash. He'd banked millions from a TV show that was even more pathetic. But worse still, the sperm-lucky imbecile had been born into a family that wallowed in undeserved wealth.

The five young, fertile-minded entrepreneurs had drunk the Kool-Aid. As far as they were concerned, the slate of any prominent family should be wiped clean with each new generation. The group had adopted its own form of elitist socialism. Subsequent generations in a family shouldn't be allowed to horde inherited wealth for accomplishing nothing. One's reputation and lifestyle should equate only to one's current value to society.

There were no fools like overinflated fools. The outcome from New Hampshire was even better than Anthony Lafferty had anticipated.

Chapter Twenty-One

"Have you had the pleasure of meeting my aunt and uncle yet?"

"No, they're due to arrive in Hanover later this evening," the special agent responded.

"Then please allow me to apologize in advance … and remember, I can't stand being around them either."

C.J. Matthews started to chuckle but caught herself. "Mr. Tremont, I am duty-bound to demonstrate full respect toward two victims of unprovoked vandalism."

"I assure you, Miss Matthews, by the end of your time with Aunt Morgan and Uncle George you'll find it difficult to classify any criminal activity involving them as unprovoked … and you'll understand the real victims of Hanover are the people who are forced to interact with them on a regular basis."

"I'll refrain from commenting, but I do commend you for maintaining your sense of humor after another tough weekend." Webb sensed she was looking for a safe, neutral segue into a more serious conversation about the events of Tremont Farms. But he still couldn't help himself. "What makes you think I was trying to be funny?"

In truth, by the time the two connected by phone on late Monday afternoon, Webb's spirits were higher than they'd been in weeks. The beloved Cop Show Copycats were at last being recognized for what they really were, at least by most people. Since midday on Sunday, Webb had been glued to a leather chair in his coach house with a television remote in one hand, while the other busily worked his laptop. Everywhere he surfed or scrolled, debates were waging over the copycats. The group was being eviscerated by the talking heads because of their senseless destruction of property. For the majority of the copycats' loyal fan base it was like losing Santa Claus, the Easter Bunny, and the Tooth Fairy all at once. But for others, it was too soon to toss their heroes under a bus—confident that given time, the Cop Show Copycats could justify their vandalism of a preposterous collection overseen by a pair of new-age aristocrats who never had drawn a paycheck.

Webb and his family had become integral parts of the national discourse. Because of where the weekend's crime had occurred, the media quickly connected the dots from past copycat activity, which further indicated the Tremonts were central to the copycats' overall purpose. It now was obvious the motivations of this unknown group ran deeper than Webb Tremont's association with a prime-time cop show. In parodying the original crime case from Nashville, the copycats could have targeted thousands of places that housed sports memorabilia in one form or another, but they chose Tremont Manor and its venerated antique accoutrements. Then they'd left their not-so-subtle message: "To the privileged, the rest of us are nothing more than playthings."

Journalists now had reason to explore each of the preceding weekends more intensely and uncover details previously overlooked. Webb Tremont's longtime girlfriend hailed from Highwood, where the copycats had left a cryptic note that suddenly carried a more ominous meaning: "Any girl from Highwood needs to be careful." The five churches targeted in Ohio had been Presbyterian—the denomination of Webb Tremont and his immediate family. What kind of vendetta did these copycats have toward Tremont and his billionaire family, and how far might they go to exact satisfaction?

Social commentaries abounded. Writers and vocal members of the public weren't content to simply opine and conjecture on the Cop Show Copycats. Anyone with an axe to grind toward the Tremonts, or the wealthy in general, now had been granted free license. But living under a microscope was nothing new to Webb or his family members; they were accustomed to being dissected.

C.J. Matthews offered Webb an obvious possibility. "The choice of Tremont Farms might mean the copycats are targeting the entire Tremont family rather than you specifically. But we shouldn't pretend the FBI understands these characters. They just as easily could be trying to intimidate you through attacks on your family."

Webb concurred. "I don't know about intimidating me, but they've definitely gotten under my skin. On top of everything else, now I find myself trying to guess which Tremonts these lunatics might go after next … gosh knows, they have hundreds to choose from. Until Saturday, I was only worried about Corrie and Sprig, my dad, or my brother and sister. Heck, I can't even tell you where a lot of the other Tremonts live."

"Don't worry … we can send you a list if you'd like," C.J. Matthews said with a smile in her voice. "Since yesterday, our local field agents have been contacting most of your extended family to suggest a few extra precautions."

"I hope you told them Cousin Webb sends his love. I would imagine most of my long-lost cousins are wondering how they can vote me out of the family."

Webb changed the subject. "What do you guys make of the contradictory messages from Hanover? How could the copycats possibly reconcile the destruction of millions of dollars in property with leaving $20,000 in an envelope marked for inner-city kids? Obviously, they knew the vandalism would turn people against them … could they really believe the public would interpret their motives as altruistic?"

"Actually, our profilers in Washington suggest these conflicting signals could lead to something positive … at least for the investigation," she responded. "The mixed messages may indicate the copycats are not as harmonious as previously assumed. Maybe factions are developing that eventually will cause the group to implode. For months, they've been living under a great deal of pressure, so they could be losing cohesion. Perhaps they'll start making mistakes or call it quits altogether."

Webb was less optimistic. "Or like other schizophrenics under emotional stress, these creeps could become more impulsive and unpredictable. Now that they've crossed the threshold into committing their first serious felony, what new limits might they push? The public turning against them won't make the copycats any less resourceful, but it might make them a helluva lot more dangerous."

The next Wednesday night would serve up another platter of raw meat for the Cop Show Copycats, so the events in New Hampshire prompted a number of community groups around the country to petition CBS to suspend all broadcasts of *Serve & Protect*. As Webb could have predicted, the network had no intention of killing its golden goose and instead released a statement on Wednesday morning asserting that the raised concerns would be thoroughly studied over the coming weeks. He was confident the network would find a group of behavioral experts to conveniently conclude the actual telecasts played a minor role in what the copycats were up to. Either way, millions of Americans collectively sighed with relief because the party wasn't about to stop.

Though the prime-time series was launched and promoted as Webb Tremont's *Serve & Protect*, the network retained the latitude to feature crimes that hadn't been profiled in any of Webb's books. The episode scheduled for January 6 was purely the brainchild of Elmore Brogan. While the show was in its development stage during the early months of 2015, Brogan instructed his writers to create a script based on a recent murder that had garnered a great deal of national attention due to the victim—a legendary rock star who'd been revered by a whole generation of baby boomers. Webb hadn't been given an opportunity to input on how the case was handled, but he at least was shown the courtesy of receiving a final copy.

In a canyon north of Los Angeles, the lead guitarist from a classic Seventies rock band was found dead on the front porch of his ranch house during November of 2014. The crime scene had the makings of a drug deal gone awry. As details were released, the public's reaction may have been one of sadness, but hardly shock. Zig Lloyd's fondness for experimental substances never had been a well-guarded secret. Nor were his repeated arrests for possession over the years.

The surprise came several weeks after his death, when detectives concluded the septuagenarian rocker hadn't been buying crack cocaine but instead selling it. By the kilo. It turned out Zig Lloyd had become one of the biggest "independent" dealers in

Southern California, and this independent status likely prompted his death warrant. The man who shot Lloyd was a foot soldier for a Central American drug syndicate, but by the time US officials tracked him down in Zacatecas, Mexico, he also was dead.

The Wednesday night episode was long on drugs, groupies, sex parties, and aging rock-star stereotypes, but short on quality. But Webb knew that the tens of millions who watched wouldn't care. The public only wanted to see what subject matter would be presented to the now-erratic copycats.

What they did with their latest subject matter was revealed three days later, on Saturday, January 9, when a visit was paid to Henlopen Acres, a tiny unincorporated town near the Atlantic shoreline of Southeastern Delaware. The area's median income happened to be the highest in the state, which made it a logical community for finding another member of Webb's family—this time, fifty-four-year-old Jacob Tremont Townsend. His grandmother had been the sister of Winford Blake Tremont, Webb's grandfather. Thus, he and Jacob were second cousins, though the two never had met, because Jacob hadn't left the state of Delaware in more than thirty years. Following a series of drug arrests during his six years of college, Jacob Townsend was holding fast to the counsel of the prominent legal team his parents had hired to defend him.

The whole story had been kept neatly locked in the family closet, but every Tremont seemed to be fully familiar with the sordid details. Cousin Jacob's attorneys had earned their substantial fees by getting him off scot-free after his first and second arrests for possession, and bargaining for two hundred hours of community service following his third. When they advised him to maintain a low profile for a few years, he took their words to heart. Since 1983, he'd secluded himself in the five-bedroom home his parents purchased for him. He avoided further temptations by remaining unemployed. The family bankers assured Jacob that if he was careful with his spending, his trust fund should hold up for another century or two—which meant that if he was less than careful, he still could push the envelope on lifestyle for the remainder of his earthly existence.

Jacob Townsend was well-known in the community for his partying ways, which included the nightly festivities he hosted for his eclectic circle of acquaintances. The local liquor store had a standing order for three weekly deliveries to his address.

The house was equipped with a high-end security system that linked directly to a full array of emergency services. At 4:16 on Sunday morning, an alert requesting EMT's was received by the fire department in nearby Rehoboth Beach. The standard follow-up call to verify the need for medical assistance didn't go through, because the phone line was malfunctioning, which only heightened the sense of urgency. An ambulance, a fire truck, and two squad cars from the Sussex County Sheriff's Office quickly were dispatched.

As emergency personnel converged on the property, they were treated to the sight of lights flipping on in various corners of the dark, sprawling home. Jacob and that particular evening's overnight guests had been awakened by the approaching sirens and flashing lights. There was no emergency, medical or otherwise. Nor had anyone inside the house pushed the alarm button. But on the front porch of Jacob Townsend's house there was an awaiting crime scene. Or what appeared to be one.

Several feet from the front door was the image of an adult male corpse, reproduced in full color on a thin layer of Mylar and laid neatly across the porch's cedar planking. The pictured man looked familiar. There was a bullet hole in his forehead, and another in his chest. Stemming from the wounds on the flat image were pools of a red, hardening substance that looked exactly like dried blood. Additional splatter marks were visible on the front door, threshold, and adjacent exterior wall. A string of red drops, some of them smudged, trailed off the porch, down the step, and onto the sidewalk. Next to the faux corpse was an upended planter, with what looked to be a flowering cactus plant beneath a pile of soil that had spilled over it.

A number of the arriving emergency personnel had watched *Serve & Protect* a few nights earlier and quickly recognized what they'd happened upon. They were staring at the Cop Show Copycats' latest reproduction. The crime scene from Zig Lloyd's murder had been replicated in precise detail. The figure reproduced on Mylar was that of Lloyd. The bullet holes and blood splatters were identical to those found at his canyon ranch. The position of the planter and cactus were the same, and even the spilled dirt. Only one element had been added—a bulky envelope taped to the front door.

Sheriffs cordoned off the porch area and marshaled everyone inside the home to await the arrival of federal agents—to whom the assembled group was glad to relinquish full responsibility. The local authorities weren't quite sure how to proceed with a criminal investigation, because they weren't certain what crimes had been committed.

In this instance, the copycats' illegal acts consisted of breaching a home security system, triggering a false medical emergency alert, and temporarily disabling Jacob Townsend's phone line. The laws broken had been minor. Their actions in Henlopen Acres served up a stark contrast to the previous Saturday at Tremont Farms in New Hampshire.

The cash in the envelopes, all in hundreds, totaled $50,000—two and a half times the largest amount the copycats had left to date. A simple directive typed on the rear of the envelope specified that the money should be turned over to a Delaware non-profit that found jobs for teens and adults who successfully completed drug rehabilitation.

A card inside the envelope carried a more detailed message that was much less benevolent: "The damage done last week in Hanover is indefensible. What occurred was a mistake of emotion and stands in contrast to our continued intentions. We violated the outpouring of support we've enjoyed from the public. We wrongfully destroyed property belonging to a prominent family—regardless of how undeserved that prominence might be, or how deplorable their behavior. Our group will do better in the future. The same cannot be said for the Tremonts."

The media needed no time at all to figure out why the Cop Show Copycats had chosen the specific address in Henlopen Acres. As reporters delved deeper and deeper into Jacob Tremont Townsend's background, more and more details emerged about his arrests from younger years and the indulgent lifestyle he'd maintained ever since.

His drugs of choice in college went well beyond what would have been considered recreational. He was busted for methadone and cocaine before finally working his way up to heroin. His third arrest was the result of a party he hosted. Police were called to his off-campus apartment by neighboring residents who reported fireworks being shot off his fourth-story balcony. One of the party guests invited the arriving officers inside, where more than 10 grams of a light-brown powder was openly displayed on a coffee table. The heroin was meant as a token of Jacob Townsend's friendship to the seventeen fellow students in attendance.

After each of Jacob's arrests, the family attorneys went into overdrive. Calls were made, strings were pulled, quiet visits were paid to judges and prosecutors, and substantial contributions were made to political campaigns. At no time was there even the remote possibility that Townsend would spend a day in jail, despite the stern courtroom admonishments he received after arrests one and two. Though the third judge instructed him to log two hundred hours of community service, young Townsend must have interpreted the sentence as optional. Thirty years later, reporters were unable to dig up a single record or recollection of Jacob Townsend putting in his first hour. Webb wasn't the least surprised, based on what he'd learned through the years from the family grapevine.

The pictures painted by the media weren't pretty, and not because of any bias in reporting. The facts alone were enough. Here was a man who for fifty-four years had served no interest other than his own. He'd never held a job. No charities or causes occupied his time. His home was a revolving door for full-time revelers.

Though Jacob Tremont Townsend had avoided subsequent arrests since college, stories were rampant about his insatiable appetite for good times. He remained devoutly faithful to his personal trilogy of women, alcohol, and better living through chemistry. If there were boundaries to his devotion, he'd yet to reach them.

Jacob Tremont Townsend epitomized wealth at its ugliest—a poster child for avarice, entitlement, and hedonism. Stick a laurel wreath atop his head, and the world had been given Nero reincarnated. He now had surfaced as the darkest of sheep for Webb and his family at precisely the wrong moment.

Webb recognized the brilliance of the copycats' choices. They had given away $50,000 to a worthy cause, owned up to their wayward acts from the previous weekend, and simultaneously refocused the public's scorn to a more fruitful target—the richest of the rich. The timing couldn't have been better. Attacks on the top "one percent" were commonplace. It was an election year, and candidates across the country were stoking the inflammatory inequities of power and privilege.

The Tremonts were sitting ducks, firmly ensconced at the pinnacle of the economic food chain. Just when the tide had turned against the copycats, they'd pulled off another masterstroke.

Webb suffered through one news story after another that dismembered the life and lifestyle of cousin Jacob Tremont Townsend. Reporters also used the occasion to revisit his aunt and uncle. Throughout their privileged adulthood, Morgan Selby Tremont Patterson and her husband, George, had done little more than bounce between three homes and their time-share villas in St. Moritz and Cabo San Lucas. Not a salary between them. Only trust funds and annuities. They were Jacob Townsend without the debauchery.

Any tawdry detail in the entire family's past was now fair game. Lawsuits settled out of court. Business dealings gone awry. The public was left wondering if there was a living, breathing Tremont who might have committed a worthy act or drawn a legitimate paycheck.

The note left by the copycats asserted the damage done in Hanover was "indefensible." Many average citizens weren't so sure anymore. Maybe this prominent American family did deserve to have their precious lives disrupted. The final words in their message loomed more ominously. "Our group will do better in the future. The same cannot be said for the Tremonts."

Just as daylight seemed to be peeking over the horizon, Webb's nightmare had gotten worse.

———————

Delaware accomplished everything Anthony Lafferty had hoped. The drive back to Boston was nothing like the previous weekend's return from New Hampshire. On Sunday night, as the group gathered in front of T-Man's television, Lafferty watched his five associates flip from channel to channel as though they were a political team following the early returns to an election. Live interviews with regular citizens seemed quite favorable. Commentators were backing away from earlier rebukes of the copycats and shifting their focus to Jacob Tremont Townsend's unusual lifestyle and affluent family.

The mood among the former business partners steadily elevated as it became clear the trip to Henlopen Acres had produced the desired results. The group had reclaimed a considerable amount of their public support and could build upon this momentum over the weeks ahead. Plus, now the entire country finally was recognizing the Tremonts for what they genuinely were—a family of no-account sponges who'd been poaching the fruits of a lopsided financial system for generations. Just like the other elitist families with whom they cavorted.

As feelings of success solidified, Blake O'Meara spoke up. "Anthony, you were right to insist on keeping the note short. The message was received and we didn't have to bare our souls with an apologia." Her eyes fixed on him in predictable fashion. Once again, she was looking for the slightest signal of appreciation from him. Her affirmation of him was of little consequence, but he decided to reward Blake's loyalty with a slight nod in her direction. Her continued allegiance would be important over the weeks ahead.

Chen, the sniveling pantywaist, offered a more tempered concession. "We might be winning back the public, but the authorities won't forget the damage you did in Hanover." Lafferty maintained his silent indifference.

Gregory Beaumont chimed in. "Michael, the public's reaction is the only thing that matters. The potentiality of criminal charges is irrelevant, because we're never going to be caught. Laffy won't allow his emotions to get the better of him again … and don't forget, he backed up his apology by kicking in the full fifty grand we left on that porch. So, I suggest it's time we declare victory from the weekend and move on like before."

Everyone nodded in agreement, even Chen. With harmony restored, Lafferty brought the conversation to a close. "Then we're all on board … and from here on out, no deviations from the original game plan. You have my solemn word."

It was agreed. Just as with prior weeks, the six would meet the following night, Monday, to begin preparations for the coming weekend. Anthony Lafferty had a strong suspicion it would be the last such gathering for some members of the group. Downsizing was likely to start very soon.

Chapter Twenty-Two

Nothing about the most recent two weekends was sitting well with Webb Tremont. The final sentences of the copycats' latest note remained especially unsettling. "Our group will do better in the future. The same cannot be said for the Tremonts." Sure, it was an obvious shot at his family, which many people resented for its inherited advantages. But the words also implied a pending harm to some of those Tremonts, and that seemed like the natural progression of where the copycats were headed.

Besides lugging around the onerous feeling of responsibility for placing every living Tremont in a precarious situation, Webb also felt useless because of his inability to advance the investigation. The actions of the Cop Show Copycats over the preceding ten weeks would rank as one of history's strangest crime sprees, and something from his past had provided them their impetus. Mind-numbing, to say the least. But Webb was familiar with the quirks of fate.

By late August of 2002, the citizens of Lake Forest no longer were giving much thought to the February rampage of Ronny Mason or the happenstance of a local officer who shot an enraged ex-husband and saved four lives inside one of the town's east-side mansions. Because the intended victims had escaped serious harm, the lifespan of the news story was mercifully short for Webb.

But as a new school year ramped up, memories of 1999 were again revived around the country. In Jefferson County, Colorado, twelve students and one teacher had been senselessly murdered, with twenty-one others wounded in gunfire at Columbine High School. Since that time, students or outside intruders had opened fire inside eleven more schools across the United States, leaving ten dead and thirty-three injured. The beginning of a school year had become a frightening time for parents and non-parents alike. As in most cities and towns, officers from the Lake Forest Police Department now were providing fortified security around school properties.

Webb was assigned the local junior high. He patrolled the school's public areas for the hour preceding first bell and then made sure all the exterior doors were securely locked before exiting the premises. He returned each afternoon, thirty minutes before classes ended, to again patrol high traffic areas until the students vacated the building.

On this particular Tuesday morning, Webb already had slid back behind the wheel of his patrol car and was heading out of the school parking lot. To the side of the building, he saw an adult male trying to open a rarely used exterior door. As he pulled over to the nearest curb to park, he lost sight of the obscure entrance. By the time he made his way there on foot, the man was gone. He probably was a teacher who'd left the building for some reason and had been readmitted by a student or another teacher. Or perhaps the man had run off when he saw the police car. Webb could think of plenty of possibilities, but he had only one immediate responsibility—to make a beeline for the front door and re-enter the building, radioing for backup as he ran.

For the second time in six months, Webb Tremont learned the concept of backup support was a standard procedure that didn't apply very well to non-standard situations. As he rounded the inner hall toward the section of the building where the door in question was located, he saw the unidentified adult male. Unfortunately, that lone figure now was brandishing a rifle. He was Caucasian, early to mid-thirties, and disheveled. Webb unsnapped his holster and screamed for the man to drop the weapon and freeze. Instead, the intruder darted toward the nearest classroom.

Here was an uncooperative armed individual hurrying into a roomful of kids. For the second time in six months, raw instinct took over. Glock in hand, Webb once again called out to the man. Instead of stopping, the intruder pointed his rifle toward Webb and fired while he was on the move. The discharge was accurate. To Webb it felt like his lower body had been blown out from under him. As Webb fell to the floor, he aimed and went for the kill shot, firing twice. Somehow he was on the money—one in the chest, and one in the head.

The chaos that followed was a blur to Webb. Between the trauma of being hit by a high-impact bullet, the attendant shock, and a significant loss of blood, his recollections were jumbled. There were distant sirens and familiar faces of fellow police officers talking about tourniquets. More sirens and emergency personnel lifting him onto a stretcher. The sound of a PA system in the background with a voice repeatedly instructing teachers to keep their students in their classrooms. Then suddenly he was waking up in a hospital room with his mother sitting next to him, holding his hand and explaining that his father was en route from Zurich.

Once lucid, Webb learned the intended shooter had been a sad case, a lifelong whack job. Like too many others, he was inspired by Columbine. Based on a spiral notebook journal found in his knapsack, he'd hoped to make a name for himself. The twenty-seven-year-old had been living week-to-week doing odd jobs. His mom and dad in Oklahoma hadn't heard from him in three years—after he had stopped taking his meds and disappeared with one of the family cars. The parents were shocked and saddened but not angered by the news of the death. Instead they were grateful that a police officer had done his job, relieved that their son was stopped before he could accomplish his end goal and wind up dead just the same. As difficult as the outcome was to absorb, a more dreaded infamy for him and his family had been averted.

The media glommed onto the story and Officer Webb Tremont. For the second time. After all, this was the same suburban cop who'd earned national attention earlier in the year. The resulting headlines went way over the top.

"BOY WONDER COP DOES IT AGAIN"

"MOVE OVER SUPERMAN"

"GET THIS GUY A MASK & SOME SILVER BULLETS"

All Webb had ever wanted to be was an unsung public servant, but newspapers around the country were turning him into a comic-book crusader. The fact that he'd been shot in the line of duty only made the details sound more heroic. Experts from every corner of the social sciences started blathering on and on with their "what if" scenarios—hypothesizing as to the number of kids and teachers that might have been shot. For a card-carrying introvert, the situation was totally dispiriting.

The bullet that struck Webb was from a Hi-Point 995 carbine rifle, the same model used by one of the two Columbine shooters. Strapped under the intruder's jacket was an Intratec 9-millimeter semi-automatic handgun—the same model as one of the weapons carried by the other Columbine killer. Webb was struck in the upper thigh, shattering his femur and much of his left hip socket. After two lengthy reconstructive surgeries and the insertion of multiple artificial parts, he faced sixteen months of recuperation and physical therapy.

Almost immediately, a slew of public officials started doing handsprings. The governor convened a press conference in the lobby of Lake Forest Hospital and personally pushed Webb in his wheelchair to a specially constructed podium. For several days Webb was on the phone at all hours from his hospital room, dutifully doing interviews with anyone who happened to host a radio show anywhere in the fifty states. From Webb's perspective, the nation was embarrassingly short on things to talk about.

The staffers in the state capital were impressed with how Webb handled himself with the media, so they urged the governor to bring the wounded hero along on his upcoming ten-city tour of the state. Webb Tremont could deliver a canned speech on curbing crime, and the popularity of this new favorite son would help gain support for a proposed tax increase. Webb was a strong supporter of curbing crime but noticed that none of the governor's budgeted spending increases were earmarked for law enforcement. He politely declined the offer. Ironically, a few years later, the subject of law enforcement took on a whole new meaning for the state's leading politician, as he joined the parade of Illinois governors escorted off to prison on corruption charges.

After a few weeks of celebrity and restricted mobility, Webb was itching to get back to police work. Regrettably, it would be more than a year before he was deemed physically eligible for patrol duty. The department couldn't force him to take an office job in the meantime, but he was more than willing to tackle paperwork and phone investigations in relative obscurity.

But escape from attention proved hopeless. Anyone he called on the phone. Anyone who stopped by his desk. Anyone who saw him in the parking lot, at the vending machines, or standing at a urinal; they all peppered him with questions. More disturbingly, they couldn't resist laying on plaudits and praise. He'd done nothing more than any other cop would have done in the same two situations, but people went on and on as though he'd singlehandedly rescued civilization from the forces of evil.

Returning to routine assignments of any kind would be impossible. Webb knew it and his superiors knew it. Anonymity had been lost. Even fellow police officers found it difficult to treat Webb Tremont like a normal human being. At Squandered Opportunities, his Highwood watering hole, there wasn't a back table or corner booth dark enough to enjoy a burger or beer in quietude. Webb recognized he never again could be the nameless everyday cop he had strived to be. Apparently when a Tremont attempted to become an Average Joe, the natural balance of the universe somehow was disrupted.

The city's top brass offered to place Webb on paid medical leave, or even creatively make the case for an extended long-term disability. Webb would have no part of it. His incapacity to remain a cop had nothing to do with injuries. The simple truth was he had become a public figure, and properly serving that public no longer was feasible. A strange incongruity. As to going on the public dole with disability payments, it was out of the question. He'd been born into one of the country's wealthiest families. The optics would be horrendous, and deservedly so.

Webb quietly submitted his resignation. Gone were the dreams of notching thirty years and retiring to a cabin in the north woods of Wisconsin. The police chief recognized the occasion of his final day on the job by holding a private cer-emony with Webb's fellow officers. He was presented his badge and semi-automatic as keepsakes. Webb accepted the badge but declined the gun, which by now had become famous in its own right. Webb Tremont had no intention of ever firing another weapon. That night he rooted around and found the shotgun his father had given him on his fourteenth birthday for sport shooting. He dismantled the classic Remington and tossed it piece by piece into the trash.

Six months short of his thirtieth birthday, Webb Tremont had made enough front-page headlines for a lifetime. Unable to continue in law enforcement, he stum-bled into a career as a crime writer, passively observing the real police work that others still were doing. A dozen years later, he had grown surprisingly comfortable with his sideline voyeurism. But for reasons he couldn't begin to fathom, he was back at center stage again—and this time as anything but a hero.

———◇———

With the media ravaging the Tremont name in the aftermath of the week-end events in Delaware, Corrie stopped by Webb's coach house unexpectedly on Monday evening to see if she couldn't take his mind off the copycats. She possessed special talents for distraction.

An hour or two later Corrie was nuzzled contentedly against his chest. During the silence Webb's thoughts drifted back to the unavoidable realities. Muttering to himself, he verbalized the question that had been eating at him for weeks: "What are we missing?"

Corrie wasn't ready to let him refocus his attention. "Pardon my ignorance, mister, but from my vantage I thought our combined efforts seemed pretty complete just now. At least I know they were for me ... so if you were faking things on your end, I must have misunderstood a chapter or two in high school biology."

He laughed. "Hardly ... and I'm guessing you were in the advanced placement class, because you taught me a few things we never covered in regular biology."

"Those who don't know must learn from those who do." Corrie let him wrestle with the quote for a few moments before finally adding, "Plato."

"I'll be damned … I never knew he wrote about sex," Webb deadpanned.

Then the silence returned until Corrie slipped out of bed. She knew he again was fixated on figuring out who might be responsible for the torment being wrought upon his family. While getting dressed she asked, "Have you heard from Theo yet? Maybe he'll be able to jog your memory about some mortal enemy you made during a dodge ball game in seventh grade."

He appreciated her light-heartedness. "I put another call into the grand wizard this afternoon. No answer, though, so I left him another message … which now makes nine. He often forgets to check his voice mail, but he never has gone this long. I only can imagine what unsolvable perplexity has been tossed his way."

Corrie shrugged and smiled. She always smiled when speaking about Theo. They'd hit if off from the moment they met during one of his fly-through visits to Chicago.

Webb Tremont hadn't expected Theo Kleyser to become his closest friend while they were growing up. The two had nothing in common. Theo was one of those intellectually gifted rockets that every school seemed to have, but to whom the rest of the student body couldn't properly relate. While normal adolescents might have been fretting over prom dates and acne medications, Theo was more likely to be pondering the intrinsic properties of quarks or the inconsistencies in the theory of light pollution within the Triangulum Galaxy. He had started elementary school at age five and skipped another two grades along the way, so he was much younger than anyone in seventh grade when Webb took notice of him. But Theo's mind was light years ahead of practically everyone in town. Even as a self-absorbed teenager, Webb remained fascinated with how Theo's genius mind functioned. While most classmates ignored Theo Kleyser, because he truly did appear to be living in another dimension, Webb would pester him with questions whenever the chance arose, which was often.

Years later, as a self-absorbed adult, Webb still couldn't resist probing Theo about the vagaries of science, math, and other such matters his own brain refused to process. While writing his *Serve & Protect* books, Webb had called Theo Kleyser too many times to remember. Theo patiently would navigate him through the technicalities of a computer crime, the limits of forensic science, or countless other topics.

Theo had bid farewell to Lake Forest High School midway through their junior year of high school in order to start college studies at Carnegie Mellon—where he was awarded his undergraduate degree before the ripe old age of nineteen. By his twentieth birthday, he already was working on a second master's degree. With the string of fellowships that followed, Theo tacked on graduate degrees from two more elite schools before accepting a position in Colorado—at what Webb described as "one of those secretive think tanks buried inside a mountain."

As yet, Webb had failed to extract a decipherable explanation from Theo about what he actually did for a living. He was left to presume that Theo was some sort of secret oracle for the government. But regardless of whatever metaphysical mysteries he might be exploring to alter the course of human evolution, Theo somehow found time to take calls from his high school friend on a private line otherwise reserved for G-20 leaders and Nobel Prize candidates. Webb couldn't understand why their tight bond endured, but he tried not to abuse his access to the uncharted reaches of Theo Kleyser's mind.

When Special Agent Matthews first had challenged Webb to recall potential enemies from his past, he immediately phoned Theo for assistance. Not only was his IQ off the charts, but his memory was essentially photographic. He'd been punching Theo's speed dial since before Thanksgiving with no results, but there was no other way to reach him. Theo wasn't allowed to share the name or location of where he was employed, and he didn't accept emails or texting.

The message on the other end was always the same, "Theo Kleyser's voice mail here. For an unspecified period, I am not accessing messages. Upon return, I will respond in no particular order. Upward."

"Upward." By the age of twelve, Theo Kleyser had dispensed with hello, goodbye, please, thank you, and all other obligatory social expressions. His brain functioned differently than normal folks. "Upward." By uniformly applying this word, he took the efficiencies of "aloha" and "shalom" and multiplied them exponentially, creating a word for all seasons. One ubiquitous term for every purpose. Webb was convinced his friend had long since forgotten other perfunctory human manifestations still existed. Happy, sad. Coming, going. Strangers, friends. "Upward" was the only sentiment Theo required.

In Theo's line of work, whatever it was, Webb had learned that "an unspecified period" of absence could mean anything from a long lunch to months away on some remote assignment. He'd been uncomfortable about leaving a message describing the true purpose of his call. *"Hey, Theo, I was just wondering whether you might remember which kids I ticked off enough that they decided to vault to the top of the FBI's Most Wanted List?"*

Earlier that day he'd waited once more for the proverbial beep and repeated his message. "Hey, Theo, Webb again. Not sure when you might resume contact with the outside world, so I'll persist. Please call as soon as you return from your latest secret mission. Important we talk. Sideways."

"Sideways." That was Webb's patented response to Theo's "Upward"—and the product of Webb's unpatented sense of humor back in high school. All these years later, it still got a chuckle out of the only super genius with whom he'd ever been acquainted. For all he knew, Webb was the only living person capable of providing Theo Kleyser a juvenile distraction from the weighty issues he hauled around inside his overdeveloped gray matter. For the time being, Webb couldn't worry about which multifaceted world crisis Theo might be off tackling. He was stressed enough wondering about what surprises the Cop Show Copycats still had in store for him and his family. If the earth's sparse supply of thulium or lutetium suddenly was running low, he didn't care to add that to his list of problems.

Chapter Twenty-Three

Blake O'Meara handled the hosting duties for Monday evening, January 11, and Michael Chen could sense the mood was upbeat as everyone arrived. Public sentiment was swinging back in their favor after Delaware, plus Laffy seemed really committed to toe the line going forward.

There was no rhyme or reason for where the group assembled each week to kick off their next round of activities, except everyone knew it wouldn't be at Lafferty's. He'd resided in Boston for four years, yet none of the others had seen where he lived. Even Blake had once confided that she and Anthony never went to his place. He would take her to a restaurant or club of his choosing, and if the chemistry was right to warrant acts of intimacy, he would invite himself to her high-rise, or on occasion spring for a hotel room. From what Chen could surmise, Laffy's sexual appetites bordered on unusual, just like the rest of his personality. Lafferty surrounded himself with secrecy, but Chen didn't really care to know about the guy's private life anyway. Though surprisingly, since his major screw-up in New Hampshire, Anthony Lafferty's actions seemed to suggest he truly did care about the rest of them.

The next episode of *Serve & Protect* would feature a case from 2011. Michael Chen and the others booted up their respective laptops to collectively research every facet of a murder that had taken place in Utah.

Shortly after one in the morning, three adult males entered a twenty-four-hour convenience store in Ogden. A few days earlier, they'd noticed an attractive young female who had started working behind the counter. Since then, the three had traded observations about the woman's sexual potential and after a night of drinking they allowed their imaginations to run wild. Two of the men forced this lone female employee to join them in the backroom of the store, where she was gagged and repeatedly raped. The third intruder manned the cash register until one of the others took his place. For two hours they rotated, taking turns until every lustful desire had been fulfilled and the twenty-six-year-old woman's life was ended by a knife across the throat.

One of the more bizarre aspects to the twisted ordeal was the flow of late-night customers who continued to enter and exit the store. Each customer was served courteously by one of the cold-blooded killers, while a few short feet away the other two were committing unthinkable atrocities.

The murder was solved in no time at all. While seated at a nearby bar the prior evening, the three perpetrators had been extolling the physical virtues of the "sweet young thing" now working the late-night shift a few blocks away. One of the men already had served eight years on a rape conviction, so the bartender contacted Ogden police as soon as the story hit the airwaves. The youngest of the suspects came clean in just the second hour of his interrogation.

———◆———

Though Michael Chen and the others found the savagery of the killers repulsive, they were pleased to be presented a colorful case. It allowed their inventive minds to explore myriad possibilities for the weekend ahead.

Standard practice was to first deal with location. Where could a more benign version of the crime best be enacted? They promptly agreed it should be a convenience store of some sort. For several weeks Gregory Beaumont had been building a database on the entire Tremont clan. But despite decades of concerted family diversification, there wasn't a single convenience store among its business interests. So Conks linked into a few of her favorite databases on names.

As it turned out, there were dozens of convenience stores with the name

"Tremont" in their addresses due to the hundreds of Tremont Streets and Tremont Avenues across the country. Plus, more than half the states had cities, towns, or neighborhoods named Tremont. She also uncovered a handful of convenience stores owned in part or in total by persons named Tremont—individuals who happened to share the surname but not the wealth of the better-known strain.

The group again decided to keep their activities within reasonable driving distance of Boston. They wanted to put a few solid weeks behind them before resuming more ambitious travel challenges. This stipulation narrowed the options considerably.

Ultimately the choice was unanimous. They settled on a convenience store on the outskirts of Richmond, Virginia. "Cappie Tremont's" was open until 1 a.m. on weekdays, 3 a.m. on weekends, and sold bait seven months of the year.

A pivotal consideration was that none of the six had spent significant time in Richmond. The city had earned a reputation for nightlife among hipper, younger crowds, and the group felt they should check out the buzz. A suggestion from Michael sealed their decision.

"How about wrapping things up early and leaving time to hit the clubs? We can check out Shockoe Bottom, the Slip, and the other reputed hot spots. It will be fun to observe the all-night brain drain in a whole new geography."

<hr />

By now it was a foregone conclusion the group would continue harping on the Tremonts. Antipathy toward the family and what they represented had intensified dramatically since the pranks began. Lafferty no longer bothered injecting the Tremont name at opportune moments. The others were able to work themselves up without any assistance.

During Monday night's deliberations, Gregory Beaumont made reference to something he noticed while researching the Tremont family. "Were any of you aware that our old pal, Webb, has been residing in the coach house to his daddy's mansion since he graduated from college? Here's a forty-one-year-old adult with trust fund money coming out his ass ... he's made tens of millions more as a so-called author

147

… yet he can't pry himself away from the family teat. How pathetic is this guy? These rich parasites are a breed unto themselves."

Anthony Lafferty knew exactly where Webb Tremont had lived during the entirety of his pitiful privileged life—but as usual, he elected to remain silent. His knowledge of the Tremonts was far more encompassing than these five supposed geniuses ever would understand.

For eighteen years, Webb Tremont had been deftly sidestepping questions about where he chose to reside. Only with Corrie did he share how out of place he felt living behind the ivied walls of the family estate. His father probably had a strong suspicion, but as with most subjects, he and Webb avoided anything resembling candid dialogue.

Early in the first semester of his senior year at Eastern Illinois University, Webb began applying to big-city police departments around the country—the farther away from the Chicago area, the better. He wanted to start a career in law enforcement where no one would recognize him as Brandon Tremont's son. But that was before he received the unfortunate phone call. It had been a stroke.

Medically speaking, his mother's condition was termed a left hemiplegia, which meant the left side of her body had been paralyzed by an aneurysm that burst and caused hemorrhaging inside the right hemisphere of her brain. The brain cell damage affected her ability to judge distances, as well as the size and speed of moving objects. As she grew tired during the day, even routine analytic functions became difficult.

Janice Emerson Tremont was fifty-seven when life took this unforeseeable turn. Her life expectancy shortened considerably. Prior to marrying into the Tremont clan, Webb's mother had been raised an Emerson—of Emerson Publishing fame. But the immense wealth of the two families didn't matter; no amount of money was going to restore her vigorous lifestyle.

Even partially paralyzed, the vestiges of her former beauty remained evident. As a young woman, the editors of the social pages had featured her photos with regularity to enhance readership. But after the stroke, her face half-frozen, the smile was gone. That smile instantly had signaled to people that Webb's mother was the real deal, a genuinely caring human being, not some upper-crust Barbie doll.

For as long as his mom was alive, Webb was committed to reside on Tremont Estate. He finished his degree at Eastern, but dropped off the wrestling team during his final year so he could make it home on weekends. Upon graduation, he accepted an hourly position handling desk duties during the overnight shift at the Lake Forest Police Station. Every afternoon he hiked over to the main house to see his mother, but sharing the same roof had been out of the question. He settled into the coach house, which for decades had been used for nothing more than storage. The run-down rooms were ample for a twenty-three-year-old who worked nights and slept while the sun was out. More importantly, the four hundred yards of separation from the big house provided the asylum he needed to retain his sanity while living on the grounds of Brandon Tremont's private domain.

He'd been prepared to slog along with LFPD for whatever number of years Janice Tremont had remaining. Then he would hook up with some big city police department.

He owed that to his mother. He and his siblings had agreed that some family member besides Brandon Tremont needed to be there with her. Her mobility was limited, so a bevy of nurses was hired to tend to her physical needs. But the non-physical ones were the more important concern. Webb's sister was married and living in Philadelphia, and his brother was only a year into his college studies out East. The responsibility fell to Webb. Otherwise the emotional well-being of a woman who had showered her three children with unconditional love would rest squarely upon their father. Totally unacceptable. Taking up residence in the coach house was a small sacrifice compared to the years of effort Janice Tremont had put forth to counterbalance the numbing stoicism of her husband.

Webb Tremont took what he had expected to be temporary residence in a coach house consisting of four upstairs rooms, plus a first floor which over the history of the estate had accommodated carriages, vintage roadsters, and eventually tractors and maintenance equipment. He was determined to live inside the budget of the limited wage he earned at the police department. He calculated what a fair market rate should be for rent and a sizable chunk of his income went toward monthly payments he insisted upon making to his billionaire father—which served to irritate the man. Exactly what Webb had intended.

He hit rummage sales during his off-hours to find furniture and kitchen supplies, making do with a second-hand sofa bed, old crates functioning as end tables, and a card table in the kitchen. He mostly grabbed meals at the police station or with friends at Squandered Opportunities.

A few years later his financial picture improved when he earned a shield and became a patrol officer. Then, of course, the money started arriving in wheelbarrows after he stumbled into his second career as a writer. Along the way, he purchased the coach house outright from his father and even managed to upgrade his living conditions—to a modest degree. As years passed, he continued visiting the main house like clockwork, not once regretting his decision to live in close proximity to his mother.

Janice Emerson Tremont outlived even the most optimistic projections. Nearly ten years after Webb had moved into the coach house, his mother slipped away in 2006. By then, the third edition of _Serve & Protect_ had gone to press. Money was no longer an obstacle, and he finally could take residence wherever he damn-well pleased.

For a decade, he'd been certain he would permanently distance himself from Tremont Estate when the time arrived. For as long as he could remember, the opulence of the grounds, central mansion, and various outbuildings had made him squeamish. Every member of the staff still refused to call him Webb, or even Webster. He was to be addressed as "Mr. Tremont"—or, at best, "young Mr. Tremont." The standing instructions had been issued by his father. Just another reminder to Webb that he was living inside the man's hallowed realm. But at last the time had come to move on. Out of respect, he decided to allow a few months to pass before finding a place in the north woods, or on some remote island in the Caribbean.

But during those months, the realization hit. His father needed him near. Not that this powerful man ever could have said so in words. No, Webb saw it in the distant forlorn stares, the new sag to his once-square shoulders. Five months after her death, this man for whom money could buy most anything seemed utterly lost without his wife. Self-deceit had placed Webb at an unexpected crossroads. Since childhood, he'd mostly viewed his father as the other parent. He never had wanted to be the least bit like Brandon Tremont. The foundation of their relationship had been more mutual tolerance than admiration. Yet now he was enveloped with a feeling of inexplicable, unexpressed devotion.

He couldn't dare tell Brandon Tremont that he'd decided to stay put. Such a declaration might have destroyed the whole stubborn tension they'd worked so hard to maintain over the years. Webb came up with a better idea. He would hire a decorator to redo the coach house from top to bottom. Once his father noticed that his son was tossing out his discount furniture and spending a sizable chunk to spruce up the place, the message would be clear enough. He would know that Webb wasn't going anywhere.

He called a few friends for names of people he might hire to handle such a project. Moments after he walked into the office of one of those recommendations, he didn't care if the woman inside knew the difference between granite and granola. Corrie DiMarco was going to redesign his coach house.

That first session lasted more than two hours, and they even got around to talking about the coach house for part of that time. Webb had brought along a few pictures of the space he was asking her to renovate.

Before leaving that first meeting, Webb figured he might as well complicate their business relationship from the very start. "Corrie, would you consider having dinner with me?"

She hesitated before responding, "I'd be flattered … on one condition. Having seen your taste in decorating, I get to choose the restaurant. I don't want to wind up eating in a soup kitchen."

One couldn't teach that kind of brazenness. Webb was even more smitten.

Following their first dinner a few nights later, they each stopped dating other people. The subject never was raised; they simply lost interest in being with anyone else. Within a year the two were discussing marriage—or more accurately, why they needn't bother.

In his past relationships, Webb had circumvented the unpleasant subject of matrimony. But he and Corrie saw things the same way. If either woke up one morning feeling a strong urge for a more formalized union, they could pull the trigger then. Otherwise, they saw no reason.

Corrie already had been burned once, even without a trip to the altar. She didn't say much, but Webb could tell the guy had been a world-class jerk. As far as Sprig was concerned, her father didn't exist. She'd never met the man, didn't know his name, and refused to speak about him.

Though Webb could be a borderline recluse, he hadn't been a monk. He'd dated an interesting array of women over the years, but with Corrie he realized that he'd never experienced anything approaching genuine love. With others, he had avoided the "L word" completely—no matter how much a timely declaration of devotion might have advanced a pressing agenda. With Corrie, hardly a day went by that he didn't tell her he loved her. Previously Webb had operated under the assumption that his earthly allotment of positive karma had been consumed by his two near misses as a police officer and the nonsensical success he'd achieved as a writer. Clearly the cosmic forces weren't paying close enough attention, because having Corrie and Sprig in his life made his prior good fortunes pale by comparison.

The rehab to the coach house turned out better than he'd ever envisioned. By the time Corrie drew up the plans, Webb was so infatuated he didn't bother reviewing them. He wanted to be surprised. During the two months of construction, he forced himself to sleep in the big house, but the end result was worth every clumsy interaction with his father.

Upstairs, she turned his dust-filled junk room into a warm, comfortable office space that had all the trappings of a professional writer. The new kitchen was modern, efficient, and man-friendly, which Webb hadn't thought possible. The main living area was filled with furniture that certifiable adults would want to sit in, and there was a custom entertainment center loaded with electronic equipment that could be operated from control panels built into the arms of two oversized leather chairs. The control panels were a nice touch, but the incredible part for Webb was that every piece of equipment actually worked. He'd never owned a TV set capable of receiving all the local channels.

He was completely blown away when she escorted him to the first floor, which had been transformed into a gigantic rec room containing everything a man would want out of life. Since Webb couldn't relocate to Wisconsin, she brought a north woods lodge to Tremont Estate. Corrie had missed nothing. On one of the knotty pine walls was a neon sign: "Squandered Opportunities, Two." The owner of his favorite Highwood hang-out had provided written consent for use of the name, with one stipulation. From time to time, Webb still needed to stop by the original.

Chapter Twenty-Four

On Wednesday night, January 13, forty-four million households had tuned in to *Serve & Protect*—the highest number to date. The enthusiasm of this massive audience soon was dampened by the featured rape and murder in a convenience store backroom. The national debate over capital punishment was likely to wage on in perpetuity, but on this particular night Webb assumed most Americans were glad the 2011 killings had taken place in Utah. The appeal process was exhausted, and four years later the three men responsible were executed.

By the next morning, Webb knew those viewers were putting the episode behind them as they anticipated a more upbeat rendition of the crime from the anonymous creeps who had recaptured their favor. The Cop Show Copycats would fashion another silk purse for their appreciative public. From the gory details of the original case, something positive was sure to emerge.

Except that's not the way the weekend turned out. What did occur had been Webb Tremont's worst nightmare from the beginning.

> The entire CBS family expresses its sorrow to the family and friends of Natalie Meriwether, who was murdered senselessly near Richmond, Virginia on Saturday night. We regret that incidents leading up to her tragic death bear similarities to a case depicted on *Serve & Protect* this past Wednesday.

Over recent weeks, CBS Television has contended with difficult issues related to its responsibility to serve the public interest. Certainly, we have been aware of speculations pertaining to unknown parties who, of their own accord, committed criminal acts resembling those dramatized on television. However, CBS Television has neither instigated these criminal actions nor encouraged the public to follow or embrace them. We have remained focused on our obligation to air quality programming.

While speculations surrounding these lawless individuals have concerned us, we have held to our moral responsibility as a television network, which includes maintaining an open forum for free speech. We thus had determined that altering our programming schedule because of the derelict acts committed by an anonymous few would have established an undesirable precedent for the entire broadcast industry. One only can conjecture as to how other groups with special interests might build on such precedence.

However, out of respect for the victim, Miss Meriwether, the airing of *Serve & Protect* has been suspended indefinitely. This suspension is not a direct response to the malicious acts committed by unknown individuals. Consistent with the spirit and content of *Serve & Protect*, we at CBS Television continue to strongly support the efforts of law enforcement, and hope these criminals are finally brought to justice before additional harm can be done.

James B. Dewitt
President of CBS Television

155

The press release was issued on Sunday. The same letter was scheduled to run as a full-page ad in the Monday editions of *The New York Times*, *The Wall Street Journal*, *USA Today*, and dozens of newspapers in major metro areas. Webb shook his head in disgust. A woman was dead and all CBS could think about was covering its backside. Typical disingenuous garbage. The network's well-crafted apologia had lawyers written all over it. Webb found no satisfaction in the fact *Serve & Protect* finally was being yanked off the air. The impetus for this long overdue announcement had been too costly.

The unfortunate victim was a forty-eight-year-old African-American divorced mother with four children.

***

Five and a half years earlier, Natalie Meriwether had convinced her older brother to call his new venture "Cappie Tremont's." She was proud of Devon's service to his country and the rank he'd attained.

Captain Devon Tremont retired from the Marines in 2010 with a military pension and every intention of never taking orders from anyone again. He was determined to open his own business. After kicking around ideas for months, he settled on a combination convenience store and bait shop near Lake Anna, where he and his sister had fished with their parents as kids. He bought an abandoned gas station for a song and tackled most of the renovation himself. Natalie would receive a portion of the profits, so she volunteered to arrange for the signage. Seeing his nickname emblazoned in lights across the roof wouldn't have been his first choice, but she knew he ultimately would acquiesce. Devon always gave in to his baby sister.

Now that her kids were old enough to take care of themselves, Natalie tried to work the evening shift whenever possible. She liked having the daytime free to volunteer at the local pet shelter. Besides, she preferred interacting with the nighttime customers, who typically weren't in as much of a hurry as the sunlight crowd. While working, she kept a radio playing in the background—usually R&B and oldies stations, or occasionally a ballgame. In January, Lake Anna didn't offer many reasons for folks to be out and around, even on weekends, so Natalie was anticipating an-other dull Saturday night.

At 11:10, when the three young men dressed in top hats and tails strolled through the front door, she perked up. They looked to be a spark to an otherwise uneventful evening. The trio obviously had been partying. Each wore a partial mask over his face, like she'd seen in *Phantom of the Opera* on one of her trips into Washington DC. The first man even had a cane that he was twirling like a baton. As they made their way toward the counter, one of them, who looked to be Asian, playfully shouted to her, "You wouldn't happen to have any French champagne would you? Maybe a Salon 1995 ... or a Krug 1990?"

She laughed. "I'll check our wine cellar. But in the meantime, you may want to look in that cooler over there on the wall. We just happen to have some fabulous Budweiser 2016, and probably a few cases of Coors Light held over from 2015."

As the threesome arrived at the sales counter where Natalie was stationed at the cash register, the frivolity suddenly ended. The man in front no longer was twirling his cane. He instead was pointing it directly at her chest, a blade protruding from the end.

The Asian-looking guy next to him spoke again. Oddly, his tone still seemed light-hearted. "Ma'am, I assure you nothing untoward will happen to you. If you've been following the news stories pertaining to the Cop Show Copycats, you should know you have nothing to fear."

Instantly her expression turned joyful again. The words had registered, which caused the one doing the talking to straighten up and puff out his chest a bit.

Natalie Meriwether felt surprisingly relaxed. She saw no harm in following their instructions. They seemed like perfect gentlemen. Whatever these characters had in mind, it was sure to be a fun adventure.

Though he didn't have an accent, she now was positive this one copycat was of Asian extraction after seeing him up close. He politely asked her to move aside and then took her place at the cash register. His two partially masked friends directed her down the short hallway to the rear of the store.

Inside the backroom that served as an office and storage area, she was escorted toward the desk chair which one of the young men pulled out with chivalrous exaggeration. He made a sweeping gesture, inviting her to sit down.

She played right along. "Why, thank you, kind sir ... I don't mind if I do."

The taller of the two reached into a cloth tote bag he was carrying and pulled out a lengthy strand of gleaming gold. Five more followed. They looked like extra-long chain necklaces. Expensive ones. The real things. Twelve or eighteen carat. Maybe twenty-four. She was beginning to understand the extra benefits this evening might hold for her.

When he asked her name, she responded without hesitation, "Natalie."

"Oh, you're the owner's sister. Nice to meet you, Mrs. Meriwether. We apologize for not introducing ourselves, but I think you can understand why we want to remain nameless." The comment gave her a chuckle. This second man had a rather interesting accent—from somewhere in Europe, she thought.

The shorter, somewhat stockier gentleman finally spoke for the first time. He wasn't as friendly. "Okay, T-Man, let's get on with it. I'll put the chains around her while you explain what's going to happen."

She figured they used initials when they spoke to each other in order to preserve their true identities. But she also noticed that the one he called "T-Man" seemed a little put out that his friend had identified him at all.

This "T-Man" told her that her arms, legs, and torso were going to be bound to the chair with the gold chains. Tight enough to hold her, but loose enough so that she wouldn't be in any discomfort. "The chains are a gift, so you don't want to struggle or work yourself loose, because you're likely to damage them."

She understood. "No problem here, I'll sit tight."

He continued, informing her that she would be released shortly after they left. "Once we're safely away from the store, we'll call your local police and alert them to an emergency situation in the backroom of Cappie Tremont's. They'll arrive in no time, to find you safe and sound ... along with these nine envelopes that contain notes and money. The police will understand what they're supposed to do with them." As he made this last comment to her, he pulled the envelopes from the inside pocket of his tuxedo.

She knew practically everything about the Cop Show Copycats. "How many hundred-dollar bills are you giving out this week, and what persons or organizations are going to receive them?" She had watched the most recent episode of *Serve & Protect* and understood exactly what the copycats were up to. They were doing an upbeat version of that appalling crime from Utah. These young men were very creative.

She watched as the less-friendly copycat busily wound the chains around her and fastened each in place with metal collar clasps. Meanwhile, the taller one answered her questions. "Each of these envelopes contains $5,000. They are to be given to nine women from the Richmond area who have been raped since the beginning of the year ... just sixteen days ago. To say the least, we have an epidemic of violent sexual assaults in this country." He then placed the envelopes on the floor, forming a neat circle around her chair.

After a few minutes, all the chains were secured and the two mystery men were readying to leave. Natalie Meriwether felt compelled to make one final comment. "I applaud what you boys are doing. You've been helping our whole country take notice of a great many important issues."

"Thank you ... I truly mean that," said the taller, friendlier young man standing directly in front of her. The other copycat had slipped behind her for some reason. A moment later she heard him say, in a mockingly sweet tone, "Say good-bye to your girlfriend, T-Man."

They were the last words she ever would hear.

———◇———

"Would somebody please tell me what's going on with you guys? You're all acting so strange." Blake O'Meara was looking back from the passenger's side of the front seat of the van, eyeing Lafferty, Chen, and T-Man, who were seated in the rear. Gregory Beaumont was driving. The two of them had been waiting in the parking lot of Cappie Tremont's with the engine running. It was Teresa Conkle's turn to handle central control duties back at a motel in downtown Richmond. Conks was counting on a punctual return so that the six of them could hit a few night spots.

The five had made their way to Lake Anna shortly before 11:00 p.m., where they pulled over to the side of the road a hundred yards from their target destination. They waited there while Beaumont traveled on foot to disable the store's security system—which was nothing more than a camera Devon Tremont had installed in the ceiling. Not much happened in Lake Anna, so the former Marine apparently opted to go the cheap route. As it turned out, Beaumont merely needed to detach a connector cable that ran through a hole near the base of the building's exterior rear wall. From there, the cable dropped underground and ran to a telephone utility box at the back of the property. But those five inches of exposed cable made disconnecting it a snap.

After Beaumont rejoined the others, they drove the final hundred yards into the parking lot. Through the window they watched a customer buying lottery tickets, so they waited for him to exit and drive off. Then Anthony, Michael, and T-Man climbed out of the fan in their goofy outfits and started their fun and games with the woman behind the counter.

From the front seat, she and Beaumont watched as events unfolded according to plan. The African-American woman looked to be having a great time as the three of them walked toward the counter. Moments later, the woman was escorted to the rear of the store, and Chen took his positon behind the cash register.

While sitting in the van, they kept an eye out for the police. If a patrol car pulled into the parking lot or even drove by the store, Blake was to send a text to the others inside. But none were seen during the twenty-minute wait.

Another car did swing into the parking lot and stop with the engine running. The driver, an older adult male, went inside to buy cigarettes while a female passenger remained in the car. Chen handled the transaction easily enough—even striking up what looked to be a friendly conversation with the customer.

Before long, Laffy, T-Man, and Chen were back in the van. All according to plan. Beaumont drove out of the parking lot and slowed a few hundred yards later, preparing to stop at the side of the road. The plans called for him to circle back and reconnect the security cable. But from the seat directly behind him, Anthony barked, "Don't bother, Greg, just keep going. Let the police reconnect the bloody cable." Silence followed as Beaumont obeyed Lafferty's instructions.

A few more minutes passed, and Blake reached into the front console for a disposable cellphone and began punching in the number to the local police station. The woman in the store needed to be released. But again, Anthony piped up from the back seat, this time even more abruptly, "No need to call, Blake. I've already taken care of that. There's no need to drag this out."

Anthony's comment made no sense. How could he have taken care of calling the police? Blake turned to discuss the change in plans, and that was when she saw how weird the three of them were behaving. Michael looked like he might vomit at any second. T-Man still was wearing his mask as he sat motionless, staring out the side window of the van. But the really frightening sight was Anthony. She'd never seen him like this. His eyes, his smile, his very being appeared evil and gleeful at the same time. At that instant Blake O'Meara realized her sometimes lover had never intended to live up to his promises to the rest of the group. Whatever he'd done, she was sure that this time the group's trust had been broken in ways which could never be restored.

⸺◆⸺

C.J. Matthews arrived at the crime scene with the early-morning sun, having flown in on a Gulfstream from the FBI fleet. The Lake Anna Police had been the first to reach Cappie Tremont's shortly before midnight. When they discovered the body of Natalie Meriwether, the flow of blood had slowed to a trickle. Based on the gaping wound in her neck, this well-liked local woman looked to have died quickly. Her clothing was saturated, the pool at her feet was six or seven feet in diameter. The killing appeared as if it had been ritualistic. Sacrificial. Gold chains adorning a dead form in the center of a dotted circle of envelopes. And the blood. So much blood.

The two patrol cars had arrived within seconds of one another, at 11:56. They were responding to a radio dispatch prompted by a call from a local citizen. Thomas Fairbury knew something was amiss when he had stopped for his late-night cup of coffee on the way home from work. "Nattie would never leave the store unattended for this long," he had said to the desk officer on the phone. "I've been standing here almost ten minutes. Her music's still playing, but she's nowhere around. You'd better send somebody over to check things out."

As Mr. Fairbury waited for police in the parking lot, he hadn't seen another soul. But by 12:30 a.m., Cappie Tremont's convenience store and bait shop was teeming with people. The State Police sent a dozen cars and the first FBI agents from Richmond arrived briefly thereafter. Others soon were on their way from Washington DC and elsewhere, including Special Agent Matthews.

The store's surveillance camera had gone down at 11:03. According to the state's centralized lottery system, ten tickets were sold inside the store at 11:08. The ticket purchases were a cash transaction, so there was no receipt to indicate who had bought them. Perhaps the buyer would come forward once the horrific story hit the airwaves. However, thirteen minutes later, at 11:21, a credit card was used to purchase a carton of cigarettes.

Roberta and Ernie Sanders were sound asleep when they were roused from bed by the doorbell. After hearing what had happened, the two were more than willing to accompany two federal agents back to Cappie Tremont's. "I did think it was kinda odd when I saw that young man standing behind the counter. He was wearing some sort of fancy tuxedo and a mask, of all things. But he sure was friendly. Said he was paying off a crazy bet he'd made with Devon over the Washington Wizards. That sure sounded like something Devon would do."

The retired roofing contractor was able to provide a partial description of the man, who presumably was one of the Cop Show Copycats. This was a first for an investigation that now would be taken much more seriously by millions of folks who once reveled in the lack of leads. "I couldn't see his whole face, but he definitely looked like he was an Oriental of some sort. He sure sounded American, though. But I guess a lot of those folks are born and raised over here nowadays."

Mr. Sanders placed the stranger's height at around five-foot-six. "Probably average for that part of the world." In terms of weight, "He couldn't have been more than a hundred and thirty pounds soaking wet." Otherwise, "Sorry ... not much more I can say. Really black hair, of course ... and thick. No tattoos, earrings, or nothing. I hate all that crap, so I woulda taken notice."

Had he heard any voices or noises from the back of the store? "Nah, my hearing ain't what it used to be ... plus that damned music was playin' so loud. She loved to blast that radio of hers."

Mrs. Sanders had remained in the car while her husband was buying "his disgusting cancer sticks," so she couldn't offer any additional details about the man in the tuxedo or what might have taken place inside the store. But she did notice a van at the far end of the parking lot. She thought it was gray or silver and reasonably new. "No, I couldn't see who was inside. The windows were dark, tinted maybe." When asked if she might have noticed the license plate number or the state that issued it, she seemed offended by the question. "Why would I pay attention to such a thing? I had no idea that poor woman was going to get murdered."

The converted gas station's slab foundation had settled over the years. The floors weren't level, so as the blood had run off Natalie Meriwether's body, the resulting pool skewed to one side. Four of the envelopes left by the copycats were totally immersed, a fifth was partially covered with blood, but four others were unaffected.

The names on the outside of the envelopes again reflected the group's ability to infiltrate secured files. The identities of the nine rape victims had been highly protected. Only the total number of sexual assaults experienced in the area was released by city and county officials, and those reports wouldn't be issued until the end of each month. Yet the copycats had accessed the data on the nine recorded rapes since January 1—with five of those occurring on New Year's Day, following the prior evening's booze-fests. Each victim's name and address was accurately printed on an envelope.

C.J. Matthews had investigated her share of rape-related crimes. She knew the message sealed inside those envelopes couldn't possibly erase the horrible memories of sexual assault for those nine victims. A small slip of paper read: "Sexual predators care nothing about ruining lives. Do not allow yourself to become a shameless conquest." The $5,000 in hundred dollar bills was small compensation for the emotional pain and indignity. Perhaps in a different context, this gesture by the copycats might have been viewed as a start, as an act of compassion. But when a tenth woman was savagely murdered to convey the message, only one conclusion could be drawn. For months, the American public had been manipulated by a group of sadistic psychopaths.

Chapter Twenty-Five

How many times had he watched their eyes roll as he offered them advice they so desperately needed? How often had he listened to all their nonsense about how lucky he was to be part of their precious new business venture? Yet without him they'd still be chasing their tails. Still, he'd tolerated all their wallowing bullshit because of the potential he saw from that very first day, when he'd flown in from Pittsburgh to meet with Chen and his personal nursemaid, Teresa Conkle.

The break-up now would begin. Strangely enough, Anthony Lafferty would miss having all of them around. Not because of the comradery or cohesiveness to which the others so pitifully clung. No, Lafferty would miss the amusement of toying with five self-important supercilious geniuses. They were the neediest, most foolish creatures with whom he'd ever come in contact. A subspecies unto themselves.

During the twenty-three months that the software company existed, Lafferty had cultivated them patiently, planting thoughts and ideas which were bearing fruit these many months later. Each unknowing partner had fulfilled their appointed roles to near perfection, but it was time to pare down. The reactions to his destructive tirade in New Hampshire and the events since had confirmed which ones he could count on over the weeks ahead. And who was now dispensable.

For as long as he could remember, Lafferty had wanted to extract retribution on a grand scale. Since early adulthood, he had conjured up a broad array of imaginative plans, but the ones that would have a lasting impact called for significant funds—much more money than he'd ever earn as a college professor. Patience was required. With the connections afforded him at the esteemed Carnegie Mellon, an opportunity eventually would present itself. He just never envisioned that right opportunity would stem from one of his meaningless diversions—a sexual fling with an emotionally impoverished former student. Blake O'Meara's introduction to Chen and the others had resulted in more than enough capital in practically no time at all.

Once his big payday was looming, the notions he had been shaping and reshaping since his teens were no longer distant fantasies. His plans became more concrete—and though his five malleable partners didn't know it, they unwittingly had volunteered to become his accomplices. But that wasn't the end to the serendipity.

Just as the group was dotting the i's on a deal that would pocket them tens of millions apiece, Webb Tremont was signing away the rights to his idiotic crime books to a television network. The god-awful TV show was heaven-sent, a perfect vehicle for Lafferty's vengeful plotting.

On Saturday night, the behavior of Chen and T-Man had been rather surprising. He hadn't expected the two of them to keep their mouths shut during the van ride back into Richmond. Shock did funny things to people. How frustrating for poor Blake, practically convulsing as she tried to pry out the details of what had happened inside the convenience store.

Beaumont's attitude had seemed strange. He just kept driving—tuning out, like he'd rather not know what might have occurred. The whole lot of them were basically cowards. Sheep. He'd banked on that, but he still found such weakness repulsive.

Still, he hadn't anticipated the quick vanishing act from Michael Chen. Chen had jumped out of the van as soon as it came to rest in the motel parking lot. The weasel practically sprinted toward his room. Ten minutes later the others were gathered in Teresa Conkle's room as they'd agreed, but not Chen. According to the pimply-faced kid at the front desk, a guy matching Chen's description called for a cab and jumped into it carrying a duffel bag. Lafferty could address Michael Chen later. It wasn't like any of his so-called friends would go running to the police. They didn't have the balls. They all had too much to lose.

The discussion in Teresa Conkle's room was surprisingly short and controlled. Blake finally got T-Man to open up. He methodically recounted the sequence of events involving the woman in the store. The banter at the check-out counter. The comfortable conversations in the backroom. Her upbeat spirit. Even her words of encouragement. Everything was sounding so positive to the other three as T-Man babbled on. Lafferty enjoyed reading their minds. They were thinking that whatever was still to come couldn't possibly be that bad.

But as T-Man neared the end, his voice began to break. He struggled to get the words out. "From nowhere, Laffy pulled out a utility knife and cut the woman's throat. She was still smiling as the blood began gushing out of her neck. Then he started laughing, telling me how glad he was not to have to listen to her nonsense anymore."

T-Man continued in starts and stops. "There was nothing I could do to save the poor woman ... it was horrible. Then suddenly the reality dawned on me ... I'd just become an accomplice to murder. But before I could even ask Laffy why he had done such a senseless thing, he was shoving me out the door ... and toward the front of the store. When Michael saw us, he could tell something was wrong. He started yelling at Anthony, asking him what kind of crazy crap he'd done this time. That's when Laffy started laughing again ... shouting back, 'Why don't you go see for yourself, Chen?' Then a few seconds later, Michael came out, looking like he was in total shock."

T-Man admitted that those minutes were hazy. His mind had stopped functioning once he saw the knife blade glide across the poor woman's skin. Chen seemed to have the same reaction while the three of them were standing inside the store staring at one another. It was Lafferty who dragged them out to the van. He and Chen no longer were capable of making decisions on their own.

Conks, Blake, and Gregory Beaumont instantly understood a key aspect of what T-Man had experienced. After hearing what took place in the store's back room, they were speechless. Each of them also had become an accomplice to murder.

Lafferty had grabbed the lone desk chair in the dreary motel room and stationed himself by the door, in case someone did something impulsive. None of the four could even look in his direction as they sat motionless on the edges of two double beds, dumbfounded as they stared at one another. Watching the realities sink in was great sport. How much good were all those fellowships and fancy degrees going to do them now? Why weren't they prattling on and on about the miraculous feats that the Cop Show Copycats had pulled off this time? Perhaps they no longer cared where they stacked up against the great minds of history. Their need for affirmation was so desperate … hoping to prove they could soar with the eagles. Watching their fall to earth was more entertaining than he'd expected.

No one was talking. What more could be said? Satisfied that everything had properly registered in their prolific little minds, Lafferty stood and moved toward the door. "It would seem the group has lost its appetite for late night bar-hopping in Richmond, so I suggest we not wait until morning to leave for Boston … we may want to get out of the area ahead of schedule. Everyone take some time to freshen up or grab a little sleep. Let's meet at the van in one hour."

Sleep. Lafferty knew that was impossible, but he enjoyed taunting them. The others would be lucky ever to experience another restful night. As for his own state of mind, the satisfaction was overwhelming. He could feel the blood pulsing through his veins. After returning to his room to gather his belongings, the stimulation intensified and he decided to pay an unannounced visit.

After opening the door, she was taken aback at first. But then she gave him that timid smile. Blake was so predictable.

Anthony Lafferty reached out and stroked her hair. "Blake, I've never needed to be with you as much as this very moment. I want you with me always."

The lovemaking was intense. Frantic. The unbridled energy was only a faint resemblance to past intimacies. The acts were more than carnal, more than bodily urges. The fulfillment was unlike anything Anthony Lafferty had experienced previously—the adrenaline rush of committing premeditated murder for the first time and knowing more would follow. Blake also seemed to get off in ways he'd never seen, probably because she believed the events of the evening would make them inseparable.

The Ohio church had been different. Lafferty wasn't intending to kill anyone at that stage. The stupid janitor made the mistake of walking in on Blake and him while they were completing their assigned tasks. The guy started screaming in Spanish and wouldn't stop. What was he to do? He had worked too hard to put his grand plan in place. He couldn't be derailed by a maintenance man. Grabbing the heavy brass candlestick seemed like the best available option. Sure, he'd feigned panic and remorse for Blake's sake. And she, of course, had bought it. Her clinging was annoying, but Blake O'Meara's loyalty was easily preserved with a modicum of attention.

After Saturday night in Richmond, he would need a little time to determine for sure who still might be of use to him. During the long drive back to Boston from Richmond, Beaumont and T-Man had shown promise. Neither said much, not even chiming in when Conkle flew into her repeated rants. Absorbing the new reality, she had allowed herself to become worked up. Somewhere in Pennsylvania she started letting loose about how he'd ruined their lives. Babbling on senselessly. She didn't know what next steps she might take, but she was going to make sure justice was served. Lafferty recognized the hollowness of her threats, but precaution was best. Unchecked emotions were dangerous. His first order of business upon reaching Boston would be dealing with Teresa Conkle.

Public reaction to the news reports from Virginia was nothing short of a national catastrophe. On Sunday, crowds were sparse in malls and restaurants. That evening, two of the major networks pre-empted regular programming to provide special coverage of the situation in Richmond. Known facts were repeated ad nauseam. But hearing the same accounts again and again seemed to help millions of people come to grips with what had transpired.

The questions posed by newscasters were no different from the ones being pondered by everyday citizens. What kind of people could commit such a heartless act of murder? What sick satisfaction could be gained from taking the country on the eleven-week joyride that had led up to a savage killing? And most chilling was the question of whether their joyride was over. What might they do next?

CBS moved quickly to make its announcement. The Cop Show Copycats no longer would have weekly episodes of *Serve & Protect* to serve as the basis for any future torment. But that hardly mattered; Webb recognized this group was capable of anything. A random killing in the rear of a convenience store couldn't have been their ultimate endgame. The sobering possibilities left the public on edge.

The new realities were sure to hit the FBI investigation like a tsunami. For months, the absence of leads had been toasted coast to coast as a testament to the copycats' brilliance. But now politicians would come out of the woodwork, looking for answers and probably a scalp or two. The competency of the entire Bureau already was being called into question. How had this group of renegades been allowed to roam free since November? Wouldn't Natalie Meriwether still be alive if federal law enforcement had done its job?

Webb Tremont could only watch from Lake Forest as his worst nightmare played out. A group of individuals with no regard for the law had at last shown its true colors. In all likelihood, they'd killed before in Ohio, but this time murder was a certainty. Precious life had been lost. A family had been deprived of a mother and sister. The pillars of law enforcement again were being tested by the groundswells of anger. He felt great empathy for C.J. Matthews. The special agent would be lucky to survive the coming days with her career intact. She no doubt had bureaucrats breathing down her neck from every direction.

Despite his ominous feelings about the copycats from the beginning, Webb not once had anticipated the level of brutality being described in Richmond. The murder was more than premeditated. It had been calculated for its shock value. Yet still these characters had insisted on emulating the actual case from Ogden, Utah. But this was no parody. This was a real woman's life cut short for sick amusement.

While Natalie Meriwether was being bound and killed in the back room of her brother's convenience store, one intruder had reportedly manned the cash register— exactly as in Utah. In the original case, there had been three perpetrators, so Webb assumed three copycats likewise had entered Cappie Tremont's. Whichever copycat wielded the knife, he or she had paid close attention to the police photographs from the Ogden crime scene. The angle, length, and depth of the fatal slash to Natalie Meriwether's neck was practically identical to the original victim's.

Natalie Meriwether's maiden name had been Tremont. She and her brother had the misfortune of sharing a surname with the family at the center of the copy-cats' contempt. But unlike other messages from recent weeks, the typed notes in Richmond made no allusion to Webb or his family.

"Sexual predators care nothing about ruining lives. Do not allow yourself to become a shameless conquest." On the surface, a noble enough thought. But considering the context in which it was delivered, the words seemed to be figments of a cult group's psychosis.

In terms of the investigation, the FBI at least had its first relevant eye witnesses. Roberta Sanders was able to describe a vehicle, so authorities were looking for a gray or silver van believed to have transported an unknown number of killers. Webb recognized the odds weren't good that this lead would turn up anything, since there were thousands of vans fitting the description. By mid-day on Sunday, the vehicle in question probably had traveled hundreds of miles from Richmond.

One of the culprits apparently had been a male Asian-American, at least according to an elderly gentleman who wasn't quite sure of his facts. But this partial description was a start. While committing their ruthless crime, the copycats for the first time had allowed one of their members to interact with outside parties. It seemed odd that such an unprecedented risk would be taken on the very weekend they turned the entire country against them. Perhaps the additional risk enhanced the thrill of their latest insanity. Whatever the reason, the arrogance of the Cop Show Copycats looked to be spiraling out of control.

By the time Tuesday rolled around, Agent Matthews still hadn't called Webb about the weekend events. She did, however, respond to a text message he'd sent: "Appreciate your concern. I'll be okay, and these bastards will be caught. Keep thinking, Tremont, just keep thinking about people from your past."

Theo Kleyser still hadn't returned his calls, so Webb phoned him again, fully prepared to leave his eighth or ninth message. He'd lost count. But his friend's voice mail box was full. He would have to wait until Theo emerged from some secret Afghan cave where he was breaking Al-Qaeda codes, or he reentered the earth's atmosphere after studying global warming patterns from an international space station. Such were the inconveniences of counting a modern-day wizard among one's closest mortal acquaintances.

But Webb did coincidentally notice a news item that reminded him of his life-long friend. He was bouncing through his regular internet news sites when he noticed a small posting from the Wall Street Journal.

BOSTON, MASS: Teresa W. Conkle, co-founder of Secure Applications for Financial Encryption (S.A.F.E.), died on Monday from an apparent drug overdose. The company revolutionized computer security across the financial services industry and was sold to Fiserv, Inc., of Brookfield, WI, in January of 2014 for $497 million. Her body was found by a cleaning service employee in the downtown condominium where the thirty-one-year-old tech wiz lived alone.

In 2007, Ms. Conkle was recognized by Wired Magazine as one of the nation's "Top Twenty Up & Coming Techies." At the time, she was enrolled at California Institute of Technology (Caltech), where she graduated in 2008 with a degree in Applied and Computational Mathematics. She later attended Carnegie Institute of Technology as a Steinhall Scholar, receiving a M.S. in Electrical and Computer Engineering in 2010. In early 2012, she joined forces with Michael Chen, another tech world wunderkind, to launch S.A.F.E., which became one of the fastest companies in history to achieve over $400 million in market value. Conkle and Chen, along with four other principals, sold the company just 23 months later.

Webb hadn't heard of the woman or the company she helped create and sell. Though disheartened to read of such an accomplished individual dying so needlessly at a young age, Webb's mind had become preoccupied. The only reason he'd stopped scrolling long enough to read the article in the first place was a name that popped out like a neon sign. "Steinhall Scholar."

Theo Kleyser had been the first and only Carnegie Mellon student to receive the Steinhall grant while still an undergraduate. Despite the context of a death announcement, Webb smiled when he spotted the reference to the award.

Theo hadn't bothered to pull away from the lab or library long enough to even apply for the scholarship, but the selection committee chose him anyway because so many Carnegie Mellon faculty members had submitted unsolicited recommendations. Through a special arrangement, Theo was allowed to complete his undergraduate studies while simultaneously applying the Steinhall grant toward work on his first graduate degree.

Theo never bothered to mention the award to Webb or his own family members, but the local Lake Forest newspaper received a press release from the university and ran an article about the town being home to a high-tech prodigy. Webb purchased two hundred copies and convinced Theo's parents to let him paper the walls of Theo's bedroom in advance of his next holiday visit. After reading the same headline two hundred times while he meticulously taped each newspaper clipping onto painted plaster, the words "Steinhall Scholar" would forever be etched into Webb's memory.

———————

Convincing Teresa Conkle to invite him inside her condo turned out to be a piece of cake. She was pretty wiped out from the whole ordeal in Richmond and that made her susceptible to hearing what he might have to say. The hardest part had been walking up and down the forty-three flights of steps to avoid the building's security cameras.

The news of her death would help Anthony Lafferty divide the men from the boys with Beaumont and T-Man. Would they actually believe she'd committed suicide? And if they didn't, how would they react?

Too bad Teresa had shown such weakness. She had so much to offer for the coming weeks, but she just couldn't stomach the murder of a meaningless woman. One shouldn't panic over collateral damage. Left unchecked, it was only a matter of time before her emotional state would have caused a major slip-up.

During one of her rants on the drive back to Boston, she'd verbalized what the others must have been thinking. "Lafferty, you killed that man in Ohio, too ... didn't you?" He hadn't responded to the accusation, but he sensed how the realization added to her torment.

Everyone in the group had been aware that their beloved "Conks" fooled around with drugs from time to time. With her state of mind after Richmond, Teresa might understandably have turned to alcohol and pills. The presence of those substances would be confirmed by a medical examiner. Beaumont, T-Man, and Blake could decide for themselves how the overdose occurred.

If Beaumont and T-Man chose to stick around, Lafferty would be fine with that. Or if they headed for the hills like their spineless buddy Chen, he could deal with that also. At this point, he simply was curious as to which route each would pick. Either way, Anthony Lafferty was in complete control. Of course, he always had been, but now that truth was properly understood by all parties.

Chen had reacted faster than anticipated. Usually the timid mouse was incapable of making decisions on his own, but in this case his innate cowardice had prevailed. By Monday evening he had liquidated and transferred a substantial portion of his assets and flown to China, where apparently he felt safe. Such naïveté.

Lafferty had all the bases covered. Back in October, the group had made special arrangements with their respective financial advisors at his suggestion. Each of them opened bank accounts in Switzerland and the Caymans. Separately, Lafferty worked through discreet connections of his own to set up additional accounts for his associates in other foreign countries, but in these instances the registered names of the account holders were aliases. Through another of his resources, they each had procured a handful of alternate identities with corresponding documentation and passports.

174

Persuading them had been a piece of cake once the five were committed to the weekend crime parodies. If any of the adventures went awry and the group was forced to flee the country, they would need to shift resources into off-shore accounts on short notice. From their respective accounts in Switzerland and the Caymans, each of the five could then direct a series of complicated transfers that he had walked them through. By the time authorities picked up on the money trails, the young millionaires would have liquidated their original international accounts and begun conducting financial affairs under new identities, with virtually all of their wealth intact. Now Chen had been the first to pull the trigger.

Ironically, China was an ideal place for his youngest partner to be stashed away. Chen obviously wanted to keep his whereabouts concealed, so he wasn't about to make any noise from the other side of the world. Lafferty had more pressing issues. He would deal with Michael Chen later.

He wasn't concerned about the others bolting off to places unknown. He could follow their movements with special locator software he had embedded in each of their cellphones many months earlier. In 2014, he'd paid thirty grand to a German programmer who previously worked for Interpol. His five former partners were addicted to their damned iPhones, but they were prone to laying them carelessly around when the group was together. He discreetly borrowed each of their phones for fifteen or twenty minutes. Recognizing each was obsessed with upgrading to the latest available iPhone models whenever they became available, he embedded the tracking software into their contact files—knowing those files would be transferred to any new devices they might buy. His theory had proven correct with each new purchase since.

Five naïve geniuses had gone above and beyond in serving every one of his purposes. Out of the sheer need to validate their egos, they'd bought into the ridiculous notion of committing bogus crimes for two months. How blissfully convenient it had been to have such able assistants share the workload and even the expense of the preliminary phase. The first part of the ride had proven to be rather entertaining—not only for him, but for the hundreds of millions of lemmings who'd followed their every move. The next stages, however, weren't likely to carry much favor with the public.

Anthony Lafferty was moving forward no matter who chose to ride along. Teresa and Chen definitely were out. Blake would make her pitiful self available to him for as long as he felt like keeping her around. With the other two, he would learn soon enough. Preparations had been thorough. His plans afforded him ample flexibility. Whether there were two, three, or four copycats didn't much matter to him. Even one copycat would be fine. It was only a matter of time before things reached that point anyway.

Eventually the infamous Cop Show Copycats would need to be retired. But certainly not yet. The public still had much to learn about the vaunted Brandon Tremont and his coddled clan. The anguish for those arrogant parasites was barely beginning.

Chapter Twenty-Six

T he one-time Robin Hoods were being pulverized. Small consolation to Webb following the senseless murder, since the copycats should never have been placed on a pedestal in the first place. But now Webb was experiencing the swinging door of media opinion on a more personal level. One moment a talking head would praise Webb Tremont for his early recognition of the Cop Show Copycats as "arrogant punks." Then in the next, a set of flapping lips would concoct some new theory on why Tremont and his books had provided the impetus for the group's total obliteration of moral boundaries.

Two weeks earlier, the nation couldn't stop blathering about what the copycats might do next. Now everyone hoped the anonymous cretins were calling it quits. After all, *Serve & Protect* had been yanked off the air. The Cop Show Copycats no longer had a cop show to copy.

Webb, like the totality of law enforcement, feared otherwise. Whatever the group's name might suggest, it wasn't a moniker they'd chosen for themselves. From the outset, their intentions went well beyond a series of mock crimes. That now had become obvious. How much beyond was anybody's guess.

On the Thursday following Natalie Meriwether's murder, Special Agent Matthews finally found time to place a call to Webb. "Mr. Tremont, I feel bad that you and the Tremont name are such prominent parts of the media coverage. Are you doing okay?"

"I'm not inclined to go out much. But as you know, this isn't the first time I've been thrown under the microscope. I never deserved the acclaim I received as a cop, or the support I stumbled into as a writer, so I guess it's payback time. Being roughed up by the media this time around is only fair."

She chuckled. "I never had you pegged as a self-loather. Where do you keep your stretch rack and thumbscrews?"

"Up until this week, special devices weren't necessary. If I wanted to torture myself, all I had to do was turn on my television on Wednesday night."

He didn't wait for a response and instead moved on to more sobering topics. "I always knew these clowns were up to no good, but I never had them pegged for premeditated murder. We know they might have killed Jorge Cabral in Ohio … but if they killed him, it probably resulted from unforeseen circumstances, because they didn't exploit his death to make one of their grandstand statements. But the way they killed that poor woman in Richmond … that was meant to be some sort of sick message."

"I'm curious, Tremont … what do you think the copycats hoped to accomplish last Saturday night?" The special agent was adept at steering conversations so that Webb did most of the talking. He understood the game. He wasn't an official part of the FBI's investigation, so she wasn't at liberty to overtly share many of her team's working theories. But with a few well-chosen probes and reactions, she managed to keep him in the loop, as much as her comfort level allowed.

Webb had given this last question much thought. "To begin with, they were showing off again. How preciously clever to find a convenience store with the Tremont name, and once again infiltrate confidential police files to come up with every reported rape victim in the county since the first of the year."

C.J. Matthews interrupted, "As usual, we have no idea how they did that. They may have been showing off, but their skill level is impressive. What else?"

Webb continued, "I hear all these experts opining over the contradictions be-tween the copycats' actions and the messages and money they keep doling out … and how these inconsistencies are reflective of a psychotic nature. But I'm not buy-ing that. Groups aren't psychotic. Individuals are. I agree with the FBI's thinking from a few weeks back ... that split factions have developed inside the group. One side goes into a weekend expecting one thing, and the other side surprises them with a separate set of actions. I believe that happened in Hanover, at my aunt's house ... and I have a feeling that's what happened in Richmond."

"Interesting."

From the tone of her voice, Webb could tell she agreed. He continued, "First off, the gold chains. They were a symbolic statement about wealth. Jewelry chains can be snapped or broken with relative ease. You don't use them to bind a woman who fears you might harm her. I think the expensive chains were meant to be a gift for Mrs. Meriwether, and she understood that, so she went along. That's why none of the chains were twisted or damaged. She never felt the least bit threatened."

He paused, and the agent said nothing. Interpreting the silence as encouragement, he went on, "Then there were the notes, the cash, and the vile mixed signal of envelopes in a pool of blood. No one could believe that they could slash an innocent woman's throat and still hope to impress the public by leaving money for nine rape victims. Not even a bunch of psychotics would throw away $45,000 to demonstrate how crazy they are. I've gotta believe part of the group thought they were committing another mock crime and that the copycats would come away looking like rock stars again."

This time when Webb paused, Agent Matthews interjected, "Let's say you're right ... that the group came into the weekend with divergent expectations. What happens now? They've crossed a line that can't be uncrossed."

Webb didn't hesitate with his response. "That's the million-dollar question, isn't it? Intended or not, every person in the group is now a party to murder. I'd like to think that at least one of them might come forward and confess to what happened, in exchange for a lighter sentence. The remorse must be overwhelming. But it's already been five days and no such luck. Apparently, the thought of jail time of any duration is a non-starter ... not to mention the public disdain to which they'd be permanently subjected ... from rock stars to evil villains. So now they have to wrestle with the consequences ... the guilt over a dead victim, probably two ... and the constant fear of being identified and captured."

"What about the group as a whole, Tremont? Do they stay together? Are they done committing crimes?"

"I can't conceive of how a group like this could stick together after what they've done. Some portion has to be abandoning ship. They clearly have access to resources, so maybe some of the copycats will head to some remote corner of the world, never to be heard from again. I only wish it would be all of them, but I expect that's not the case. Some element of the group isn't done yet. Whoever that element is, they merely have been setting the table, and I hate to think what lies ahead."

"I regret to say the FBI is operating under the same set of assumptions. And, Mr. Tremont, none of this bodes well for you and your family … but I guess you already recognize that."

Webb sidestepped the personal implications. "Well, at least there's a bright side for the top dogs at CBS. Nothing would make them happier than to see the copycats continue. Since Saturday, they've been blasted by the press for sticking with the show as long as they did. If the illustrious Cop Show Copycats go on to demonstrate that their antics were destined to continue with or without a TV show, then CBS is off the hook."

"Which raises an intriguing question," said the agent. "With *Serve & Protect* off the air, where might the Cop Show Copycats turn for their next crimes?"

Webb hadn't gone that far with his thinking, but the answer seemed obvious. "Between all the other lame cop shows and movies, there's no shortage of inspiration. Not to mention the thousands of new crimes reported around the country each week."

C.J. Matthews was pulled into a meeting, so the call came to an abrupt close. Usually after a phone conversation with the special agent, Webb would enter a blissful world of suspended animation, allowing her voice and associated visual images to linger a few moments longer. This time was different. His mind immediately went back to work on the copycats, contemplating what might come next.

The events in Richmond also were weighing on his father. Brandon Tremont added security teams on the home front, claiming he did so to protect the family's privacy from the endless stream of gawkers who now drove by Tremont Estate at all hours. But Webb suspected otherwise. The copycats were known murderers with an unmistakable vendetta, and Brandon Tremont was concerned for his son's safety. Whoever these enemies were, they wouldn't hesitate to murder again. Webb's days as a hero were long past. For once Webb didn't take issue with his father.

Webb's father also made another special appeal to Corrie, paying her an office visit to deliver his latest invitation in person. He practically insisted she and "Melissa" move onto the estate until the copycats were captured. This time he even thought to confer with Webb in advance. But based on recent events, Corrie responded that she and her daughter might be in greater danger living with the Tremonts than living apart from them. Her logic was hard to refute, so Brandon quietly doubled the protection assigned to the two of them.

With ever-present security details and constant media coverage, Sprig was becoming an even bigger celebrity inside an alternative universe inhabited exclusively by teenagers. According to Corrie, Sprig did nothing to encourage the attention; it simply was unavoidable. Details of her personal life had become public fodder. Sprig was unfazed by the endless inquiries about her mother's pregnancy and the fact that she had no idea of who her father was. Webb had observed it first hand; Sprig relished her mom's independent nature. Due to recent circumstances, those same qualities were becoming a stronger and stronger part of the young girl's personality.

The subject that Sprig really enjoyed addressing with her peers was Tremont Estate. She faced repeated questions about what went on behind the ivied walls. According to Corrie, she liked regaling her friends with stories about the "awesome" Brandon Tremont. Webb was a bit disappointed to learn his name didn't come up much.

A slight from local teenagers wasn't the only indignity Webb was forced to endure. The FBI assigned a team of agents to stay by his side. More accurately, they were strapped to his hip. Besides providing protection whenever he ventured away from the coach house, the pair was instructed to assist Mr. Tremont in reconstructing his past in order to identify possible enemies he'd yet to consider. Walt Briggs and Daniel Kaufman didn't use electrodes or waterboards, but their methods were equally inhumane.

The two agents looked like they'd stepped out of a government recruitment brochure. Both were mid-thirties to early forties, professionally courteous, and strictly business. Webb hoped for their sake that they occasionally took a walk on the wild side. Maybe they might order a steak without a potato. Or unbuckle their seatbelts before the plane came to a complete stop at the gate.

With the help of his new pals, Webb compiled another master list of individuals with whom he'd been well-acquainted during his forty-two years of drawing breath. Classmates from kindergarten through college. Work associates from assorted summer jobs as a teenager all the way through his years with the Lake Forest Police Department. Freelance researchers who'd assisted him with his books. Family interests. Romantic interests. Guys he'd simply kicked around with. Webb found it hard to imagine that he might have given any of the listed individuals a reason to initiate a national crime spree in his honor. The effort failed to produce a single name that he hadn't previously considered during his many sleepless nights since November.

Nonetheless, if any amount of uncertainty was evident, that name was turned over to Bureau experts for appropriate "background checks." Webb supposed the FBI was doing all the secret things that regular citizens feared—electronically searching credit card receipts, airline records, missed days of work, adherence to the basic food groups, potty training as a toddler, and so forth. In a few instances, deeper dives were required to verify facts or circumstances. But one by one, the potential suspects fell by the wayside.

Asterisks were placed next to names of people with whom Webb had been especially close. These individuals received personal phone calls or visits, in the hopes they might offer a different perspective on potential enemies Webb might have made. In chasing down several of these folks, Webb suffered indignities that clearly violated his human rights according to the Geneva Convention. He was sure of it.

Ultimately, he concluded that Briggs and Kaufman were driven by a perverse sense of humor. The three of them made a series of trips together. No insights were gained to further the investigation, but his stone-faced companions were afforded frequent opportunities to watch Webb grow visibly uneasy. A number of his purported friends shared fond memories of Webb that consistently included descriptors like "irreverent" and "cavalier." Not to mention "insolent" and "sarcastic." Or lest he forget, "dismissive" and "flippant." Webb had to admit that most of the people in his life had been paying closer attention than he'd ever realized. He couldn't argue with any of their characterizations.

They called on one woman that Webb had dated during his freshman year at Eastern Illinois. Despite the fact that he'd broken off their relationship after a couple of months, the two had managed to remain reasonably good friends through the balance of their college experience. A decade later she became one of his most ardent book fans, ordering them in bulk for reasons he never understood and didn't want to. Though they'd exchanged emails from time to time, Webb hadn't seen her in person since graduation day.

When they arrived at her townhouse at the appointed time in Rockford, ninety miles west of Chicago, her greeting at the front door was rather exuberant. She laid an awkwardly long kiss on Webb before proceeding to hug Briggs and Kaufman. She'd even dressed up for the occasion—in a low-cut satiny blouse that a lot of women wouldn't have thought to wear at ten in the morning on a Tuesday. But it did go well with the short skirt and heels. Webb was fairly certain he'd told her in advance that he would be accompanied by FBI agents.

Though he wondered if her husband and three children would have approved of the wardrobe selections, the revealing ensemble did remind Webb of why he'd been in such a hurry to end their college romance. She definitely had been one of those gals that a guy was inclined to write letters about. Not home to Mom and Dad, mind you. More like *Penthouse* and *Hustler*.

When probed by the agents, she couldn't remember a soul on campus whom Webb might have irritated during their days at Eastern. By the time they bade her farewell, Briggs and Kaufman were convinced the woman was uniquely qualified to render such a sweeping opinion. She seemed to have become intimately familiar with a rather high percentage of the student body.

Two of the other personal visits were closer to home. Webb and the agents grabbed early morning coffee at the Lake Forest Police Station, where they met with some of Webb's former colleagues before they headed out on duty. Webb had stayed in touch with most of them by hoisting a beer or two whenever he had a yearning for cop-to-cop banter. He knew his fellow cops could be counted on to deliver unadorned truth.

One by one they did. With both barrels. Nothing they said held much relevance to the investigation, but Briggs and Kaufman didn't seem to mind. For Webb, they clarified things that Corrie and his siblings had been trying to tell him for years. Vern Dinnsen was a particularly weathered veteran who was a few months shy of thirty years and full-time retreat to his lakeside cabin outside of Fond du Lac. He'd been the nightshift supervisor during Webb's first year out of the Academy. Vern had a way of cutting to the quick.

"Hell, most guys with Tremont's smarts, looks, and family money … they'd have been walking around with some enormous chip on their shoulder. They would have wanted everyone to recognize they were something special. Not Tremont, though. He always did the opposite. He went around putting himself down all the time because of the good breaks that life had dealt him. But at the end of the day, the result was no different. By going overboard to deny his advantages, people focused even more on how lucky he was and resented him just the same."

The man clearly cared about Tremont and ended his dissertation by looking directly at him. "Webb, I always wanted to tell you that you didn't need to work so hard at coming off as anti-arrogant. A more effective approach would have been humility … with a little gratitude thrown in for good measure. But I figured you'd be better off learning that lesson for yourself."

Webb's eyes got a little watery as he saw the compassion slipping through Dinnsen's crusty armor. Finally, he responded, "I can't argue with you, Vern, and I would have been."

Another gentleman who'd long dealt in unvarnished truths was his high-school wrestling coach—probably the closest thing to a mentor that Webb had ever allowed himself to have. He was the final stop on the whirlwind tour through Webb's past. The meeting took place at Squandered Opportunities—the original one, not the knock-off version on the first floor of his coach house. Roy Maggard was waiting at a back table and nodded a welcome when he saw the three of them arrive. The man was seventy-four years old, had been retired from coaching and teaching mathematics for over a decade, but looked like he still could show a bunch of cocky teenagers how to execute a proper take-down. His hair had turned more silvery, but he sported the same military cut. The same flat stomach. His biceps were smaller than in his prime, but enviable by most standards.

As soon as they sat down, Walt Briggs asked what Webb had been like in high school, which was all the encouragement Maggard had needed. Coach took it from there. "Shoot, Tremont ... he practically apologized to every guy he ever pinned in a wrestling meet. I can't remember anybody I coached who worked so hard at not making enemies. The kid went out of his way to be friendly to the whole blazin' high school, like he was planning to run for office someday.

"Then he was the same way after he became a cop ... being all polite to everybody around town. Just about anyone he'd run into, he'd start calling 'em 'sir' and 'ma'am' right off the bat ... like he was worried he might get people mad by doing his job. I don't think there was a person in Lake Forest who couldn't see through it, though. Webb here, he was compensating for being a Tremont ... like it was some incurable disease.

"You know, if what those copycats have been doing wasn't so darn tragic, it almost would be funny that Webb managed to get a group so worked up. I can't imagine him, of all people, making those kinds of enemies."

To say the least, Webb was grateful when the conversation came to a close. Coach Maggard confirmed what he'd started to recognize about himself. A few weeks of intense self-examination will do that. He now could admit, if only to himself, that he'd spent too much of his life working hard at being a pleaser. He may have tried to hide this inner need behind a glib sense of humor. But deep down he had wanted people to like him—or more accurately, not to dislike him. He didn't want to be resented for the good fortune he'd been born into. To make matters worse, he had fallen into one success after another since becoming an adult, but he hadn't had the guts to carry his successes with either pride or confidence. And now the irony. These truths finally had become clear to him because some anonymous group was plotting his demise. So at least on one level the investigation was producing something.

Well actually, two levels. Walt Briggs and Daniel Kaufman had been thoroughly entertained.

Friday night, January 22, passed without any reported activity from the copycats, so Webb transitioned into Saturday still weighted down by the dread that had become part of every weekend. To divert his attention, Corrie suggested they take in an afternoon movie with Sprig. On a whim, she invited Brandon Tremont to come along. When she informed Webb, he laughed, wondering whether his father had ever seen the inside of a movie theater. Miraculously, he accepted. More surprisingly, he seemed to enjoy himself—once he got comfortable with the notion of eating popcorn from a communal cardboard tub. At one point, he started passing it around to perfect strangers before Sprig reeled him in.

On Saturday evening, Corrie made dinner for Webb at her apartment. After Sprig went to bed, she found other imaginative ways to keep his mind preoccupied. He floated home at some unknown hour and on Sunday morning flipped on his coffee pot and went into alert mode. The TV was tuned to cable news, his cellphone was at his side, and he busily searched his standard news sources on his laptop.

He instinctively knew the copycats had struck somewhere, but a looming question remained. Where would they turn for criminal inspiration? Before the first word hit the newswires, C.J. Matthews called with the answer. An answer that should have been obvious.

Chapter Twenty-Seven

T he absence of a weekly cop show posed no hardship whatsoever for the Cop Show Copycats. It wouldn't have taken a prophet to foresee this likelihood, since a manual of modern-day crime practically had been handed to them. The intricate details of over two hundred cases were chronicled across eleven volumes of _Serve & Protect,_ and the copycats certainly didn't need to watch them played out on television.

One such case featured Sam Bigelow, a dirty cop from Lancaster, Pennsylvania. When Webb included the investigation of Bigelow's murder as the final chapter to his eleventh book, it was the first and only time he wrote about an officer of the law who had tainted the uniform. Not that Sam Bigelow deserved to die because he succumbed to the primal temptations of working vice. In fact, his illicit activities might only have warranted a temporary suspension if his superiors had known about them while he still was alive. Unfortunately for him, Sharon Bigelow convened her own private review board and dealt her husband the death sentence. Lieutenant Samuel G. Bigelow was bludgeoned and dropped into a storm sewer in May of 2003.

Sam Bigelow and his wife, Sharon, were both thirty-eight years old. They'd started as high school sweethearts and wound up with six kids and a beagle named Bogart. Once he was dead, a few of his fellow cops admitted they had suspected that Sam occasionally crossed the line while working vice. Opinions varied as to when he first strayed from his matrimonial vows of nineteen years.

Until Bigelow's body was discovered by a city worker on a wet spring afternoon, he hadn't been reported as missing. No one at the police station had seen or heard from him in three days, which hadn't been unusual since he started working undercover in 1997. Sharon Bigelow also had grown accustomed to her husband's prolonged absences. Lancaster, Pennsylvania, was hardly a major crime center, but there were enough vice cases to keep a veteran lieutenant occupied.

The dead officer's neck was broken and his skull was battered in several places by a blunt object the size and shape of a baseball bat. The investigation immediately turned to a number of unsavory characters whom Sam Bigelow had played for fools during undercover operations, plus other criminals he'd helped bring to justice during his earlier years as a regular detective, and before that as a uniformed patrol officer. Month after month the intensive investigation kept coming up empty.

Meanwhile, Bigelow's widow seemed especially eager to move on with her life. In the weeks immediately after her husband's brutal murder, Sharon Bigelow was surrounded by Sam's LPD friends and their wives—which was normal practice within a community of police families. But she separated from the close-knit group and dispensed with outward mourning much sooner than usual. Her behavior prompted one of Sam's detective pals to start connecting a few dots.

Sam Bigelow's closest colleagues were aware that their former comrade had played around on the side. But over the course of interviewing pimps and prostitutes whom Bigelow had befriended while working vice, Detective Dennis Cunningham was surprised to learn how frequent and twisted those occasions became. The detective also knew Sharon Bigelow was more suspicious than most wives. If her husband's lifestyle had progressed as recklessly as Cunningham now understood, Sharon would have picked up on the signals.

Their circle of friends knew Bigelow's wife held to a rather rigid view of morality. The notion of a cheating husband would not have settled well. Cunningham started paying unannounced visits to Sharon Bigelow on an almost daily basis, irritating her with seemingly innocent and curious probes about her relationship with Sam. What had been the keys to their happiness when he was alive? Did she realize how much Sam had talked about her when he was out with the guys ... how much he had loved her? Was she aware how easy it might have been for a man in his line of duty to slip off the straight and narrow?

Dennis Cunningham worked her like a made-for-TV detective. Regardless of how annoyed she grew, he continued pestering her in his softest, most compassionate tone. Cunningham wasn't sure whether guilt finally overcame the poor woman, or if she merely lost patience and wanted to shut him up. But Sharon Bigelow eventually broke. More accurately, she burst.

Sordid details came spewing out. The packages of condoms she'd found in Sam's pants pockets too many times to count. The time she followed her husband and watched him disappear into a sleazy motel room with two ladies of the night. The baseball bat she had brought in from the garage just days before she worked up the courage to confront him—for protection in case he didn't like being confronted. Finally, the night her world caved in. The way Sam Bigelow stumbled into the house, stripping off his clothes as he made a path to the bedroom. His naked body, face-down on the bed, passed out and reeking of alcohol. Reeking of sex. The sounds of wood making contact on bone, her arms flailing uncontrollably as though propelled by alien forces.

Through sheer adrenaline, the hundred-and-thirty-pound woman was able to wrap Sam Bigelow's hundred-and-eighty-pound body with blankets and drag it to her SUV in the home's attached garage. During the pre-dawn hours, she drove the city's downtown streets looking for a deserted spot to dump the body. The inner city was where a vice operation most likely would go down. It was where a cop like Bigelow might turn up dead if an operation went badly.

Peering through her fogged-up windshield, she spotted an open manhole on Prince Street. A work crew from the day before had left the heavy cast-iron cover off to the side, which Sharon Bigelow interpreted as divine intervention. A beacon of righteous providence. She positioned her vehicle with the rear hatch directly above the opening to the storm sewer, removed the blankets, and maneuvered her husband's naked corpse until it tumbled twenty feet below street level. Using a tire iron and sheer will, she worked the manhole cover into place—closing the most painful chapter of her life. Until Dennis Cunningham started his irritating assault on her privacy. The next chapter of Sharon Bigelow's life would start in prison.

Now, more than a dozen years later, another unclothed body had wound up in the exact same manhole in the 800 block of Prince Street in Lancaster, placed there by the country's most-wanted criminals. Following the slaying of Natalie Meriwether in Richmond, the Cop Show Copycats had shot to the number one spot on the FBI's list. Just as Webb feared, these sadists were determined to continue toying with the nation's collective psyche. This time out no one was killed, but the principal victim might have wished he had been.

———◦———

Saturday night, January 23, was no doubt a rough one for Lancaster's Howard C. Kykendall. Sunday morning was even worse. Special Agent C.J. Matthews and her team were called to Pennsylvania, where they uncovered a great many details about Kykendall.

According to coworkers, Howie Kykendall took unusual pride in his appearance. He kept his hair and mustache neatly trimmed, his face and hands always were scrubbed to a shine. Unlike many of his fellow realtors, Kykendall wore well-pressed business suits while on the job—in the same meticulous way he once had donned his blue uniform as a beat cop for thirteen years with the Lancaster Police.

When Howie Kykendall was assisted out of the storm sewer on Sunday morning, draped only in a blanket, not a single newspaper photographer had been present. No TV crews were around to document the emergence. But a series of iPhone photos taken by a female onlooker would be enough to throw the ex-cop's life into a total tailspin. Before noon on Sunday, she sold the images to the city's largest paper for fourteen hundred bucks. By the end of the day on Sunday the pictures had gone viral.

Kykendall had been rendered unconscious before he was placed into the storm sewer the previous evening. When he awoke in total darkness, his hands were shackled to a metal structure of some sort. His screams for help had gone unnoticed. As dawn broke a few hours later, Howie Kykendall recognized the hole-pattern of a manhole cover some twenty feet above him and realized he was handcuffed to the bottom step iron. With rays of light now piercing through the openings, he also saw that his cell phone had been positioned in such a way that he could stretch his leg and rake it in with a bare foot. After exhausting every effort to free himself on his own, he finally maneuvered the phone into one hand and placed a 9-1-1 call.

When the first arriving officers lifted the manhole cover and beamed their flashlights downward, they saw a nude male figure that appeared unhurt. Crouched into a ball on cold concrete, trying to preserve what dignity and privacy he could, the man looked strangely familiar to them. The reason became clear as soon as he called out his name and former precinct. Out of respect for a one-time cop, the officers dimmed their lights. Kykendall was tossed a blanket and set of master keys to free himself. In the meantime, a few early-rising citizens were gathering to check out the action.

During Kykendall's ascent from the dank chamber, the black letters printed across his forehead weren't yet distinguishable. But the moment the ex-cop's head rose above street level, the word practically screamed in the early morning sunlight. "ADULTERER!"

An EMT at the scene tried to remove the letters from his skin with various cleansing agents from a medical kit. To no avail. The permanent ink used by the copycats required a special solution. "ADULTERER!" was front and center in every picture snapped by the lone bystander who thought to pull out her cellphone. The word was front and center in every colorful account repeated by the handful of other witnesses who observed the rescue. Then front and center as those same pictures and first-hand descriptions went national in the hours and days that followed.

Also found at the scene was an envelope—sealed inside a waterproof pouch and suspended by wire from the bottom of the manhole cover. The bulky packet was addressed to Tricia Kykendall, wife of the cop-turned-realtor. Inside was a stack of hundred-dollar bills that totaled $20,000 and a note that read: "Hire a good attorney. Husbands must pay for their philandering." Poor Howie didn't stand a chance.

His wife of nineteen years now could afford any divorce attorney in the area, with an entire country assuming she had justifiable cause.

When C.J. Matthews and the FBI contingent arrived in Lancaster at midday on Sunday, Howie Kykendall still was struggling to understand how his life had been turned upside down so abruptly. In fragments, he revealed how he'd shown up a few minutes early for an appointment at nine o'clock on Saturday night to visit a recently listed condo in the downtown area—assuming things went well. The other party wasn't a potential buyer; she was a married woman he would be meeting for the first time.

It was to have been a blind date, set up through an internet dating service. The woman was supposed to be waiting inside her car in the secluded parking lot he'd used for such trysts in the past. They'd agreed he would lock his car and walk to hers, which he assumed to be the red sedan that was parked in the agreed-upon space. In their email exchanges, she had insisted upon taking her car during a planned evening of dining, clubbing, and whatever might naturally follow. After taking two or three steps away from his car, he felt a cloth against his face and multiple sets of hands grabbing him from behind. The next thing he remembered was awakening to total darkness and cold concrete against his buttocks. Due to the aftershock of the previous night's events, Kykendall's defenses were down. He poured out his soul to the agents who interviewed him.

The romantic rendezvous was arranged through one of the four online match-making services to which Kykendall subscribed under assumed names. In recent years, he had discovered these services were ideal for hooking up with the right kind of sex partners—that is, once he'd learned how to decipher the veiled jargon used in the dating profiles. An insatiable philanderer, Howie Kykendall liked sneaking around with married women who were bold enough to employ dating services. He figured they were apt to have as much to lose as he did if proper discretion wasn't practiced by both parties.

The odd and unpredictable hours associated with a successful real estate practice provided Kykendall perfect cover on the home front whenever an appealing computer match materialized. Plus, his ready access to empty residences supplied him an ever-changing array of suitable playpens.

The copycats evidently had posted some veiled jargon of their own. Under the guise of being an interested female party, they lured Kykendall to the isolated parking lot where he was incapacitated. Executing the abduction and depositing his unconscious body into a storm sewer must have been relatively easy for this now accomplished group of criminals.

The tougher task would have been identifying an appropriate target who could be turned into a public spectacle. The copycats clearly had wanted to approximate the original Lancaster crime as closely as possible, so they would have searched for a cop who was an adulterer. In the end, they must have decided that an ex-cop was the best they could do. Or perhaps they simply thought Howie Kykendall was the most deserving candidate among whatever slate of contenders they identified.

The population of Lancaster's metropolitan area was a half-million, with thousands of cops and ex-cops living around the city. Ascertaining the names of police officers, present or past, who repeatedly cheated on their spouses would have been no small challenge. It wasn't the type of inquiry one simply put to Siri or typed into Google.

The copycats repeatedly had demonstrated their skills for infiltrating systems of any type and accessing secured data. In the first 24 hours after Kykendall was rescued, the FBI's computer specialists determined the group this time had hacked into the databases of several internet dating sites, deciphered their various data codes, and screened for married males from the Lancaster area with a pattern of contacting willing married females. The trickiest part would have been sorting through the posted names these individuals used and working back to establish their true identities to determine which ones might have been police officers.

This degree of searching and verification required not only extraordinary technical skills, but also significant time. At best, weeks. More likely, months, according to cyber-forensic experts. Which meant the Cop Show Copycats had prepared in advance for a time when they wouldn't have episodes of *Serve & Protect* to parody. The group had known a line eventually would be crossed and that the network would be forced to suspend the program. They had planned ahead for just that occasion. As soon as their situation changed, they set the wheels in motion to entrap and expose a philanderer like Howie Kykendall. The poor fool never had a chance.

Compared to the prior weekend in Richmond, the events of Lancaster seemed almost comical. Except, of course, to Howie Kykendall. Or to Webb Tremont. Almost immediately, the press made the connection to the more tragic Lancaster crime case profiled in Webb's most recent edition of _Serve & Protect_. No additional explanation was required. First his TV show, now his books. The public knew with certainty that Webb Tremont was the target of the copycats' venom. Several among the cable news drones even hypothesized that the copycats had chosen the Lancaster case because it allowed them to humiliate an unlikable character who happened to be an ex-cop. Just like Tremont.

One of the grandstanders on CNN couldn't resist stretching further. "The Cop Show Copycats are more and more fixated on Webb Tremont with the conscious choices they're making. What is unclear is whether they are relaying messages to him or about him. Either way, I don't envy Mr. Tremont for having to defend himself with the woman in his life. One has to wonder if they might be insinuating he, too, is a philanderer."

Nothing like a little false empathy from a media vulture while he casually casts aspersions upon a man's fidelity. Fortunately for Webb, Corrie shrugged off the speculation as nonsense. At least, he thought she was shrugging.

Meanwhile, things weren't looking up for his favorite special agent. As the copycats continued to dominate the news, the FBI kept searching for a misstep, large or miniscule, that this anonymous group might have made in setting up Howie Kykendall. A computer trail they might have left with one of the online dating services. A fingerprint, a footprint, a tire track somewhere in Lancaster. A witness at the parking lot where Kykendall was abducted. Or near the storm sewer where he later was deposited. A purchase code on the handcuffs placed around his wrists.

Something. Anything. But results were the same. Nothing. More obligatory wastes of time that Bureau spokespersons tried in vain to sugarcoat.

———◦———

Anthony Lafferty always had suspected T-Man was different from the rest of them. Even though the guy never opened up about his past, he'd been the first to jump on board when Lafferty started railing against old-line families and all their old-line wealth. He'd done his own digging and learned that T-Man came from a family with its own serious money. But over time it had become clear that T-Man detested the upper crust almost as much as he did. In fact, this secretive partner even helped sway the others. Chen and Teresa Conkle actually wound up believing it was their idea to start taking shots at the Tremonts with the messages left in envelopes. But, of course, Teresa had wanted to believe virtually everything was her idea.

Not surprisingly, Gregory Beaumont had checked out after Richmond—disappearing just hours after Teresa Conkle's body was discovered on Monday. Lafferty was comfortable with a group that now numbered three—at least for a few more weeks. Blake and T-Man had provided more than enough support in Lancaster, especially since he'd locked and loaded all the key pieces many weeks earlier.

In fleeing, Beaumont turned out to be reasonably resourceful. Like Chen, he'd liquidated his investments and bolted the country with millions transferred into offshore accounts. Beaumont's first stop was Key Biscayne, a logical place from which to slip away and start island-hopping toward South America under a new identity. Lafferty would continue tracking this ex-partner's stealth journey for a few more days before taking a jaunt of his own to the islands. He'd visited the Caribbean only once in the past, for an academic conference in Nassau. He looked forward to a second trip and a surprise reunion with his old pal Gregory.

———◦———

Webb Tremont had held onto the faint possibility that the Cop Show Copycats might leave him alone once they'd successfully knocked *Serve & Protect* off the air.

They couldn't have known how much he abhorred the show, so he was hoping they might view its cancellation as an important victory and move on to harass some other hapless soul—some other spineless writer who sold out to greed, or some other lucky seed with a succession of birthrights.

That slim hope vanished once the news was received from Lancaster. They had chosen case number 222 from the book series that had provided Webb his day-to-day existence for over a decade and the first real purpose to his life. Due to the self-reflection of recent months, he finally could admit his strong desire to become a cop had been a sham. Sure, he always had harbored a fascination with crime and law enforcement, but he never really possessed the same inner drives as other cops—the real cops he respected more and more with each new book. In researching criminal cases, he time and again had observed a selflessness in the manner with which committed police officers went about their duties. He was missing that gene, that inner capacity. Becoming a cop had been nothing more than a convenient holding pattern—a place to occupy time until he might conjure up a real career and irritate Brandon Tremont in the meantime. The role his father played in his decision-making was probably more pivotal than he ever would understand, or dare to admit.

Eerie. For days following Lancaster, the eeriness seemed universal. The media and the public no longer had guideposts. The pervasive dread of a coming weekend was palpable. For hours on end, Webb sifted through the eleven books he'd authored. He practically could recite the cases from memory. Which cases might the copycats choose? Would they depict their next crime light-heartedly or commit acts more deviant than the original ones? By Friday, Webb's every waking hour was consumed by this mental spiral. The unexpected phone call was exactly the pick-me-up he had needed to restore a modicum of balance to his life.

"Upward!"

When he heard that voice, Webb's mind invariably filled with pictures of Teddy Roosevelt riding a horse down Main Street and barking out greetings to everyone in sight.

Theo Kleyser neither owned a TV set nor bothered with the daily news unless it pertained to one of his assigned projects. So, Webb wasn't surprised to hear his closest friend knew nothing about the Cop Show Copycats or the attacks he and his family had been weathering. But he was downright shocked to learn Theo had not been off on a professional mission.

For as long as he'd known Theodore Samuel Kleyser, Webb couldn't remember him taking time away from work. Yet Theo had gone on vacation—a bona fide personal holiday. The trip had been one of those unimaginable, once-in-a-lifetime opportunities. At least for someone who'd mastered calculus and organic chemistry by the time he was halfway through seventh grade.

Normally, Theo Kleyser wasn't one to show much emotion. Mostly because his mind would have been simultaneously processing fifty or sixty of humankind's most complex unanswered mysteries. So ,Webb was somewhat taken aback after he asked Theo about his extended absence. The guy went giddy on him. Not as in transitory exuberance. No, this was mile-a-minute, two-octaves-higher, faint-at-any-moment, little-kid euphoria. Between gasps, gulps, and other exclamatory emissions from the other end of the phone, Webb was able to piece together a vague understanding of where Theo had been.

There was this massive chunk of ice called the Mertz Glacier, which apparently was named for some Antarctic explorer who got lost in 1913, never to be seen again. Well, in 2011, an iceberg crashed into this big old glacier and caused a large piece of it to break off. Lo and behold, biologists, botanists, and oceanographers from every continent dropped what they were doing and scurried down to the bottom of the world just to dive into the frigid waters of an enormous new hole that had been created. For almost five years, the scientific journals had been filled with articles that described entirely new species of fish, sponges, sea stars, and other life forms still being discovered.

Dying to get into the action, Theo had networked his way up a ladder of VIP's in the scientific community to wrangle an invitation onto one of the study ships. Even to someone like Webb, who had detested every science project since dissecting an earthworm, Theo made the prospect sound too wondrous to miss. He actually found himself getting wrapped up in Theo's infectious enthusiasm.

But then Theo went and destroyed the magic. His friend hadn't been the least bit interested in sea stars the size of hubcaps, neon-colored sponges, or a new marine animal called a sea pen that actually sprouted feathers underwater. No, his scholarly friend had expended two months of saved-up vacation time and tens of thousands of his own hard-earned dollars to observe phytoplankton. Microscopic plants, no less. Algae. Miniature oceanic weeds. Talk about a buzzkill. Webb wrote it off to the idiosyncrasies of an overdeveloped brain.

Unfortunately, he'd managed to wind up Theo. He was obliged to listen to another twenty minutes of uninterrupted phytoplankton-speak. Webb could envision his pal waving his hands wildly as he cradled the phone between his shoulder and chin. He likely was clad in one of his trademark black t-shirts, maybe worn under a black sweatshirt, with black denim pants and black cushion-soled shoes. Black socks if he'd remembered to put them on. Black was the only color he owned. Theo wasn't making any kind of fashion statement. A closet full of black clothes was simply more efficient. Less time needed for shopping and less time deciding what to wear. He probably was sporting several days of dark stubble. Shaving also took valuable minutes away from more important matters. Since eating, too, could be a distraction, Theo's weight hadn't climbed above a hundred and seventy pounds since puberty. Not much, considering the guy stood six-foot-six. Not that Theo Kleyser stood a lot.

The marvels of polar plant life. Webb was on the verge of gnawing off the fingers of his left hand when Theo finally got around to asking about the repeated messages that had been left in his voice mailbox. At last the conversation could move on to something more enjoyable, like whether Theo could think of anyone from their mutual past who might want to put an end to Webb and his entire family.

Webb hit him with what had become his standard battery of questions about past recollections. Theo's response was the same as all the others. His longest and closest friend couldn't think of a soul from their junior high and high school days who might carry this degree of animosity, or any animosity at all for that matter. But opinions from Theo never were rendered without complications. In the world of The Cerebral One, there was no such thing as a simple judgment.

"Webb, during our younger years your standard behavior patterns didn't really leave much of an opening for the other kids to dislike you. I'm not suggesting you were equipped with a particularly pleasing disposition, as we can agree you were not. But if anyone might have been inclined to say something derogatory about Webb Tremont, you already would have said it for them. In high school, you were inexorably self-deprecating. You still are. You are burdened with an underlying revulsion toward your family's wealth and reputation. I've never understood such wretched insecurity over what are enviable advantages ... but look at me. Who am I to judge?"

"What do you mean by that?" Webb interrupted.

"Patience. I'll get to the relevant parallels momentarily. As a Tremont, you were the recipient of obvious benefits ... money, family connections, prestige. Plus, as much as I'm reluctant to concede, you also were endowed with reasonable intelligence and what many misguided females might have described as boyish good looks. Yet still you feel this constant urgency to compensate for your good fortunes ... and not just the financial ones. You've somehow managed to transform every advantage into a handicap."

He was on one of his patented rolls, so Webb could only listen. "A prime example was high school athletics. You were gifted enough to make any number of teams ... realms I'll never understand in the first place ... but I digress. So, what did you do? Without mentioning a word to anyone, you tried out for wrestling ... a sport completely foreign to you. A sport to which no one besides other wrestlers paid notice. Out of pure, unmitigated overcompensation, you worked harder than the rest of the team and pushed yourself to the State semi-finals."

Theo continued, "And let's face it, Webb. I've been prone to similar tendencies. I overcompensate for having been gifted with an advanced IQ. Think of how I conducted myself in junior high and high school ... I walked around pretending my head was in the clouds, trying to make people believe I didn't notice or care about the normal things teenagers cared about. I was a fraud. I was so worried about being different, because of the classes I took, that I put on airs. It was safer than trying to be normal and run the risk of being rejected. You treated me like I was just another classmate. Hence, as banal as this may sound, our friendship continues to mean a great deal to me."

Webb couldn't let that pass. "Pardon me for interrupting, Socrates. Did you ever stop to think I treated you that way because you were doing the same with me? Granted, your mind always has blown me away, but not once did you ever care about who or what my family was. As teenagers, I wasn't even sure you knew. With so many others, I've had to endure the perpetual glad-handing, or worse yet, the jealousy and resentment. Not because of anything I did or didn't do, but merely because of some name typed onto my birth certificate."

Theo voiced agreement as only he could. "Upward, Tremont! I've given the subject a great deal of thought during this phase of life we mistakenly label adulthood. Everyone encounters natural prejudices of some sort … it is absurd to evade those realities or be intimidated by them. By doing so, we allow those prejudices to confine us from experiencing the satisfactions of our own fuller potential."

Webb let his words sink in. "Like I said, Theo, your mind constantly blows me away. You're right, I've wasted a lot of energy hoping to avoid the preconceptions of others. If anything, I inflicted my own onto everyone around me by making presumptions about how they might view me because of who my family was."

"Upward, Tremont, upward!"

Two "upwards" from Theo Kleyser. For Webb Tremont, life couldn't get much better than that, so it was a perfect place to leave the conversation. "I'll let you go, Theo. You probably have all kinds of pictures of phytoplankton you want to get posted on YouTube. But please give a little more thought to anyone from our school days who still might have it out for me."

Theo couldn't resist the opening to tee up one relationship the pair had been bantering back and forth for twenty years, "You mean besides Kimberly?"

"That reminds me, I saw her scurrying around town a few weeks ago. I can't believe she has all those kids ... she still looks as hot as she did when she was a teenager."

"Hey, watch it—that's my kid sister you're talking about." The mock annoyance in his voice was right on cue.

They'd reenacted the exchange dozens of times. It was Webb's turn. "You claim she's younger than you by seven minutes, but I still haven't seen the proof. You're positive your parents weren't lying about the whole twin thing?"

Now it was back to Theo. "She got the looks, I got the brains."

Webb laughed. "Poor thing, she didn't have the fortitude to go for her PhD ... called it quits after a mere Ivy League MBA." Every kid in Lake Forest had known Kimberly Kleyser was the total package.

"Well, Tremont, you have to live with the fact you could have married her." Then the required pause. "Or at least taken her out a few times."

"I couldn't, Theo ... she was your sister. Don't you think that might have been a little weird?"

Theo gave Webb that point, just like he always did. "I suppose. But she sure had a big enough crush on you."

"And let the record show, I did nothing to encourage her or take advantage. I was a perfect gentleman."

"You were a perfect something, but I don't think Kimberly would have categorized your behavior as gentlemanly."

Webb was ready to say goodbye when one last thing popped into his head. "Theo, did you know that Conkle woman I read about ... the one who committed suicide a few weeks ago? She was a few years behind you at Carnegie Mellon, but she was awarded the Steinhall Scholarship, so I figured the two of you might have met at some fancy alumni thing."

"Teresa Conkle took her own life? I missed that while I was away." Theo paused momentarily to absorb the news. "I only met her once, but she was a definite tech star. As I recall, she'd been on a nice run career-wise. Too bad ... the highly-tuned mind can be fragile. Upward." And like that, the conversation was over.

Chapter Twenty-Eight

In the early hours of Sunday, January 31, Webb received word that he and the rest of America had been dreading. The copycats were responsible for another homicide. This time, the murder took place inside a health care facility near Riverhead, New York. Webb had never spoken with the victim, but he'd spent time with the man's family several years earlier. After hearing the news, he reached to the shelf above his desk, knowing exactly where to look. He pulled down a copy of his eighth book, turned to chapter three, and reread every word he'd dedicated to a remarkable public servant. With due respect to all the other law enforcement officers he had profiled in his books, Webb once admitted during an interview that Kelso Estabrooke was his favorite.

> On the furthermost end of the island, posting signs to warn visitors they are entering private properties would be unnecessary. Utterly superfluous. Anyone traveling east of Calverton or Flanders is well aware of where they're headed. The Hamptons. As if by law, every square inch of this rarefied sliver seemingly is attached to a sprawling summer home, a private golf club, or a marina filled with oversized pleasure craft. Uninvited guests would have no reason to venture out this far unless they were looking to feel terribly out of place.

Conversely, most folks know little about Long Island's other finger, the North Fork. Weekenders from Manhattan who wind up on this out-of-the-way peninsula are usually lost. Or on occasion, some well-meaning couple might be trying to show their citified kids what rural really looks like. Here, just seventy-five miles from Wall Street, the rolling acreage is filled with orchards, vineyards, and pumpkin farms. The local business owners don't worry much about selling biscotti or sunscreen; they're more concerned with smudge pots and tractor parts.

In September of 2003, Kelso Estabrooke had been chief of the Southold police force for seven years when a call came in that trespassers had driven through Herm Talbert's potato field, a few miles west of Peconic. In all, Kelso had put in twenty-nine years with the department, and no one questioned whether he was deserving of the top job. He arguably should have been promoted much sooner, but the guy before him had wanted to reach his fiftieth year before retiring. Kelso didn't mind the wait. The previous police chief was his father, Lydon Estabrooke.

The call was received late in the day and Kelso would be passing by the Talbert farm on his way home for dinner. He'd handle this one himself. Herm was standing by his damaged fence, carping to a pair of locals who had parked their cars on the side of the road so they could get out and commiserate. In these parts, carping and commiserating were the standard responses to damage done by outsiders. As yet, no one in the group had bothered to walk more than a few yards into the field to determine how many potato plants were damaged. Kelso needed that information to file his report. It was growing dark, so he grabbed a flashlight from his patrol car and began stepping off in measured strides.

Fifty yards inside the fence the weaving tire tracks continued. Whoever the pranksters had been, they'd taken it to an extreme. Seventy-five yards, a hundred yards. Finally, as he looked ahead, Kelso could see where the car had turned and started a parallel set of tracks back toward the break in the fence. His steady paces followed the turn of the car, but suddenly Kelso Estabrooke stopped; the beam of his flashlight froze several feet to the side of where the vehicle had traveled. Scattered amongst matted down potato plants were seven dead dogs—pit bulls covered with blood, their internal organs spilling through gaping holes where teeth had ripped apart skin.

Those were the opening paragraphs to the twenty-six pages Webb Tremont devoted to Kelso Estabrooke and an unusual Long Island crime case. The title of his eighth book was _Serve & Protect: Blue Blood Runs Deep_. One didn't need to wear an actual police uniform, blue or otherwise, to be considered a blue blood—but one did need to be a second-generation cop of some type. Or in a few cases, third- or fourth-generation. "Blue blood' was the unofficial label given to the select breed of cops who carried on the family tradition. Once these individuals demonstrated they were badge-worthy in their own right, they achieved a different level of respect, a special form of reverence from their peers.

This volume in the _Serve & Protect_ series was dedicated solely to criminal cases in which blue bloods had played a pivotal role. A few of the featured police officers had sacrificed their lives during the line of duty. While doing his background research, Webb felt as though he'd ventured onto sacred territory. By tying their latest crime to the Long Island case, the Cop Show Copycats had struck another of Webb Tremont's deepest nerves.

204

The last thing Chief Kelso Estabrooke ever had expected to investigate was a network of secret locations where well-heeled gamblers could gather to wager on dog fights. But entrepreneurism took many shapes. A group of six seasonal workers from Latin America had possessed the vision and requisite expertise to seize an untapped marketplace opportunity. These were farm hands, caddies, kitchen workers, and members of lawn service crews who spent summers on Long Island, pocketing as much money as possible to take back to their families once the season was over.

For three summers, the group had organized and hosted clandestine Friday-night dog fights. The venues moved around Long Island. One week the ten or twelve matches might be held at a secluded spot along a shoreline; the next week could be slated for a deserted warehouse or an empty field. The Latinos were smart enough not to get in the middle of the actual gambling that took place—as that kind of greed tended to alienate more organized crime factions. They were content to charge interested parties a hundred dollar entry fee for the privilege of witnessing the death matches, and then sell premium-priced liquor and cigars throughout the evening to those in attendance. Betting on each dog fight was handled in the style of the open market, one gambler to another. Or when an outside middleman paid the gate fee, he could insert himself in whatever manner he might choose—making it his problem if a more organized syndicate were to take exception.

Word-of-mouth had spread through underground channels. On any given Friday night, hundreds of people—mostly male, from the New York area—were willing to journey out to Long Island and drop huge sums of cash. The combination of gambling, carnage, and illicit thrills was a natural. The Latinos were making a fortune for their families back home—until two of them got careless.

It was the weekend after Labor Day of 2003; the last dog fights of the season had been held the previous evening. Outside dog suppliers already were headed south to set up winter operations, so the Latinos could only line up fourteen pit bulls, enough for seven bouts. By the end of the month, they and most of their fellow Latinos would be packing up and heading to their respective home countries until the following spring.

As a rule, the dead dogs were discarded carefully—due to all the crazy hot buttons Americanos had about their animals. It was a country filled with "Bobolicones" … dumb asses who found it easy to look down their noses at anyone with darker skin, yet would scream bloody murder over the way some mangy dog was treated. Even dogs that had been bred for fighting for hundreds of years.

But following the festivities on this final Friday night, the two amigos assigned burial duty had decided to drain much of the season's remaining liquor supply. By the time the sun started rising, the duo was in no state or mood to work up a sweat with meat saws and shovels. When they rounded a bend in the highway, Herm Talbert's potato farm beckoned ahead. Either by whim or by accident, their pick-up traveled through the fence and eventually came to a halt inside a field thick with plants, which at the time seemed a perfect place to deposit seven bloody carcasses.

For several years stories and speculations about illegal dog fights had made the rounds among Long Island police departments. Until this incident, Kelso Estabrooke had seen no reason to believe hordes of New Yorkers would travel as far as Peconic in search of sick thrills on a Friday. Whoever the organizers might be, they surely wouldn't have scheduled any of their bloodbaths way out on the North Fork.

Eyeing the mutilated pit bulls, the police chief knew he'd miscalculated. That part didn't bother him. Years on the job had taught Kelso never to underestimate what people might do for a few dollars or a few laughs. Still, he was agitated. Sure, he liked dogs and couldn't condone the frivolous, vicarious brutality. But Kelso Estabrooke's immediate reaction was much more parochial. Provincial. He hated anything that violated the tranquil isolation of Long Island's most-forgotten extremity. His number-one priority always had been preserving the desolate solitude of his jurisdiction. Kelso Estabrooke liked the fact that most folks characterized the Southold Town Police Department as dull and sleepy. He took pride in that reputation and would assert the full legal authority he'd been granted to protect the slumbering normalcy of North Fork life.

Working solo, the police chief diligently dug up details throughout the autumn and winter months that followed. He tirelessly chased down the accumulated rumors, separating facts from the growing lore surrounding a dog-fight ring. Pursuing one lead after another, Kelso hop-scotched around the broader New York City metropolitan area. By March of 2004, he'd identified each and every one of the migrant organizers—sharing his information with no one. Back in September, at the time of the incident, Chief Estabrooke had asked the local paper not to print anything about discarded dogs or damage to Herm Talbert's potato field. He didn't want the culprits to suspect someone might be looking for them.

Kelso Estabrooke patiently waited through April, when three of the Latinos returned to Long Island for another season of warm weather employment. Then through May, when two more made their way north. He bided his time until the first week of June, when the last of the six finally arrived from Guatemala. Then on a Wednesday morning, he had lengthy phone conversations with his counterparts in various towns across Long Island. Just after lunch, the six organizers simultaneously were arrested. They subsequently were tried, imprisoned, and deported. Future seasons of North Fork serenity had been preserved by a one-man police investigation that was as effective as any conducted by the largest, most sophisticated law enforcement agencies in the nation.

The story of the arrests barely made the papers on Long Island, let alone elsewhere. Kelso Estabrooke did everything possible to see that the whole episode was downplayed—further protecting his beloved quietude.

Webb Tremont learned about the case through the network of sources he had built over his years of writing books. The police chief from a neighboring burg on Long Island called when he heard about the anthology Tremont was compiling on blue bloods. He'd been a long-time friend and admirer of both Kelso and his now-deceased father.

The more Webb researched the case, the more he, too, came to admire Kelso Estabrooke. He was moved to probe deeper into the man's past by traveling to Long Island. He interviewed Kelso's friends, fellow police officers, and lastly his wife and eldest son—who was serving Southold as a third-generation blue blood. In story after story related to him about Kelso Estabrooke, the police chief personified duty, humility, and persistence. Webb had been certain Chief Estabrooke would have tried to persuade him to omit his name and the entire case from his next book. But unfortunately, he was unable to speak directly to the man at the center of the case.

In autumn of 2007, Kelso Estabrooke had fallen from the roof of the municipal building that housed his modest police department. He'd wanted to save the taxpayers a few bucks by clearing leaves out of the gutters during one of his many slow afternoons. The head injury left him permanently incapacitated—confined to a wheelchair, unable to communicate.

<hr>

Nearly eight years after his tragic fall, Kelso Estabrooke slipped into a coma in July of 2015. He was placed on life support at a regional health care center and six months later a heated debate still was being waged among the residents of Southold. Many argued this well-respected man's dignity would be better preserved if a plug was pulled, while others upheld the morality of life in any form. Further fueling the intensity were the staggering medical costs which inevitably would have to be borne by taxpayers in one manner or another.

Anthony Lafferty decided the last Saturday in January would be the appropriate time to bring the issue to a close. Late that evening, T-Man made the necessary adjustments to a monitoring device attached to the machine keeping Kelso Estabrooke alive. The breathing tube then was detached without a warning signal being transmitted to the nurse's station down the hall.

Blake wrapped up the envelope duties and the three of them were in and out in less than six minutes. It was easily the simplest mission since the inception of their weekend adventures, but the impact was sure to be felt.

<hr>

The lifeless body was discovered by an attendant making midnight rounds, who was afraid to touch anything more once she was certain Chief Kelso Estabrooke had no pulse. Even the local police kept their distance, because of the three boldly numbered envelopes pinned to his hospital gown. This one belonged to the FBI.

When C.J. Matthews arrived at the Long Island health center, she was escorted to a conference room where agents from the New York field office were clustered around a computer. The messages inside the envelopes pinned to Kelso Estabrooke's chest already had been bagged and sent to a forensics lab. But photos first had been taken, and those pictures were uploaded onto a laptop.

The card inside the first envelope captured the sentiments of many area residents: "May Kelso Estabrooke be remembered for having served his fellow citizens with dignity and humility, not for the manner in which he was left to die."

The second, larger envelope contained twenty thousand dollars in hundred dollar bills and another typed note: "For the chief's widow, in recognition of the legitimate contributions made by each generation of the Estabrooke family." These words also would strike a positive chord with residents along the North Fork.

The typed words on the third envelope carried little significance for the local citizenry. Its message was directed to an audience 850 miles to the west: "How pathetic that an unworthy exploiter dared to write about a family of genuine blue bloods." An additional card had been enclosed in the envelope with this note, and its content was the focus of the discussion among the huddled agents staring at the computer screen.

The 5X7 card contained a computer-generated illustration. The tiny detailed drawing mirrored the original police photo that Kelso Estabrooke had taken years earlier of seven dead pit bulls sprawled across Herm Talbert's potato field. But when this illustration was enlarged, the seven dead figures weren't dogs at all. They were emaciated and disfigured human bodies who were portrayed as four-legged animals by the placement of their limbs. As those seven minute figures were enlarged further, recognizable faces were revealed in microscopic detail. The likenesses were disturbing.

The faces on the two most mutilated bodies were those of Webb Tremont and his father, Brandon. The faces on three of the others belonged to Webb's mother, sister, and brother. The final pair depicted Corrie DiMarco and her daughter. The expressions on each of the renderings reflected exaggerated pain. Save one. Janice Emerson Tremont was drawn to look peacefully asleep.

After studying the illustration for a few moments, the special agent pulled out her phone. After relaying the news about Kelso Estabrooke, she informed Webb Tremont that a blow-up of an illustration left by the copycats had just been emailed to him. "I think you should prepare yourself not to overreact. These deviates are trying to play with your head ... don't let them get the better of you."

———◇———

The images were a lot to absorb with sleep still in his eyes. Webb trudged over to the main palace to fill in his father, who took the news as though he were being briefed on one of his business deals. Brandon Tremont went into immediate action. He called the outside security company to once again increase the manpower assigned to Tremont Estate. Webb wondered how long it would be before barracks and a mess hall were erected.

The FBI would instruct its field office in Philadelphia to provide round-the-clock protection for Webb's sister and her family—which probably was overkill considering the number of armed guards already arranged by Brandon Tremont. Webb figured they all could run themselves silly trying to keep up with Brooke and her efforts to save the world, one checkbook at a time.

His brother was another matter. Since Brandon Tremont had directed his youngest son to stay in Europe until the copycats were captured, he was outside the FBI's jurisdiction. Sheffield Armstrong Worthington Tremont would have to suffice with the two full-time bodyguards that his father had sent along with him. Webb's youngest sibling normally resided in a Chicago high-rise, worked reasonably hard for the family business during the day, and played exceedingly hard for himself at night. At thirty-seven, Sheffield, or Spud, was single, thought he was twenty-five, and had accumulated the necessary experience to idle away whatever time required on whichever continent his father selected for him. Among all of Webb's worries, his brother wasn't one of them.

That left Corrie and Sprig. Brandon Tremont thought another appeal in person was worth a try. This time he brought Webb along. When they showed Corrie the illustration left behind by the copycats on Long Island, she finally agreed. Mother and daughter would take residence in Brandon Tremont's private military compound until the danger passed. Sprig was ecstatic and Webb shared her enthusiasm.

The close relationship between his father and his girlfriend had been a fascinating journey to watch. The two first met in early 2007, after Webb and Corrie DiMarco had been dating for months. By then she'd been to the coach house often, even spending the night on a few occasions when Sprig was invited to sleepovers at friends' homes. Sprig had joined her mom on many of her more regular visits. The three played games or watched movies, with Webb giving no thought to the fact that his father was going about his daily routine several hundred yards away. To maintain sanity, he had become accustomed to ignoring the proximity.

It was Sprig who started pestering Webb about making the introductions. She wanted to see first-hand the mystery man who lived in the big house—the one who sat in the back seat while someone drove him around in a big black Mercedes. Finally, Webb succumbed and on an impulse suggested the three of them stroll over to the main palace on a chilly March evening. Unannounced. Nessie wasn't quite sure what to do after she opened the immense wooden door and saw the trio standing there. She gave Webb one of those you're-on-your-own looks, as if to say, "I accept no responsibility for whatever might happen as soon as you bring these two nice ladies across this threshold."

Moments later, his father joined them in the foyer. Corrie couldn't help herself. "I've heard so much about you, Mr. Tremont. But then again, who hasn't?"

Before he could speak, Sprig, who was seven years old at the time, added her own special touch. "Yeah, even the kids at my school talk about how much money you must have."

Brandon Tremont maintained his standard even keel. "For quite some time I've been hearing rumors that Webster was seeing an attractive woman with a rather adorable daughter. The loyal informants who work here thought I might be interested ... with him being my son and all." He glanced in Webb's direction, tilting his head downward to duly register the admonishment. He then shocked his son by turning back to Corrie and Sprig with a broad smile, of all things. He extended his hand to each with a slight bow, "You must be Miss DiMarco, and you must be Melissa. I am honored by this long-overdue introduction."

Webb was at a loss. His father had attempted charm. He'd made the effort to say things that real people might say. As if that wasn't enough out of character, he then did something more unthinkable. He asked Corrie and Sprig for their jackets, with Nessie standing right their next to him. Brandon Tremont walked over to the guest closet, opened the door, slipped the garments onto hangers, hung them in a vacant space, and closed the door. He did all this using his own two hands. Even Nessie was dumbfounded.

And that's when the serious fun began—at least for Webb. He'd never known Corrie to wear a bra and was fairly sure she didn't own one. Her breasts were firm and shapely, but not particularly large. Most of the time it would be hard to tell if she was sporting any kind of added support. But the cold air during the walk across the property had induced a biological reaction, a certain perkiness that remained visible through the fabric of Corrie's cotton blouse.

Brandon Tremont obviously was distracted. Monumentally distracted. Webb could sense how much his father wanted to stare, but above all else, the elder Tremont was well-bred. Throughout the hour-long conversation in the mansion's spacious living room, Webb watched his father's awkwardness in quiet delight—not that he could have gotten many words into the mix anyway.

He was pleased, and more than a little relieved, to observe the instant chemistry. But what he really enjoyed was watching his father's eyes. Whenever the dignified Brandon Tremont spoke to Corrie, he didn't know where to gaze. The man liked to look people squarely in the eyes whenever he addressed them, but in this case, caution made that impossible. He was fighting an irrepressible urge to let his eyes drift downward. His only hope to avoid succumbing was to focus his full attention on Corrie's forehead.

It was amusing to watch his stiff-collared father fumble a bit. Yet as a male, Webb couldn't help but be proud. At the time, Brandon Tremont had been a few months shy of seventy. In all his years as a son, Webb had never known whether libidinous thoughts would even dare form in the head of his powerful father. Frankly, it was something he preferred not to think about. To the man's credit, he'd never done or said anything remotely off-color in his son's presence. He stood as an unwavering paradigm of propriety. Yet there he was, possessed with natural curiosities, desperately wanting to leer at the bosom of his son's girlfriend and indulge in the female form.

Later that evening, in a more private conversation, Webb probed Corrie, "Didn't you find it uncomfortable to have my father staring a hole through your forehead?"

He had expected one of her snappy barbs about men and their childish tendencies—the kind of comment regularly elicited by his own behaviors. Instead she went all gooey on him, "Of course not, Webb. I was completely aware of your father's predicament and found his gentlemanly conduct endearing. You could learn a lot from that sweet man."

And so began their indestructible bond of mutual admiration. No longer could Webb count on a sympathetic ear or the blind allegiance of his girlfriend when he wanted to rant about the idiosyncrasies of Brandon Tremont. He had no one to blame but himself. He'd known it was a mistake to take that fateful walk.

Now, eight years later, the two women in his life would be under the roof of his father's mansion. A captive audience for Brandon Tremont. By the time the whole copycat thing was behind them, Corrie and Sprig would be completely brainwashed.

On the other hand, Webb anticipated certain other benefits. Since the beginning of their relationship, he and Corrie had worked overtime to manufacture opportunities for late-night intimacies. Both had agreed it inappropriate for Webb to spend the night at Corrie's apartment when Sprig was around. When he did stay late, a degree of caution was required in case Sprig were to wake up and walk into a delicate situation. Or worse yet, an indelicate one.

With the pending new living arrangement, Webb's brain went into overdrive— along with other relevant body parts. The second night on the premises, he invited Corrie to go out on a date. He picked her up at midnight, once most everyone in the main palace was sleeping soundly. He knew Nessie always slept with one eye open. Nothing behind the ivied walls escaped the Scottish woman's special powers, but he had counted on her discretion too many times to count. If Nessie had been called upon to rat out Webb or his siblings during their youth, she more likely would have cut out her tongue. Her devotion to Corrie and Sprig was just as evident.

A nightly routine quickly established. Webb would escort Corrie to his coach house, where snifters of brandy, romantic music, and candlelight awaited. Hours later he would accompany her back to the main palace, sometimes with a slight limp after pushing the limits of his reconstructed hip. Granted, late-night security personnel roaming the property also were aware of these off-hours visits, but sworn secrecy was part of their job description. In the event Sprig might wake up during the night and find her mother's room empty, Webb had armed Corrie with a surefire alibi. She simply needed to claim that she'd been restless and dozed off elsewhere in the house. He'd learned as a teenager that evading accountability for one's presence at odd hours was relatively easy inside a mansion of twenty-eight rooms.

Hours alone on a nightly basis was a wondrous concept. Webb and Corrie dusted up on a few forgotten moves from their earlier years together, and possibly invented two or three new ones. He couldn't be sure. For the first time in twenty years, Webb Tremont was genuinely grateful to be dwelling inside his father's kingdom.

<hr />

On Monday morning, Anthony Lafferty would board a plane to tend to one of his loose ends. The momentum from recent weeks was boding well.

Saturday night on Long Island had gone like clockwork, as he, Blake and T-Man were back in Boston well before dawn. The cooperation from Todd Swinford was especially encouraging. T-Man had gone along with the killing of Natalie Meriwether in Richmond, but in that case his compliance was after the fact. He'd had no idea her death was coming. But this time he and Blake were fully complicit, Lafferty had made sure of that. Premeditated murder was a whole different matter. Some people might not take to it as well he had. He chose to ease them in with a mercy killing. Savoring the final moments of a human life was a feeling of triumph unlike any he'd ever known. Blake was too messed up to experience that kind of euphoria, but the look in T-Man's eyes was obvious. The rapture was undeniable.

Lafferty had hoped that would be the case, but there'd been no way to know in advance. The guy was an enigma. During their four years with the group, Todd Swinford had been reluctant to share much about himself. So Anthony Lafferty had paid handsomely to have someone else uncover the details of his past. Over the years, Lafferty had developed relationships with several such resources.

On the surface, Swinford was thirty-three with blondish hair and Scandinavian features—a square jaw and prominent cheek bones. He'd lived in various cities across Europe as a child, and likewise while he accumulated an impressive array of scholarly credentials as a teenager and young adult. Leaving academia, Todd worked for a small tech consultancy on the outskirts of London until he was recruited by a big Boston firm at the age of twenty-seven. But those basics had been shared with all the partners when S.A.F.E. took shape.

Beneath the surface were the more promising facets to T-Man's personality. He'd been born Tiede Svinhufuud, in Cyprus. The name Tiede was Dutch, like his mother. Svinhufuud and his father were Swedish. The very day he turned eighteen, he legally changed his name to Todd Swinford. This act of independence, protest, or both, was especially encouraging for Lafferty's purposes.

The Svinhufuud family had been rolling in kronor for generations. By the time young Tiede was thirteen, his parents had lived in seven different countries, but these repeated dislocations were seemingly irrelevant to their lone young son. He'd been sent off to exclusive boarding schools since kindergarten. According to former teachers, Tiede's home was nothing more than a place for the young prodigy to visit on holidays.

Swinford's first year of college was spent in Finland, at the University of Helsinki. He needed just two more years to earn his degree from the Swiss Federal Institute of Technology in Zurich. From there, it was off to the prestigious Humboldt University in Germany for graduate work.

Copies of transcripts revealed Todd Swinford had been at the top of his class during every stage of his education. Confidential files, which turned out not to be so confidential for the right amount of money, revealed Swinford had been "studious, quiet, and respectful." There were no disciplinary issues of note. Still, Todd Swinford was described as an extreme loner by a number of his advisors. He'd never married, his sexual preferences were unknown, and he had no police record.

Swinford's parents currently resided in a Tuscan villa outside Montepulciano. When discreetly contacted, the Svinhufuuds acknowledged they hadn't heard from their son since he accepted his first position in London. Their interaction had been minimal for quite some time. His parents were unaware the young man had relocated to the United States.

Lafferty's private investigator contacted numerous individuals from Swinford's past. To the best of anyone's recollection, Todd Swinford had no close friends while growing up—male or female. None of his acquaintances could explain the urgency with which he'd changed his name upon reaching legal age, or the reasons he had become estranged from his parents.

For more than a year, Anthony Lafferty had understood there were dark corners to T-Man's psyche. He had hoped to see them play out in his favor. On Long Island, they did. Todd Swinford showed no reluctance in reworking the electronics inside the life-sustaining machine at Kelso Estabrooke's bedside, or subsequently in pulling the tubes to end his life. Lafferty knew the coming weekends would reveal even more about this mysterious partner.

<hr />

After the hideous black and white drawing from Long Island went public, the media hounds were strangely sympathetic toward the Tremonts. At least for a day or two. The accompanying note was one thing—"How pathetic that an unworthy exploiter dared to write about a family of genuine blue bloods." By virtue of previous messages left by the copycats, Webb Tremont had been deemed fair game. But illustrating his family, his girlfriend, and a teenaged girl in such excruciating fashion made no sense. It was a tasteless act of intimidation.

But as each day passed, Webb saw the sensitivities slowly shift. More and more attention was paid to the blue-blooded reputation of the Tremonts. On Thursday evening, NBC launched a full-frontal attack with the anchor story on *Backdrop*, the network's weekly news magazine show.

From the first run-on sentence oozing out of the host's lips, Webb knew it was going to be a tough night for the home team. "Since this past weekend, when the Cop Show Copycats left a picture depicting Webb Tremont and his wealthy family as mutilated dogs, more and more people are wondering how the Tremonts could elicit this degree of hostility from a group of unknown criminals. One of our investigative teams went looking for possible answers, and you may be surprised to learn how many others share their contempt."

Webb recognized that an in-depth piece of this nature couldn't possibly have been pulled together over the three days since Kelso Estabrooke's death. The network's news department apparently had been building their archive of assorted nastiness on the Tremonts, waiting for the opportune moment to string them together into a thirty-minute hatchet job. The head honcho of NBC News must have decided the time was ripe. The family already was reeling from the dead dog illustration, so why not kick 'em while they were down?

A perfectly coiffed female reporter started with Webb's brother, who provided an easy foothold because of his colorful reputation as a partier. A second glib voice took over and tore into Brooke and her husband for their aristocratic lifestyle, before another of the story's contributors delved into Corrie and her out-of-wedlock pregnancy. The segment's producers at least had the decency to go easy on Webb's mother—the only jab being a reference to the "double-barreled wealth that came her way through the Emersons and the Tremonts." They saved their heaviest artillery for the big crescendo.

Responsibility for the final portion of the exposé was handed back to the eager program host. Poring through Brandon Tremont's past, he practically scoffed, "This man has been blindly allegiant to every Republican president and presidential candidate since Richard Milhous Nixon." Webb had been using essentially the same words to rip on his father for years, but now he found the accusations offensive for some reason.

There were clips of Brandon Tremont in the rose garden of the White House, as well as sitting before a Congressional subcommittee. Special attention was given to his financial dealings, and on this subject the facts were edited to leave the audience with a desired impression. Issues of accuracy were incidental.

The business interests of other Tremont relatives were woven seamlessly into the story. With more than two hundred and forty living family members, cherry-picking unsavory or contentious holdings was an easy exercise. There was the one distant Tremont who owned eleven riverboat casinos and acted as a silent partner in eight more that could be found on Indian reservations. Webb had a cousin who'd sold overpriced licenses for a chain of spray tan studios that wiped out dozens of mom and pop franchisees, and another octogenarian cousin who had been leasing New Jersey warehouse space to the largest gray-market automobile operation on the East Coast since 1977. But even Webb had been unaware of the sweatshop factories in Thailand and Laos, the medical marijuana farms, or the lucrative online dispensary of erectile dysfunction medications that operated out of Canada.

Brandon Tremont had nothing to do with any of these shadier investments. Webb knew his dad approached business with the same meat-and-potatoes philosophy he brought to the dinner table, not to mention life in general. But the pieces fit neatly into a preconceived mosaic of a billionaire family. Viewers would be left to assume that at the end of each day, Brandon Tremont retreated to a private counting room staffed by undernourished orphans.

The program got under Webb's skin for obvious reasons. Corrie and his siblings should have remained off-limits, and the overall bias was more blatantly skewed than the usual snark directed at families like his. But what really bothered him was how his own name barely drew mention. He was the one at the center of the whole stinking debacle, and each week those closest to him were paying a greater and greater price.

Brandon Tremont's reaction to the lopsided journalism was typically stoic—sheer indifference, as though similar roads had been traveled too many times to remember. The burden of wealth, Webb presumed.

To calm his son, Brandon Tremont offered a dose of fatherly wisdom. "Webster, compared to what most people contend with, wouldn't you agree that a few random misrepresentations hardly merit our protests? There always will be a tenuous, arbitrary line between rightful satisfaction and unwarranted pretension. In striving for one, we invariably fall victim to the other. We shouldn't dwell."

Webb found himself nodding his head in solid agreement, but he wasn't sure why. Conundrums always had been one of Brandon Tremont's signature talents. Growing up, Webb would get dizzy trying to decipher his father's words. This time, though, he had a grasp on the basic gist of his father's message. Or at least he thought he did.

Some number of copycats were still out there, plotting. Whoever they were, Webb knew they were somewhere laughing. Snickering at him, chortling derisively at his family. Even cackling out loud as more and more critics continued to pile on. Payback would come eventually. Then those same copycats could rollick twenty-four hours a day from the confines of their prison cells.

A short trip to the islands was exactly what he'd needed. Gregory Beaumont had seemed duly surprised to see him. Anthony Lafferty had watched from the cabin of Beaumont's boat while his former partner cleared customs inside a small cinderblock building at the end of the pier. It took a few minutes to adjust to his former partners new appearance, but he had to admit the transformation was effective. Beaumont's head was shaved and a full beard was taking shape on the face below.

Anthony Lafferty thought his younger associate could have shown at least some measure of deference when he found him waiting inside the cabin, holding the duffel bag that Beaumont had come back to collect for an overnight stay in Antigua. "Hello, Gregory ... you know, I never had you pegged as a water lover."

Like the others, Gregory Beaumont routinely had discounted Lafferty's mental acuity over the four years they'd known each other. Faced with the reality that he'd been completely outmaneuvered, the condescending loner didn't even bother to ask how he'd done it, how he had managed to track him to his sixth port since leaving

Key Biscayne and crossing fourteen hundred miles of open sea.

On one level, he'd always been willing to forgive a certain amount of Beaumont's off-putting nature. It couldn't have been easy growing up as an urban Black kid with an off-the-charts IQ. His aloofness probably developed first as a coping mechanism that helped him overcome the odds and escape his environment. But on another level, Beaumont's background angered him. The guy should have been attuned to the possibility that Lafferty had confronted similar adversities as an unusually perceptive kid in a small town where private lives became an open book. It was of no consequence now; this loose end had been properly addressed.

Returning to the States at midweek, he was glad to see the media had taken the bait—at first sympathetic to the Tremonts, before methodically ripping into the rich bastards and everything they represented. Not that Lafferty really cared, but even the backlash to the murder of Kelso Estabrooke seemed modest. After all, pulling the plug was the humane thing to do.

He tried to keep his feelings of satisfaction in check. The challenges would be riskier after he and his two remaining partners made their way to Illinois.

Chapter Twenty-Nine

T he rattle of the cellphone on the nightstand interrupted a surprisingly deep sleep. He had crawled under the covers less than an hour before, after escorting Corrie back to the main palace. The display read 4:07 a.m. His mind wasn't quite hitting on all cylinders, but Webb was fairly certain the morning was Friday, so the FBI was unlikely to be calling about the copycats striking again. He couldn't imagine who else could be phoning at such an ungodly hour, so he hardly was prepared for the greeting on the other end. But then he was never adequately prepared for Theo Kleyser. "Upward!"

Webb shook his head in amazement. The time was 3:07 in Colorado, if that was where Theo happened to be. Regardless, it was a ridiculous hour for calling a friend. Or calling anyone, for that matter. But Theo often went days without checking a clock. His active mind was unconstrained by the concept of time.

"Top of the morning, Theo … and I do mean the very top."

"If you say so." Theo was undeterred by Webb's sarcasm. "Since our conversation last week I've been occupied by other commitments. But a few minutes ago, I got around to what you asked of me."

Webb was caught off guard. "Which was?"

"To give additional thought to people from our school days whom you might have alienated, of course."

Theo sounded confused as to why Webb wasn't tracking with the specifics from their most recent phone call. Theo Kleyser's skills for compartmentalizing were pronounced.

To him it was like they'd just hung up from the week before. When they last spoke, Theo already would have been consumed with a full docket of issues requiring significant think time, so he would have placed Webb's situation into that part of his brain where thoughts were held in a suspended state. Six days later, this special request from his oldest friend had cycled to the top of his to-do list—or in Theo's case, his to-ponder list. Moments later, he was reaching for his phone during the pre-dawn hours. Once Theo Kleyser had something to share, time of day was of no relevance whatsoever.

Webb was eager to hear what Theo had to offer. "So you've remembered someone from high school who hated me enough to come after me twenty-five years later?"

"No, this particular individual is from our college years," he responded.

"Theo, I doubt I need remind you that I attended Eastern Illinois and you matriculated at Carnegie Mellon? There wouldn't have been a whole lot of overlap with the friends we made in college."

Theo was very matter-of-fact. "Webb, what friends we did or didn't have in common is immaterial. You asked about potential enemies ... and we definitely shared one college acquaintance who qualifies."

As often the case, Webb was clueless as to where his good friend was leading him. But this time the confusion was not a result of any intellectual disparity. "Come on, Theo ... what are you trying to tell me?"

"Not what, Webb ... whom. Please try to stay with the conversation. I'm referring to Laffy. I apologize for not thinking of him when we spoke last week, but you specifically asked me to think about relationships from our junior high and high school days ... and like some simpleton, that's all I did."

The exchange wasn't getting any easier for Webb. "That's all well and good, Theo. But who the hell is Laffy?"

His voice rose. "Anthony Lafferty ... you remember, the college roommate who came to visit me in Lake Forest."

Webb Tremont rifled through past memories as fast as his mind allowed, but he wasn't coming up with anything.

Finally, his genius friend grew impatient with the silence. "Come on, Webb, think back to the summer after my freshman year. Lafferty phoned me because he wanted to acquaint himself with Chicago ... he felt it was a city worthy of his consideration for eventual employment. He practically begged me to convince my parents to let him stay at our house for a couple of weeks. While he was there, the three of us hung out a few times. We even went bar-hopping ... illegally, I might add."

Webb's memory at last kicked in. "Oh, him. Tell me his first name again."

"Anthony. Anthony Lafferty."

"Theo, I appreciate you calling back, but I barely knew the guy. Why would he harbor negative feelings toward me?"

"This is where I really feel stupid, Webb. Near the end of our last phone call, we even discussed the precise reason he took an immediate dislike to you. My sister ... Kimberly. As soon as Lafferty met her on day one, he became infatuated. Anthony Lafferty was bright and decent enough looking, so at first Kimbie was kind of interested. But by the second or third day, he started creeping her out. And believe me, Lafferty could do that to people."

"So what does any of this have to do with him not liking me?" Webb interrupted.

"I'm getting there, Tremont." Theo explained, "His resentment toward you was unavoidable—for three reasons, actually. First, it became obvious to Lafferty that my sister had feelings for you ... and in your own way, you had feelings for her. There always was this chemistry, this friendly sexual tension between the two of you. So, after Kimbie started giving Lafferty the cold shoulder, it really bugged him to see her being so playful with you. That made him jealous, which only added to the envy he already harbored toward your family's wealth. And that was reason number two. Anthony Lafferty came from no means whatsoever and intensely resented anyone who did."

Theo paused, searching for the right words before proceeding. "Third, let's simply say your endearing wit left a deep impression on Lafferty. Over the course of his two-week stay in Lake Forest you managed to call him, Gear Head, Propeller Head, Little Einstein, Brain Boy, and assorted other epithets."

Webb jumped in. "My God, Theo, you guys were going to Carnegie Mellon ... you both were freakin' rocket scientists from my vantage. I wasn't trying to be a wiseass ... I was complimenting the guy on being brilliant."

"He wouldn't have seen it that way because of the negative baggage he carried around. He was convinced you were poking fun at him, because that's what he was accustomed to. But what really hurt him was when Kimbie laughed every time you tossed one of your cute little nicknames his way. He didn't care that she laughed at practically everything you said, because as we both know, she thought anything that toppled out of your unfiltered mouth was clever. No, he assumed both of you were laughing at him, because that's where his mind naturally gravitated ... no matter how much I tried to tell him otherwise. So, he not only resented the obvious feelings my sister had for you, but he concluded your barbs were causing her to pull away from him."

Webb was dumbfounded. "You can't be serious."

"Trust me, Webb, I couldn't be more serious. When we returned to school the next fall, I had to listen to him rant and rail any time your name came up. I'd explain that you didn't mean anything ... that you assigned innocent nicknames to every-one. I tried to convince him you were a decent guy. But my defending you only made him angrier. And meanwhile he was calling Kimbie so often that my dad finally had to get on the phone and insist he stop."

"Why didn't you tell me about any of this at the time, Theo?"

"You hadn't done anything wrong ... why should I bother you with another guy's hang-ups? I simply started avoiding conversations with Laffy which involved you, my sister, or Lake Forest. But there still were plenty of other subjects that ir-ritated him. I made it through the end of the next semester with him, then moved into a house with other classmates after Christmas break. To the best of my ability, I avoided Anthony Lafferty for the balance of my time at Carnegie Mellon."

"Was this guy all there in the head?" Webb asked.

"Intellectually, he was brilliant ... just like you said earlier. But emotion-ally, Anthony Lafferty was a freak of nature. From out of nowhere, he might throw a tantrum one minute, then start sulking and pouting the next. His moods were unpredictable. Trust me, you wouldn't have been the first or last person to set him off. Laffy was equipped with a full menu of epic complexities ... especially when it came to girls or money. He always seemed to reach for girls who were out of his league, then go ballistic when they'd shoot him down. The money thing was even stranger. Though he'd grown up poor in some small town in West Virginia, he was sailing through college on a full academic ride. Laffy knew he was going to knock down serious bucks in the years ahead. But he just couldn't let go of the bitterness, the bile he carried around for people who already had their wealth."

Reflecting further on his last point, Theo added, "You can't imagine how fixated he became during his two-week visit to Lake Forest. It was irrational. The cars, the homes, the expensive boutiques ... every aspect of the town disgusted him. But oddly enough, despite his stated desire to become familiar with the city of Chicago, he spent virtually all of his time hanging around Lake Forest ... checking out the very people and places that made his stomach turn. And to make matters worse, the guy had a photographic memory. With you, for example ... when I told him we were going to meet up with you the first time, Lafferty recognized your name and started babbling about all kinds of stuff from your family's history. It was like a sick compulsion. He would read everything he could get his hands on about the mega-rich and hold on to every cancerous fact, almost as though he wanted those details to keep eating away at him."

Theo stopped before remembering one more thing. "One of the times the three of us went out ... it was my turn to drive, so we swung by your house to pick you up. We were early, but rather than wait in the driveway, he insisted we go inside. While you were still upstairs getting ready, he said he needed to use the bathroom and took off before I could even tell him where it was. He was gone for an unusually long time ... I remember having the feeling he was snooping around the whole first floor."

Everything relayed by Theo Kleyser came completely out of left field to Webb.

"Wow, who'd have guessed I could have made such a powerful impression? What happened to this Lafferty character after college?"

"Like many of our classmates, he stuck around academia and collected a few more diplomas. He wound up on the faculty of Carnegie Mellon for a number of years. But then he became part of some tech start-up that hit it big. I heard from one of my classmates that Lafferty made tens of millions from the deal."

Webb found this last bit of news encouraging. "Well, hopefully success took the edge off of his hang-ups."

"Maybe, but like I said, the guy was a freak of nature."

Webb was compelled to ask, "If Anthony Lafferty was such a strange bird, how did the two of you wind up as friends ... why'd you agree to live with him in the first place?"

"Good question, Webb. We met during our first week on campus, when he grabbed a seat next to mine at an orientation session. We had a few laughs, but then it was like he started seeking me out wherever I went. You have to remember that we of the propeller-head genus aren't particularly proficient at attracting friends. So even a weird friend is better than none. I just didn't realize how weird he would turn out to be."

A wake-up call at four in the morning about an odd character he barely remembered made about as much sense as most things in recent months. Webb decided to wrap it up. "I've gotta believe that after all these years Anthony Lafferty has managed to overcome whatever petty animosities he might have harbored. I doubt he even would remember me. But thanks for the call, Theo ... truly. Let me know if anyone else pops into that propeller head of yours."

"I hope you're right, Tremont. But just the same, I'd suggest you ask your friends at the FBI to do a little digging. It can't hurt. Upward!"

"Sideways, Theo. Sideways."

Once they'd hung up, Webb didn't budge as he kept replaying the conversation about Anthony Lafferty. He wouldn't have recognized the man's name without the added details from Theo, and he still was having difficulty picturing the guy. Surely no one that brainy, who now was worth millions of dollars, would launch a nation-wide crime spree because of some misguided college-age crush. He tried to dismiss the possibility out-of-hand. But his subconscious couldn't let go. Drifting back to sleep was out of the question.

Al Capone was rumored to have had an IQ approaching 200. Leopold's and Loeb's were said to be well above 160, and the two of them wound up with life sentences for kidnapping and murder. Ted Kaczynski, the Unabomber, was a noted researcher and mathematical genius. High intellect wasn't a disqualifier to criminal behavior. Anything was possible.

Webb had no idea where a certain special agent might be sleeping at the same ungodly hour, but he had a strong suspicion she wasn't sleeping that well anyway. He once again picked up his phone from the nightstand.

Chapter Thirty

Some leads will break a case faster than others. From researching thousands of crimes, Webb Tremont could cite scores of newly discovered facts that had become the pivotal turning point to an investigation. During her years as an up-and-coming federal agent, C.J. Matthews had experienced this phenomenon first-hand. But neither of the two could have anticipated a middle-of-the-night miracle. Theo Kleyser's phone call didn't just crack the door on a stifled investigation, it blew the walls off.

After receiving Webb Tremont's call about an odd acquaintance from his past, Special Agent Matthews immediately started awakening agents and research specialists from their pre-dawn slumber on Friday, February 5. By the dawn of Tuesday, she and the powers inside the J. Edgar Hoover Building were preparing for a firestorm. Photographs and profiles of six individuals believed to be the Cop Show Copycats were being released to the public at 8 a.m.

One detail after another had fallen neatly into place and Matthews was able to convince her superiors that the unknown perpetrators had been identified. Apprehending them would be a different matter, so a barrage of information was to be unleashed with no advance warning in the hope that the remaining copycats might be spotted before they could seek adequate refuge. The weekend's round-the-clock investigative effort already had determined one of the six suspects was deceased, apparently from suicide.

The identity provided by Theo Kleyser had done the trick. C.J. Matthews promptly had issued instructions to dig up every possible fact about a graduate of Carnegie Mellon named Anthony Lafferty. Quick inquiries revealed his academic achievements were beyond impressive. FBI staffers also started searching for his name among airline databases, while digging into his credit card activity and finances. The most important connection was made to five other individuals with stellar academic backgrounds. The six had formed a business partnership that netted each of them close to fifty million dollars. In practically no time at all, investigative teams had produced a cohesive group with brainpower and resources. The fit seemed almost too perfect. In a matter of hours, the most gaping questions from three months of futility had produced viable answers.

By late Friday morning, the special agent was presenting the case file to her immediate supervisor. An army of federal agents was sent into overdrive. The last known address for each of the six former partners was in the Boston area. A search of airline manifests from November and December revealed all six flew separately to various airports within reasonable driving distances of several cities where copycat crimes had occurred, on dates that bookended the respective weekends. For other weekends, no such bookings could be found, but perhaps alias identities had been utilized.

Everyone in the group likewise had flown to Las Vegas in mid-October, which corresponded to a working hypothesis on where the copycats might have amassed an unending supply of hundred-dollar bills. Other financial facts aligned in rapid succession as FBI personnel accessed credit card and bank statements for the six individuals.

The FBI ordered their respective financial accounts frozen, to little avail. Only small portions of the group's accumulated wealth from their software venture could be isolated. In recent weeks, the vast majority of their investments had been liquidated, with those funds transferred to foreign accounts, and from there directed to multiple entities using methods outside the normal purview of US authorities. Picking up on the money trails would take weeks or months, if they could be tracked at all.

As field agents conducted interviews, other dominoes dropped. Security guards, doormen, and neighbors of the six suspects confirmed each of the young millionaires were repeatedly away on weekends. Building records indicated their cars hadn't left their assigned parking spaces on a Friday, Saturday, or Sunday since October.

After selling S.A.F.E., their software encryption company, most of the group had moved on to new jobs or entrepreneurial endeavors, but coworkers couldn't remember seeing any of the six logging time over a weekend in months. A few of the alleged copycats had spoken to their family members on occasion, but not a single relative had seen any of the six in person since the previous summer. These neighbors, associates, and family members didn't view any of these behaviors as unusual. The young millionaires were universally described as loners, and in some cases as having peculiar tendencies.

Former S.A.F.E. employees credited thirty-one-year-old Teresa Conkle with convincing another of the partners, Michael Chen, to form the business in the first place. She was found dead in her apartment just two days after the copycats committed the heinous murder of Natalie Meriwether. Boston authorities ruled that Miss Conkle had taken her own life with drugs and alcohol, either accidentally or on purpose. Feelings of guilt stemming from the Richmond killing now might explain why such an accomplished young person with every reason to live would fall prey to melancholy. Nonetheless, the government would open a more extensive investigation into her death.

One new detail already seemed suspicious. The memory to Teresa Conkle's computer had been wiped clean on the date of her death. Whether done by her or someone else, that person's technical skills were exceptional. The FBI's computer forensics teams couldn't reconstruct any portion of her former files.

On the same day as the young woman's death in Boston, twenty-nine-year-old Michael Chen had flown to China. He had liquidated most of his investment accounts and booked a flight to Beijing, also within forty-eight hours of the Richmond murder. With assistance from the State Department, authorities were able to confirm

Mr. Chen had traveled to the city of Xian, where he remained a guest of the Chinese government. The State Department further revealed Chen's well-educated parents hailed from the Xian Region, but they had pulled strings and immigrated to the United States during the 1980s in order to elude China's one-child policy.

Michael Chen's features matched up with the partial description provided by the elderly customer in Richmond who had said the man working behind the counter on the night of Natalie Meriwether's murder was of Asian descent.

A third member of the group, Gregory Beaumont, also appeared to have separated abruptly from the others. On the day after one partner died mysteriously and another took off for China, Beaumont flew to Miami, Florida on a one-way ticket purchased just ninety minutes before his flight. The thirty-two-year-old transferred close to forty million dollars out of three Boston banks just hours before his departure.

Perhaps the original six partners had recruited others to join them in implementing their copycat crimes, but for now C.J. Matthews would focus attention on three individuals who seemed to be continuing the efforts that the full group had started: Anthony Lafferty, Blake O'Meara, and Todd Swinford. Agents in Boston determined none of the three could be found at their known addresses. But it was a weekend. They likely were off in another city, committing a mock crime of some sort.

Search warrants were issued so that fingerprints and DNA samples could be collected for all six suspects. These specimens held little value for establishing whether members of the group had been present at previous crime scenes, because those investigations had failed to turn up comparative samples. But perhaps future events would be different.

The copycats were as careful inside their respective residences as they had been in their travels. No items were found that would qualify as hard evidence. Whatever materials might have been used to plan or commit their crimes were either destroyed or retained elsewhere. If anything existed in writing, it probably was kept on their computers—all of which were absent and presumably with their owners.

Meanwhile, multiple teams of federal agents were stationed around the residences of the three copycats still believed to be active, ready to arrest them upon their return from the weekend. But Sunday and Monday passed with none of the three making an appearance. On Tuesday, the entire nation was to be placed on full alert.

———◆———

Like millions of bewildered Americans, Webb Tremont tried to absorb the details as they were unveiled across his TV screen. Six individuals who would qualify as geniuses by anyone's standards, having each achieved colossal success in the worlds of academia and commerce, collectively had decided to apply their talents toward nefarious ends.

They looked like Main Street. Not a single tattoo across a single forehead. No bizarre facial piercings. Not a dreadlock or hair spike among them.

Photographs of the late Teresa Conkle revealed a great smile. Her mid-length hair was light, her face thin and perky. She'd grown up in the suburbs of Denver.

Michael Chen was an Asian-American raised near Palo Alto. In most of the pictures gathered by the media he wore wire-rimmed glasses and t-shirts with designer jackets. Chen looked to be on the diminutive side.

The more regular-sized Greg Beaumont was a light-skinned African American from Oakland who had a roundish face and close-cropped hair. He appeared younger than his thirty-two years.

Webb studied the features of the three remaining copycats more closely, since each represented a more imminent threat. Blake O'Meara was a thirty-year-old female from a small town in Kentucky. She had long dark hair and probably carried a few extra pounds. None of the available photos showed her smiling.

Thirty-three-year-old Todd Swinford looked like a member of a Nordic ski team. In terms of background, his sounded the most complicated. He'd been estranged from his parents since reaching legal adulthood. On the morning of his 18th birthday, he filed paperwork to legally change his name. On that same day, he took possession of a trust fund that made him independently wealthy. The millions he'd earned from the subsequent software venture was minor by comparison. The FBI estimated Swinford's total worth at two hundred million dollars or more—most of which was stashed away in European banks.

That left Theo's former classmate. Anthony Lafferty had grown up in Lewisburg, West Virginia. At forty-one, he was the oldest copycat by eight years. Unlike Blake O'Meara, there were plenty of pictures with him smiling—but none of those smiles could be described as warm or friendly. Granted, Webb was naturally biased, but the man somehow looked disingenuous, if not outright sinister. Seeing more recent images of Lafferty, Webb remembered having similar reactions when he'd been around him twenty years earlier. Back then his dark narrow eyes had darted from person to person, as though constantly seeking attention or approval from the people around him. Two decades later, his face looked much the same. He had olive skin, now with a few wrinkled creases around his eyes and forehead. His bushy eyebrows had gone salt and pepper, as had the thick hair atop his head. His long, flat nose looked slightly oversized against the backdrop of his narrow eyes and thin-lipped mouth. He was about six feet tall. Overall, not an unappealing physical appearance, but one Webb found easy to dislike.

Reporters were practically tripping over one another to uncover new details about the six former business partners. Webb Tremont grew more astonished by the minute. How, before the age of twenty, could he possibly have incurred this much wrath from Anthony Lafferty through a few casual interactions? And how could this Lafferty character have convinced five brilliant minds to go along with him on a protracted criminal rampage? Having actual names and faces now made the whole situation even more surreal.

Chapter Thirty-One

On Thursday morning, the three of them had hit the road from Boston, prepared for a prolonged period of travel. Lafferty drove the used luxury RV he'd purchased in July. Blake and T-Man rotated every few hundred miles between riding shotgun in the RV and driving the trailing sedan, which had been procured the prior week. Both vehicles were bought directly from former owners through cash transactions. According to their titles and registrations, the Winnebago Meridian and Toyota Camry now belonged to a gentleman from West Roxbury.

Friday was spent in downtown Chicago, shopping Michigan Avenue and the Gold Coast during the day, taking in the city's blues clubs after dark. Lafferty had planned a rather prankish crime for the weekend ahead that required little preparation. This time he hadn't choosen a case from any of Webb Tremont's crummy books. He instead borrowed two absurd incidents from the useless worm's real-life experiences.

At the stroke of midnight on Saturday, Lafferty tossed fireplace logs through two windows at the rear of a stately mansion in Lake Forest—the very residence where years earlier Tremont had stumbled into a violent situation and prevented a raging lunatic from killing his ex-wife and three others. At precisely the same time, T-Man and Blake were throwing three logs through the windows of a classroom in the central corridor to Lake Forest's junior high school—where Tremont somehow had managed to stop another madman hell-bent on killing the kids and teachers inside. Webb Tremont had been an ambitionless amoeba hiding from the real world as a suburban cop, yet still wound up with people viewing him as some sort of hero.

Lafferty instructed Blake to prepare a special note for each of the two locations. To appease her and T-Man, he also had agreed to leave packets of cash behind—but he insisted on setting the amounts. Attached to one of the logs used at the mansion was an envelope addressed to the family of Natalie Meriwether. Inside was $20,000 in hundred-dollar bills, and a card that read: "Given in memory of the Lake Forest Tremonts, who always took more than they gave."

A second envelope containing the same sum was attached to a log at the school, this one addressed to the family of Jorge Cabral. Enclosed was the same note. The money for the janitor's family would give the media something new to chew on, while the typed messages were intended as a more pointed torment.

On the Sunday and Monday that followed, Lafferty watched with amusement as media pundits pondered the implications of the cash left in memory of Jorge Cabral. A like amount had been directed to the family of Natalie Meriwether, as well as the family of Kelso Estabrooke on the previous weekend, and they were two acknowledged murder victims of the Cop Show Copycats. Were these anonymous killers admitting to a third homicide of the church janitor? And did they believe it remotely possible that these gifts of money could be of consequence to anyone?

Lafferty was amazed by the amount of imbecilic banter. All because the news networks were forced to fill twenty-four hours of airtime. Of course, the copycats were responsible for all three. And stay tuned folks, the dreaded Cop Show Copycats weren't even close to being done.

"Given in memory of the Lake Forest Tremonts, who always took more than they gave." The media's deciphering of his carefully worded ascription was entertaining to watch. The plural nature of the reference seemed to indicate the copycats' hostilities ran deeper than Webb Tremont alone. Plus, the wording suggested these particular Tremonts were no longer around. Were the copycats making a direct threat on the lives of Webb Tremont and his immediate family? Anthony Lafferty thought it insane that so much time could be wasted debating something so obvious.

Unlike his former business partners, Lafferty had paid little attention to the incessant media coverage devoted to the Cop Show Copycats. Until now. Killing time in an RV required new diversions. But he still had a few regular pastimes to help overcome the monotony. Like preying on Blake's emotions.

When Tuesday rolled around and the FBI went public with their big announcement, he was relieved. It was about damned time. How naïve that the other five could have convinced themselves their clever parodies could continue into perpetuity without anyone discovering their identities. Lafferty was surprised the charade had lasted as long as it did, but nonetheless was curious as to who or what had provided the authorities their pivotal lead. Even as feeble as the FBI had proven to be, something was bound to have fallen into its lap eventually.

Lafferty had prepared for this eventuality by vacating his brownstone months earlier and taking cover in a cheap Boston motel. Fortunately, he also had been able to convince Blake and T-Man to clear out of their condos in recent weeks. Surely, federal agents had figured that out by now. For the time being, the best thing for the three of them was to remain mobile—like nomads, moving from city to city.

The RV afforded them plenty of basic comforts. They would continue rotating driving duties to each of his planned locations. Maintaining effective disguises would be easy enough. He found it amazing so many criminals were inept. Avoiding capture wasn't that difficult. But he had to admit, their virtually unlimited resources provided them significant advantage.

Though their identities now were known, authorities wouldn't be able to touch most of the group's assets. From the day the software company was sold, Lafferty's personal wealth had been stashed away in remote foreign countries. Todd Swinford had nothing to worry about, considering the trust fund dollars he had socked away in Europe. Of course, T-Man had no idea Lafferty was aware of those sizable accounts, or that he was in possession of the account numbers and passcodes.

Blake had done the best she could to exit Boston with her cash in tow, and as usual, her best efforts had fallen short. She'd been able to transfer only half of her holdings before they were frozen. What a pity to see the rest go to waste. She personally wouldn't need much money in the years ahead, but Lafferty had hoped to wind up with a higher percentage of the group's total assets, for no other reason than sheer pride.

By now, Webb Tremont would have made the connection to their shared past. But what about his father, the imperial Brandon Tremont? Either way, both Tremonts now could put faces on the individuals who had to be occupying their every waking thought. How it must irk the two of them to recognize that over the weekend these now known persons, who were intent on ending their family's very existence, had been tossing logs through windows just minutes from their precious estate as they soundly slept, dreaming their opulent dreams. That reality alone should be enough to hold them until his next visit to Lake Forest.

Chapter Thirty-Two

Webb tried to take it all in. The internet, talk radio, the television drones. He almost could hear the muffled conversations in eleven thousand Starbucks. Dialogue everywhere centered on one subject—the inconceivable answer to a question that had held a nation spellbound since November. Who were the copycats? Media commentators marveled over their academic accomplishments and business success, while struggling to explain the non sequitur that any one of them would have chosen to become a wanted felon. Let alone all six.

For months, nothing—then instantly the public had received full descriptions in living color. It was a lot to absorb. Still missing was a reasonable rationale. What had these young millionaires hoped to accomplish? The FBI was reluctant to release details about Webb's past dealings with Anthony Lafferty. That connection was far too tenuous, and it did nothing to explain the involvement of the other five. The authorities needed to fill in more blanks before a supportable theory would be advanced to the public. Besides, developing a coherent explanation wasn't the top priority. The backstories could come later. The remaining Cop Show Copycats needed to be captured before harm could be inflicted on more innocent victims. One thing for sure, a very attractive special agent wasn't getting much sleep.

Local law enforcement and the public at large were cautioned to be on the look-out for Anthony Lafferty, Blake O'Meara, and Todd Swinford—each being described as armed and dangerous. The FBI issued special instructions to airport, ground transportation, and border authorities at hundreds of potential points of departure from the country. C.J. Matthews had little doubt the remaining copycats would alter their physical appearance, and at this point no one was questioning their skills for adapting to any situation.

Soon after the media volcano erupted, police in Miami received a call and the special agent's team was promptly notified. On January 21, an independent boat broker in Key Biscayne had sold a previously-owned 40-foot Hinckley to a man who looked like Gregory Beaumont—or at least the pictures of him on television. That boat buyer had claimed to be Eric Thompson, which matched the name on the driver's license he brought to the closing, along with a cashier's check for the listed price of $714,000.

With full payment in hand, it wasn't surprising that the boat dealer didn't require additional verification of the purchaser's identity. By asking around, Gregory Beaumont wouldn't have had much difficulty finding an eager businessperson willing to hurry the paperwork for an easy sale.

Beaumont looked to be fleeing the country. Probabilities were high that he'd acquired documentation that provided him multiple identities for his planned disappearance. There was no shortage of profit-minded sources in Boston or Miami who could address such needs.

The Hinckley purchased by Beaumont was one of the most reliable powerboats on the market for open-sea travel, and it could be operated by a single individual. He had the craft and fuel capacity to disappear most anywhere in the Western hemisphere. With access to nearly forty million dollars, he also could arrange for a charter flight to anywhere in the world once he was outside the jurisdiction of the United States.

An alert was issued to all ports within a reasonable radius of Key Biscayne. Just hours later, C.J. Matthews received word that a Hinckley matching the description was moored overnight in Key West on January 22. The boat's name and identification number were different from those specified in the alert, but a steady hand and two cans of marine paint could explain those discrepancies. Marina forms filed in Key West listed the owner as Duncan Hutchison, but his physical description matched those of Gregory Beaumont and Eric Thompson.

As additional responses were received, the FBI was able to chart the route traveled by Gregory Beaumont through the first of February. From Key West, he made his way as Duncan Hutchison to Exuma, in the Bahamas, where he docked for two nights. Then Port of Providenciales, in the Turks and Caicos Islands, for a few days, followed by Anguilla and St. Maarten—skipping stops in the US territories of Puerto Rico and the Virgin Islands, where he would have been subjected to tighter screening. Finally, on February 1, he reached Antigua, clearing customs in the late afternoon. But after several days, the Hinckley still had been moored in the slot temporarily assigned to Mr. Hutchison. Finally, the craft was impounded by authorities. Local police had been searching for the missing visitor ever since. At the request of the FBI, Antigua officials inspected the Hinckley's identifying markings more closely and concluded they had been altered in recent weeks.

Meanwhile, field agents in Pittsburgh paid a visit to Jeannette Lafferty, the ex-wife of Anthony Lafferty. The former professor had been married for four years during his tenure at Carnegie Mellon—long enough to father a daughter and son. In the six years since the divorce, his former wife and kids hadn't seen or heard from Lafferty—nor had they received a dime from the man. It was a trade-off she was more than willing to accept. Reports that her former spouse was wanted for murder were both sobering and satisfying. She looked forward to the day when Anthony Lafferty would be locked away. The ex-wife showed similar hostilities toward Blake O'Meara, whom she'd always assumed to be one of her husband's extracurricular playmates. According to his wife, there had been many, and most of them students.

Agents in Boston dug deeper into the recent career pursuits of the now-known copycats. Before exiting the country, Michael Chen had completed the development of a new encryption methodology that would allow companies to enhance the benefits to promotional gift cards by allowing them to more securely add targeted incentives over the life of the cards. A number of major retailers were eager to test his latest concept, before he began missing a series of scheduled meetings. According to experts, his latest brainchild would be worth many more millions to the young entrepreneur.

Gregory Beaumont had gone to work for a toy company, inventing intricate puzzles and games. But the company's president received an unexpected resignation by phone on the same day Beaumont took off for Florida.

Both Todd Swinford and Blake O'Meara had been working independently since the sale of S.A.F.E. Swinford was producing a pilot for a kids' television show, while O'Meara earned $4,000 a day as a free-lance IT troubleshooter.

Anthony Lafferty rented the top two floors of a brownstone in Boston's South End. No lobby, no security desk, no system to track his coming and going. The building contained a second rental unit on the ground level, plus there was an old shared garage in the rear. The other tenants, a young working couple, described Lafferty as moody and often distracted, at least on the rare occasions they happened to see him. They'd become accustomed to Lafferty's being away for extended periods over the three years he had resided there. Neither of the pair could remember seeing him or his old Jeep in months. Inside, agents found his refrigerator empty, his houseplants dead, and weeks of mail piled under the letter slot at his front door. His rent, like most of his bills, was paid automatically from a checking account that carried a balance of ninety-four thousand dollars.

Webb knew C.J. Matthews had her hands full, so he was caught off-guard when he received a text on Wednesday morning to ask if she could stop by later in the day. He assumed the special agent was swinging through Lake Forest to check out the events from Saturday night, when the copycats had hurled their logs and messages. Webb was surprised she wanted to schedule time with him, but he wasn't one to look a gift horse in the mouth. He welcomed any opportunity to meet with her in person. Or so he thought.

She arrived at the coach house shortly after 2 p.m., accompanied by Walt Briggs. The usual pleasantries were skipped. Both agents appeared uncomfortable, with Miss Matthews seeming slightly agitated. This definitely wasn't going to be courtesy call.

As soon as the three of them were seated, the special agent took the lead. "Mr. Tremont, I'm sorry to be abrupt, but we're heading over to meet with your father as soon as we're done here ... and we felt obliged to spend a few moments with you first."

Webb sensed a dark cloud moving into his life. "Why would you need to meet with my father?"

C.J. Matthews ignored the question, instead giving a head nod to Walt Briggs, who proceeded to fire a question from left field. "Mr. Tremont, what do you know about Marion, Ohio?"

Webb's mind was racing to come up with any idea of where the conversation might be leading. "It's located somewhere between Lake Erie and the Gulf of Mexico, I suppose ... and it also was one of the towns where the copycats broke into a church."

"That's all?" asked Briggs.

"I swear, that is the sum and substance of my knowledge of Marion, Ohio."

C.J. Matthews took over. "Mr. Tremont, maybe I can prod your memory. Have you ever had occasion to speak with your father about his business dealings in Marion ... or were you even aware he'd conducted business there?"

Wherever this conversation was headed, he now was dreading that destination. "Over the years, my father did business in dozens of places I wouldn't have had reason to know about. I don't recall the town of Marion ever coming up."

She continued, "Based on your responses, can I then assume you are unaware that Anthony Lafferty was born in Marion, Ohio?"

"No, that can't be. Theo told me Lafferty was from West Virginia ... and the media reports have been referencing the fact he grew up in Lewisburg." Though not sure why, Webb Tremont was grasping for shreds of hope.

Her voice softened. "He grew up in West Virginia, but he was born in Marion, Ohio. His mother moved to Lewisburg when Lafferty was an infant."

The FBI was aware and clearly concerned that his father had spent time in the birthplace of a psychopath with a vendetta against his entire family. Webb didn't need a sixth sense to recognize the dark cloud that had been approaching was about to unleash a downpour.

Marion was a town of thirty-five thousand people, about fifty miles north of Columbus. That much he could glean from an atlas. The two agents filled in the rest. For twenty-four years, one of the Tremont family's holdings had been a local bank in Marion—which Brandon Tremont picked up as a remnant piece from a deal struck with a prominent Ohio family to gain control of their principal banks in Cincinnati and Dayton. He ultimately sold the Cornerstone National Bank of Marion in 1995.

The business transactions sounded like routine ones for Webb's father. But from there, things took a radical turn. Walt Briggs pulled out a photo the FBI had found in Cornerstone National's personnel files. It looked dated and featured an attractive young woman with long hair and dark features. After Webb studied the picture for a few moments, Special Agent Matthews spoke up. "This photograph was taken in 1969, when the young woman shown was hired by the bank."

"Who is it?" Webb instinctively asked.

"Her name is Diana Lafferty, the mother of Anthony Lafferty. She worked for Cornerstone National as executive secretary to the bank's president until 1975, when she was fired at the instruction of your father."

Webb sighed before asking his next question, not really wanting to hear the answer. "For what reason?"

C.J. Matthews let Briggs handle this one. "We're not sure what reasons your father may have had, but the explanation listed in her employment record states: 'Unwed motherhood is inconsistent with the reputation and community standing of Cornerstone National Bank.' Four months after leaving the bank, Miss Lafferty gave birth to her first and only child."

Webb stared at the floor as he asked his next question in a near whisper. "Was my dad the father?"

"We don't know for sure. There's no father listed on the birth certificate, but Diana Lafferty maintains your father was not responsible," replied C.J. Matthews

"So why would you doubt her?" asked Webb.

The special agent's tone suddenly turned softer. "Because, Mr. Tremont, we've learned it was common knowledge at the time that your father was having an extended affair with Diana Lafferty." She allowed that to sink in before continuing, "Plus, Miss Lafferty received a severance package that was unusually generous for 1975. She was paid $20,000, which according to the bank's files was awarded to her in response to a specific directive from Brandon Tremont."

The time period had been the early Seventies, and the town was Marion, Ohio. Webb realized Brandon Tremont and the bank executives reporting to him wouldn't have worried much about a discrimination lawsuit from a pregnant female, due to her unmarried status. Agents in Ohio, as well as West Virginia, had been gathering a great deal of background on Diana Lafferty and more details from a growing dossier were shared with Webb.

As a consequence of her termination and tarnished reputation, Diana Lafferty was unable to find another administrative position or anything comparable in Marion. She had cousins in West Virginia and decided to relocate, but again ran into problems finding suitable employment as an unwed mother. From that point forward she struggled to make ends meet. Mostly she worked as a waitress or restaurant hostess at the historic Greenbrier Hotel, just thirteen miles away. According to sources who wished to remain nameless, during her off-duty hours Diana Lafferty "traded favors from time to time" with male guests seeking diversion from the conventions or business meetings that had brought them to West Virginia.

Diana Lafferty definitely hadn't led the life one typically associated with a son who attended Carnegie Mellon on a full academic scholarship. Now Agents Matthews and Briggs would meet with Webb's father to better understand how he fit into this curious history.

Once the agents left the coach house, Webb phoned Nessie and asked her to call him as soon as the two were done meeting with his father. The next ninety minutes felt like an eternity as his mind wandered to places never anticipated. Finally, he got the call and made the slow trudge over to the main house.

Brandon Tremont met him at the door, a dire expression on his face, knowing what his son had come to discuss.

This time there would be no chat in the wine cellar. Brandon Tremont showed Webb into his private study and closed the door behind them. He took his seat behind the antique mahogany desk as Webb pulled a chair up to the opposite side, facing him.

"Marion, Dad. Tell me about it."

Brandon Tremont slowly nodded his head up and down, "I am prepared to do just that, Webster … but first I need to assure you that I had no reason to think my long-ago indiscretions could have had any bearing on this whole copycat situation. If I'd known, I would have been completely forthcoming. I wouldn't put the lives of innocent people at risk because of any personal embarrassment I might suffer … not to mention, jeopardize the safety of the people I hold most dear."

From his father's demeanor, Webb recognized how hard the next minutes were going to be and tried to be sympathetic. "I know you well enough to believe that, Dad. Still, it would seem there are some aspects to your personal life I might have misjudged."

He nodded again. "Until now, there was no reason to burden you with my past mistakes. Son, I wasn't always the husband I should have been to your mother."

His father paused to let that sink in and to gather the strength to continue. "Like any young couple, your mother and I experienced highs and lows as we adapted to married life … it is fair to say we both exhibited frustrations and intolerances at times. We each had been pampered … spoiled in our childhoods. Eventually we worked through these differences and I honestly can say that during the last twenty-five years of your mother's life, we were entirely contented and committed to one another. However, in the early years of our marriage there was a period when I strayed from our vows—convinced my actions were justified by difficulties we were having at home. But make no mistake, it was pure selfishness and weakness on my part. Your mother deserved much better, and I've always regretted my infidelities."

The last word had been plural. His father was admitting to affairs with more than one woman, but Webb didn't need to hear about the others. He didn't want to. "Dad, just tell me about Diana Lafferty."

"She was the private secretary to the president of the bank we owned. It was a minor holding for our family, and he was the only person with whom I really needed to meet whenever I visited Marion. But I couldn't see him without passing Miss Lafferty's desk outside his office. She was attractive and appeared receptive to an after-hours relationship. As a young man, I was rather full of myself. I no doubt flaunted the fact I personally had negotiated the purchase of the bank. So, I cannot blame her, by any means. I took liberties in exploiting my position. For almost a year, we met secretly. And during that time, I scheduled more business trips to Marion than should have been warranted by that bank's relative unimportance as a business asset."

Webb tried to reveal no outward reaction, to appear non-judgmental. Inside, though, his thoughts and feelings were exploding in a thousand directions. This was not only a man he'd always considered a paragon of propriety, this man was his father. Husband to his mother.

Brandon Tremont continued, "Our relationship ... our affair ... lasted until the summer of 1974. Diana became more and more careless and demonstrative during my visits to the bank. I no longer could risk how she might behave or what she might say when I wasn't present, so I chose to cut off the arrangement."

The timing of this "arrangement" made Webb even more uncomfortable. He had been born in the spring of 1974, which meant Brandon Tremont was dashing over to Ohio to satisfy his sexual urges throughout his wife's second pregnancy. But this wasn't the time to dwell on how his father could have been so duplicitous, so he moved on. "And what about Diana Lafferty's pregnancy?"

"That came later ... by maybe a year. Webster, I never meant to suggest I was her only romantic interest. Miss Lafferty was rather active in that regard."

"So, Dad, you're telling me Anthony Lafferty is not your son ... and you're absolutely convinced of that fact."

Brandon Tremont's expression grew more forlorn. "I understand the FBI's asking me that question, but I was hoping you would have given me the benefit of the doubt. Of course Anthony Lafferty is not my son." His elderly father caught himself. He was in no position to become indignant. "I'm sorry, Webster. Considering the circumstances, you had every reason to draw that conclusion."

Webb was confused. "Then why did you order the firing of Diana Lafferty a year after your affair ended ... and why was she given such a generous severance package?"

He looked startled by the amount of information his son already knew. "It seems the FBI has brought you into their confidence. Webb, times were different. Towns like Marion were very parochial ... Diana was pregnant and unmarried. We couldn't risk the stigma of having the private secretary to our bank's president being talked about all over town. Important customers might have moved their business if we didn't take appropriate action ... I was given no choice. As for the twenty-thousand-dollar payment the bank made to her, I funded that out of my own pocket. I'm sure you can appreciate why I was concerned for her well-being."

"What was her reaction?"

"Webster, she wasn't living in a bubble. I remind you, times were different ... she understood the difficult situation in which she'd placed the bank. She left amicably ... I was told she was most appreciative of the sizable payment she received."

Webb was stunned. "You didn't speak with her. You left that to other people ... my God, Dad, did you ever hear from her again? Did you even bother to check on how she was doing?"

His father's response was straightforward. "No. To be honest, I can't remember the last time I even thought about her until this afternoon, when those agents started asking me questions. I've been reading about Anthony Lafferty for several days and never thought to make the connection. What does that tell you?" His tone turned sheepish. "I had no idea that she'd moved to West Virginia, or whether she'd given birth to a boy or a girl ... or maybe had an abortion. Webster, I know how callous this all must sound, but the fact that his last name didn't even register with me should tell you how little she meant to me ... and how ashamed I now feel."

Webb stared out the window behind the desk. He didn't want to make eye contact as his father's words and demeanor sank in. Brandon Tremont seemed genuinely remorseful about the infidelities to his wife, but completely indifferent when the conversation had turned to Diana Lafferty. So much for remaining non-judgmental; emotions took over and Webb Tremont allowed his pilot light to get lit.

"Dad, how could you have been so insensitive, so detached, about this woman? She was interesting enough when you were looking for a little something on the side. But once your sexual appetite had run its course and she found herself in trouble, all you bothered to do was put a price tag on what those past intimacies had been worth to you. You didn't give her a second thought. You gave her money ... worse yet, you had someone else give her the money on your behalf. Money ... the easiest, most natural method that the great Brandon Tremont always has used to deal with issues which weren't to his liking. Guilt, embarrassment, moral responsibility ... any of those silly, petty annoyances can be swept away and forgotten for the right dollar amount. Hell, twenty thousand bucks ... how many of your old paintings or rare books are worth more than that?"

Some default switch had flipped inside his head. Webb couldn't believe what was spewing out of his mouth, but he was unable to stop himself. At a time when Anthony Lafferty was looking to do harm to everyone close to him, Webb suddenly was more concerned about how the damned lunatic's mother had been treated forty years earlier than the emotional state of his own father.

The reaction on the other side of the desk was disquieting. Brandon Tremont was unaccustomed to being talked to in such manner—especially from his son. Over the years, the two had argued too many times to count. Webb certainly had tweaked around his father's edges on a routine basis. But never had he outright insulted the man; not once would he have even thought to attack his moral character. Now, basking in self-righteousness, Webb had lost control. Instantly he wished he hadn't.

Webb could have dealt with retaliatory anger from his father, or one of Brandon Tremont's deep, piercing stares. Even tears might have been okay. Instead, he watched as the proud man practically withered in his chair—abandoned by his own son at a moment of bitter truth, and looking thoroughly despondent. Finally, he spoke in a meek, quivering voice that Webb wouldn't have recognized as his father's if he hadn't been sitting across from him.

"Son, I'm so horribly, horribly ashamed. There is so much I wish I could undo … so much I wish I'd better understood when I was younger. Webb, I'm not like you—and oh, how I've wished I could be. I don't feel the things you feel. I've never had your sense of humanity, your compassion. I envy those traits … the qualities you and your mother shared. I always wanted to be more …." His voice trailed off and Brandon Tremont sat staring at his hands folded on his lap.

Webb saw the anguish on the face of his father, who for the first time looked old to him. As a writer, millions of words had flowed from his fingertips onto a keyboard, but when he needed them most, Webb was unable to push a single sound through his lips. After a few moments, Brandon Tremont interpreted the silence as his son's final reproach for all of his admissions. He slowly rose from behind the desk and walked toward the door, his upper body slumped to one side. He had his hand on the doorknob and his back to his son when Webb finally managed to speak. "Dad …"

His father turned around, looking as though he expected to be laid into again. Webb stood, approached him and reached out with both arms. They hugged for the first time in more than thirty years. "Dad, it's not too late."

—— ◦ ——

C.J. Matthews felt like Brandon Tremont had held nothing back during their private session. He volunteered every embarrassing detail about his extramarital relationship and was resolute about not fathering a child with Diana Lafferty. Nonetheless, she still gave Briggs the nod before they wrapped things up. He pulled a swab kit from his pocket and requested a DNA sample in order to verify no paternity issues existed. The powerful billionaire didn't object.

Investigating agents in West Virginia and Ohio continued their full-court press. Diana Lafferty never had married and still lived in the three-room Lewisburg apartment where her lone child had blossomed into a genius. Starting in kindergarten, teachers and administrators in the public school system had recognized her son's potential. Anthony Lafferty was placed into every available special program. He graduated from high school more than a year early. After his enrollment at Carnegie Mellon, Lafferty allowed whatever relationships he might have had with friends and relatives back in West Virginia to lapse. Those who bothered to ask would receive occasional updates from his mother, but nothing more.

Following college graduation, Lafferty's contact with his mother dwindled to periodic phone calls. Diana Lafferty hadn't seen her son in person since she visited him in Pittsburgh in 2009, while he was married. To say the least, she had been shocked by the most recent revelations. She recognized that her son often could be difficult and aloof, but the thought of him being party to cold-blooded murder was incomprehensible.

Despite her spotted past, the agents interviewing Diana Lafferty developed a respect for key aspects of her character. Going all the way back to her unexpected pregnancy in 1975, she accepted responsibility for her indiscretions. Surprisingly, she harbored no outward bitterness toward Brandon Tremont, the Cornerstone Bank that had employed and terminated her, or the unnamed Marion male who actually did father her son. She'd done everything possible not to burden her gifted child with pointless animosities. But she admitted that it would have been impossible to shield him from the gossip that followed her wherever they went.

According to a number of long-time Marion residents who also were interviewed, Diana Lafferty's relationship with Brandon Tremont had been widely recognized around town—in great part because she rarely hesitated to talk about her devotion to the man. He was so different from the others in her past, and there had been many. Details of her personal life made for a juicy story in a small community. Not-so-casual observers had wanted to believe her affair with Mr. Tremont continued long after 1974. When the bank summarily fired a pregnant Diana Lafferty in 1975, many assumed the rich and powerful Brandon Tremont had been the father of her unborn child. After forty years, some locals still wanted to believe those original rumors—rumors that followed Diana Lafferty to Lewisburg, West Virginia.

After relocating to a new state for a fresh start, Diana Lafferty applied for a wide range of office jobs. Repeated calls for references were made to people in Marion and the undercurrents of her past spread from one potential employer to another. Too many provincial folks were unwilling to give an unwed mother the chance to prove herself, so eventually Diana was forced to accept her first waitress position. And then her second. Over time, gossip about her past affairs melded with stories of her continued free-spirited lifestyle. Many of the men who joined Diana Lafferty for late night reveling in rural West Virginia were out-of-towners. But not all. She enjoyed plenty of in-town companionship as well. Anthony Lafferty surely must have become aware of his mother's revolving-door relationships.

Growing up, Anthony couldn't have avoided the rumors and speculations about his mother's past. A few of Diana Lafferty's closest confidants from Lewisburg even made reference to her romantic fling with Brandon Tremont back in Ohio. Diana had talked about it as though she had been Cinderella to his Prince Charming. One current friend was convinced that Diana still carried a torch for the celebrated billionaire.

Miss Lafferty acknowledged to federal agents that during his teenage years, Anthony had confronted her repeatedly about her past. He was intent on uncovering details about his father. He would go through her phone directory and call listed individuals from Marion and catch them off-guard with a string of questions. Then he would pester her about some new piece of information he might have gleaned. No matter how adamant Diana Lafferty became with her son, Anthony wouldn't stop conducting his personal inquisition. Nor did he ever seem to accept that the man who fathered him still lived in Marion, and that this male friend had been nothing more than a married philanderer. The man still owned and operated two convenience stores that barely broke even. She'd slept with him a handful of times after drinking together at a local tavern. They were bar buddies, nothing more. She hadn't wanted to ruin his marriage, so she never even told the man about her pregnancy.

One agent who interviewed Diana Lafferty made special note of how, after all these years, she still spoke about Brandon Tremont with reverence. He clearly had been her greatest romance. It would have been impossible for Diana Lafferty to disguise those deep feelings during her son's persistent questioning.

———◇———

The day after her meeting with Brandon Tremont, C.J. Matthews was willing to share additional information about Diana Lafferty and the childhood afforded her son. For Webb, these details filled in puzzle pieces about the relationship Anthony Lafferty had struck up with Theo Kleyser upon their arrival at Carnegie Mellon. Lafferty's eyes must have lit up when he read that one of his classmates hailed from Lake Forest, Illinois. He would have glommed onto Theo as soon as they arrived on campus.

Lafferty wasn't the least bit interested in checking out Chicago when he weaseled an invitation out of Theo to spend two weeks in Lake Forest. He had wanted to scope out where Brandon Tremont resided—the man who had used his wealth and power to take advantage of his mother, to satisfy his libidinous urges. The man who had seen fit to send her packing once she became pregnant. The man who just as easily could have been the father he didn't know. To Anthony Lafferty, Brandon Tremont was the unscrupulous prick who had forced an unwed mother to scrounge for work while he merrily moved forward with his own privileged lifestyle. She and her son lived from meager paycheck to meager paycheck, while Brandon Tremont earned tens of thousands a day on interest alone. Visiting Lake Forest, he finally saw the affluence in which the Tremont family was immersed. Such randomness of fate could only intensify his resentment. In Anthony Lafferty's mind, a share of that wealth might rightfully have been his, and such thoughts must have been torturous.

To make matters worse, Theo Kleyser's closest friend had turned out to be the son of the same Brandon Tremont. Lafferty was forced to endure this younger Tremont's presence on multiple occasions during his two-week stay in Lake Forest. Webb Tremont had been a contemporary in age, brimming with glibness, and unable to hold a candle to him intellectually. Yet there he was, affirmed and protected by a family name. No wonder the guy couldn't suppress his disdain every time the name of Webb Tremont came up in subsequent conversations with Theo.

Still, as much as Webb tried to understand the emotional triggers for Anthony Lafferty, his mind kept returning to his father. He couldn't dislodge the image of Brandon Tremont as a womanizer, but this gaping character flaw suddenly made it easier for Webb to humanize the man, to want to connect with him. During their gut-wrenching conversation, his father had dropped every vestige of pride or pretense and openly revealed the most human of his frailties. Not just the infidelities, but his unshielded feelings, his self-described incapacity for experiencing a full range of emotions, and the private disappointment over this yawning void.

In Webb's own complicated way, he'd always loved his father—in some ways even silently and stubbornly adored him. Paradoxically, he now felt closer to his father than at any time in his life. This was Brandon Tremont in a whole new light. The irony was not lost on him. His father had confessed to repeatedly cheating on his mother. He had admitted to wholesale emotional shortcomings. And what was Webb's reaction? He started liking his father for what he wasn't, rather than resenting him for what he was. Fate had an odd way of shuffling the deck.

Chapter Thirty-Three

"That son of a bitch!"

He knew Niu Tsen was sleeping soundly in the next room, but he couldn't hold back. He was sitting on the floor with his legs folded, staring at his open laptop on the coffee table. Tears formed in the corners of his eyes, a combination of anger and sadness.

"It's the middle of the night … what's wrong, Michael?" she asked in a soft voice.

She was standing in the doorway from the bedroom, a silk robe thrown hastily over her shoulders and covering little of her nakedness. Despite his family's heritage, Michael Chen had never dated a woman of Chinese extraction, or Asian extraction of any kind, for that matter. Now he'd fallen head-over-heels for Niu. The two of them had been introduced by his cousin and had been together practically nonstop since his second day in Xian.

Michael always had viewed romantic relationships as a complication, as a distraction from studying or building out new ideas. Yet already he found himself wondering what life might be like with Niu in California or Boston on a permanent basis. Not that he ever would be able to return to the US, thanks to his asshole ex-partner, Lafferty. The expensive apartment in downtown Xian was the most impressive place in which he'd ever lived, but it never could feel like home. The prospects of a lifetime in exile only added to his feelings of sorrow.

He still was reeling from the news a few weeks earlier. His closest friend,

Teresa Conkle, had been found dead in her condo, just two days after Richmond. He knew damned well that Conks wouldn't have taken her own life. Lafferty had killed her and made it look like suicide. And now, as of Tuesday, pictures of all six of them were popping up across the internet, their identities fully revealed. Since the Chinese government blocked so much content, Chen was forced to navigate a series of obscure links to stay abreast with news in the US, gathering his facts in bits and pieces. Just a few minutes earlier he'd come across an item about Beaumont having gone missing in Antigua. He was sure Lafferty somehow had tracked him down. Michael Chen was certain that another of his close friends had been eliminated. He felt personally responsible. He never should have invited Anthony Lafferty to join them in the first place. It all seemed so obvious now. How could they have allowed themselves to be so easily manipulated?

Webb figured the public's preoccupation with the copycats had to be creating a number of unusual challenges for the FBI. The Feds wanted to keep the faces of the five remaining suspects as visible as possible. They would release any new facts that could expedite their capture. Yet at the same time, the Bureau would want to withhold information that merely contributed to an overall frenzy. The FBI committed to weekly press conferences to update the public on the investigation and field questions from the media. The news networks promptly announced they would broadcast them live.

Webb Tremont abhorred the need for such distractions, but he credited the brain trust in Washington DC for making at least one prudent decision. As head of field operations on the case, C.J. Matthews would share the weekly podium with the Bureau's regular spokespeople. If the FBI wanted the public to feel positive about its overall efforts, putting her face in front of a camera was a huge step in the right direction.

The federal authorities chose not to disclose the details about Anthony Lafferty's mother and her affair with Brandon Tremont. There was no reason to invite millions of people to trample through their private lives. Webb and his father certainly didn't disagree, and Diana Lafferty probably was appreciative as well. But Webb knew the point was moot.

Thousands of reporters and wannabe reporters were treading over the same turf, digging into the background of every copycat. Many of the folks from West Virginia and Ohio who had spoken with FBI agents were now in a talkative mood. Even individuals who had wished to remain nameless when questioned by the FBI became less concerned about their anonymity once they were offered the chance to appear on national television. After all, how many times was one given the opportunity to go split-screen with Anderson Cooper?

The photos and names of the Cop Show Copycats had been emblazoned across the American landscape since Tuesday, February 9. By Friday, February 12, the faces of Webb's father and Diana Lafferty were almost as familiar, thanks to probing reporters. The privileged lifestyle of a powerful billionaire didn't sit well with a sizable portion of the population to begin with. The stories of his marital indiscretions pushed the negative needle even further. Brandon Tremont obviously was a scoundrel.

The mother of Anthony Lafferty didn't fare much better. Her challenges as a single mother evoked some degree of empathy. But human nature being what it was, several of those interviewed in Lewisburg thought it might be interesting to comment on the more colorful aspects of her personal life, both past and present. Diana Lafferty didn't help the situation when she agreed to a string of television interviews. She came off as utterly indifferent toward her son and his alleged crimes, while making repeated fond references to her memories of Webb's father and even suggesting a willingness to meet up with him again for old time's sake. After all, he no longer was married.

The revelations about Brandon Tremont and Diana Lafferty handed the talking heads another reason to revisit the copycats' past crimes. The choice of Presbyterian churches in Ohio now seemed attributable to Brandon Tremont rather than Webb. His father had been much more regular in his church attendance over the years, plus he continued to underwrite a number of Presbyterian mission projects.

Notes left by the copycats at their various crime scenes suddenly took on greater meanings. The message found among the rubble of damaged antiques at Tremont Farms now was viewed as a commentary on the manner in which Brandon Tremont had treated Anthony Lafferty's mother: "To the privileged, the rest of us are nothing more than playthings." Then the next weekend, in Delaware, the message left on the front porch of another Tremont had admonished the family for its "deplorable behavior"—which clearly was another backhanded reference to Brandon Tremont's indiscretions with Diana Lafferty.

In Richmond, amidst the pool of blood surrounding Natalie Meriwether, money had been left for nine rape victims. The note inside each envelope had read: "Sexual predators care nothing about ruining lives. Do not allow yourself to become a shameless conquest." The words now could be interpreted as a scathing allusion to the interactions between Webb's father and Diana Lafferty. However, the general public as yet remained unaware that the selection of Cappie Tremont's convenience store as a crime scene carried additional significance. Diana Lafferty had confided to federal agents that her son was fathered by a man who owned and operated convenience stores in Marion, Ohio.

A week later, the copycats had struck in Lancaster, Pennsylvania. "Adulterer" was printed across the forehead of Howie Kykendall and the note attached to the manhole cover chided: "Husbands must pay for their philandering." In more recent weekends, the messages continued to be laced with negative commentaries on the superficialities of the Tremont family.

As the copycats had become more pointed in their choices and messages, the cash left inside their envelopes repeatedly totaled $20,000. Hardly coincidental, considering the same sum had been paid to Diana Lafferty upon her termination from the bank in 1975—the amount Brandon Tremont had decreed as the appropriate compensation for his inappropriate conduct.

Webb, along with millions of his fellow countrymen, had been given a new prism through which to interpret the copycats' actions. If questions remained as to how Anthony Lafferty might feel about his mother and the decisions she'd made over the course of her life, many of those were answered on the second weekend of February.

———◦———

Just three miles across the Mississippi River from St. Louis, Missouri sits the conveniently named town of East St. Louis, Illinois. This small municipality of 27,000 and the surrounding county of St. Clair rank as one of the poorest and often most troubled districts in the country. In 2001, the New Gateway Food Shelter lost its largest benefactor when the dotcom bubble burst and the stock market took a nosedive. Hundreds of East St. Louis families suffered the trickle-down consequences of unchecked greed. At least, that's how Darnell Cooke saw things. Darnell had been executive director of the local food bank for fourteen years and felt a paternal responsibility for the neighborhoods it served. Those residents counted on the grocery goods he and his limited staff distributed four afternoons a week to lengthy lines that formed outside the shelter's rundown facility.

Well-intentioned bureaucrats got busy, hoping to arrange alternative funding for New Gateway, but month after month the efforts proved fruitless. Meanwhile, the area's families needed to eat. Darnell and two of his associates couldn't bear the thought of turning folks away any longer. They knew most of those families by name, and with each name, the unfortunate circumstances they confronted. To maintain the pantry's commitment to the community, the three decided to bend a few laws—or, more precisely, break them outright.

Over a three-month period, Mr. Cooke and the other two paid late-night visits to four warehouses across Illinois, Missouri, and Iowa. Next up was to be Kansas— that is, until four guys in uniform stopped by the food shelter with a search warrant. In retrospect, Darnell and his fellow night-raiders had pushed their luck when they'd decided to hand out frozen turkeys a full month before Thanksgiving. People in the neighborhoods tended to talk about such windfalls. A local cop overheard the buzz on the street and remembered an alert received from the Des Moines Police Department. Two hundred missing Butterballs wasn't something a beat cop was likely to forget.

The wholesale cost for the stolen food from the four heists totaled $37,412. Darnell and his two associates pled guilty to four charges of grand theft at their arraignment. Meanwhile, members of the East St. Louis Police Department continued digging into the burglaries and the men behind them. Due to a great deal of off-hours legwork, these officers determined Cooke and his coworkers hadn't made a cent from a single can of green beans or box of pancake mix. In fact, to complete their illicit forages, the three had spent their own money to put gas in New Gateway's rusted-out van.

After strong encouragement from the district attorney's office of St. Clair County, the operators of the four targeted food distribution centers abruptly decided none of their managers could be made available for their scheduled depositions. This was no small task, considering state lines had been crossed and the FBI was involved. Each of the distributors instead reclassified their missing inventory as a charitable donation.

Even the media cooperated. Local reporters were encouraged to walk a careful line, so as not to turn three guilty parties into heroes for breaking the law. The trio received two years' probation, along with the gratitude of hundreds of families throughout their community. The New Gateway Food Shelter had been oversubscribed with private and corporate underwriters ever since.

As a chronicler of crimes, Webb Tremont routinely combed newspapers from every part of the country. He had locked onto the New Gateway story because the three principal characters offered a fresh counterpoint to the hardened criminals featured in many of the cases in his books. The sixth volume of _Serve & Protect_ included the chapter "Hindsight in St. Clair County."

Yolanda Salotich and her daughter, Rose, were starting their fourteenth month at Welton House. They were permitted to live there for up to twenty-four months, plus an additional six if the right people petitioned on their behalf. Yolanda knew a women's shelter was no place to raise a six-year-old. Nonetheless, she was grateful to the judge who'd pulled strings so that she and Rosie could get away from the toxic environment of the duplex owned by Ruffo's family. Ruffo had served his jail time for kicking her to the ground at a Labor Day picnic, and was back living with his mother, sister, and her two kids.

Welton House had been serving an important need in the East St. Louis Community since 1983 by providing temporary sanctuary to abused women constrained by financial hardship. The old Victorian home had a maximum legal capacity of twenty-five residents. Including infants, the current occupancy was thirty-four. The residents shared household duties, which included the preparation of communal breakfasts and dinners. Due to limited funding, the meals often were short on portion size and nutritional balance. So, when a food distribution truck pulled up to the curb shortly after dawn on February 14, a Sunday morning, Yolanda and the other residents who happened to be awake were more than curious when the driver and his associate came to the front door.

The cheery men informed Yolanda that they'd been instructed by their supervisor at Petros Brothers Wholesale Foods to deliver a substantial order of food goods, which had been purchased by a group of anonymous donors. All they needed was a signature and instructions on where to unload the cases of food. Yolanda gladly complied and noticed on the acceptance receipt that the donated items were valued at more than $37,000.

The next half-hour was like Christmas morning. One of the older kids hurried through the upstairs halls, pounding on doors and shouting for everyone to come join the fun. As residents assembled, they formed a human conveyor belt to help empty the truck. Once the pantry and store room were filled, furniture was rearranged and the remaining boxes were stacked in the living room. Thanks to some magnanimous group, the women of Welton House would be preparing complete, healthy meals for weeks to come. Their kids would be able to eat from each of the basic food groups at a single sitting.

One of Yolanda's friends, Angela, noticed that Noreen Shipley and her infant son were missing from the celebration. She scurried up to the third floor to roust the young mother from her bed. The baby could be heard wailing from outside the door, but Noreen didn't respond to knocks or calls from the hallway. The door was unlocked, so Angela slowly pushed it open. The sight awaiting her was gruesome. Noreen Shipley's neck had been sliced from ear to ear. The pillows, sheets, and mattress were soaked in blood. Her four-month-old son was crying from the crib next to his mother's bed.

⸺⬦⸺

Two of the patrol officers responding to the call at Welton House were on the force in 2001, when stolen food at New Gateway Food had tested the compassion of local law enforcement. There was no such ambiguity about the bloody scene awaiting them in the bedroom of Noreen Shipley. The responsible parties were heartless monsters, and within moments of arrival, the police on the scene knew exactly who those individuals were when two unopened envelopes were spotted on the nightstand. The FBI immediately was notified.

By the time C.J. Matthews made it to East St. Louis, medical examiners already had drawn preliminary conclusions. Miss Shipley likely had been sleeping when her head and upper body were restrained from above, with a chloroform cloth placed over her mouth. Any struggle was minimal. The lengthy incision across the neck would have been made rapidly, before she had time to adequately comprehend what was happening to her. In that position, it might have taken up to a minute for her to lose total consciousness, but only seconds to lose the strength and will to resist. Her killer or killers probably had waited and watched, to make certain she was dead.

Inside the adjacent crib an empty baby bottle was found, but it was different from the others scattered among Noreen Shipley's baby supplies. Analysis of residue inside the bottle revealed the formula was not the one normally purchased by the young mother. The infant must have awakened during the ordeal and been contented by a bottle brought by the intruders as a precaution.

The envelopes left on the nightstand had been bagged and rushed to a forensics lab. Photos of the contents were emailed to the special agent. Inside a larger envelope were hundred dollar bills that totaled $20,000, accompanied by a note that read, "To help find a suitable home for this motherless boy." The second smaller envelope only contained a typed message. "Just as lowlife men must be held account-able for wantonly satisfying their biological urges, women must be held accountable for their misplaced attempts at raising unwanted children."

At this point, the FBI investigators couldn't be sure how many of the six known copycats might still be active, or if others had been recruited along their journey, but it seemed abundantly clear that Anthony Lafferty remained among them. He apparently took issue with some of the choices that had been made by Diana Lafferty.

The initial exploration into Noreen Shipley's background revealed this twenty-six-year-old woman had led a promiscuous lifestyle since her early teens. Opinions among her fellow residents at Welton House were split on whether the unwed moth-er was capable of changing her ways and accepting the responsibilities of a baby. It now was a moot point. The remaining copycats had passed irreversible judgment on the young female's fitness for motherhood. No doubt, Lafferty weighed in heavily on that death sentence, as well as the selection of the victim. Diana Lafferty also had been twenty-six when she gave birth to a son and was confronted with the op-portunity to straighten out her life.

Special Agent Matthews accompanied the team of agents who paid a late-af-ternoon visit to Alex Petros on Sunday. Mr. Petros was head of Petros Brothers Wholesale Food, a third-generation family business. She had hoped to gain a de-scription of at least one member of the copycats, but that wasn't to be the case. On Saturday morning, a package had been delivered to his home. Inside was cash total-ing $37,412, in assorted denominations. The weathered condition of the currency suggested the money had been raised through some sort of grassroots fund-raising effort. The accompanying letter invited Petros Brothers to partner in a charitable endeavor that was extremely important to a nameless group of benefactors.

According to the letter, all that needed to be done was deliver as much food as the wholesale food broker saw fit to provide for the enclosed amount. "Since your respected family has made meaningful contributions to this community for genera-tions, we are confident you will price the food items accordingly. Please know, steps are underway to assure extensive media coverage of your efforts."

262

The letter went on to itemize the specific brands of food to be delivered, as well as the time and location. Alex Petros did his part by instructing his warehouse manager to load a truck with food goods having a wholesale value of closer to fifty thousand dollars. Unfortunately, he hadn't envisioned the type of extensive media coverage that would follow.

Weeks earlier, C.J. Matthews had downloaded electronic copies of Webb Tremont's books onto her laptop. She pulled up the sixth edition of _Serve & Protect_ and jumped to the relevant chapter about the New Gateway Food Shelter. As she expected, Anthony Lafferty and the other copycats were remaining true to their parody crimes. The brands of food specified in the letter to Alex Petros were the exact products Darnell Cooke and his associates had lifted from four food warehouses in 2001. The amount of cash left for Mr. Petros, and printed on the delivery receipt left at Welton House, was the wholesale cost assigned to that stolen food.

His plan once again had required all three of them to participate. Entering the room and killing the woman easily could have been handled by two persons. If necessary, he would have pulled off the killing alone. But Anthony Lafferty enjoyed dragging his associates further down the dark hole. Tending to the baby kept Blake occupied with something she couldn't screw up, and more importantly, she was given no choice but to witness the final moments of the young mother's life. T-Man had agreed to hold the woman down on the bed while her mouth was covered with the chloroformed cloth, but Lafferty was a little disappointed by Swinford's reaction when he offered him the utility knife. The even-keeled Scandinavian actually freaked out at the prospect of applying the blade to the woman's throat. Perhaps next time. Soon enough there would be another opportunity to plumb new depths with their degradation.

In the meantime, arrangements were progressing nicely in China. Michael Chen wouldn't be a loose end much longer. Anthony Lafferty appreciated how each stretch of his long-anticipated journey was providing unique challenges and satisfactions.

Insanity. There was no other word to describe the depravation. The copycats were toying with the national psyche—one weekend playing childish pranks, the next committing random acts of murder. Most of the media's talking heads were running out of words, which dampened neither their zest for prattling on, nor the public's appetite for soaking up the morbid details.

Webb Tremont barely could remember his personal interactions with Anthony Lafferty from twenty years earlier, but he was feeling an intimate connection to the man. They were inside each other's heads. He was sure of it. With each new revelation, Webb bristled over how the sick bastard must be reveling in self-satisfaction. Worse yet, Webb knew his mounting frustration was precisely the reaction Lafferty intended him to have.

Just as the message next to Noreen Shipley's body left little doubt about Lafferty's attitude toward his mother, the brutal slaying reaffirmed that the remaining copycats were more than comfortable taking innocent lives. Whatever past signals may have suggested the group was experiencing discord in committing serious crimes, those issues had been resolved or eliminated. Such unity of purpose did not bode well for the family of Brandon Tremont.

The media profiles on Todd Swinford and Blake O'Meara continued to expand as journalists dug deeper into their backgrounds. But nothing explained why either would have become party to heinous murders. Both were blessed with brilliant, fertile minds in which unhealthy seeds somehow had taken root. Neither ever had been in any kind of serious trouble. Each tended to keep to themselves, according to acquaintances, but otherwise they'd behaved like model citizens throughout their lives.

With their only child wanted for murder in the United States, Todd Swinford's parents made several brief statements to the European press—mostly attempting to dissociate themselves. They in no way condoned the unconscionable acts and quickly attributed blame to the liberal practices of the educational institutions to which their son had been entrusted, along with the culture of violence in the United

States. Mr. and Mrs. Svinhufuud were confident that any number of dignitaries across the continent would vouch for the family's long-standing moral integrity.

Mr. and Mrs. O'Meara, of Owenton, Kentucky, weren't worried at all about damage to a family name. They simply didn't believe their daughter could have played a role in the string of crimes ascribed to her and her former business partners. There had to be another explanation. Contact with Blake had been infrequent during recent years, and they conceded she was prone to periods of moodiness, even depression. Despite the academic achievements of her youth, "Our Blake at times tried too hard to win the approval of her peers—especially boys." But what young person hadn't? Her four siblings, who at first had resented their sister's newfound wealth, dismissed any possibility of her involvement. The O'Mearas were more fearful that Blake faced danger from some trigger-happy law enforcement officer or vigilante citizen because she hadn't come forward to incriminate the other five. Or worse yet, maybe she already was dead like her friend, the young Conkle woman.

Meanwhile, one of Special Agent Matthews' lieutenants informed Webb that the State Department was making progress with officials in China. Within days, a letter from the US Department of Justice was to be presented to Michael Chen. He would be offered a suspended sentence for pleading guilty to his role in the copycats' non-lethal crimes in advance of Richmond, Virginia. Plus, if it could be proven that he wasn't directly responsible for the murders of Jorge Cabral or Natalie Meriwether, he would be afforded substantial leniency with regard to those homicides. In exchange, he must testify and give a full accounting of the group's activities for the period he was with them.

The idea of a deal had been broached with the US Attorney General's office after a great deal of deliberation inside the senior ranks of the FBI. Going easy on one of the copycats potentially could backfire in the court of public opinion, but the prevailing theory among those actively involved in the investigation was that Michael Chen probably had been an unwilling participant in whatever serious felonies occurred prior to his separation from the others. Why else would he have liquidated his accounts so quickly, then booked a flight and fled the country after the Meriwether murder? If Chen could provide details that led to the capture and successful prosecution of the other copycats, the trade-off was more than warranted. Fearing for the safety of everyone close to him, Webb agreed wholeheartedly with the government's conclusion.

Chapter Thirty-Four

Over the previous two weekends the copycats had smashed windows to the north of Chicago, then murdered a young woman in her bed just 300 miles to the south. Members of C.J. Matthews' team were speculating on whether the remaining copycats now were confining their activities to a smaller section of the country. Traveling shorter distances at odd hours would reduce the risk of being recognized. Lafferty and his cronies also could be tightening the noose around their ultimate targets on Tremont Estate.

Concerns over the fates of Brandon and Webb Tremont hardly were allayed by the group's next weekend jaunt. Special Agent C.J. Matthews received notification that the copycats had hit Cedar Rapids, Iowa, just 263 miles west of Lake Forest. She this time pulled up her digital version of Webb Tremont's seventh book, in which he had profiled three murders that dated back to 2005, in Ridgewood, New Jersey.

It was a home break-in that took a fatal turn. The burglar had been a forty-four-year-old professional loser with two prison sentences already to his name. He pried open the back door of a secluded Tudor owned by an investment banker and his wife. The couple had taken their daughter out for dinner and a movie. The contents of the spacious home were better than anticipated. The guy got greedy, even for a thief, and made one too many trips to his van parked behind the large house, loading up silver, furs, electronics, and anything else that would fetch a decent price. When the homeowners walked through the front door, all four parties were caught off guard. The husband and wife's natural reaction was to start screaming at the intruder. Sadly, his was to panic. He pulled a handgun from his back pocket and started firing before the father, mother, or daughter could flee through the still-open front door. He moved closer and fired several more shots, to make certain. No one in the family survived.

In Cedar Rapids, the Cop Show Copycats paid a visit to the home of a more traditional banker. Bryan Duncan was president of a local retail bank not far from their upscale address on Cottage Grove Avenue. Agents on the scene started drawing comparisons to the homicides in New Jersey as soon as they arrived.

C.J. Matthews made her way there within hours, and by then her teams had theorized that Mr. Duncan and his wife, Shannon, were asleep in their upstairs bedroom when intruders entered the home through a rear door on the first floor. Their twelve-year-old adopted son, Andrew, was likewise sleeping in his room. The parents were rousted from their beds and shepherded down to the living room, where the curtains had been drawn. Bryan and Shannon Duncan were shot to death by what looked to be the same caliber handgun as had been used in Ridgewood, eleven years before. The locations of the bullet wounds on both bodies were virtually identical to those of the murdered parents in New Jersey.

Bryan and Shannon Duncan's lifeless bodies were arranged in the same position and proximity to one another as the original murder victims. Twelve-year-old Andrew was found near them, in the same position as the murdered daughter from Ridgewood; but in this case, he still was breathing. When police arrived, responding to an anonymous call, the officers first assumed Andrew also was dead. But what looked like three bullet wounds and corresponding blood was merely make-up and liquid dye. The 120-pound boy had been heavily sedated, probably from a hypodermic, before being carried downstairs.

For punctuation, the front door to the Duncan home was left wide open after the murders were committed, just as the door had been found in Ridgewood.

Next to the body of Andrew Duncan was an envelope with his name on it. The enclosed note read: "Better to be fatherless than to be raised the son of a banker."

A second envelope was addressed to Gallagher Place, a residential community for orphaned children that served a ten-county area in Eastern Iowa. Inside was $20,000, in hundred-dollar bills, and another note: "To help kids learn the importance of fending for themselves. The nuclear family is a farce."

As usual, the horrid details from Iowa were everywhere by noon the following day. For most Americans, waking up and waiting for the latest installment from the copycats had become more routine for Sunday morning than going to church. Webb assumed his normal position in front of the television, laptop at his side, and tried to make sense of the unfolding story. Though the murders automatically were attributed to the copycats, no physical evidence had been found to firmly establish that Anthony Lafferty, Todd Swinford, or Blake O'Meara were anywhere near the Cedar Rapids homicide. Trace evidence was unlikely to emerge, so it didn't much matter that the FBI was equipped with fingerprint samples and DNA profiles of the presumed perpetrators.

As far as the talking heads were concerned, Anthony Lafferty might as well have left a business card inside the Duncan home. A bank president had been murdered in cold blood. The envelopes contained resentful allusions to bankers' sons and nuclear families. These choices screamed of Lafferty and the hang-ups he surely carried toward Brandon Tremont and his own mother. The fact that Andrew Duncan had been adopted was probably no coincidence either. There clearly was another layer of psychological shrapnel bouncing around inside Lafferty's head about his mother's decision to raise him rather than put him up for adoption. Unfortunately for hordes of law enforcement teams working the investigation, none of these provocative assumptions equated to hard evidence.

Thankfully, medical personnel called to the scene had been able to transport Andrew Duncan away from the home before he regained consciousness and saw the manner in which his parents had been killed. According to a child psychologist who interviewed him, the adolescent had no recollection of the night's events. He neither heard nor felt a thing when his room was entered by the copycats. Nonetheless, the late hours of February 20 were certain to haunt the preteen boy for the rest of his life.

———◆———

As he replayed the events from Cedar Rapids in his mind, Anthony Lafferty only could shake his head. The clueless bastard actually had believed his pleas might make a difference. At one point, the weasel even started offering huge sums of money for their lives to be spared. Typical banker. Money was their answer to everything.

Observing the guy's pitiful brain at work had proven to be entertaining. Especially when he finally accepted that the situation was hopeless. Watching one's wife get shot at point-blank range would convince most men.

Originally, the plans had called for the unconscious son to be brought downstairs after his parents were dead, but the temptation was too great. Lafferty called an audible that caught Blake and T-Man by surprise. Nonetheless, as soon as he instructed them to retrieve the kid while the Duncans still were alive, the two of them went into action without raising a question. He felt good about the progress both of them were making.

Lafferty had extended the father a choice. "Banker Man, you decide who dies next. You or young Andrew here?"

Well, at least the whimpering loser got his wish. The next three bullets were fired into Bryan Duncan's head and chest, even though the first one would have been sufficient. The man died believing his son's death was a certainty. Lafferty smiled. Hauling the kid down and laying him next to his piece-of-shit father had been a nice touch.

He had changed his mind about asking T-Man to handle one of the killings. He'd wanted the pleasure all to himself. Besides, it wasn't like T-Man or Blake could dissociate themselves from Saturday night's murders. Or any of the other murders, for that matter.

He'd always been able to outthink the people around him because of his ability to remain focused. Those so-called geniuses, Leopold and Loeb, had killed one lousy kid back in the Twenties. Counting Conkle and Beaumont, he now was up to eight. The fact that all the known murders were being attributed to the Cop Show Copycats as a group merely demonstrated how perfect his crimes had been. Soon enough he'd distance himself from the others completely, and the total mastery of his accomplishments would become evident. There was bound to be outrage and rebuke at first, but Anthony Lafferty was confident history would treat him well. Ultimately, his ingenuity and determination would have to be recognized.

Chapter Thirty-Five

For another week, the media had one more horrific murder to dissect ad nauseam. The lives of Bryan and Shannon Duncan were recounted through the eyes of friends, neighbors, and family members. The future of their adopted son was pondered by television's standard cadre of sociologists and psychologists. After the first forty-eight hours, Webb tried to tune out the noise. He didn't need to hear the brutality and randomness underscored at the top of each hour.

Of course, the media feasted on the juicy elements that could be connected to the Tremonts in some fashion. The Cedar Rapids murder emulated another case taken from one of Webb Tremont's books. Instead of an investment banker, the copycats targeted the president of a retail bank—like dozens of banks in the business portfolio amassed by Brandon Tremont. Then there was the message: "Better to be fatherless than to be raised the son of a banker." And once more the copycats had seen fit to leave $20,000 for a charity—again reprising the amount Brandon Tremont had paid to wash his hands of Diana Lafferty.

Meanwhile, Tremont Estate was on virtual lockdown. For Webb, living in close quarters with his father, his girlfriend, and her daughter had taken some adjustment—though he recognized most folks would find it difficult to think of confinement to a 28-room mansion and coach house on ten scenic acres as much of a hardship. But most folks didn't know his father.

Sprig was ushered to and from school during the week, but otherwise the FBI wanted everyone to avoid leaving the premises unless absolutely necessary. Corrie's clients understood the circumstances, and she was able to proceed with her design projects through phone contact and email.

As for Brandon Tremont, from wherever he chose to operate, his staff had no option but to conform. Every few hours, some new face seemed to arrive with files for his father's review or contracts that required his signature. Webb figured that for the foreseeable future, his dad could get by without daily trips to his royal counting house. One of his devoted portfolio managers could phone him at the end of each day with an updated tally on the family fortune. For years, Webb had envisioned a huge tote board suspended above the desk in Brandon Tremont's office, the figures rapidly spinning in an ever-upward progression. He had no idea what devices his dad did or didn't use, however, because he'd never had occasion to visit his father's place of work.

Out of concern for Corrie and Sprig, Webb started spending more time over at the main house. He wasn't sure what kind of brainwashing his dad might attempt if left unchecked. Early on Wednesday morning, Webb and Corrie were seated at the kitchen table. Nessie and two of her cooking crew were doing prep work around a nearby island. Brandon Tremont strolled in and asked as normally as if he were inquiring about the weather, "So what are our plans for this afternoon … you know, once Melissa gets home from school?"

Webb had just taken a big gulp of coffee and most of it shot through his nose. From behind he heard a suppressed gasp from the general direction of Nessie. Only Corrie remained unfazed. "Oh, good morning, Mr. B."

His girlfriend couldn't possibly have understood the significance of what had just occurred. Brandon Tremont most definitely wasn't a morning person—not that Webb thought his father was an especially enjoyable afternoon or evening person either. For more than fifty years, his dad routinely had emerged from the upstairs master suite without saying a word. At most, he might issue a barely audible grunt if something wasn't to his satisfaction—like, say, one of his six morning newspapers had been placed outside the bedroom door with a frayed corner.

Growing up on Tremont Estate, there'd been no such thing as "our plans for this afternoon." The everyday roles in the family were tacitly understood. There was a mom, a sister, two brothers, and one mega-important billionaire who lived in an alternate universe. Special appointments were required when Brandon Tremont slipped into the role of father. Now, after all this time, he wanted to become Ward Cleaver or Cliff Huxtable.

Compounding the complexities of this new uncharted galaxy, Corrie somehow had been granted special permission to call his father "Mr. B." If any of Brandon Tremont's employees had taken such liberty, that man or woman was unlikely to be heard from again. None of his dad's friends had ever dared to give him a nickname. The same with Webb's mother. He'd never heard her call him anything other than "Brandon."

His morning metamorphosis continued. "Surely there is something we might do together to make proper use of this glorious day." Webb only could stare. The man's mouth had been moving and the voice sounded exactly like his father's.

Webb's speechlessness could last only so long. "Gee, Dad, I was thinking we might call some sort of emergency meeting so you could run us through a few balance sheets. Maybe put together a new tender offering … or we could go real crazy and launch a couple of hostile takeovers from the living room."

His father retained what appeared to be a smile. Webb was unaccustomed to the notion of Brandon Tremont smiling, so he couldn't be sure. "Now don't be pugnacious, Webster. I simply submit that we might be better served by remaining occupied instead of idly waiting and wondering about our friends, the copycats."

Pugnacious. This was still Brandon Tremont, all right. With one perfectly chosen word, the man could seize or maintain control of most any situation. Besides, Webb recognized that pugnacious was exactly what he was being. He had underestimated his father and his sudden interest in afternoon activities. Following the events of Cedar Rapids and the string of prior weekends, the man merely was looking out for the mental well-being of the loved ones under his roof.

The three of them decided the selection of afternoon activities should be left to Sprig. Arriving home from school, she didn't hesitate. "Darts." Webb chuckled to himself over the randomness of her unexpected choice as the four of them migrated to the coach house and Squandered Opportunities II. Who could have guessed that dartboards had been popular in bars frequented by Dartmouth students? Or that Brandon Tremont might have patronized such establishments in his younger years? He and Sprig made short work of Webb and Corrie. Six straight games at a buck apiece.

While forking over the money to his father, Webb felt it would be unsportsman-like to suggest he and Corrie had been set up. He was further caught off guard when Sprig asked if they might like an opportunity to get their money back. "How about we meet here tomorrow afternoon for a few games of pool?" Her accompanying smile was anything but innocent.

"It's surprising that until this afternoon Mr. B didn't even realize you owned a pool table, Webb. You and your father should talk more."

<hr />

The attorneys he had retained in both China and the United States were review-ing the offer letter. There would be requested tweaks to the necessary assurances, but Michael Chen was optimistic that acceptable terms could be reached. His fate miraculously had reversed, and the prospects of returning home were real.

As long as he couldn't be directly tied to the murder of Natalie Meriwether or that janitor in Ohio, the price he would pay for his outrageously bad judgment would be incidental compared to that of his friends. Michael was confident the evidence would show he wasn't in the room when the poor woman was murdered in that convenience store. He had been completely unaware of Lafferty's intentions. Surely T-Man and Blake wouldn't throw him under the bus. They eventually would testify that Lafferty was fully responsible. There even was a witness who reported that the man working behind the store's check-out counter was of Asian descent. He alone fit such a description, which placed him outside the back room while the killing took place.

As to Jorge Cabral, nothing possibly could connect him to whatever occurred in the Dublin church. He would rely on his attorneys to prove he'd been occupied at a different location more than fifty miles away. He might never learn what happened to that poor janitor, but his instincts had been right from the moment they got back to the motel. Lafferty and Blake were covering up what really had gone down that evening.

So many bright possibilities now seemed within his grasp. He would be free to see his parents and siblings again. Free to develop algorithms and software that pushed new envelopes and made bundles of money for anyone involved. After a few breakthrough concepts, no one would remember or care what early role he might have played with the Cop Show Copycats.

Plus, Niu would be with him. Her two years at Cornell had left her hoping for a return to the United States on a more permanent basis. Plenty of opportunities existed for a talented architect in whichever city they decided to settle. Or, hell, with her looks she could just as easily make a fortune posing for magazine covers.

Lastly, there was Lafferty. Returning home and testifying was the only way to make sure the prick got everything he deserved.

Chapter Thirty-Six

Sergeant Jake Weddington was a twenty-three-year veteran with the Lake Forest Police Department. Whenever he ran into Webb Tremont around town, he would remind him that he had been responsible for Webb's first notable accomplishment as a rookie cop. After Jake sprained his ankle, Webb stepped in as quarterback in the annual flag football game against the Lake Forest Fire Department. At the time, the cops were up by three touchdowns, and thanks to Webb's inspired play-calling, they were able to hold on and eke out a one-point victory.

His latest connection to Webb wasn't likely to produce much clever banter in the years ahead. Weddington had volunteered to the take the late-night shift on the last weekend of February, filling in for an officer friend who was off on his honeymoon. Shortly after 2 a.m. on Sunday morning, he entered the gates of Lake Forest Cemetery to do a quick drive-around. From the asphalt roadway that snaked through the cemetery's thirty-two acres, he noticed a light beam shooting skyward from a section of gravesites situated on a wooded knoll overlooking Lake Michigan. Progressing on foot, he discovered the source was a large halogen flashlight wired to a marble cross that marked the final resting spot of Janice Emerson Tremont. Of more immediate concern was the female form resting against an adjacent marble cross, which was the twin headstone marking the site where Brandon Tremont would someday be buried. The woman was dead, her arms extended outward from her torso. Each wrist had been lacerated and the grass beneath the two open wounds was damp and reddened. Lying next to her right hand was a bloodied utility knife.

277

Minutes later, Weddington was joined by a swarm of other officers and EMTs, and soon thereafter federal agents. The face of the lifeless body was drained of all color, but the young woman was no less recognizable to everyone present.

———◆———

Webb couldn't believe what he was hearing from C.J. Matthews on the other end of the phone call. He had come to expect the unexpected from the copycats, but this was madness.

"You're telling me that Blake O'Meara committed suicide on my father's gravesite? Why the hell would she do that?"

The special agent responded calmly, "I didn't say she committed suicide ... I said her death looks like a suicide. It's way too soon to draw any conclusions."

The related details were just as mind-boggling. A thick envelope was found in the pocket of Blake O'Meara's jacket. It contained a printed message and 200 hundred-dollar bills. The note simply read: "He no longer requires my services." But unlike previous envelopes, no instructions were given as to where or to whom the $20,000 should be directed.

To the side of her body was a cardboard box. Inside, sealed in plastic, was a laptop computer connected to a portable printer.

Okay, maybe Blake O'Meara no longer could handle the guilt and wanted out. But why on his father's grave? Why the twenty grand? And what might the cryptic note mean? *"He no longer requires my services."*

Or if she hadn't taken her own life, why would the remaining copycats go to all the trouble of making it look like she did? If this O'Meara gal had somehow ticked them off, why not just quietly get rid of her? The copycats certainly were capable of disposing of a body. But instead, a freaking spotlight had been used to draw attention. What kind of statement were they hoping to make?

In theory, Webb should have been encouraged that the number of copycats continued to dwindle. But a dead body on his parents' gravesite didn't bode well.

———◆———

By mid-afternoon on Sunday, Special Agent Matthews received confirmation of a theory posited by a member of her team. Forensics technicians had determined the computer and printer next to Blake O'Meara's body was the equipment that produced not only the note found in her pocket, but also the printed cards left at all the copycats' previous crime scenes. If the copycats no longer would be issuing their messages, perhaps they were throwing in the towel, and the crime spree was over.

But more likely the abandoned equipment was itself a message—that the copycats were done being copycats. From here on out they planned to commit crimes of their own, the first of which was the elimination of Blake O'Meara. The specifics surrounding her death didn't match up with a case from any of Webb Tremont's books or any of the thousands of cases on file with the FBI. And, as yet, no additional weekend crimes had been reported that could be attributed to the copycats. So, if they were intent on maintaining their weekly timetable, the demise of one of their own had constituted the most recent weekend's activity.

By dawn, the streets of downtown Lake Forest were crawling with media vehicles. At the behest of Washington, C.J. Matthews held a Sunday press briefing as dusk approached. She was bombarded with questions about the relationship between Blake O'Meara and Anthony Lafferty.

Over recent weeks, reporters from around the country had found their way to college acquaintances of O'Meara. It had become common knowledge that she once enjoyed a romantic fling with her Carnegie Mellon professor. Lafferty was reputed to have participated in numerous teacher-student entanglements, and this one had represented the final straw to a strained marriage.

Speculations were running rampant as to whether the two copycats still had been emotionally involved. Now it appeared almost certain they were, but for some reason their relationship had faltered. *"He no longer requires my services."*

The special agent only could acknowledge the possibilities. Similarly, she was in no position to offer an official opinion on whether Blake O'Meara took her own life or was murdered by former associates. However, Matthews was able to reveal that medical examiners had confirmed Miss O'Meara died exactly where the body was discovered—having bled to death from the lacerations on her wrists. Further, those lacerations had been made with the utility knife at her side. But as yet, no physical evidence had been uncovered to suggest a recent presence of other persons at the gravesite where she was found.

In the mid-afternoon on Monday, Matthews was once again in front of reporters, this time relating that the sole fingerprints on the utility knife had belonged to Blake O'Meara. Also, the depth and angle of the incision, as well as the position of the discarded knife, were consistent with suicide. But besides the blood of Miss O'Meara, two other miniscule traces were detected in the seams of the device's handle. The same utility knife appeared to have been used in the killing of Natalie Meriwether in Richmond and Noreen Shipley in East St. Louis.

The revelation about the blood traces had surprised the special agent—a reaction she kept to herself. Keeping an incriminating murder weapon in one's possession for such a prolonged period was inconsistent with the demonstrated proficiency of the copycats. Unless, of course, certain members of the group had been planning to implicate one of their own all along. In fact, the knife combined with the computer and printer were the first hard evidence that directly tied any of the six copycats to the past crimes—and that lone individual now was dead.

In the Monday briefing, C.J. Matthews also shared key points from the autopsy. Blake O'Meara had consumed an excessive amount of tequila combined with methylenedioxymethamphetamine, or Ecstasy. The same substances had been found in the system of Teresa Conkle a month earlier in Boston. Taken together, the alcohol and narcotic could accentuate emotional volatility and evoke suicidal thoughts among persons who were so inclined. But the same combination also might render an individual malleable or vulnerable to someone she trusted. For the time being, the cause of Blake O'Meara's death was to be categorized as uncertain.

"Do you think the guilt could have become too overwhelming for her?" one reporter asked.

Matthews handled the question matter-of-factly. "Perhaps, but if she indeed killed herself, the suicide note suggests her reasons may have related more to feelings of detachment from a male in her life."

This response prompted inquiries about the role Anthony Lafferty might have played. "You've heard the public opinion, I want to know if the FBI shares the view that Anthony Lafferty was the man who no longer required her services?" asked another reporter.

Then another piled on. "Do you believe these unspecified services related to their shared criminal activities, or was she intimating something of a more personal nature?"

C.J. Matthews had definite opinions, but her responsibility was to maintain the party line. "Without more facts, we'd only be speculating."

The questions about Lafferty became increasingly pointed—and more aligned with strong beliefs held by the FBI's lead investigator. The special agent simply smiled as reporters expressed what she couldn't.

"Though the copycats in general seem to have issues with the Tremonts, it does seem odd that Blake O'Meara would select Brandon Tremont's gravestone as the place to end her life. Doesn't the location of her body point more directly to Anthony Lafferty?" asked one.

Then from another, "Knowing the manner in which Brandon Tremont abruptly ended his affair with Lafferty's mother, aren't the parallels becoming rather apparent? Wasn't $20,000 the amount Diana Lafferty received after Mr. Tremont no longer required her services?"

And finally, "Isn't it just plain obvious that Anthony Lafferty killed Blake O'Meara?"

The entire population was reaching the same conclusion, but C.J. Matthews retained her game face. "I only can assure you that as the investigation moves forward, proper attention will be focused on Anthony Lafferty and Todd Swinford. We ask citizens in the Chicago area and across the country to keep an eye out for both men … and caution everyone that both are highly dangerous individuals."

⸺◈⸺

As the day wound down on Monday, Brandon Tremont received a call from C.J. Matthews asking if she could stop by to meet with him and his son. Showing such deference to his father was commendable, but Webb recognized that even a fast-rising federal agent needed to be careful when dealing with a powerfully connected billionaire.

Special Agent Matthews and Walt Briggs arrived precisely at 6:00 p.m. As soon as Webb saw that she'd brought reinforcements, he feared his father might be in for another bumpy ride.

They moved from the entry hall to Brandon Tremont's personal library. Once the four had taken their seats amidst the walls lined with valuable rare books, Agent Briggs pulled two 8x10 manila envelopes from his briefcase and placed them before Webb and his father.

As the senior investigator, Miss Matthews kicked things off. "Our computer forensics group has analyzed the laptop computer found next to the body of Blake O'Meara. The principal files and memory of that computer were effectively erased … and whoever performed the task knew what they were doing. None of the former contents can be reconstructed. But after the hard drive was cleared, three small files were uploaded shortly before the estimated time of Miss O'Meara's death. And what you have before you in the envelopes is the content of those files."

Webb stared at the two manila rectangles on the coffee table as though they were cursed. Walt Briggs spoke up, "Gentlemen, if you'll be kind enough to open the envelopes, we'd like to know if you recognize any of the women shown in the enclosed photos?"

Practically in unison, Webb and his father picked up the envelopes, unclipped the flaps, and slid out the contents. There were three photographs that showed individual females from the shoulders up. Webb estimated the ages of each to be late sixties or early seventies. The three grainy close-ups appeared to be enlarged sections from pictures taken at a distance. Printed along the bottom border on each photo was a typed name and city.

Elsa Greene—Austin, Texas.

Maxine Willis—Savannah, Georgia.

Suzanne Henderson—Winnetka, Illinois.

Webb studied the photographs several times before responding, "I don't recognize any of these women and can't say that I've ever heard their names. I'm sorry, I wish I could be more helpful. Who are they?"

The two federal agents looked toward Brandon Tremont, waiting to hear from him before addressing Webb's question. The elder Tremont didn't look up. He slowly shuffled from picture to picture, his eyes moving from face to face and name to name, almost trance-like.

After more than a minute, the special agent addressed his father. "Mr. Tremont, can you help us?"

Again the room went silent, as the two agents and Webb stared at the elder Tremont—unsure whether he'd heard a word directed his way.

Finally Agent Briggs spoke up. "Mr. Tremont, these women appear to hold some sort of relevance for you. We need your assistance, sir."

More silence.

Webb thought he should give it a try, "Dad, please ... what can you tell us? Who are they?"

The sound of his son's voice prompted Brandon Tremont to look up, first directly at Webb, and finally toward the two agents. The shakiness in his voice reflected bewilderment. "How could they ... how could they have come up with these names ... and their pictures? It isn't possible."

The three waited through more silence before Brandon Tremont again looked up at his son. Sheepishly. Apologetically. "Webb, I told you I wasn't a faithful husband to your mother during the early years of our marriage. When these three women were much younger, I had sexual relations with each of them." He paused, before continuing in a tone of utter despondence, "To comprehend the thoroughness ... the tenacity with which someone has delved into my past, you have to trust that these are the only three women with whom I ever strayed ... that is, besides Diana Lafferty. This is incomprehensible. After so many years, I couldn't even have told you the last name of one of these ladies … Elsa Greene, in Texas. We met at a cocktail party and spent a few hours together after too much drink … that was all. My God, the effort … the digging ….” His voice trailed off as his attention shifted back to the photographs on his lap.

The room went quiet once more as the two agents and Webb worked through the same thought processes that Brandon Tremont had. They contemplated the persistence and resolve required to trace the totality of another man's adult life and uncover his most private indiscretions with 100% accuracy. For weeks, hundreds of eager journalists had been dissecting Brandon Tremont's past, yet none of these extramarital relationships had surfaced.

Webb's mind raced down a path toward one individual, and he finally let loose. “What a sick son of a bitch! Think of the weeks, the months, even the years that Anthony Lafferty must have invested to isolate the various time spans of your life … the places you traveled, the people you met. How many trips must he have made … how many people must he have contacted to identify these three specific women? Dad, how many of your friends or acquaintances were aware of your sleeping around … how many of them might have taken a stranger like Anthony Lafferty into their confidence?”

Brandon Tremont was still shaking his head in disbelief. He tried to answer but didn't get very far. “Looking back … I admit to not being especially careful about my indiscretions … but for him to ferret out … he would have needed ….” He trailed off again, unable to complete his thought.

Agent Matthews interceded, a bit more delicately. “Mr. Tremont, you said these were the only women with whom you were intimate during your marriage. I must ask, have there been others since your wife passed away? Others that Anthony Lafferty might have learned about?”

“No.” At first, he seemed content to let his terse response suffice, but then realized additional explanation was owed—not necessarily to the two FBI agents, but to his son. “Webster, the woman from Winnetka … Suzanne Henderson. She was among your mother's closest friends … at least, until I destroyed their friendship in the late Seventies. We allowed ourselves to become reckless with our rendezvous-ing and word got around. Eventually your mother confronted me … deeply hurt on multiple levels. For several years, we sought counseling through the pastor at our church, and I was fortunate that Janice was able to move forward. Whether or not she ever fully forgave me, I can't answer … and either way, I wasn't seeking or de-serving of absolution. But I vowed to your mother that there would never be another woman. My commitment to her didn't end with her death."

To keep the discussion from becoming mired in emotions, Agent Briggs pro-ceeded along a different line. "Mr. Tremont, how about these three particular wom-en … did you maintain contact with any of them after your romantic interludes had run their course?"

Brandon Tremont quickly retorted, "I certainly did not." Then he recognized he was in no position to stake the moral high ground. "As my son can attest from recent conversations regarding Diana Lafferty, I wasn't prone to allowing my off-hours entanglements to linger. No, once my selfish purposes had been served by these women, I moved on with minimal consideration for them or their situations." His embarrassment, his self-disgust were obvious.

Briggs dispensed with any personal judgments and plied onward. "The three pictures were taken outdoors, quite possibly without any of the subjects' knowl-edge. In fact, the three women may be completely unaware that anyone has discov-ered their previous relationships with you. Two are married, the third is a widow. We have agents in each city prepared to call on Ms. Greene, Ms. Willis, and Ms. Henderson. Before any of those meetings take place, we'll want to share what we've learned from you with those agents. Obviously, the conversations may prove rather awkward, but we need to determine whether any of these three women met with or remember seeing any of the copycats … or perhaps have been contacted by an outside party working on their behalf."

Brandon Tremont nodded. "I understand. I only hope it won't become necessary to embarrass them with their husbands and families. Or worse yet, go public."

C.J. Matthews intervened rather sharply. "Rest assured, Mr. Tremont, we don't plan to release the details of these computer files. Anthony Lafferty obviously wants to continue tarnishing your reputation, and we'd rather keep him off-guard by not playing into his hands."

"Forgive me, Agent Matthews; I didn't mean to suggest I was concerned about my reputation. I only was thinking about the disruption these three ladies might be forced to endure. As for me, I'm prepared to accept whatever additional tarnish that comes my way. None of it is undeserved."

Her response was much softer this time. "We appreciate that, Mr. Tremont. I imagine Mr. Lafferty already has derived a great deal of satisfaction out of seeing your name and your family's name besmirched. I can't think of another reason why these three pictures would have been placed on Blake O'Meara's computer other than to see your name dragged deeper through the mud."

"So what possibly could be next?" asked Webb.

The question was meant to be rhetorical, but Walter Briggs was cut from FBI cloth—which meant all questions were taken literally. "First off, if we assume Miss O'Meara's death was no suicide, then we have to anticipate Anthony Lafferty is moving closer to whatever end game he has in mind … either with or without Todd Swinford. Based on where her body was found, he would seem to be even more focused on bringing harm to your father, you, and possibly others around you."

C.J. Matthews tagged on. "In fact, with the O'Meara murder, Lafferty and Swinford seem to be telegraphing that they're no longer interested in parodies or twisted spoofs. In essence, Saturday's murder was a declaration that they're moving on to crimes of their own making … and as we now know, they're capable of anything."

The four talked for several more minutes before wrapping up. Mostly they just thought out loud as a group—alarmed by the clearer picture of Anthony Lafferty that was taking shape.

Brandon Tremont escorted the agents to the front door. Webb waited in the library, pondering how one would go about dissecting a half-century of another man's life with such precision. Anthony Lafferty was a psychopath of unusual resourcefulness and financial means. The combination was frightening. One without the other wouldn't have allowed Lafferty to put such a complicated plan into action. How long had he plotted, biding time until he'd accumulated the necessary funds?

Webb glanced around his father's library, knowing everything in view epitomized the old-line wealth abhorred by Anthony Lafferty and others like him. Brandon Tremont never had declared that this room should be treated as his own private sanctuary. He hadn't needed to. Webb's mother, Nessie, and anyone living or working inside the family estate, instinctively referred to this hallowed chamber as "your father's library." Every square inch exuded affluence—from the polished brass hardware on the doors and windows to the perfectly mitered joints in the crown molding. The chair on which Webb was perched, along with two others that matched, plus a small sofa and dark cherry coffee table, were all classic Queen Anne pieces. Webb wouldn't have been surprised to learn they'd actually belonged to the original Queen Anne.

One whole wall consisted of leaded-glass windows and plush English draperies. The other three walls were fronted with dark walnut bookcases climbing fourteen feet from floor to ceiling. But not just any ceiling. Two hand-hewn walnut beams bisected the overhead expanse from either direction and crossed at the room's exact center point to form equal quadrants—each with inlays crafted from a different exotic wood. Ebony from India, teak from Burma, rosewood from Africa, and a rare mahogany from South America. The large panels featured ornate carvings done by native artisans in the countries from which they'd been commissioned. The end result was emblematic—three thousand editions of civilization's most acclaimed literary works housed beneath a ceiling constructed from the four corners of the world.

The fine leather-bound volumes on the shelves mostly dated back to the eighteenth and nineteenth centuries. Tastefully situated among the expensive books were small animal figures, which Brandon Tremont had collected during his travels. But not just any animals. Webb's father had a penchant for two particular earthly beings—camels and turtles. Wherever he might journey, if he saw an interesting camel or turtle crafted of crystal, ivory, jade, precious metals, or gems, he purchased it for his private menagerie. He claimed to have been drawn to this pair of odd creatures by what they symbolized in many foreign cultures. The camel embodied strength, survival, endurance, and self-sufficiency. The turtle epitomized tenacity and longevity. Brandon Tremont had wanted to surround himself with reminders of what he believed to be worthy attributes. But Webb and his siblings secretly had maintained their father related more closely to another shared characteristic. Their perceived lack of emotion.

The pegged hardwood floor in the room was covered with an enormous Tabriz rug from Northern Persia. The assorted lamps and an ornate dictionary stand were likewise limited editions, now valued at extraordinary sums. Two French Impressionist oil paintings rested on a pair of hand-carved easels stationed along the innermost wall, shielded from the sunlight.

Nothing much had changed in the library during Webb's lifetime. The same was true for most of the rooms inside Brandon Tremont's domain. Preserving the ageless elegance of the privileged class was an inbred sixth sense. Both of Webb's parents possessed it—as did his sister. But this gene, like plenty of others, had skipped right past Webb. Without Corrie, his coach house still would have looked like a bunkhouse.

There was a light rap on the door frame. "Son, shall we talk for a few minutes?"

Only Brandon Tremont would be so formal as to knock before entering his own library, the same room he'd exited just minutes before.

Webb couldn't resist. "Good thing you knocked, Dad. I wouldn't have wanted you to catch me in a compromised state with one of your racy volumes of Balzac or D.H. Lawrence. Believe me, I remember exactly where to find them from my teen years."

As usual, Brandon Tremont ignored the sophomoric sidebar, "About the three women, Webster—"

He clearly felt he owed his son further explanation, and likely anticipated a verbal assault similar to the one received in his study after the revelations about his affair with Diana Lafferty. But Webb's mindset had changed. The past was in the past, and he was happy to leave it there. He cut his father off. "Nah, Dad, we're good. Let's go find Corrie and Sprig. I think it's time we grabbed some chow."

Webb knew the past hour, not to mention the past several weeks, had been painful for Brandon Tremont. But in that instant, his father dropped the protective mask of stoicism and smiled a genuine smile. But only briefly, before regaining his normal demeanor. "You may 'grab some chow' if you wish, Webster. Personally, I'm looking forward to a proper dinner with two delightful young ladies."

Chapter Thirty-Seven

In the days following Blake O'Meara's death, Webb watched and listened as the national conversation about the copycats seemed to be reduced to one individual—Anthony Lafferty. At first, few dared to utter the question on everyone's minds, but by Wednesday the guardedness was gone. "Will this be the weekend Anthony Lafferty finally brings harm to Brandan Tremont?" It was a foregone conclusion that the billionaire's demise was the intended end game. What concerns existed about the most recent act of murder were overshadowed by curiosity over how this Svengali might accomplish his goal, since the media had reported at length on the tight security at Tremont Estate.

With previous copycat efforts, Lafferty and his cronies had enjoyed the element of surprise, the advantage of choosing their victims and locations at random. Going after one man in a known, heavily secured setting was something else entirely. Carrying out this final crime would prove or disprove how much of a genius Anthony Lafferty truly might be. The public wasn't necessarily rooting for this acknowledged criminal mastermind—or at least Webb hoped that to be the case. For the most part, Lafferty was viewed as vile and despicable. But for some, the prurient fascination of following his every move addressed a primeval urge buried inside the human psyche.

To say that Thursday morning changed everything would be an outlandish understatement. Shortly after 11 a.m., Webb's phone rang. Even in the midst of serial murders and fears over his family, a call from C.J. Matthews was still a welcome event.

"I hope you're sitting down, Mr. Tremont."

He hadn't been, but moments later he fell into a chair.

Almost two hours earlier, at 10:06 Eastern Standard Time on the third day of March in the year 2016, Anthony Lafferty had strolled into a Boston police station and turned himself in. This crazed man who seemed determined to bring serious harm to Webb, his father, and everyone close to them had been taken into custody. The arrest required no S.W.A.T. teams, high-powered weapons, or acts of heroism. On his own initiative, Anthony Lafferty asked to see the senior duty officer and promptly identified himself as one of the famed Cop Show Copycats.

Webb should have been elated. Dance-in-the-street jubilant. At a minimum, he should have been numb or confused. But he was none of the above. Instead, internal warning signals were sounding off at full blast. He was skeptical as hell. He hadn't seen Anthony Lafferty in twenty-three years, and he'd barely known him then. But during the twenty-seven days since his fateful phone call from Theo Kleyser, Lafferty had taken permanent residence inside Webb's head. This lunatic genius wouldn't have surrendered himself to police without some deep, dark ulterior motive. Going to the authorities had to be part of Lafferty's devious master plan, a wildly unexpected act that somehow would unleash pestilence, famine, or plagues upon all of humankind.

C.J. Matthews already was heading to the airport when she'd called Webb. In casual discussions with the Boston police, Lafferty had offered up a few surprising details regarding his whereabouts over recent months. But he'd quickly been handed over to the FBI and the official interrogation would get underway as soon as the special agent arrived.

Anthony Lafferty claimed to have an ironclad alibi, asserting that he'd been holed up inside a cabin on a remote corner of Cape Cod during the entire period his fellow copycats were committing multiple murders. He had retreated there weeks earlier, when he realized where his former associates were heading with their destructive plans, fearful of what they might have planned for him.

His story couldn't possibly be true. Webb had convinced himself that Anthony

Lafferty was the root of all evil. The mental images had been vivid—the ones of Lafferty committing senseless murders in Richmond and on Long Island. In East St. Louis and in Cedar Rapids. Faking the suicides of Teresa Conkle and Blake O'Meara. Smashing antiques in New Hampshire. Throwing logs through windows in Lake Forest. Loading photos of his father's former lovers onto a laptop. Webb had felt Lafferty's presence in every sinister deed. He'd sensed him lurking in close proximity to Tremont Estate. Now suddenly the guy walked into a police station and Webb was supposed to believe this psychopath was in Cape Cod the whole time, that he had hightailed it away from the rest of his smarmy little group out of concerns for his own personal safety. The whole idea was preposterous.

Webb feared the worst, a new and bigger nightmare. Lafferty had concocted some plausible alibi and was planning to outsmart the totality of US law enforcement. The possibilities were mind-numbing.

The next day, Webb Tremont was invited to Boston to take part in the interrogation of Anthony Lafferty. Lafferty had been fully cooperative during the first two sessions on Thursday afternoon and Friday morning. With an accomplished attorney at his side, he calmly had answered each and every question in thorough detail. Regardless of the subject matter or manner in which questions were posed, Lafferty maintained his composure and provided responses that were utterly convincing. At least on the surface. His impeccable explanations served only to convince the panel of veteran interviewers that this suspected serial felon was a world-class liar. Special Agent Matthews wondered if the presence of Webb Tremont might elevate Lafferty's body temperature a few degrees and melt his cool exterior.

Webb wished she had been right. When he was escorted into the interrogation room late in the afternoon on Friday, Lafferty's attorney objected to the presence of an outsider in an unofficial capacity. The federal attorneys caucused a few minutes before coming down on the side of caution. They agreed that Webb Tremont should be restricted to the designated observation area. It had been a well-orchestrated exercise to let Lafferty know his nemesis would be watching from the other side of a one-way mirror. Unfortunately, Webb's being there didn't bother Lafferty in the least. If anything, he seemed to enjoy the additional audience, so halfway through the following day Webb was dismissed.

Webb hadn't anticipated what it would be like to see Anthony Lafferty in person. The experience had been disturbingly eerie. Physically, Lafferty looked much the way Webb remembered him, allowing for a couple decades of wear and tear. His hair was brown and curly, with thin gray arches taking shape around his ears. During the two interrogation sessions he observed, not a single one of those hairs slipped out of place. Not the smallest bead of sweat formed on his olive-toned skin.

His eyes were brown, almost black. Twenty years earlier they constantly had darted in every direction from behind their narrow slits. Eye contact had been rare. The uncertainty and awkwardness of a younger Anthony Lafferty had been evident. Now those same eyes were steely and focused.

His eyebrows were neatly trimmed. Slight wrinkles were forming around his eyes and a faint crease was weaving across his uppermost forehead. His dark, thick beard was closely shaven. According to the arrest sheet, his height was five feet eleven inches. He wasn't overweight, but his body looked soft, like it rarely was used—as though physical exercise and mental genius were mutually exclusive.

Arriving home after midnight on Saturday, Webb was in desperate need of cheering up. At that hour, he was surprised to run into a familiar face amidst the rambling acreage of Tremont Estate. Of all people, Corrie was standing inside the upstairs entrance to his coach house. There were definite advantages to having one's girlfriend living inside the ivied walls. She was holding two glasses of eighteen-year-old Macallan, clad only in a dress shirt from the back of Webb's closet. His instincts had been good. Months before he'd almost thrown out the tattered old garment but decided it still might come in handy. By the time Webb walked Corrie back to the main house several hours later, he wanted to erect a shrine to the faded white shirt and dedicate sonnets to every missing button. A night with Corrie was exactly what he'd needed.

———◆———

Once C.J. Matthews arrived in Boston, she'd met with two senior federal attorneys assigned to the Lafferty case. They agreed the first order of business was to assure that this alleged copycat remained in custody. For one thing, the public needed to be protected from a man believed highly dangerous. But secondly, the feds wanted to continue questioning him over a prolonged period until he tripped over some random detail. Regardless of IQ, any guilty party eventually screwed up if given enough opportunities, and Lafferty's story was an especially thin tightrope to walk.

Holding him had proven easier than anticipated. Formal charges were brought forward at a special arraignment hearing. The list of charges was lengthy because of the numerous crimes committed by the copycats during their early months, before the murders began. These lesser crimes weren't the ones for which the attorneys ultimately hoped to indict and prosecute Anthony Lafferty, but they hopefully would be adequate for justifying an arrest and remand.

Special Agent Matthews observed the proceedings as the unforeseen situation continued to take unexpected turns. None of the accusations were even contested when Lafferty declined to enter a plea. His lawyer likewise made no bail request, asserting that his client preferred incarceration in order to remain safe from the retribution of his former colleagues.

The feds outwardly toiled to stretch the interrogation over as many days as possible. In truth, there were only a finite number of questions that could be asked, so Lafferty was forced to confront many of the same ones over and over in different forms. Any time his attorney began to protest, Lafferty waved him off. He was content to indulge them their fun and games. C.J. Matthews and the others kept waiting for the first inconsistency, figuring fatigue eventually would set in. But from her vantage, only the teams of attorneys who grilled him were exhibiting any weariness. From beginning to end, Anthony Lafferty looked like a million bucks. Or more accurately, tens of millions.

Never leaving the side of Anthony Lafferty was Elliott Fingerman, his defense attorney. Fingerman had joined his client at the police station just moments after he'd surrendered himself. In selecting his lawyer, it was as if Lafferty had placed a call to central casting. If Elliot Fingerman hadn't been an actual attorney, C.J. Matthews was convinced he could have made a fortune portraying one in Hollywood.

His large head was completely shaven and rested on an abbreviated neck, giving him the appearance of a bulldog. His torso could best be described as rotund. He was uniformed in custom-made worsted wool suits. He had an odd habit of shoving his wire-rimmed glasses to the top his shiny head, and then allowing them to slowly slide down to the bridge of his nose. Fingerman's age was anybody's guess. Fifty, possibly eighty? There was no way to tell, but newspapers suggested he was somewhere around sixty-seven. Especially notable was the man's British accent. Not just any British accent. No, Elliott Fingerman's was elegant and finely polished, somewhere between Sir Laurence Olivier and the queen herself. Ordinary sentences sounded like Shakespearian verse when they floated off his tongue in a voice that surely had soothed and assuaged hundreds, if not thousands, of jurors.

One of the federal attorneys asked Lafferty about his selection of legal representation. Anthony Lafferty explained that he previously had not had occasion to employ a criminal attorney, but he remembered Mr. Fingerman's name from the media's coverage of several high-profile trials in the Boston area. Remarkably, he retained this highly-sought barrister just ninety minutes before he dropped into the police station. Lafferty managed to get through to him on his very first call to the law firm. C.J. Matthews could imagine how that went. *Mr. Fingerman, there's a gentleman on line three who claims to be one of the Cop Show Copycats.* Calendars quickly would clear for what was sure to be one of the most closely monitored court cases in US legal history.

Details were revealed in dribs and drabs as Lafferty and his attorney fielded the unending questions; eventually his complete story took shape. She had to admit it was masterful. If his story was to be believed, it would vindicate Anthony Lafferty of everything outside of his admitted role in what began as a series of elaborate and harmless hoaxes. His most heartfelt confession was when he declared that he had been taken in by his former business partners, that he had failed to understand their true character and not foreseen the depravity in their plans.

According to Lafferty, the whole copycat thing had started as nothing more than an intellectual exercise. Disdain for an over-hyped TV show had prompted a

295

succession of hypothetical conversations. None of the group seemed serious, or so he'd thought. But then their collective ambitions kicked in. Out of sheer boredom, real plans took shape. "After selling the software company, we hadn't kept ourselves adequately stimulated, which was sure to be a problem when six overdeveloped brains were spending a great deal of time together." No one was to be harmed, and in fact, many folks would be monetarily rewarded for whatever inconveniences they might endure. Important messages were to be delivered, with the group of fertile minds having every intention of capturing the nation's attention. By the time they were finished, the six was to have left an indelible mark on contemporary culture by pulling off what never had been attempted, let alone accomplished. Not just one perfect crime, but an elaborate series of them. But not real crimes, mock versions. More intricate, more ingenious than any real ones ever perpetrated. Sure, laws would be broken, but that didn't matter, because their identities were to remain a mystery. They never would be identified. Of that eventuality, they'd been certain.

Weekend after weekend, they'd executed their pretend crimes flawlessly. The money, the messages, the media coverage. Everything according to plan.

Lafferty was asked if things had gone wrong in Ohio. Had Jorge Cabral, the missing janitor, walked in on them? "No," claimed Lafferty. "As a matter of fact, I personally was assigned that church in Dublin ... along with Blake O'Meara. We didn't see a janitor or anyone else inside the building on that particular Saturday evening." Upon hearing the media reports of Cabrera's disappearance in the after-math of their Ohio visit, he and the other copycats assumed the man had fled the area due to his fears over deportation. After six weeks on Cape Cod with no access to media, Lafferty had been surprised to learn the janitor's whereabouts were still unknown, or that the copycats had claimed responsibility for his death. Seeking credit for a murder they hadn't committed was further corroboration of how irrational the others had become, and why he was content to remain in custody.

According to Lafferty, everything changed in New Hampshire, when the copycats paid their visit to the farm occupied by Brandon Tremont's sister and her husband. "The plan was to assemble the family's idiotic artifacts from around the property, and attract public attention to how out of touch the whole Tremont family really was ... plus leave some money for inner city kids, so they'd have access to legitimate athletic equipment. At least, I thought that was the plan. But out of nowhere, Todd Swinford and Gregory Beaumont showed up with sledgehammers and started whaling away at all the items we'd gathered. Teresa, Michael, and Blake simply watched in amusement. As much as I might have wanted to join in, I knew at that moment we were crossing an irreversible line. The group was committing a real felony with real consequences. I managed to stop Swinford and Beaumont ... but not before too much damage already was done ... most of the antiques had been destroyed."

He maintained that by the time they returned to Boston, he'd decided to part company with the group. "I explained to the others that I no longer could condone what they were doing, but gave them my word that I wouldn't go to the authorities. They promised the events of New Hampshire had been a one-time mistake ... that they'd gotten carried away with their abhorrence of the Tremonts. They pleaded with me to reconsider ... and Michael Chen suggested I take a week or two to think it over. I reluctantly agreed.

"So, I didn't join them for the next weekend, when the five of them went off to Delaware and restaged that crime scene on the porch of Jacob Townsend, another Tremont lowlife. Things seemed to be returning to normal, but I remained skeptical, so Michael agreed I should skip the next weekend as well, when they traveled to Richmond."

At this point during the interrogation, Anthony Lafferty paused and asked for a bottle of water. He continued, "I guess we all know what happened in that store outside of Richmond. I heard the news reports while my five former partners presumably were making their way back to Boston. I realized how insane the situation had become. These five individuals had been my closest friends, or so I believed. I was repulsed by the details of that poor woman's death, but at the same time fearful of what they might have planned for me upon their return. By suggesting I sit those weekends out, they'd been toying with me ... playing a sick game. They knew

297

exactly what they were going to do in Richmond, and that I never would have agreed to any part of it. That's why they'd busted up all those antiques in New Hampshire in the first place ... to scare me into taking a few weekends off. And then after Richmond, because of what we'd done together over the previous months, they figured I'd feel trapped, that I would be forced to go along with them ... or if not, they could address my circumstance in a different manner. And at this point, I knew they weren't averse to taking lives."

Special Agent Matthews tried to put herself into the mindset of a potential juror. Facing the aforementioned complexities, it seemed like a normal person would make a beeline to the police. But there was nothing normal about Lafferty or any of the copycats. After weighing his options, a certifiable genius apparently settled on an alternate approach. He decided that vanishing was the best way to guarantee his personal safety.

The details regarding his hideaway meshed perfectly with his improbable alibi. Lafferty's three-room cabin had no televisions, no radios, and no computers. The property was intentionally isolated from outside intrusion. He'd quietly purchased the place three years earlier for the sole purpose of escaping the distractions of the real world whenever he needed to free his mind.

As his former associates were driving from Richmond to Boston, he threw some clothes into a suitcase, jumped into his old Jeep, and headed straight to Truro, on the furthest outreach of Cape Cod. None of his partners were even aware of the cabin—including Blake O'Meara, whom he admitted to dating from time to time when asked by his interrogators.

The cabin stood by itself at the end of a dirt road rarely traveled by anyone—especially during the winter months. He claimed that over the course of his six-week stay there, he'd made occasional trips into Truro for provisions, but otherwise remained securely inside, reading and painting. Lafferty kept a sizable collection of books in the cabin and liked doing abstract paintings to relieve stress.

When he went into town to shop, he would hurry through a limited number of local stores, purchase what he needed, and exit quickly, trying not to be noticed.

On his most recent trip into Truro, during the late afternoon on Wednesday, he'd seen the front page of a newspaper near the check-out counter at the local grocery store. On it was a picture of Blake O'Meara and a headline indicating she was dead. He purchased the paper and raced back to his cabin. That was when he learned the group's six identities had been revealed weeks earlier, and a whole series of innocent people had been killed since his separation. Plus, two of his former associates apparently had taken their own lives and two others were missing. Worse yet, authorities and the public believed him to be the party most responsible for these random killings. "I immediately recognized I had no choice but to turn myself in."

On his drive to Boston the next morning, he'd stopped at a pay phone and called Elliot Fingerman. Lafferty claimed his cellphone had gone dead soon after his arrival on the Cape. In his haste to get out of Boston, he'd forgotten to grab his recharger cord—which he said was immaterial. "While in hiding, I would have removed the phone's battery anyway. My former associates are technically resourceful. I wasn't about to activate a digital device that could be traced through any number of methods."

Only since his surrender to police had Lafferty understood the scope of the crimes committed by the other copycats after their weekend in Richmond. "Obviously, there was much to catch up on. Mr. Fingerman's staff has provided me stacks of clippings and I've been granted supervised internet access for ninety minutes each evening. The accounts I've been reading are horrifying …to think these deplorable acts stemmed from something that started out as a sheer lark among friends. It's all so inconceivable."

Day after day, C.J. Matthews watched in amazement. The assorted pieces of Lafferty's story entwined perfectly with the timeline of copycat activities. If his outlandish version was to be believed by a jury of peers, his only involvement with a serious felony had been the destruction of property at Tremont Farms—and even then, he asserted that he was an unknowing accomplice who stepped in to stop the others. But the very notion of a jury of peers was out of the question. Anthony Lafferty was unlike any person to ever serve on a jury.

She didn't believe a single word. He pushed lying to levels previously unattained. While weaving his absurd tale, he exhibited all the right emotions in all the right places. But the sincerity was too sincere. The disappointments were too disappointing. The shocks were too shocking. The conveniences were too convenient. And he knew it. Anthony Lafferty was posturing. Showing off, just as he and his merry band had been doing for seventeen consecutive weekends. Constructing such an intricate alibi had required planning and preparation that was beyond comprehension, and now he was taunting the FBI to try and prove him wrong. When he'd walked into that Boston police station, the fun for him was just beginning.

The special agent was painfully aware that her massive investigation had yet to turn up any hard evidence that could debunk a single premise in his ridiculously contrived proposition. Anthony Lafferty reeked of confidence, knowing the FBI had nothing. But in his arrogance, he seemed to have forgotten one loose end. Michael Chen.

Chapter Thirty-Eight

As Special Agent C.J. Matthews sat through the days of interrogation in Boston, she issued endless requests for government personnel to dig into every piece of nonsense that oozed out of Anthony Lafferty's mouth.

Forensic accounting teams were able to determine that his Truro cabin and the surrounding eight acres were owned by an LLC with the innocuous name of MIDI. The purchase had been made in January, 2014—at a price of $691,450. The LLC had been formed seven months earlier, through a Grand Cayman law firm. All the shares were owned by A. Lafferty. At the LLC's inception, he deposited fifty thousand dollars into his new entity. Substantially more was added a week before the cabin's purchase. Nothing in the legal filings indicated what MIDI meant, so the question was posed directly to Lafferty by one of the federal attorneys. He clearly had been waiting twenty-seven months for the right person to ask. The smugness was palpable as he delivered his succinct response. "It's an acronym that stands for Money I Didn't Inherit." No further explanation was necessary.

The LLC currently held no additional properties or investments, but records revealed a cash balance of several hundred thousand dollars still sitting in a Cayman bank account. Where Lafferty had stashed the balance of his wealth remained a mystery. When probed during the interrogations, Lafferty's attorney interjected, "My client has no obligation to divulge how he spends or invests his available funds. He can bury it in a tin can in his backyard if he so wishes. The IRS should be able to confirm that Mr. Lafferty paid all applicable taxes when he and his partners sold their company, and that for every year thereafter he has filed tax returns accordingly."

The timing of the LLC and the cabin purchase made perfect sense to anyone involved in the investigation. The copycats' business had been sold in January of 2014, so Lafferty would have had plenty of available funds from which to transfer over a million dollars to the Caymans. The more telling aspect to his intentions had been when the LLC actually was formed—during the summer of 2013, months before he and the others would sell their company. But by then the partners already were shopping S.A.F.E. to the highest bidders. A big payday was imminent, so Lafferty started making the necessary preparations. Plans he'd probably been formulating for years could soon come to fruition, since the only thing he might have been lacking were the resources to put his wheels in motion.

C.J. Matthews read report after report as they were emailed to her. Unfortunately, her contempt for Anthony Lafferty was matched only by his brilliance.

Lafferty apparently had a special knack for timing. The sequence of events over the week leading up to his surrender to police on Thursday was unusually convenient.

He just happened to drive into Truro for supplies on the Wednesday after Blake O'Meara's body was found in a Lake Forest cemetery. Only then did he discover that he was the most-wanted man in the United States and realize he needed to turn himself in. O'Meara's death occurred in the early morning hours of Sunday. He easily could have driven the thousand miles from Lake Forest to Cape Cod in that amount of time.

FBI teams were able to confirm that a man fitting Lafferty's description had been seen on the streets of Truro during the late afternoon hours of Wednesday. In fact, reports from the field agents who interviewed Truro locals suggested Lafferty had gone out of his way to be noticed while he was in town shopping. And not just on the Wednesday in question.

Lafferty owned a 1965 Jeep Wagoneer, one of those oversized classics with wood side panels. His just happened to be bright blue, in near mint condition. That type of vehicle was sure to stand out in a small town along the Eastern Seaboard. So of course he'd been spotted when he pulled up to the local grocery store. The drugstore, too.

A few of the locals definitely had observed him and his vehicle on other occasions during the recent winter.

"Sure, I remember him being around here once or twice."

"Nice enough fella, but never said much."

"You know, I never made the connection to all those pictures of the copycats on TV. I guess I can see the resemblance, but that's not exactly the way he looked when I saw him. But I sure remember that Jeep of his."

The agents inquired as to whether any of the townspeople could attach a specific date or day of the week to any of Lafferty's prior trips into Truro.

"Can't say that I can."

"You know, after a while the days all sorta run together."

None of the local retailers could recollect what Lafferty might have purchased, but they willingly agreed to allow agents to go through their credit card receipts for as far back as they wanted. Nothing with Anthony Lafferty's name was found, which meant he had paid cash for anything he might have purchased.

One of the FBI teams finally interviewed a young man who could offer a few explicit details about Lafferty's first trip into town, at the onset of his alleged six-week stay on the Cape. Jamie Geist was a nineteen-year-old grocery store clerk. When shown a photograph, he remembered that Lafferty had gone through his check-out line.

"It was a ways back. He wasn't as clean-shaven as he is in that picture … he was letting his beard grow, I guess. And he was wearing a hat … one of those floppy fishing deals. But I'd have to say it was him, okay. He bought all kinds of food and supplies, and wanted me to pack everything into boxes. His bill was over $800, and he paid it with cash. Biggest wad of hundreds I've ever seen. We don't get a lot of those. He even handed me one of 'em just for loading the boxes into the back of his car … one of those old Jeeps. Sweet. Biggest tip I ever got."

The next step proved easy—finding the cash receipt. Eight hundred-dollar bills were a rarity at the Truro grocery store. It was dated January 12, a Monday, at 3:24 in the afternoon—two days after Natalie Meriwether's throat was slashed in Richmond. The day after Lafferty claimed to have fled Boston and driven to his secluded cabin. According to his version of events, he was going into hiding for an unspecified period, until he figured out what to do about his former associates. So, of course, he would have needed to load up with provisions.

The optics were perfectly ambiguous. His classic old Jeep was sure to be noticed. He was flashing a wad of hundred-dollar bills. He spent $800 at a store where most customers got change back from a twenty. He tipped the clerk a C-note. Anthony Lafferty did everything possible to assure that his first trip into Truro had registered with the locals.

As things stood with the investigation, specific dates could be assigned to Lafferty's first and last trips into Truro, the ones that bookended the period of his supposed hiding. During the six weeks between, his car and someone resembling Lafferty had been observed in town at least two more times—yet no one could stipulate a date for those visits. If someone were able to confirm that just one such occasion had fallen on a Friday night or Saturday, it would mean Lafferty couldn't have been in some other city committing a crime with the copycats. A single cor-roborated weekend sighting would confer at least a hint of veracity to Lafferty's preposterous tale. But none of the locals could offer anything specific.

The ambiguity served up another possibility that seemed far more plausible to C.J. Matthews and her FBI cohorts. Anthony Lafferty could have traveled the country on weekends, scoring headlines with his friends, and still found time to make a few random trips out to the Cape during the weeks between. Not long stays, just enough time to tend to a few details in his cabin and pop into Truro so that he could be observed by folks on the streets.

Most of Cape Cod slowed to a near halt during wintertime. Lafferty's cabin was located at the end of a long, rarely traveled dirt road. Truro Police didn't even bother to drive all the way back most of the time.

The officer who handled the occasional patrol duties remembered a paneled blue Jeep being parked on the east side of the cabin throughout the most recent month or two. The vehicle sometimes was covered with enough snow to suggest it hadn't been driven in weeks. The officer hadn't personally observed Lafferty or anyone else around the property, "but it sure looked like someone was living in there. Lights were on ... smoke was billowing out of the chimney. We don't have a name for who owns the place ... just some company or something. I figured whoever was inside was the real owner or one of his friends. There was no reason to slop through the mud and bother people ... everything looked fine. Out here we're used to people wantin' their privacy."

The facts again seemed to line up in Lafferty's favor, but once more, an alternative scenario seemed more likely. Lafferty purposely had left his very identifiable Jeep where it could be seen for the duration of the period he claimed to be in hiding inside the cabin. He could have used a second vehicle to shuttle out to the Cape in order to make his witnessed trips into town with the Jeep, then before surrendering to police, properly dispose of the extra car.

A technical genius was more than capable of rigging timers and thermostats to make a cabin appear occupied. A review of utility company records verified that electricity and gas consumption for the isolated address was consistent with someone living there. Not surprising in the least, considering the sophistication of Lafferty's overall preparations.

Obtaining a search warrant presented no obstacle, because Anthony Lafferty encouraged the FBI investigators to spend as much time in the cabin as they wanted. The circumstantial evidence that was gathered reinforced his version of the events. Bed linens and towels showed signs of usage. The ample food supplies purchased in early January had dwindled significantly. Trash cans were full. There were indications that cleansers and other household products had been used on a somewhat regular basis. Plenty of footprints matching Lafferty's boots were found in outside areas surrounding the cabin. Open books rested on furniture, or were strewn about the floor. Sketches and paintings, in various degrees of completion, were left leaning against walls or taped to flat surfaces. But once again, all these telltale signs could have been manufactured with a few brief visits by Lafferty.

In Boston, a half-dozen federal agents were unleashed on the streets, in the futile hope of finding someone who might have seen Anthony Lafferty during the weeks he purportedly was stowed away on Cape Cod. Over the period in question, Lafferty would have avoided places in Bean Town where people might have recognized him. Due to the cold weather, it would have been natural to see someone bundled in scarves, hats, and even sunglasses—providing Lafferty easy cover. Maybe he'd also used partial disguises and rented some fleabag apartment or motel room. Who says a person couldn't be in two places at once? Especially a guy who was convinced that he could commit perfect crimes on a weekly basis.

Lafferty acknowledged that after cashing his millions from the software company, he had elected not to jump back into the workplace like his partners did. The investigation indicated he also didn't become involved with anything or anyone outside this circle of former associates. He seemed to have kept his life free of entanglements. The agents in Boston found no one who'd seen him, or anyone who would have expected to. None of his monthly accounts were past due, since all of his bills were paid automatically from a checking account. His two credit cards last had been used in December. Neither his business attorney, doctor, nor investment advisor had heard a word from him in months, but that wasn't unusual. Special Agent C.J. Matthews and her team were convinced that at some point since mid-January, as Lafferty bounced from city to city, he would have made a mistake that could prove he hadn't remained on Cape Cod. But whatever needle he might have left out there, it was buried deep inside a haystack.

The interrogation of Anthony Lafferty dragged on for six days. The same ground was covered countless times. Finally, Lafferty was given a two-day hiatus. When the questioning picked up again, a new face was inserted into the government's line-up. And not a pleasant one.

Her name was Sylvia Dougherty. Characterizing Ms. Dougherty as unfeminine seemed harsh, so Special Agent Matthews would keep this opinion to herself. But the woman's presence likely evoked disturbing images for any adult man in her presence—images that had been etched into the subconscious of every adolescent male during high school biology. C.J. Matthews vividly remembered the reactions of boys to those dreadful videos. No guy really wanted to watch a female praying mantis rip the head off a male and devour her partner as the final act of their mating ritual. That hideous slow-motion photography must have left indelible scars across generations of males.

It didn't help that this middle-aged attorney was tall and lean. Or that her arms and legs were disproportionately long, and her joints unusually angular. She looked as though she would have been really adept at climbing out to the farthest reaches of a tree limb in her younger years. Upon hearing her voice for the first time, C.J. Matthews thought she saw two male lawyers reflexively cupping their hands over their crotches.

Sylvia Dougherty began her questioning, "Mr. Lafferty, let's presume for a moment that you're telling us the truth about not traveling with the others to Richmond. By now, I hope my able associates have made it clear that you still could be convicted as an accomplice in the Natalie Meriwether homicide for having assisted in the planning of the events that took place inside the convenience store. Would you not agree that her murder occurred during the commission of another crime of which you were fully aware and to which you were a contributor?"

Elliot Fingerman must have forgotten they were sitting in an interrogation room. His courtroom instincts kicked in as he rose from his chair. "Miss Dougherty, I find it most astonishing that you would expect Mr. Lafferty to render a legal opinion. He has neither seen the manner in which your team intends to present its feeble case ... nor has he the benefit of knowing which of the multitudinous facts we will utilize to defend the unfortunate predicament in which he found himself back in January."

Fingerman then placed his hand on his client's shoulder. "Mr. Lafferty is keenly aware of the difficult situation into which he was placed by the unforeseen actions of Todd Swinford and the rest of his associates. That is precisely why he separated from his former companions as soon as physically practicable. It was a matter of personal safety, and I'm confident any impartial assembly of peers will appreciate why my client elected to isolate himself for a period of sufficient duration to adequately deliberate his options."

Special Agent Matthews had to hand it to this Fingerman character. He could make cow vomit sound like Chaucer. She also found it interesting that he chose to single out Todd Swinford. Perhaps Anthony Lafferty's plan called for Swinford to be set up as the primary culprit in the murders committed by the copycats.

Sylvia Dougherty continued to pepper Lafferty with questions about the weekend crimes that occurred while he claimed to be in hibernation. As usual, he displayed a nice array of reactions. Surprise, dismay, consternation. From time to time, he remembered to throw in righteous indignation.

"For my benefit, Mr. Lafferty, can you tell us again how you learned Miss Conkle had died?"

He glanced at his attorney, as if to tell him he had this one covered. "The articles in the newspaper I purchased in Truro last Wednesday made reference to the fact she was dead. But it wasn't until Thursday, while driving back to Boston, that I heard her death was classified a suicide. I was listening to a radio station in my car that was doing a sloppy profile on the six of us. But I'm not buying that Teresa would take her own life. She wasn't the type … she had too much to live for. On the other hand, she did like to toy around with drugs and alcohol, so maybe she was pushing the limit and made a tragic error in judgment."

Dougherty quickly pivoted to the death she really wanted to probe. "What about Miss O'Meara, then—was she the type?"

Lafferty allowed his voice to quiver on this one, but just a trace. "I'm afraid she was. Poor Blake … she had such a big heart, but was very much a lost soul. She tried painfully hard to emulate Teresa over the years, so it's not surprising that she ingested the same substances before putting a knife to her wrists."

"Mr. Lafferty, federal agents have spoken to several sources who have commented on the relationship you and Blake O'Meara enjoyed back in Pittsburgh." Condemnation filled the air, as Sylvia Dougherty appeared eager to bust his balls.

He met her head-on. "We don't need to rely on second-hand reports, Ms. Dougherty. I can confirm that we enjoyed an intimate relationship. In fact, our private interactions often could be exceedingly enjoyable." He punctuated his final point with a self-contented grin.

But Dougherty was just getting started. "Is it accurate that you became acquainted with Miss O'Meara while you were her professor?"

He also was warming up. "Both of us had reached the age of consent ... so, yes, we became very well acquainted away from the classroom. Which worked out rather nicely, thank you."

Dougherty didn't miss a beat. "Not according to your wife."

Nor did Lafferty. "Ex-wife. I hope your agents gave Jeannie my best."

Elliot Fingerman finally interceded. "Perhaps, Miss Dougherty, you could proceed toward a more constructive destination with your line of questioning."

Sylvia Dougherty slowly slid her reading glasses down her thin nose and glanced condescendingly over the top of the tortoise-shell frames toward Fingerman, before pushing them back into place. "If your client could please describe the nature of his relationship with Miss O'Meara while they were working together ... and then later, after the company was sold?"

"If you're referring to the romantic aspects ... those were on again, off again." Lafferty sported another glib smile as he stared down the female attorney, quite pleased with his double entendre.

Sylvia Dougherty was impervious. "I see. Prior to her death, Mr. Lafferty, can you specify the last time that you might have been 'on' ... if I may be so crass?"

"Blake and I hadn't been intimate in many months. To be honest, her mood swings grew tiresome ... along with everything else about her. She sought more from our relationship than I did." He practically was boasting that Blake O'Meara had been nothing more to him than a sexual plaything—taunting his female adversary to try harder.

She did. "Which may explain the note that was found with her body … 'He no longer requires my services.' Would you have been that 'he' to whom she was referring, Mr. Lafferty?"

"Me, Todd Swinford, Greg Beaumont … or maybe the last guy who stood next to her in a cab line. I'm afraid Blake would have been susceptible to any number of 'he's' who showed an interest. She was desperate for attention. Sad so many women can be like that … isn't it, Ms. Dougherty?"

Seams were cracking. C.J. Matthews watched as the hardened federal prosecutor allowed her exasperation to show. Anthony Lafferty had won the bout and looked ready to go another twenty rounds. One of the male attorneys jumped in. "Mr. Lafferty, let's move on to a subject we've yet to discuss. Our forensics experts have determined the computer and printer found next to Miss O'Meara's body were used to produce the notes left behind at the copycats' various crime scenes."

Lafferty cut him off before he could even finish the backdrop to his question. "I don't know much about those details, unless they were reported in the media … but I can confirm that one of Blake's responsibilities was preparing the notes each week … at least while I was still a part of the group."

A young female attorney handled the follow-up. "Might you speculate as to why Miss O'Meara would want authorities to find this computer equipment upon her death?"

"To be honest, I haven't given Blake's actions much thought … but if the FBI is correct and she and the others were responsible for four additional murders after Richmond, then her guilt may have become overwhelming." The unflappable genius dialed a hint of sorrow and pity into his tone. "She wouldn't have been one to cope very well with the attendant remorse and shame. Leaving that computer for the authorities may have served as the final confession her conscience demanded."

No mention was made that Blake O'Meara's computer memory had been wiped clean. Likewise, there was no reference to the new files that were uploaded shortly before her death—the pictures and names of Brandon Tremont's three former lovers. The federal attorneys had avoided those specifics, hoping Lafferty might slip and allude to them on his own, or at least appear curious as to whether anything was found on O'Meara's laptop. He did neither.

Finally, a few hours later, C.J. Matthews watched as one more government attorney took his seat. The neatly dressed middle-aged man placed a folder on the table and folded his hands atop it. "Mr. Lafferty, do you recognize the names Elsa Greene, Maxine Willis, or Suzanne Henderson?"

"I certainly do. I'm familiar with all three."

The questioner was surprised by Lafferty's straightforward response, but continued as though nonplussed. "Then can you please tell us who they might be."

"I would imagine everyone here already knows exactly who they are, but I'll indulge you." Lafferty glanced back and forth across the battery of lawyers seated across from him before continuing, "They are three of the four women with whom Brandon Tremont had extramarital affairs." After providing the answer, his expression turned solemn, in anticipation of the next question.

"And the fourth woman would be?"

Once again, Lafferty slowly made eye contact with each of the attorneys, as well as the special agent. He responded unemotionally, "My mother."

"Mr. Lafferty, how did you become aware of the other three?"

As this line of questions was pursued, Lafferty became more disengaged with his replies. "I made it my business to learn their identities."

"And how did you do this?"

"By being smart enough to find exactly the right people who had known Brandon Tremont in his younger years, and being rich enough to pay them off." Lafferty might just as easily have been telling the panel what he'd ordered for breakfast. *Coffee, black. No sugar.*

"So you admit to holding a certain fascination with Brandon Tremont?"

"I'm more inclined to think of it as a revulsion. The man ruined my mother's reputation … and as a result dictated the standard of living to which I was subjected during the entirety of my childhood." *Eggs over-easy, bacon, orange juice.*

"Do you believe Brandon Tremont could be your father?"

"I don't really know. Does it matter?" *A side order of pancakes.*

"Mr. Lafferty, did your personal 'revulsion' toward Brandon Tremont contribute to decisions made by the copycats … or any of the messages left by your group?"

"I'd say your assumption is accurate … my repudiation of Brandon Tremont and other unworthy pigs just like him was shared." *More coffee.*

"Why would anyone other than you have uploaded the pictures and names of Mr. Tremont's former lovers onto Blake O'Meara's computer just hours before her death?" The attorney clearly was trying to catch Lafferty off-guard with this one. He reached into the folder in front of him and pulled out the photos of the three women and arranged them on the table.

"Interesting fact … I wasn't aware of the contents of Blake's computer. Not having been in contact with my former associates for weeks, I have no specific knowledge of who might have been responsible or why. However, one could surmise the others chose to set me up as the primary culprit with their reckless actions … making it appear as though I was the driving force behind their recent killing spree. I did, in fact, share information about these three women with Blake last summer, after returning from my final meeting with the private investigators I hired to identify Brandon Tremont's sexual conquests. I assume by now you've confiscated my computer from inside my car, so you should be able to locate the detailed email I sent to Blake. Copies of these very pictures were attached." *Check please.*

They were all so convenient. The truths and the gaps between. Anthony Lafferty's meticulous mosaic defied reasonable common sense, but at the same time remained totally plausible. If Special Agent C.J. Matthews had been a judge scoring the lengthy interrogation process, she would have been forced to award Lafferty a perfect ten.

Chapter Thirty-Nine

Anthony Lafferty was in custody; he'd seen that with his own eyes. But there still were plenty of dark paths for Webb Tremont's mind to travel. He'd been assured every conceivable resource was being dedicated to the national manhunt for Todd Swinford. The public was on full alert for this genius-turned-murderer who remained on the loose. Maybe he was roaming the country in preparation for another killing, or perhaps he'd fled the country.

Gregory Beaumont was the other lone copycat for whom there was no accounting. The FBI had uncovered no clues as to his whereabouts since he last was spotted on the island of Antigua. His abandoned boat could mean that harm had come to him while in port, or maybe Beaumont had arranged other transportation to take him further down a rabbit hole. Or perhaps Beaumont had traveled to the islands for some other reason and now was reunited with Swinford for nefarious purposes.

Meanwhile, according to the agents assigned the hand-holding duties on Tremont Estate, greater and greater focus was being placed on securing a deal for the testimony of Michael Chen, whose location in China at least was known.

Two weeks after Anthony Lafferty surrendered to police, those arrangements took a positive turn. Michael Chen's attorneys finally felt all the relevant parties had agreed to suitable protections that guaranteed their client a better than reasonable chance of a pardon, so formal paperwork had been drawn up. Chen had divulged enough information to federal attorneys handling the negotiations to convince them the whole copycat case would reach a proper conclusion with Anthony Lafferty standing very little chance of regaining his freedom.

Michael Chen requested and was granted a few days to tie up loose ends in Xian before heading home to the US, since he wasn't anticipating a return trip to China any time soon. Not the least of his complications was a young lady with whom he'd become involved. He wanted to finalize arrangements for her to join him after the copycat mess was behind him. Chen agreed to be at the American embassy in Beijing on the first Tuesday of April, where he would meet two US marshals who would escort him on that evening's flight to Boston. Webb finally had reason to hope the walls were closing in around Anthony Lafferty.

The media continued to stir up the scandal over Brandon Tremont's indiscretions with Diana Lafferty, plus rumors were surfacing about other affairs as people from his past began to talk. Nevertheless, Webb sensed any uneasiness for his father was more than offset by the presence of Corrie and Sprig, who were filling cavernous spaces that had sat empty for years.

The mansion pulsed with conversation and laughter again, but in a different way from when Webb's mother was alive. This time his father was fully participating instead of watching from a detached distance. The change in atmosphere was especially pleasing to Nessie, whose loyalty to the family far exceeded her numerous professional duties. It had been forty-four years since Vanessa Haldane arrived at Tremont Estate as a twenty-three-year-old lass from a small borough in Scotland. In her starched gray dresses, she became a fixture in the lives of Webb and his siblings, serving the family in whatever capacity the circumstances of the time might have dictated. Nurse, comforter, disciplinarian. Her pinned-back hair was mostly gray now, and she carried a few more pounds on a stoutish frame, but her vigilance and devotion were steadfast.

Nessie's outward demeanor always had served as a bellwether for Brandon Tremont's temperament. She'd tended to his disposition and needs for so long that their biorhythms were virtually synchronized. Webb had noticed the difference in recent weeks—the subtle smiles, the bounce in her step. He heard the lilt in her brogue whenever Corrie and Sprig were near.

During an evening meal in mid-March, Webb's father went so far as to ask Corrie about sprucing up the main palace. "Nothing like you did for Webster over in the coach house, mind you. I recognize the uniqueness of that particular challenge … you know, the need he has to hide from adulthood and all. I'm hopeful you merely might infuse a fresher energy into the ambience of this home, so that persons such as yourself and young Melissa feel more comfortable here."

Sprig instantly beamed, and Corrie didn't hesitate with her response. "Mr. B., there is nothing you could do to make us feel any more comfortable than you already have … but it would be my privilege to offer a few decorating ideas." Then it was Brandon Tremont's turn to beam.

Webb had reached his limit. "Shall we all join hands and sing Kumbaya?"

Following dinner, they adjourned to the music room, which was becoming a regular routine—much as it had been when Webb's mother would play duets at the piano with her children. Music rooms didn't necessarily come standard with every historic estate, but over the years, his parents had sprung for a few extra amenities. This dedicated parlor was added when Webb was in first grade. In the center of the room's hardwood floor stood a classic Steinway—which hadn't been played since the death of Janice Tremont. Still, Brandon Tremont insisted her grand piano be tuned regularly in the hope some future visitor might honor his wife's memory by playing one of her favorite pieces. This possibility had been a long shot, of course, because entertaining essentially came to a halt after Webb's mother passed away.

The windowless room featured a built-in sound system with more than thirty custom-crafted speakers from Germany. Webb hadn't been able to get an accurate count because the darned things were intentionally inconspicuous, blending into the sculpted plaster ceiling and commissioned mural of Vienna that spanned panoramically around the four walls. He'd often wondered how a little cranked-up Zeppelin might sound inside Brandon Tremont's acoustically perfect chamber, but on this night Debussy was playing. A special request from Sprig.

Unbeknownst to Webb, and even Corrie, Sprig had been spending several hours each week in that very room, exploring the virtues of classical music with Brandon

Tremont. As far as Webb was concerned, the girl was a turncoat. The prior week, she'd gone over the moon when his father promised her a night at the symphony as soon as the copycats were arrested and reentering the outside world became viable again. Webb found himself pondering which might be worse—Symphony Hall with his dad and his highbrow friends, or another year or two of confinement.

During the course of their Debussy-backed conversation, Sprig let loose with a question that momentarily knocked the planets out of alignment. At least for Webb.

She was relating how much fun she'd been having with "Mr. B" during their discussions about the great composers. To begin with, Webb wasn't accustomed to hearing fun and his father in the same sentence. But then Sprig unleashed her bomb. "Mr. Tremont, you're different from other rich people in this town. You're not uppity like so many of them ... you never act like you're more important than anyone else. How do you stay so normal?"

Webb Tremont always had maintained there were no absolutes in life. Just the same, in this instance he was bet-the-ranch certain that over his seventy-seven years of drawing breath, no living human had ever complimented Brandon Tremont for being normal. If anything, being uppity was his strong suit. At first, Webb wondered if Sprig might not be as sharp as he'd always thought her to be. But soon it dawned on him that she hadn't experienced the same Brandon Tremont as the rest of modern civilization. Perhaps the hardened preconceptions he automatically applied to his father needed recalibration.

Though Brandon Tremont appreciated her praise, he felt obliged to offer a counter-perspective. "Melissa, I'm not sure many people would share your gracious opinion ... in fact, I'm quite convinced no one would." He looked toward his son, smiling. "Wouldn't you agree, Webster?"

Webb searched for the right words to respond. The best he could do was shrug.

His father continued, "Your sentiments are excessively kind, and it would be egregious on my part not to admit humility has never been a personal asset. Throughout much of my life, I've behaved as though a privileged upbringing made me something special. Worse still, I too often believed it to be the truth."

Corrie spoke up, her voice filled with compassion. "Please, don't be so tough on yourself. If your values weren't in the right place, you couldn't have said what you just did."

He looked at her appreciatively. "Oh, dear girl, those weren't values speaking."

Sprig piped up, "Then what was it, Mr. B?"

"What you heard was the voice of mortality."

Seeing the awkward reactions around the room, Brandon Tremont knew he needed to explain. "Regardless of how many pretensions we each might harbor, there is one force of nature that will explode every overinflated opinion we hold of ourselves ... and that's the inevitability of death as we draw nearer and nearer to it. In death, we all are the same ... and ironically, accepting that fate sooner would make our lives together a great deal more satisfying. When staring at death, the airs and self-deceits fall away like meat from a bone. We shouldn't fear the skeletal truth that lies beneath ... we should embrace it."

This was not some spur-of-the-moment commentary. Webb's stoic father had been doing a lot of deep thinking. Or to be more accurate, rethinking.

Brandon Tremont continued, "It's funny how virtually no one fears or resents people once they've grown old ... even though we manage to fear, resent, or chastise most everyone else. Slipping into our latter years, we become less threatening ... we finally lose whatever conceits and superiorities we've been parading around. We no longer answer to the sirens we once scurried toward—those temptations borne of self-importance. Instead, and at last, we are humbled by the one unavoidable siren that beckons us all. The ultimate acceptance of this reality humbles everyone ... our egos are deflated by our own natural progression. And here I sit as living proof."

Thank goodness for Corrie and Sprig. They knew exactly what to say after his father's soul-searching testament. Within moments, the three of them were laughing and jumping on to another subject. Webb, meanwhile, was unable to speak. Not because he couldn't find the right words. No, this time he was unable to get them out.

Anthony Lafferty was catching up on his reading in a well-guarded room inside an undisclosed location. A trial date likely would be set for six to nine months in the future, though the list of specific crimes for which he was to be prosecuted had yet to be finalized. Neither he nor his attorney was protesting such murkiness from the federal prosecutors. Lafferty was perfectly content to remain in custody as US law enforcement wrestled with how best to proceed.

The previous night he received confirmation that Michael Chen was still in Xian, China. Lafferty assumed that wouldn't hold true for much longer unless the feds were totally incompetent. Surely, they were trying to lure him home with offers of leniency or even a full pardon.

Lafferty received his regular updates on Chen via the internet. His supervised sessions didn't allow him to send or receive emails, and what information he could access was strictly limited. Each evening, after spending the majority of his allotted time surfing approved news sites, Lafferty routinely clicked through the icons linking to other standard fare he was allowed to see. For a few minutes, he scanned this limited number of permissible websites, including one which provided Christian support for incarcerated criminals. The site featured a section where outside parties could post general words of encouragement to all who were behind bars. But the only words of interest to Lafferty were those potentially posted by a "Father Kenneth." It wouldn't matter what the father might have to say. A posting of any kind meant Michael Chen had left China. But as of the prior evening Father Kenneth hadn't posted a thing.

Father Kenneth was actually a talented young woman he'd sought out during his recent weekend in Lancaster, Pennsylvania. She readily had agreed to monitor the locator software embedded in Michael Chen's cellphone. She had no idea what role she might be playing in abetting a potential felon, but Anthony Lafferty was confident the fifty thousand in cash had been enough to buy her loyalty—that, and the file he'd shown her which documented how she borrowed the identities of sixty-five hundred federal taxpayers and electronically absconded with their refund checks.

Waiting much longer to make his move would be unwise. Anthony Lafferty pulled out a notepad and jotted down a phone number along with a few random thoughts about suggested revisions to a text book. The next day he handed it to one of the young attorneys working with Elliot Fingerman and asked him to pass along the phone message to a former fellow professor. How could the young lawyer refuse his most famous client? No one would answer the number he called, of course. A voice mail box would receive his bogus message. Just the same, the call would set very important wheels in motion.

Chapter Forty

He was feeling a buoyancy that had been missing for months. Michael Chen always thought of himself as an optimistic sort, at least compared to most overeducated workaholics. But banishing himself to the other side of the world had taken a toll. Then tracking the activities of his former colleagues from 8,000 miles away had been downright brutal—the random murders, the bullshit suicides of Teresa and Blake, the grim disappearance of Greg, and finally the vile audacity of Anthony Lafferty. Thinking back, Chen realized this drain of positive energy really had started in October, as soon as they committed to their weekend larks. Brainstorming and romanticizing the intricate parodies was one thing, but putting such idle whimsy into action had been stressful from the beginning. The expectation that something was bound to go wrong never had left him, yet he'd been unable to muster the courage to talk his closest friends off the ledge.

Better days lay ahead. It didn't seem possible that he could be returning to the United States and in a matter of months resuming his normal life—except for the infamy that would forever follow him as one of the Cop Show Copycats. Better still, he was sure he had found his soulmate for life. Niu Tsen would join him when the timing was appropriate. That morning he had met with Mr. and Mrs. Tsen and received their blessing. As a token of his devotion, he had presented each of Niu's parents a car—a BMW convertible for her mother, and a Bentley for her father.

He and Niu had spent a glorious day together, shopping at a Chinese wine market, picnicking on a blanket in the park, napping away the afternoon with her head

320

against his shoulder and the smell of her skin and hair summoning sensuous thoughts of the many intimacies they would share over the years ahead. The next morning, he would board a flight to Beijing with agents of the US government, so the night ahead was to be their last together for whatever number of months it might take to nail Anthony Lafferty. Until the trial was over, he refused to subject Niu to the media scrutiny that anyone associated with him was likely to endure. He needed to finish packing, so Niu decided to swing by her office before she joined him at his apartment.

After he entered the lobby and headed toward the elevators, the friendly woman at the security desk called over to him. Her English was improving by the day. "Mr. Chen, I have package for you." A going-away gift from one of his cousins, he presumed. Riding up to the ninth floor, his mind still lingered on his future with Niu. He gave no thought to what might be inside the smallish box covered in plain brown paper.

Once inside his apartment, Michael went to the kitchen for a knife and there opened the tightly wrapped package. The outer box contained a smaller one with a note attached to the top. As he read the typed words Chen feared all his plans were about to change because of what the second box contained.

On the morning of April 5, when Webb Tremont received his call in Lake Forest from Special Agent Matthews, the time in Beijing was approaching 11 p.m. By then, US authorities had been on the phone countless times with police detectives in Xian. At the appointed time of noon, eleven hours earlier, Michael Chen had failed to appear at the US Embassy. Thirty minutes later, a senior diplomat had made the official request for cooperation from Chinese law enforcement.

Security personnel in the lobby of Chen's apartment building reported that the young American had been out for most of the previous day, returning in the early evening at 5:36 p.m. He took the elevator to the ninth floor, but returned just forty-three minutes later, carrying a suitcase and small duffel bag. The woman on duty saw him exit the premises and hail a cab outside the front entrance.

The disarray in Mr. Chen's bedroom indicated he had packed hurriedly, leaving several partially filled suitcases behind. In the kitchen, detectives found a package on the counter and the knife apparently used to open it. Inside a small box within a larger one was a vacuum-sealed translucent bag containing what looked to be the internal organ from an animal, or possibly a human. Next to the nested boxes was a note that read: "Gregory sends his best. Apparently, your family members on the West Coast are doing well in your absence, but it may be time for someone to pay them a visit. You decide, Michael." The message was unsigned.

The smaller box measured six inches in length, four in width, and four in depth. Through the tight plastic layer inside, a medical forensic specialist was able to confirm that the gelatinous contents had been removed from a human body ... a human who most certainly would have been dead at the time.

After hanging up with C.J. Matthews, Webb went right to Wikipedia. The parietal lobe was one of the four major sections that comprised the cerebral cortex. This particular lobe helped integrate the five senses and was highly active when individuals processed language or tackled math problems. As most persons achieved adulthood, the parietal lobe maintained its natural proportion to the rest of the brain. But for those belonging to the genius universe, the parietal often overdeveloped well into one's latter years. For example, Albert Einstein's overall brain was normal in scale, maybe even on the small side. But in the parietal lobe department, the famous scientist was impressively endowed. Where size really did matter. Sadly, one needed to be dead to flaunt such an enviable appendage.

———◦———

In view of Gregory Beaumont's mental acuity, the message for Michael Chen that he "sends his best" left little doubt about the fate of one more copycat. Nonetheless, C.J. Matthews received official confirmation within twenty-four hours. The vacuum-sealed tissue was sent to a Chinese government lab, where the DNA profile matched the one from a digital file shared by the FBI. The sizable parietal lobe definitely had been extracted from the body of Mr. Beaumont some five to eight weeks earlier. Assigning a more precise time estimate was difficult because the lobe had been frozen for much of the intervening period.

Two FBI agents fluent in Mandarin quickly headed to Xian, where they were permitted to accompany Chinese detectives as interviews were conducted. Niu Tsen, the girlfriend of Michael Chen, was emotionally distraught during her session. She had arrived at the high-rise apartment building, as planned, at around 7:30 p.m. on the evening Chen went missing. She was told in the lobby that Mr. Chen had departed an hour earlier, giving no indication of when he might return and leaving no message for her or anyone else. She waited in their favorite nearby piano bar, repeatedly calling his cellphone to no avail.

Miss Tsen confirmed that just hours earlier Chen was fully committed to making his appointment in Beijing and returning to the United States. Further, she'd never known him to turn off his cellphone or ignore her calls. When she was told about the gruesome package found atop his kitchen counter, her reaction was immediate. "Poor Michael. He feared Gregory was dead … but I don't think he considered the possibility that Anthony Lafferty would threaten his family."

None of Chen's relatives or other acquaintances in Xian had heard from him. No record could be found of him departing the district by airplane, railway, or river transport, or checking into an area hotel or hostel. Overnight, he had dropped off the face of the earth, which was no small challenge for an American guest of the Chinese government. But perhaps money was the one true universal language.

Back in the States, Michael Chen's parents had upheld their son's request not to contact the authorities. But when agents in the Bay Area paid an unannounced visit, fear overcame them. They had received a call from their son during the middle of the night on Sunday—which phone records confirmed to be 6:06 p.m. on Monday in China. Just minutes before exiting his apartment, Michael Chen had phoned to inform his parents that he had changed his mind about coming home. He also apologized for possibly placing his entire family in significant peril.

The package that changed everything had been delivered to Chen's apartment building in Xian late on Monday afternoon. The security guard on duty in the reception area had needed to visit the restroom. She was away from her station for less than two minutes, but when she returned the wrapped box addressed to Mr. Chen had been sitting on her desk. One of the lobby's security cameras revealed a figure, cloaked in dark clothes and a hood, entering and dropping off the package as soon as the guard stepped away. Enlarging the video image made no difference. Not even the gender of the messenger could be discerned, let alone any distinguishing characteristics.

As these events and their subsequent investigation took place, Anthony Lafferty remained securely in custody. Special Agent Matthews and one of the federal attorneys paid him a visit. Upon hearing Gregory Beaumont was dead and that Michael Chen had vanished, he showed little reaction. On the other hand, Elliot Fingerman was quick on the draw. "I should think the federal authorities now would agree that my client's former associate, Mr. Swinford, is a madman. Even those who were skeptical can finally understand the ruthlessness of which this man is capable, and why Mr. Lafferty felt the most prudent course of action was to go into seclusion."

<hr />

Slouched against the window so that none of the other passengers could view his laptop, he reread the comments attributed to Lafferty's high-priced mouthpiece. "That bastard is pinning everything on T-Man." Michael Chen had muttered a full sentence before he realized he was thinking aloud. Fortunately, the woman seated next to him was still breathing heavily. Not surprising, since she'd slept through each of the last two stops.

That Anthony Lafferty could pull off such an outrageous plan was unfathomable. Chen thought, *He must have been scheming for years ... laughing at us every step of the way. How neatly we fell in line for him. It had been so easy for us to underestimate him.*

Chen had called his parents, and now they wouldn't hear from him again. Nor would Niu. Their safety was too important to take unnecessary risks. Whether Lafferty was in custody or not, the lunatic was capable of anything.

After opening the horrific package, his mind had started racing. He knew at once he must disappear, but he also recognized that Anthony Lafferty was keeping tabs on him despite being in custody back in Boston. The deranged prick some- how had been tracking all of them. For God's sake, Lafferty had caught up with Beaumont on a Caribbean island. He had to have planted specialized software in their computers or cellphones. Those were the only items that the five of them had in common. At first, he was tempted to discard both devices, but then he started worrying about how Lafferty might respond.

Instead, he decided to disable the basic phone functions of his iPhone, so that Niu eventually would stop trying to reach him. Next, he disabled the standard geo- tracking capabilities built into the device and its software apps. He was sure Lafferty was using something far more sophisticated, but in this way the authorities wouldn't be able to locate him through any digital signals.

Since fleeing his apartment in Xian, he'd been traveling the public bus system into rural districts of Central and Southern China for more than three days. As he rode, Chen first scrolled though the diagnostics to his laptop, dissecting every computer drive, file, database, and software program. He worked in six-hour shifts, getting off the bus at the next scheduled town after completing each of his work sessions. There he would freshen up, grab a bite to eat, recharge the power to his computer, and board a different bus traveling a different route.

Once he'd become convinced the laptop was clean, he initiated the same pro- cess with his iPhone. Early on, he followed a logical hunch and began deconstruct- ing his contact files. There it was, the embedded locator software. He plugged the cellphone into his laptop and opened the file so he could analyze the programming code. What he found was highly impressive. Though Lafferty clearly possessed many hidden talents, software development wasn't one of them—of that, Chen was certain. But clearly his former partner had managed to connect with a state-of-the- art professional.

Once he had the answer in hand, Michael Chen extended his itinerant journey for another full day. Total anonymity and the hum of the highway were surprisingly conducive for freeing his cluttered mind. Understanding how Lafferty had been able to track his movement solved one important riddle, but he still needed a long-term plan. The obvious option was to deactivate Lafferty's embedded software, reconnect with Niu, and permanently vanish to some secluded beach along the Cambodian or Vietnamese coastline.

As easy as that choice might have seemed, Michael Chen settled on a different direction. He decided not to touch the locator software. For the time being, it was best if Anthony Lafferty thought nothing had changed.

His bus odyssey brought him to Kunming, nearly a thousand miles south of the Xian Province. It was impossible to imagine the types of henchmen that Lafferty might have working for him, even in China. The safest thing Chen could do was stay well away from Niu and his relatives up north.

Chapter Forty-One

W ebb could do nothing more than wonder and wait as the investigation slogged into mid-April. According to the Chinese government, Michael Chen still was lurking somewhere inside the country's borders—which meant the perimeter of the search for him could be confined to a mere 13,756 miles. With physical features that allowed him to blend in and a fluent grasp of the language, the young genius had concealed himself among 1.4 billion citizens.

Any trace of the other missing copycat, Todd Swinford, similarly had vaporized. If this Scandinavian was the bloodthirsty criminal Anthony Lafferty claimed him to be, he at least had stopped craving the weekly limelight as a solo act. No crimes had been committed by the copycats since February.

In Boston, Anthony Lafferty rested comfortably, waiting for federal attorneys to determine which charges they might be able to successfully prosecute. From what Webb was told, the smug bastard was knocking off one book after another from his reading list.

Public interest had perked up for a day or two as the media dwelled on the salacious details surrounding Gregory Beaumont's extracted gray matter. But otherwise attention now was occupied by a more normal diet of presidential politics and random acts of terrorism. The hiatus surrounding the Cop Show Copycats was temporary, as the TV networks and their audiences anticipated a pronounced spike in interest once Anthony Lafferty went to trial.

On Tremont Estate, the lack of new developments was producing near normalcy—that is, if one was accustomed to the constant presence of a private army. Webb's father refused to trim a single security detail until Todd Swinford was apprehended.

Each evening Webb hiked over to the main palace for dinner with the others—and not even begrudgingly. He actually looked forward to the ritual he once had abhorred. One night Webb surprised everyone, especially Nessie, by volunteering to cook dinner if Sprig would agree to assist. He allowed her to select the menu, and being a typical teenager, she opted for Mexican. Brandon Tremont had never confronted guacamole and was at a loss on the proper etiquette for consumption. The notion of scooping a viscous green substance onto a chip with one's fingers was completely alien to him. Nessie kept the swinging door from the kitchen partially open and chuckled as she followed the whole ordeal. In the end, Webb was slightly disappointed with the overall effort, recognizing that fajitas and refried beans lost a great deal of their casual charm when they were dished up on Flora Danica china that had been specially designed for the Tremonts during the 19th century.

After dessert plates were cleared in the dining room each night, the four of them became accustomed to adjourning to the music room for a classical recital, or to the living room for spirited competition. Unbeknownst to the others, Brandon Tremont had called a local retailer in late March and ordered an assortment of popular board games to help occupy their minds. Scrabble quickly provided another opportunity for Webb to be bested by his father. But Webb figured any septuagenarian banker, by definition, would be unfamiliar with contemporary pop culture. Trivial Pursuit held the promise of redemption. However, he soon learned the elder Tremont was reading more than the business sections in his daily array of newspapers.

Usually around nine o'clock, the group disbanded—Sprig to her homework for an hour or two, Brandon Tremont to whatever it was that billionaires did in private, and Corrie to catch up on her design projects. Webb would slip over to the coach house and patiently anticipate lights-out. Between the festivities earlier in the evenings and his late-night trysts with Corrie, he realized this was the most contented he'd ever felt—despite the tumult of Anthony Lafferty and Todd Swinford. Family life had grown on him.

———◦———

"Cast all your care upon Him, for He cares for you." As a kid, he remembered reading this drivel when he was thumbing through the Bible his mom had lifted from The Greenbrier. Having a photographic memory was often a curse.

But this time the italicized passage of scripture comforted Anthony Lafferty—just not in the manner the people behind the Christian website would have envisioned. The quote had been posted by Sister Anabelle, which meant Michael Chen was on the move but still inside the borders of China. Had the message come from Father Kenneth, Lafferty would have had reason for concern, because that would have meant Chen had left the country.

Lafferty smiled. The message conveyed by the small wrapped package had produced its desired result. If nothing else, Michael was predictable. The coward wasn't going to cut any deals and put his family at risk.

But there still was the matter of Todd Swinford, who had been loyal to the end. Patience. Any day now that fun chapter would kick in.

———◦———

He couldn't get over his good fortune. Though he was only twenty-two, Qiáng Jiao was sure it would be the easiest money he'd ever make, and the timing couldn't have been better. He had decided just that morning to sit out a term or two at Kunming Metallurgy College. He needed to return to his job at the copper fitting factory until he could bank enough for two more terms of tuition and books. But then *tien yi* stepped in. Divine providence.

Jiao was eating his lunch on the steps of the City Museum when the friendly man had struck up a conversation with him. This well-dressed stranger spoke fluent Mandarin, but definitely behaved more like a Westerner.

Ten minutes later, Jiao had agreed to accept 5,000 yuan a week for doing nothing more than recharging a cellphone every few days and carrying it around in his backpack. What did he have to lose? If a new cellular service provider was willing to pay that kind of cash to test its coverage patterns, he was more than willing to accept.

The whole thing sounded too good to be true, but he'd been handed 10,000 yuan on the spot to compensate him for the first two weeks. At the beginning of the third week, a courier would deliver payment that covered two additional weeks. Though the courteous gentleman couldn't say how long the test might last, Qiáng Jiao would earn enough in just that first month to get him through his final year of studies.

<hr />

Penetrating the computer systems inside the city's universities had been a snap. After an afternoon of rooting through transcripts and financial statements, Michael Chen had selected his handful of candidates. The conversation outside the museum convinced him at once that Qiáng Jiao was the best choice. For the time being, Anthony Lafferty could track the movements of a young Kunming college student.

Chapter Forty-Two

On Friday, April 22, Webb was killing time by jogging laps around the inside perimeter of Tremont Estate. His phone pinged three times in rapid succession. He disliked text messages and even the sound they made. After all, he'd made a decent living as a man of words—whole words and run-on sentences, not emoticons and bifurcated jargon. He pulled the phone from the pocket of his sweatshirt and glanced at the screen, then smiled. If anyone detested texting more than he did, it was Theo Kleyser. Yet his closest friend had just sent him a message.

Theo viewed any texting exchange as a needless diversion—just like he viewed most forms of communication. The only reason he'd consented to retaining the texting function on his cellphone was to appease his parents and sister. When he disappeared into seclusion for weeks or months at a time, they sought occasional assurances that he still could be counted among the living. Out of respect for his family, every few days he would pull himself away from whatever might be the focus of his tunnel vision and type out a single word. "Breathing." To make sure his loved ones didn't exploit this magnanimous concession, he programmed his phone to block all inbound messages. There was a limit to how much distraction a super-genius could tolerate.

But Theo's digital indulgence did produce an unanticipated benefit. He found he could reach out to other people in the precise manner he preferred: efficient one-way communication. He was able to dispatch messages to whomever he chose, but they were unable to respond in kind. No wasted time with idle chatter and insipid questions. Webb and Theo could go months without actual dialogue. Theo might send a text to Webb suggesting he check out some obscure article or simply to let him know his plans for an upcoming holiday. The best Webb could do in response was call and leave a lame message on Theo's voice mail.

With this particular missive, Theo was informing Webb that he would be dropping by Lake Forest that evening. One of his mysterious out-of-town sojourns had wrapped up early, so he was rerouting his return trip to Colorado through Chicago.

"TRAPPED IN CLEVELAND SINCE TUES. ESCAPING EARLY TO SURPRISE PARENTS FOR WKND. COMPELLED TO SPEND REQUISITE TIME WITH YOU. LET'S CELEBRATE LAFFERTY INCARCERATION BY HOISTING BREWS AT SQUANDERED OPPS (THE REAL ONE.) 7PM. FLIGHT ATTENDANT MALIGNING YOURS TRULY ABOUT TURNING OFF EVIL ELECTRONIC DEVICE. GUESSING SHE PREFERS ALTERNATIVE ELECTRONIC DEVICE FOR COMPANIONSHIP. NOW THREATENING TO TOSS ME. NORMALLY WOULDN'T CARE, BUT FEMALE ACROSS AISLE READING VONNEGUT. PROMISING. LEAVE MESSAGE IF TIMING WORKS. WILL CHECK UPON LANDING. HOPE TO HOOK UP. LATER, THEO."

The text was classic Theo Kleyser—Vonnegut and all. Webb could envision the irreverent savant pecking out his message as an angry flight attendant loomed above him. No sinister stare would ever force Theo Kleyser to cut short his sarcasm.

Webb punched Theo's number and left a voice message to confirm that he and Corrie would meet him in Highwood—accompanied by their standard platoon of security guards. Corrie and Theo had hit if off from the moment the two were introduced years earlier. Like Webb, she welcomed any opportunity to explore the inner workings of his ungoverned gray matter.

But by the time Webb finished his run, something about Theo's message was eating at him. He reread the text several times before hurriedly punching another familiar speed-dial.

Special Agent Matthews pushed back on Webb for a third time. "You're absolutely positive, Mr. Tremont? You're basing a great deal on a rather minor nuance. Your friend's behavior patterns may not be as foolproof as you think."

Webb didn't vacillate. "Trust me, Theo Kleyser's behavior is foolproof on virtually every dimension . . . but especially this one. I assure you, someone else somehow sent me that text message using his account."

Now, four hours later, the FBI's North Central Division had gone into full alert, along with several suburban police departments. So, it was only natural that a few doubts might start creeping into Webb's head. Maybe he had made too big a leap. Sitting in a police car a few blocks from Squandered Opportunities in Highwood, he reread the message for at least the hundredth time. So much of the texted banter sounded exactly like Theo. But he was convinced. The tiny discrepancies still glared out like neon signs.

"TRAPPED IN CLEVELAND SINCE TUES. ESCAPING EARLY TO SURPRISE PARENTS FOR WKND. COMPELLED TO SPEND REQUISITE TIME WITH YOU. LET'S CELEBRATE LAFFERTY DEMISE BY HOISTING BREWS AT SQUANDERED OPPS (THE REAL ONE.) 7PM. FLIGHT ATTENDANT MALIGNING YOURS TRULY ABOUT TURNING OFF EVIL ELECTRONIC DEVICE. GUESSING SHE PREFERS ALTERNATIVE ELECTRONIC DEVICE FOR COMPANIONSHIP. NOW THREATENING TO TOSS ME. NORMALLY WOULDN'T CARE, BUT FEMALE ACROSS AISLE READING VONNEGUT. PROMISING. LEAVE MESSAGE IF TIMING WORKS. WILL CHECK UPON LANDING. HOPE TO HOOK UP. LATER, THEO."

Every word, every barb, every facet of the scene described on the airplane read like Theo Kleyser. The spontaneous wording was vintage Theo. Until those final two sentences. "HOPE TO HOOK UP." Theo would never waste his energy thinking such innocuous pleasantries, let alone peck them out on a miniature keyboard. Plus, he would be more apt to speak in medieval tongues than resort to the use of "LATER."

More out of the question was the possibility that Theo would put his name at the end of an electronic communication. Once transmitted, the recipient of said message automatically would see the sender displayed as Theo Kleyser. Including his identity as part of a message was unnecessary, and Theo instinctively eliminated all forms of redundancy from every aspect of his life.

Certain laws of nature were incontrovertible. A message from the true Theo Kleyser could end but one way. "UPWARD." No sappy sentiments, and certainly not his name. The end of the text had been a dead giveaway that something ominous was underfoot. So, Webb had called C.J. Matthews.

———✦———

To a special agent who answered to a battery of stern faces in Washington DC, a few little words in what appeared to be an impromptu text message might seem like a tenuous thread from which to be dangling. But prior to the recent hiatus, the copycats had been progressing toward a dramatic endgame for weeks. Maybe the wait was over.

Within minutes of the phone call, close to thirty agents from the Chicago and Milwaukee areas were making beelines to Highwood, by highway and helicopter. C.J. Matthews jumped on a Gulfstream G-650 from Boston.

Calls were made to Colorado, only to learn that Theo Kleyser indeed had spent the week in Cleveland at a climate change summit. According to the person who booked his travel arrangements, the last session had ended that morning. However, from there Theo had flown to Miami and currently was on a plane bound for Quito. Whoever was taking liberties with Kleyser's name had made sure Theo couldn't be reached by Webb once the text message was received.

To send the bogus message, someone had managed to hack Theo Kleyser's cellular account. Not easy, in view of the fact that the communication devices used by him and his secretive think-tank associates were protected by the most sophisticated cyber-security systems available. Circumventing safeguards of that level of complexity would have been an irresistible challenge to the Cop Show Copycats. Whatever remnants of the group might still exist, their skill sets had not diminished.

At 7:02 p.m., a middle-aged man wearing a nylon jacket approached the bartender at Squandered Opportunities and asked where he might find "a Mr. Webster Tremont." The poor guy instantly found himself surrounded by four federal agents with their guns drawn.

Now trembling, the man raised his arms toward the ceiling, even though none of the agents had instructed him to do so. A small package in his right hand was hovering above his head. "What's in the package?" Special Agent Matthews demanded.

The man slowly shook his head from side to side before working up the courage to answer, "I have no idea … I only was instructed to deliver it here, to a Mr. Webster Tremont."

"By whom?" she asked.

"By my boss back at the office."

She didn't miss a beat. "And what office might that be?"

"Uhh … 24-7 Couriers. The Waukegan branch."

This time C.J. Matthew's tone softened. Her curiosity was evident. "You work for a delivery service?"

"Yes, ma'am, for fourteen years." With a finger of his suspended left hand, he pointed down toward the right side of his jacket, where the logo for 24-7 Couriers was printed on the sleeve in bright orange.

During the drive, the special agent learned that the deliveryman had never before experienced an official government escort. Nor had he previously been afforded the occasion to visit an FBI office, or an interrogation room. But he wasn't alone. Within the hour, the fourteen-year veteran was joined by his supervisor from the delivery service in Waukegan, Illinois. First individually, and then together, they described everything they knew about a package addressed to Webster Tremont.

That morning the package had been found in the overnight drop-off box. Attached to it had been an envelope containing specific delivery instructions and $800 in cash, in hundred-dollar bills—more than six times the normal service charge for this kind of delivery. The package was to be brought to Squandered Opportunities at precisely 7 p.m. that evening, and every feasible attempt was to be made to secure a signature from Mr. Tremont.

Typically, the company wouldn't accept an order without a customer completing the corresponding paperwork. But in view of the staggering amount paid up front, an exception was made. Besides, the destination for the delivery was only a few miles away. "It was no big deal … and we didn't have a customer name. If we didn't accept the order, who were we supposed to refund the money back to?" C.J. Matthews and her fellow agents at least had to admire the business integrity of 24-7 Couriers.

Meanwhile, the package was whisked away by a bomb squad. After testing negative for explosive or chemical substances, it was unwrapped while Matthews and members of her team observed. Beneath standard brown paper was a corrugated carton, approximately the size of two paperback books stacked on top of each other. Inside the carton was a vacuum sealed bag—white in color, but translucent enough to see that the contents looked like a piece of raw meat or fish. The unopened bag was rushed to a forensics lab for testing, but the agents in attendance had a strong hunch about the outcome.

Later that evening, the DNA match was confirmed. Without question, Todd Swinford was dead. It was anybody's guess where the rest of his body might be, but the parietal lobe of his brain had been sent to Webb Tremont. No card from the sender was enclosed. As with Gregory Beaumont, Swinford's brain section had been frozen since being removed sometime during the preceding two months.

24-7 Couriers was located in a Waukegan strip center. An exterior security camera was positioned above the drop-box where the package had been deposited, which happened between the close of business on Thursday and Friday morning at 7:30. The camera was stationary, and whoever deposited the package with the advance payment appeared to have been acutely aware of it. The only captured visual image showed a gloved hand coming into view and sliding the package through a one-way door panel.

Security cameras atop a light post in the shopping center's parking lot didn't pick up any cars during the night. Whoever dropped off the package had done so on foot, being careful to remain close to the building. By sliding along the storefronts, an individual could avoid the sight lines of the aerial surveillance system because of a concrete awning that covered a protected walkway.

Determining the person responsible for the dissection of Todd Swinford could be added to the growing list of FBI challenges. C.J. Matthews was informed that Anthony Lafferty had become thoroughly distraught upon learning of Todd Swinford's demise. *Of course he had.* Elliot Fingerman even felt compelled to speak to reporters on his client's behalf. "Mr. Lafferty had hoped Mr. Swinford would soon be apprehended and offer a full confession. Now there doesn't seem to be anyone left who can completely exonerate my client from having direct involvement with the murders and other serious felonies committed by his former partners."

On the flipside, no one was left who directly could implicate Lafferty either. Despite his surrender, Anthony Lafferty had remained the primary suspect in the FBI's investigations. For a brief time, there might have been a few seeds of doubt that perhaps Todd Swinford was the master culprit. But now there could be no other reasonable explanation. Anthony Lafferty somehow had prearranged a chain of events that continued to play out during his self-imposed confinement.

Regardless of what C.J. Matthews, her teams, and her bosses might believe, public opinion was swinging slowly back in Anthony Lafferty's favor. The dismembered brain lobes of Gregory Beaumont and Todd Swinford had been delivered while Lafferty was tucked away at an undisclosed location. The nation's most feared law enforcement agency still was unable to disprove a single element in the man's account of where he had spent his winter months.

Webb Tremont tried to absorb the fact that Anthony Lafferty was pulling it off. Things were unfolding exactly as this madman must have planned. He wanted the Tremonts and the whole of law enforcement to understand that he had anticipated every detail. The murders, the suicides, and the venomous symbolism all had been his. Lafferty had known exactly where the burden of proof would fall and had crafted a magic act that toyed with those boundaries. For his latest trick, all he'd needed to do was hand over the right amount of cash to convince someone to discreetly place an innocuous-looking package in a Waukegan depository at a prescribed time. The rest of the pieces would slide into place from there.

The phony text from Theo Kleyser reeked of Anthony Lafferty. During his college years, he'd seen firsthand the close friendship shared by Theo and Webb. He would have kept track of their relationship and known that Webb would spark to any invitation from Theo to meet up at Squandered Opportunities. Lafferty also knew that a legitimate message from Theo could only end with his patented "Upward." This gaping inconsistency was sure to be noticed by Webb.

Lafferty had wanted the FBI to jump through hoops. He effectively staged a spectacle whereby a throng of armed FBI agents descended upon an unsuspecting deliveryman in a public setting. The absurdity of the situation further amplified his desired message—that Anthony Lafferty was in complete control.

A few days later, Webb received an unexpected call. "Tremont, I want you to know how awful I feel about bringing Lafferty into your life."

"I trust I'm speaking with the real Theo Kleyser … one can't be too sure anymore. Trust me, Theo, you don't bear any of the burden. This whole convoluted mess traces back to my dad and Lafferty's mother."

"Yeah, but in college he played me like a flute so that he could observe your family firsthand, and I hate seeing the pain he has caused you and your father," Theo responded.

Webb was touched. "Strangely enough, this bizarre ordeal has brought the two of us closer. Everything's going to be fine, Theo."

"You know how much your family means to me, so I guess I needed to hear you're doing okay. Upward."

The phone call was over before Webb had a chance to ask Theo a single meddlesome question. But it meant a great deal to know that his closest friend had taken time away from sparing the world from another undisclosed calamity.

Chapter Forty-Three

The media feeding frenzy fueled by the special delivery in Highwood lasted a week or two. By the first of May, the investigation again was operating under the public's radar, primarily because there was nothing to report. No trace of Michael Chen had surfaced, and Chinese authorities remained adamant that he couldn't have slipped across a border without their knowledge. C.J. Matthews and US authorities were fearful that Anthony Lafferty's tentacles somehow had extended into China and Michael Chen already might be dead.

Any leads associated with the package that contained the remnants of Todd Swinford's brain had gone nowhere—like the hundreds of other dead ends produced by the case. How, when, or where this young Scandinavian had died might never be known.

Scores of agents in assorted geographies continued their efforts to disprove a single item in Lafferty's alibi, but the seams of his preposterous story remained airtight. Anthony Lafferty held the upper hand, and his smugness was on greater and greater display with his incarcerators.

As much as the FBI's top brass might have needed a scapegoat, they couldn't hang C.J. Matthews out to dry for mishandling the investigation. For six months, every conceivable resource had been thrown at the Cop Show Copycats, to no avail. Exhaustive efforts were still underway, but the potential outcome was becoming painfully obvious. Anthony Lafferty might walk.

The feds were anticipating one more shoe to drop. On Monday, May 9, it did.

Elliot Fingerman requested and received a special bond hearing for his client, asserting that Anthony Lafferty now preferred to await trial as a free man, because Todd Swinford no longer posed a threat to him. No basis for murder charges had been established, and the list of lesser charges filed against Lafferty didn't justify his continued remand. Under the watchful eye of the public, federal attorneys wanted to avoid appearing recalcitrant, so they acceded to an immediate hearing. Special Agent C.J. Matthews was in attendance.

"Your honor, our request for bail is well within any citizen's legal right," proffered Fingerman. "In this instance, Mr. Lafferty has been incarcerated for nine weeks, during which time he fully has cooperated with law enforcement in their toilsome investigation, and the only formal charges filed against him relate to what essentially were harmless pranks committed months ago."

Though on paper many of those pranks would qualify as felonies, none were likely to put Lafferty away for very long, especially after a jury was reminded of the popularity of the copycats' early crimes, the high-minded messages they left in envelopes, and the significant funds distributed to worthwhile causes. Plus, at this point no trial date had been set, because federal prosecutors were still hoping for material evidence that could build a case against Lafferty for multiple homicides.

The judge didn't really have an option. At the Tuesday morning hearing, the prosecution was given two weeks to finalize charges and schedule a trial date. Until the conclusion of that trial, Lafferty was relieved of his passport and instructed not to leave the Boston area without permission from the court. A bond of $200,000 was posted and Anthony Lafferty strolled through the front door of the federal courthouse under his own recognizance, looking as though he was checking out of a spa.

Hordes of reporters were waiting. With his attorney at his flank and an unmistakable aura of triumph, Anthony Lafferty took questions for close to an hour on the steps outside. A growing percentage of the public had swung to Lafferty's side, convinced that no one person was capable of constructing a parallel alibi of such immense complexity. Even among those who questioned his innocence, many were rooting for Anthony Lafferty out of sheer admiration for what he'd accomplished. Murderer or not, he was a genius of the highest order.

Fortunately, C.J. Matthews and her teams were too preoccupied to follow the media coverage. She could imagine how the cable news networks and their hardcore viewers were salivating over the drama that Anthony Lafferty would bring into the courtroom. She knew the anticipated proceedings already were being hailed as the "trial of the century"—or at least the next installment in an endless succession of trials of the century.

At present, unless new evidence miraculously appeared, the prosecution's case would consist of documentable charges stemming from a series of fun-filled schemes that had entertained a nation, accompanied by hypothetical claims of serial murders which any respectable judge would dismiss on arrival. Against this backdrop, an assumed psychopath was to be given the consummate platform for taking a victory lap. Several highly placed officials already were suggesting that the existing charges be dropped as quickly and quietly as possible.

<hr />

Anthony Lafferty returned to his South End brownstone for the first time since early January. During his first week at home, he established a daily routine consisting of a morning visit to a nearby coffee house, a midday trip to a deli, and a final late-afternoon venture to a local grocery store to shop for dinner. The reporters, who at first had been eager to follow every step of Lafferty's re-entry into everyday life, soon lost interest in his frightfully dull existence. By the end of the second week, the procession of annoying voyeurs who walked, biked, and drove by his address also had ceased. At last he was free to come and go as he wished.

The first important stop he made was to a storage unit where he kept his footlocker. Inside were the passports and documents that eventually would allow him to travel the world under different names. Months down the road, he would fly off to an interesting assortment of countries to close out the various bank accounts set up by his one-time partners. They had made it so easy for him to transfer their funds into his own accounts. But for now, those identity elements would stay put, along with a handful of disposable cellphones and a sizable quantity of cash. The only item he needed was the laptop that he slid into his backpack.

Next, he swung by a payphone and placed a call to Pennsylvania. For the time being, Lafferty would reassume the duties of tracking Michael Chen, so he thanked the Lancaster woman for her services. Curious to see what Chen was up to, he booted up the computer as soon as he was back inside his living room.

His young partner had made a smart choice with Kunming. A large, diverse city was ideal for someone hoping to remain inconspicuous. Then as the additional files finished uploading, he smiled at the predictability. Chen was living near a university where he bounced around campus on a daily basis. Even as he feared for his life, the software geek couldn't keep his brain in check. "Enjoy yourself, Michael. When the time is right, I'll pay you a visit."

For weeks, Chen had been keeping to himself inside the small, musty apartment. In this part of the city, questions weren't asked when a renter offered cash in advance for a one-year lease. And no one really noticed whether that renter spent most of his time holed up alone, pondering the previous six months and the three years leading up to them. Michael Chen had replayed the entire sequence countless times since he'd opened the backroom door in the convenience store and seen that poor murdered woman. What fools, what sheep they had been.

The only reason S.A.F.E. had been formed in the first place was to monetize his ideas for advanced encryption. Why hadn't he simply published them in a journal like he originally planned? Sure, he could blame Teresa for talking him into starting the business, but he had gone along without a moment's hesitation. His greed, his ego were no less intense than hers. Or any of the others'. As a result, she and three of their friends were dead and his own life would never be the same. All because of one sick bastard's hang-ups. And now, according to the latest reports, Lafferty was out walking the streets again and likely to avoid conviction. It was only a matter of time before the son of a bitch made his way to China.

He knew that the perseverance of the Chinese government would be waning.

There were more important priorities than helping US officials solve one of their own domestic crime cases. Still, Chen would hold off a few more weeks before proceeding with his plans to make a discreet exit from the country.

———◆———

"How could he disappear? I thought the Chinese were maniacal about watching over everyone."

"That's the perception they've created to help maintain control over a population that's five times larger than ours. But they're no more effective than any other developed nation. They have no leads whatsoever on where Mr. Chen is hiding, except for the fact that he hasn't left the country."

The calls from Special Agent Matthews were only a courtesy at this point. There was nothing more Webb could offer to advance the investigation of Anthony Lafferty or the pursuit of Michael Chen, but he still was a central figure in what had turned into one of the most awkward cases in FBI history. Now some of that same awkwardness was being felt by Chinese officials. Apparently, the special talents of the Cop Show Copycats were transportable to other parts of the world.

C.J. Matthews had shared everything she'd learned from her sources. Since early February, after the copycats were identified, the Chinese authorities had been monitoring Michael Chen's activities in Xian on behalf of their American counterparts. During that period, Chen met with a number of software developers who were interested in forming partnerships with him. He socialized with an uncle and aunt, plus several adult cousins who lived in the area. His interest in a promising Xian female architect had escalated into a serious romantic relationship.

Once Chen agreed to the terms of his return to the US, the scrutiny lessened. The Chinese were glad to be turning him over to his home country. But then came the abrupt disappearance. Immediately, the relevant bureaus across the country's twenty-three provinces were put on alert. Now it was early June and in the two months since, no trace of him.

The FBI's top authority on Chinese law enforcement hypothesized that Chen was either staying with an unidentified acquaintance or paying for lodging that was beneath his usual standard of living. Hotel and rental facilities in China were required to report the names of international occupants and retain copies of their passports. Only a less-reputable enterprise would risk violating this government mandate. With Chen's physical appearance and language fluency, the manager of such an establishment could claim the mistake was unintended.

He probably had chosen a large metropolitan area because the odds for undetected assimilation would be better there. For authorities, this likelihood meant the search could be narrowed to a mere 160 Chinese cities with populations that exceeded one million residents.

Chapter Forty-Four

The weeks of June passed quickly for Anthony Lafferty. Midway through the month, he and Elliott Fingerman had been invited to a private meeting with federal prosecutors where he was offered a deal. By pleading guilty to all existing charges without a trial, he would receive a five-year prison sentence with half of that time suspended. However, the government would not agree to refrain from filing murder charges at a future date if evidence were to materialize. The deal was a non-starter; Lafferty would take his chances in front of a jury. In fact, he was looking forward to it. He had the government on the run.

The prosecution had not requested any form of gag order from the presiding judge at Lafferty's arraignment or subsequent bail hearing. Lafferty knew what they were hoping—that in his arrogance, he would slip up and say too much during some future interaction with the media. A month after his release, he imagined they were regretting their decision.

Lafferty was selective about which invitations he accepted, restricting his interviews to two or three per week. The appearances drew sizable national audiences, and he felt he was becoming increasingly proficient with each new exchange. More and more people among the potential jury pool were being exposed to his intriguing tale. The ambitious fun-filled pranks that benefited so many worthy causes. The disdain the six of them had shared for sperm-lucky parasites. The sudden realization that he'd been duped by other brilliant minds who harbored ulterior motives. His compassion for the group's unfortunate victims. The disappointment over the ineptitude of the nation's most senior law enforcement officers.

Outwardly, Lafferty continued to project the sadness and confusion of someone who'd been misled and abandoned by those he trusted most deeply. He was ever-mindful of the two audiences he attracted but couldn't decide which one provided the greatest satisfaction—those who actually believed his outrageous version of the events, or those who knew he was lying but couldn't do a damned thing about it.

Inwardly, he reveled in his success. The end results from his years of planning were exactly what he'd anticipated, but the emotional gratification was far greater. He had pulled off perfect crimes on too many levels to count, and he wasn't finished yet. Once the trial was behind him, he would address the lone surviving loose end from his former partnership.

More importantly, after a little more travel, Lafferty would consolidate the group's financial assets. He had penetrated their personal computers many months earlier and monitored their progress as they dutifully set up foreign accounts under new identities. He would use their respective passcodes to his own benefit. Including Swinford's family money, Lafferty estimated his net worth soon would exceed $400 million. That kind of money could rain a lot more misery into the lives of Brandon Tremont and his empty-headed son.

———◆———

The date and time had been agreed to several days earlier. On Sunday, June 26, the four of them met on the front lawn at 2 p.m. Unbeknownst to Webb, the grounds staff had been instructed to stencil white lines around a rectangular area that measured 50 by 100 feet. Within this boundary, the grass was cut to a height of one inch. Nine white wickets and two wooden stakes were laid out in perfect symmetry. At dinner on Thursday, Sprig had suggested a croquet match, so Brandon Tremont had taken the natural next step of ordering up an official court.

Corrie and Webb arrived a few minutes late, armed with a pitcher of piña coladas fresh from the kitchen. Sprig and Brandon Tremont were waiting patiently for them at mid-court, clad in all white, sipping Pellegrino from champagne flutes.

Seated on the sidelines was a gallery comprised of Nessie and the rest of the staff—most of them giggling.

The contest was slated to run until late afternoon, with the winning team needing to take three of five games. A well-played, strategic game of croquet was likely to last thirty minutes or more if the teams were evenly matched. Unfortunately for Webb, he and Corrie barely had time to make a dent in their piña coladas, losing three straight games by 3 p.m.

The four of them adjourned to a veranda at the side of the main house, where Webb offered a sportsmanly toast to the victors. "I can't remember having a better time getting my butt kicked. Until next time."

The spirit of celebration continued until the conversation took an unexpected turn. Corrie tossed out what she thought was a casual comment. "I hope these competitions don't come to an end just because we're moving back to our apartment."

She saw from their somber expressions that she had caught the two Tremont men by surprise. "Webb, I told you last week that it didn't make sense for us to stay here any longer. Anthony Lafferty isn't going to leave Boston and the rest of the copycats are dead or in China. There's no risk to resuming our normal lives."

Webb felt just like he did as a kid when summer was coming to an end. "Yeah, but I didn't think you meant so soon ... I figured you and Sprig would be here for another month or two."

He was slumped down in his Adirondack chair, staring at the bluestone. Out of the corner of his eye, he noticed his father was pretty much in the same position. More oddly, when he glanced over at Corrie, he saw she was staring at both of them with tears in her eyes.

On the way to the airport, he needed to make one last stop in Kunming. He still faced a ninety-minute layover in Shanghai, but before the morning was over Michael Chen would exit China as Liko Hueng, a silver-haired, bespectacled citizen of Myanmar.

Chapter Forty-Five

C hinese officials lived up to their commitment of sustained cooperation. On Tuesday, June 28, C.J. Matthews received a call from her contact in the state department. At 7:16 a.m., on the same date, some eight thousand miles away, Michael Chen had gone to an ATM located in a downtown section of the city of Kunming and withdrawn 3300 yuan, or about $500, from his account in a Chinese bank. The bankcard picked up in the system had belonged to Chen and the ATM's video camera captured an unobscured image of his face.

Eighty-five days after fleeing his Xian apartment building, Michael Chen was confirmed to be alive and still residing in China. Now the country's law enforcement could magnify its search to one specific metropolitan area. The last elusive copycat likely would be located within days, or at most weeks.

These details were received especially well in Lake Forest. It was the first encouraging news for Webb and the others in quite some time. To say the least, they were discomforted when Anthony Lafferty had been released from custody. Concern continued to mount over the prospect that this psychopath might be found innocent of serious charges, if a jury were allowed to hear a case against him at all. Learning that Michael Chen had thus far avoided the fate met by four of his former partners was practically cause for celebration. Michael Chen was a certifiable genius. Once he was retained by Chinese officials and facing extradition, he surely would be receptive to another deal to testify against Anthony Lafferty.

He spent Wednesday morning doing an interview with a syndicated radio personality and fielding questions from around the country. The vast majority of callers expressed their admiration and support. A few amateur sleuths tried probing him for inconsistencies in his well-tested narrative, but Anthony Lafferty actually enjoyed these exchanges the most. He missed the cat-and-mouse games with federal prosecutors.

Arriving home, he punched in the code to his recently upgraded security system. He disarmed the interior motion sensors but kept the perimeter door and window alarms activated. Recognizing that he might be a natural target for any number of crazies out roaming the streets, Lafferty had become a great deal more cautious about personal safety.

He dropped the car keys on the coffee table and made a beeline to the kitchen. He would finish off the satay from last night's dinner and open a bottle of his latest favorite ale—which happened to be Crown Ambassador Reserve from Australia. Bottles typically ran about $90 apiece, but by ordering several cases at once, Lafferty was able to keep that cost to less than $75. Regardless of the money he'd soon be worth, there was no reason to overpay for small luxuries.

The ales were shoved all the way back in the refrigerator. Why did the damned cleaning ladies feel a constant need to rearrange things? He moved a few items near the front of the shelf and leaned inward to reach between them.

Suddenly he was pushed headfirst into the open refrigerator, his head jammed against cold metal. Lacking balance or leverage, Anthony Lafferty was helpless when he felt the cloth against his face. "Hello, Laffy ... I presume you understand how you've left me no choice." The voice was unmistakable. As the chloroform took effect, his mind was processing the unanticipated flaw that had proven to be fatal.

Food was about the last thing Michael Chen cared about as he sat alone picking at his plate. He'd been in the crowded restaurant for more than an hour before

349

two police officers finally arrived and approached his table. It was after 10 p.m. on Thursday. He'd withdrawn 2000 yuan from an ATM more than two hours earlier and then killed time window shopping the surrounding area—confident that if he didn't leave the popular block of storefronts, the authorities eventually would find him.

Walking into a Kunming police station and turning himself in would have created a certain poetic symmetry, but he needed to show restraint. Crafting a situation that allowed him to be in two places at once had provided enough of a parallel. He was sure his partners would have approved of how he had stolen a page from Lafferty's playbook.

———◆———

On Friday afternoon, Webb received the phone call he had been awaiting. The day before, Michael Chen had visited a second ATM in Kunming, China, after which he was intercepted by local police and turned over to US authorities. The discussions had proceeded smoothly and the missing copycat already was on a plane heading home. At last the pendulum had swung full tilt. Chen would testify under oath that Anthony Lafferty was present in the convenience store near Richmond and was directly responsible for the murder of Natalie Meriwether. He had proof that Lafferty was with the group on multiple weekends for which he'd claimed otherwise. The trial would now be a mere formality. By the end of the year, his family's nightmare would be over.

———◆———

It was Michael Chen's third fourteen-hour flight in less than five days, but this time he carried a single passport—his own. The fake one used on the return flight to Shanghai, two days earlier, had presented his identity as Chancai Meesang, from Bangkok. Laffy's acquaintance from Pittsburgh, who'd completed all the paperwork back in December, had allowed them to invent their own aliases. Michael selected Chancai as one of his because the name meant "skilled winner" in original Siamese. He had thought the choice clever at the time, and now he hoped it would prove to be prophetic. Since he hadn't used this particular identity with any of his hidden bank accounts, he destroyed the passport upon his return to Kunming.

But as he flew halfway around the world this third time, Chen was escorted by two travel companions. The men to either side of him seemed unusually amicable, but he had no basis for comparison on how federal deputies were supposed to behave.

His attorneys in China had tried to dissuade him from agreeing to the immunity agreement so readily. "Mr. Chen, we are confident the US government will grant you another day or two for a visit with Miss Tsen before you return to Boston." But they had no idea how relieved he'd been to receive the latest offer in writing.

It was virtually the same deal as the one struck three months earlier, before he'd been spooked off by the gruesome package. His sworn testimony against Anthony Lafferty in a court of law was still paramount to federal prosecutors. Importantly, the stated terms contained no stipulations regarding the well-being of Lafferty. Michael Chen signed the binding letter on the spot. As an indication of good faith in upholding his part of the agreement, Chen offered to board the next available flight. From his standpoint, it was crucial the deal be consummated as quickly as possible—before anyone realized that Anthony Lafferty would never be tried in a court of law.

Chapter Forty-Six

"**M**r. Tremont, you and your father should prepare yourselves for a lot of calls from the media. A press release is being issued within the hour. Anthony Lafferty was found dead inside his brownstone this morning ... apparently murdered several days ago. We'll have a more precise time of death later this evening."

Webb could think of nothing to say while he processed the news from the special agent.

"I know you heard me and I'm pretty sure I know how you feel, because I'm working through the very same emotions. It's okay to celebrate another man's death. This one had it coming. Things have a way of working out sometimes."

He remained speechless, his emotions on lockdown.

She continued, "I've gotta run ... but one last thing. We've contacted security personnel on your family's property ... to confirm that none of you were out of their sight long enough to make a round trip to Boston. I hope you understand, Webb."

"Sure," he mumbled out in a monotone. But then something hit him and his energy perked up. "I just want to make sure I heard you correctly, Matthews. Did you just call me Webb?"

<hr />

Anthony Lafferty had fired two cleaning ladies since returning home in May. Zofia Nosek had started working for him the previous Monday. When he didn't answer the doorbell, she rooted through her tote bag for the printed card the un-likable man had handed to her. She punched six numbers onto the exterior keypad and listened for the *beep-beep-beep* sound before opening the front door. Once inside, she punched six more numbers onto a different keypad and waited for the irritating beeps to stop, which signaled the alarm system had been deactivated. Then a final three numbers to secure the front door while she worked inside. The instructions were very specific. First, she must dust the books on the shelves in the living room. *So many books, and all so old in their leather covers.* Next, she was to dust the strange collection of animal figures scattered around the room. *Why would anyone want just turtles and camels ... they're not even pretty?* Each needed to be wiped carefully with a special cloth and placed back in its exact spot. *Everything so complicated with this man.*

Zofia Nosek was inside the residence for close to an hour before she finally made her way to the kitchen. What she encountered was extremely startling, but her im-mediate reaction surprised even her. *Too bad I waste so much time dusting all those things in other room.*

His body was wrapped in a tightly taped sheet of plastic. Even through the blood smears, she could see it was him. She'd watched his face too many times on the tele-vision. Zofia didn't have strong feelings about him either way until she'd met him in person the week before. The way he smiled when she took off her sweater to start working made her feel uncomfortable. She already had told her bosses they needed to find someone else to clean his home. Now it didn't matter.

From the appearance of the body inside the plastic, Zofia could tell that Anthony Lafferty been dead for some time. She had no fears about the killer still being inside the residence. But oddly, she felt no remorse about the dead man. She calmly exited the brownstone, not bothering to reset his crazy alarm system, and called the police from the sidewalk outside.

<hr />

The first arriving officers found an envelope next to the corpse. It was held for the FBI agents already on their way. Special Agent C.J. Matthews was in Washington

DC, but the message on the typed card inside the envelope was read to her over the phone: "Paid in full and in kind for the deaths of Jorge Cabral, Natalie Meriwether, Teresa Conkle, Kelso Estabrooke, Noreen Shipley, Bryan and Shannon Duncan, Gregory Beaumont, Blake O'Meara, and Todd Swinford."

Chapter Forty-Seven

The last thing C.J. Matthews needed was assignment to another abstruse felony case related to the Cop Show Copycats. But at least this time she wouldn't be in charge as the Bureau investigated the murder of Anthony Lafferty. The Director of the FBI felt she deserved to be taken out of the line of fire, but her in-depth knowledge was too indispensable to let her totally off the hook.

The list of potential suspects was far-reaching. First were the obvious persons with direct ties to the havoc wrought by Anthony Lafferty. There were plenty of Tremonts, who certainly possessed the resources to arrange a contract killing in order to provide their family more sleep-filled nights. Of course, there were the friends and family members of the four business partners whom Lafferty systematically had eliminated. Plus, the friends and family members of six other individuals who had been murdered indiscriminately by the Cop Show Copycats.

These possibilities alone produced scores of names. In addition, there were the less directly impacted prospects. Random citizens, the vigilantes who were appalled by a growing likelihood that Anthony Lafferty could escape punishment. Someone who might have decided to impose his or own sentence. Maybe a person who placed great value in the law and the legal system. Or perhaps a law enforcement officer, past or present, who resented the mockery of the preceding nine months.

The hypotheses were endless, but practically speaking, all the obvious arrows pointed in one direction only. Toward Michael Chen, who had been granted immunity to return to the United States and testify against a man who already had been dead. Much to the chagrin of the FBI, geniuses from the tech world apparently had developed a skill for being in two places at once.

No one had more to gain from the death of Anthony Lafferty than Chen. The security of his family members. His own safety upon returning to the United States. Revenge for his four former colleagues.

Elements at the South End murder scene were reflective of other crimes committed by the very group to which Michel Chen once had belonged. Chloroform was found in Lafferty's respiratory system. The lethal wound across Lafferty's throat was consistent with a utility knife. The high-end security system had been totally compromised and subsequently restored. Every room of Lafferty's residence was scoured for forensic evidence and yielded nothing. Finally, as punctuation, there was the sealed envelope and the message contained inside.

If Michael Chen were to be found guilty of killing Anthony Lafferty, his guaranteed immunity for other crimes was meaningless. Whatever acts Lafferty might have committed, his death still was a cold-blooded homicide. No matter how many attorneys Chen could afford, he'd be looking at many years in prison.

One unusual aspect to the murder was how the perpetrator had left the body. The slash across Lafferty's throat was between seven and eight inches in length. He would have bled profusely from such a wound, but the plastic in which the body was found contained less than two ounces of blood. The logical explanation was that the killer had waited for Lafferty to bleed out before wrapping several layers of plastic around the body, and then securing that plastic with duct tape. This sequence meant the killer had waited ten minutes or more for Lafferty's body to drain nearly five liters of blood before encasing him in plastic.

There also was a large stained area on the floor near the body, where the pool of blood had collected. The blood itself was mopped up, with a rinsed-out mop and bucket found near the kitchen sink.

Such time and effort after an act of murder would normally be expended only if the perpetrator wanted to dispose of the body. But in this case, the body was left at the murder scene. Perhaps the killer was a neatness freak, but more likely he or she was making sure Lafferty's downstairs neighbors didn't detect any abnormal odors in the days immediately following.

Preventing the body from being discovered for several days suggested the perpetrator would have gained some form of advantage from the interim passage of time. It was highly conceivable that Michael Chen had snuck into the country and murdered Anthony Lafferty. He would have needed those important few days in the aftermath to return to China, and then, most importantly, strike his immunity deal before anyone realized Lafferty was dead.

C.J. Matthews knew the theory was a perfect fit for investigators. Except for a few small details. Chinese officials were resisting any notion that Michael Chen could have slipped in and out of their country without detection. US Passport Services also had no record of Michael Chen entering or exiting American borders. Cameras at US Customs checkpoints had picked up no images that were a facial match for Chen. Likewise, the computerized screenings of footage from surveillance cameras located in international airports through which he might have traveled kept coming up empty.

But the biggest obstacle to charging Michael Chen as the principal suspect in Anthony Lafferty's murder was provided by the victim himself. Sitting on the desk in Lafferty's living room was a laptop that was different from the one he'd surrendered to police months earlier. On this second computer, which he secretly had withheld, forensics technicians discovered a customized software program that was capable of tracking the location of individuals anywhere in the world. The program had been set up the previous summer to monitor the whereabouts of Anthony Lafferty's five former business partners. Most of the content from four of those files had been deleted, but the sophisticated software was still actively tracking Michael Chen.

According to Lafferty's computer, Chen currently could be found in a hotel on the outskirts of Boston—which was exactly where he and the federal deputies assigned to him were staying. The program further verified that prior to his departure from China under government escort, Michael Chen had not left the city of Kunming since arriving there in early April, and for the most part had restricted his activities to a downtown district near a major university. Within this vicinity were two ATM's from which Chen had withdrawn money on the days before and after Lafferty's death. Michael Chen appeared to have an ironclad alibi. Unless investigators could come up with a witness who observed Chen in the Boston area, the available facts would cause any reasonable person to conclude that the sole surviving copycat was on the other side of the world when Anthony Lafferty was murdered.

———◆———

The terms of his agreement stipulated that Michael Chen remain in custody until the conclusion of Anthony Lafferty's trial. Since the US government was unlikely to prosecute a dead man, the timing of his expected release was now up in the air. Chen had hired a top-notch legal firm upon arriving in Boston, but he was reluctant to let them loose. He realized he was a prime suspect in the murder of Anthony Lafferty, and rightfully so. For the time being, he would let things play out. He could be patient. Eventually the federal attorneys would have no choice but to grant him his freedom.

He had engineered a perfect plan to eliminate Lafferty—one that his former partners would have fervently applauded. Every step had gone precisely as anticipated. Qiang Jiao fulfilled his obligation without a hitch, keeping the cellphone in his backpack where ever he went. Chen's first stop upon returning to Kunming from Boston was retrieving the phone and giving Qiang an extra 10,000 yuan for his efforts.

When he and the others had paid outrageous sums for the counterfeit passports and documentation those many months ago, he had thought the expenditure a needless waste. But now having exited China under one identity and re-entered under another, he was grateful to Lafferty for pushing them all so hard on the matter. The colored contact lenses, the hair coloring, the pock marks formed with make-up. Basic disguises had been more than enough to fool the security screening software. Plus knowing in advance where all the cameras were mounted around airports made it easy to keep one's head down at the right times. No wonder so many terrorists traveled the world so effortlessly.

Penetrating the computer system of the home security company that Lafferty used was harder than expected. Lafferty had hired the best available, but it still was a business operated by humans. Eventually he'd been able to extract the necessary passcodes, because humans inevitably cut corners somewhere.

Upon entering the brownstone, he'd been relieved to see the laptop in plain view on top of Lafferty's desk. Some tech team assigned to the murder investigation quickly would uncover the locator software. How thoughtful of Laffy to make it so simple for him.

Everything had been progressing flawlessly as he scoped out the rest of the apartment. Until he came to the kitchen. Laffy was lying on the floor near the refrigerator, surrounded by a pool of blood.

Chen was dumbstruck. Who else would have killed Anthony Lafferty and done so in the very same manner he had intended? He couldn't allow his mind to linger on the possibilities; he needed to remain clear-headed. Though greatly relieved that he didn't have to become a murderer, he recognized that under the circumstances, no one in their right mind was going to believe he hadn't. He had entered the country illegally and was standing in the kitchen of a man he abhorred and actually had expected to kill. He certainly wasn't about to call the police. His immediate concern was Lafferty's body. If it were to be discovered before he could return to China and implement the final stages of his plan, Chen would lose any chance of immunity and returning home for good.

The answer was obvious. He must proceed exactly as he had planned—before he had known he would have an accomplice, whoever that might be. He reached into his backpack for the sheet of plastic and roll of tape and went looking for a mop. Twenty minutes later, as he was preparing to leave the premises, he remembered one final detail. *Why not? The real killer isn't likely to mind.* He pulled out the envelope and dropped it next to the body.

As Michael Chen now idled away his hours in a lousy motel room, the ironies continued to haunt him. The whole ordeal had started over nonsense about perfect crimes, the product of senseless ego. He and his four closest friends had been sucked in by a psychopath who manipulated them to commit his own seemingly perfect crimes to serve his own sick purposes. In the end, Chen had been forced to formulate an intricate plan to prevent Lafferty from prevailing. Soon enough Chen would go free, but he knew whatever he might have accomplished, it was far from perfect. He would carry the deep emotional scars for as long as he lived.

But there was a someone out in the world who had pulled it off. The FBI had no leads and weren't likely to come up with any. Chen knew that he would remain the FBI's prime suspect, while the real killer went about his or her normal life unnoticed. Thanks to some unknown party, a perfect crime had been committed. More importantly, with the murder of Anthony Lafferty, a greater good had been served.

Chapter Forty-Eight

F or Webb Tremont, the summer of 2016 was markedly different from the previous one—or any past season, for that matter. Though the Cop Show Copycats were a closed chapter for the Tremont family, the events of the prior year continued to produce changes in his life.

The FBI was obliged to go through the motions of investigating Anthony Lafferty's death. As was typical for anything involving the copycats, no meaningful leads materialized. Webb knew the assigned agents would keep flapping their wings until some mucky-muck in Washington threw in the towel as soon as most folks stopped paying attention.

C.J. Matthews remained a bright spot. She must have enjoyed their phone conversations as much as he did, because she continued calling every few weeks. During a moment of candor the special agent disclosed that the Bureau, from top to bottom, was convinced Michael Chen had killed Lafferty. Unfortunately, the Chinese government saw the matter as closed and refused to allow investigators access to relevant information or individuals. Any evidence that Chen had exited and re-entered the country without detection would create an international embarrassment.

Webb was less inclined to pin the murder on Chen. He had watched an in-depth television interview with this sole surviving copycat. When the questions got around to Lafferty, there was something about his responses. "Sure, by the end I despised the guy. How could I not? He'd murdered my closest friends and threatened my family … so I definitely would have killed Anthony Lafferty if given the chance.

I know this sounds crass, but I'm genuinely appreciative to some unknown soul who did that for me … who did that for all of us."

From his days as a cop and then as a cop story writer, Webb had become a big believer in cop instincts. The look on Chen's face, the unguarded tone of his voice, his overall demeanor—they all strongly suggested he was speaking pure truth. The kid had been through plenty. It was reported that his girlfriend from China had joined him in The States. Webb wished them well.

Though full immunity turned out to be a high price for the government to pay, value still was received from Chen's unencumbered return. Anthony Lafferty wouldn't stand trial, but bringing closure to the public still had remained important. Chen testified under oath to federal authorities that Lafferty's assertion about distancing himself from the group in January had been patently false. In New Hampshire, Lafferty had been the copycat who destroyed the valuable antiques on his family's farm. Despite Lafferty's claim to the contrary, he didn't skip the subsequent weekend in Delaware where they restaged a rock star's murder scene on the front porch of a Tremont cousin. Most notably, on the following weekend Lafferty definitely had traveled with the group to Richmond and was the person responsible for the murder of Natalie Meriwether.

More than his sworn word, however, Michael Chen had produced pictures from each of those weekends showing Anthony Lafferty with the others in identifiable locations. Chen never had trusted the guy, so he'd discreetly taken photos with his cellphone when no one was paying attention. He thought it wise to keep something on Lafferty in his back pocket for whatever the future might hold. A genius with common sense. Webb was impressed.

Chen was unable to comment on Lafferty's role over the remainder of the weekends because he had fled to China. But the details he did provide were sufficient to discredit Lafferty's contention that he had run off to Cape Cod while the copycats were committing more serious felonies. In the court of public opinion, Anthony Lafferty wound up being viewed as the primary culprit for every heinous act.

Due to materials found on the laptop computer he'd previously shielded from authorities, the public also learned that Lafferty was guilty of unconscionable greed. He had compiled files on the offshore financial accounts of his five former partners, including account numbers and passwords set up under multiple false identities. In the weeks leading up to his death, he'd electronically transferred a portion of their funds to his own accounts. Obtaining the rest would have required his traveling to the respective countries and institutions where the monies were held. Webb had no doubt Anthony Lafferty had every intention of making those trips.

Now Lafferty's computer files would provide a convenient roadmap for the estate attorneys who represented the family members of the other, now deceased copycats. Otherwise, with Lafferty's death, much of the group's accumulated wealth might have gathered interest on foreign shores in perpetuity.

Since November of 2015, Webb Tremont's head had been spinning at warp speed. Then sanity was restored with the sudden demise of a character from his past, whom he hadn't even remembered when the whole ordeal began. Following the murder of Anthony Lafferty, Webb, investigating authorities, and millions of Americans had tried to make sense of it all. But clarity was hopeless. The totality of applied modern psychology couldn't properly explain the behavior and motivation of Anthony Lafferty, or the foolish complicity of five extraordinary minds.

As a crime writer, Webb long ago had given up on the idea that criminal behavior could be rationally explained. The entire nation now had gained an amplified perspective on an important truth he'd learned over and over. With every criminal act, there was some degree of arrogance. In this case, that level had become all-consuming.

As a Tremont, Webb was uniquely qualified on the subject of arrogance. He forever would regret whatever role he might have played in stoking Anthony Lafferty's insecurities—because at its core, arrogance was nothing more than overcompensation for one's self-perceived shortcomings.

The past year's journey had taught Webb much about his own arrogance, about his own shortcomings and overcompensations. His carefully constructed facades had revealed their many fissures. As a consequence, the stubborn underlying foundation had seismically shifted. He'd spent four decades feeling pretty crummy about himself. Unworthiness can do that. It's sneaky. Unworthiness gnaws, it chafes. It bores away at the slightest vulnerability.

Since childhood, Webb had craved absolute certainty in his life. The hard, cold facts. That's why he'd been drawn to the law. He preferred things black or white. In his work. In his opinions. In his relationships. But now his mind was opening to the uncertainties found in the rich gray areas between. He hoped to approach each day more philosophically.

Sure, many of the messages should have been as clear as rainwater long before his forty-second birthday. But he admitted to being slow sometimes. Okay, most of the time. The irony was inescapable. It had taken a bunch of serial eggheads trashing his family to discern what was most important in his life, to humanize his own father, and to fully accept responsibility for whatever came his way.

The notorious Cop Show Copycats had achieved the unachievable, though no one at FBI headquarters was likely to talk much about it. Law enforcement across the country had been completely baffled. Perfect crimes were signaled in advance and then delivered on a weekly basis. If the betrayed copycats had stopped when things first turned ugly, the identities of five young talents would have remained anonymous. Tragic. Each of the five could have launched new ventures and accumulated more and more millions, if not billions. But human nature prevailed. Anyone carrying a badge had learned through experience that human nature was their most powerful ally.

During the rollercoaster journey, Webb had gained an authentic respect for his father. He had watched Brandon Tremont weather the whole nightmare with dignity intact. Sure, the man's reputation had been tarnished but he also emerged with deeper self-awareness. Habitual stoicism had been replaced by a new enthusiasm for life—due in great part to Corrie and Sprig.

The two important women in Webb's life did go back to their apartment above Corrie's office, but only temporarily. Webb convinced the two of them to move into the coach house on a permanent basis once a new renovation was complete. Webb once again asked Corrie to redo the space, to make it more suitable for a family of three. The project was expected to take six or seven months. In the meantime, Webb bunked alone in his old bedroom in the main palace—at least until after the wedding.

The August ceremony was small. The bride and groom invited forty-seven friends and family members to join them at Squandered Opportunities. In his wildest dreams, Webb wouldn't have envisioned Brandon Tremont leaning against the bar and throwing back Sambuca with Salvatore DiMarco, Corrie's dad. At one point, he overheard the two men discussing bocce ball. Brandon Tremont didn't seem to know much about this game that predated the Roman Empire, so Salvatore volunteered to teach him how to play later in the week. Webb sensed a set-up in the works when his father asked if he could bring Sprig along as his partner.

Remarkably, Webb allowed his father to pick up the tab. The entire affair cost twenty-nine hundred dollars—less than the price of one of Brandon Tremont's tailored suits. The truth was, Webb's father would have coughed up millions for Corrie and "Melissa" to become members of his family.

A teary-eyed Nessie expressed her sentiments to each and every person in attendance. "Praise the saints, my two lassies are staying put. We're going to be a home again."

Two of those guests were C.J. Matthews and her significant other. As should have been expected, he was as attractive as she was. Webb thought the pair should have been standing on top of the wedding cake.

Webb took the opportunity to thank everyone in attendance for helping him through a tumultuous year, before bringing the crowd to tears with a toast to his bride. For once, even he felt like he managed to pull the right words out of their hiding places.

His father also offered a toast. This man of normally few words went on and on about Corrie and Sprig, as Webb had expected he would. But then Brandon Tremont segued into the subject of his son.

"Webster, a few weeks ago you confessed to me that deep down you never had wanted to be a police officer … that your initial career choice was a charade. Maybe that's true … but you were a damned good cop, and everyone in town knew it. After recent events, I know you've also been wrestling with whether you want to remain a writer. That's your choice, but I hope you do, because you have a gift, Webb … you're a damned good writer. And now, today, you've committed yourself to a marriage, and in so doing you've given me one more reason to be proud of you … because I know you're going to make a damned good husband."

Proper words scurried back to their cranial hiding places as Webb tried to respond. He instead gave his father a lengthy hug with the whole world watching, openly pleased to be Brandon Tremont's son.

But on this special day the biggest surprise, at least for Webb, was delivered by his best man. Normally, Theo Kleyser avoided public speaking like he did most forms of communication, but he chose to make an exception. Theo heaped more enthusiastic praise on Corrie and Sprig before turning his attention to Webb.

"Let's face it, folks … back in our younger years I was an academic geek. Hell, I still am. The one person who never seemed to notice that fact was Webb Tremont. He made me feel normal … and trust me, we all need to feel normal from time to time." These comments had been addressed to the room at large, but then Theo started speaking directly to Webb, as though no one else was present. "You always have been there for me, Webb … and I've always hoped I might be able to be there for you at some point."

Theo paused briefly and in that instant Webb saw it in his eyes. The final question no longer remained unanswered. A perfect crime indeed had been committed by a superior mind. There was not a fraction of doubt. Webb would never utter a word to a living soul, including Theo. The two of them would never speak of the matter. Webb knew it, Theo knew it. Their pact had been sealed through lifelong friendship.

"Please trust that someday I'll find a way, Tremont. In the meantime, I wish you and Corrie the best that life has to offer. Upward, dear friends. Upward!"

Other novels by Mitch Engel

Deadly Virtues

Stephanie Burton is a voice that pierces the din of television news. Attractive and charismatic, she eventually is hailed as "America's Moral Compass." Privately, she contends with emotional scars as sordid as the stories on which the cable networks feast. In this psychological mystery, the dissonant behaviors of an unlikely murderer unfold to a surprising conclusion.

Noble Windmills

Milo Peters has climbed to the upper echelons of corporate life, but is headed for a mid-life nuclear meltdown after battling twenty years of misdirected ambition. Now his closest, lifelong friend wants him to become a whistleblower for the government. His first-person account of what ensues is an emotional rollercoaster. You'll probably laugh, maybe shed a tear or two, but definitely fall in love with this irrepressible character.

CPSIA information can be obtained
at www.ICGtesting.com
Printed in the USA
FFOW04n1645190917
40132FF